Stand In Your Power

Power

Part 1

A Novel By

Simon P. Micallef

SIMON P. MICALLEF

KINDLE DIRECT PUBLISHING and logo are trademarks of Amazon.Com (USA) Inc.

LIBRARY OF CONGRESS CATALOGING-IN-PUBLICATION DATA:

Micallef, S. Peter 1973
Stand In Your Power / by S. Peter Micallef

KDP ISBN No: 9798665492186

Set in Manchester, Sandbach & Alsager, Stoke & London (UK), New York (USA), & Sao Paulo (Brazil)

Cover design and layout by: Akinoladimeji Toluwalope Samuel and Debbie Adeola Adekunle

Art director for Promotional Video: Levi Henry aka N.A.X.I of NewArtsNUArt

Printed in United Kingdom
Kindle Direct Publishing

First Edition

SIMON P. MICALLEF

To, KAREEN

I HOPE YOU ENJOY
READING THIS NOVEL
AS MUCH AS I DID
WRITING IT...!!!

STAY BLESSED

AUTHOR SIMON MICALLEF

(12-APR-2022)

SIMON P. MICALLEF

Dedication

In loving memory of Grandpa and Grandma Simon & Constantina Georghiou

Mother Andriana Georghiou and

Father Anthony Micallef

This book is dedicated to my son Myron Kai Micallef and my two daughters Vyienna Kerenza Nia Micallef & Saffron Lourdes Vassell-Gilzine.

Everything thing I do is for you three.

Daddy Loves you.

SIMON P. MICALLEF

ACKNOWLEDGEMENTS

First off to my family past: my late grandparents Simon and Constantina Georghiou and to my late parents, Andriana Georghiou and Anthony Micallef, your passing's laid the catalyst to the beginning of this book's creation and for all your unconditional love, thank you, R.I.E.P.

To my children, my universe, my life's purpose, my three heartbeats, Myron, Vyienna and Saffron, the love you transpire gives me the strength to do what I do, you're my life's energy and my beginning and end. To my sister Maria Khan, since we lost our parents you have been more than a rock to me, thank you, love you. To my number one cousin Selina Taylor; if there is a person that gets me period, then it's you, Love ya to da max.

Now that's my Royal family formalities out of the way! I want to express my gratitude to the rest of the kingmen and Empresses I'm about to give dedications to.

First up, to one of my best friends in the whole wide world, my sister from another mister; Nero Diamante, thank you for letting me see life in a fresh light through your precious soul, your knowledge of life knows no bounds and I know where you get it from, I can't wait until you tell the world your story. I'm getting Goosebumps as I write this, Love ya more than words can say! To My brother from across the pond and fellow author, David Adekunle, your intelligence and work ethic is an inspiration, you truly are a magnificent human being, I can't wait to read your Trilogy of books about an ancestral story of amazing characters. To my Soul-Sister in this life Journey Ninah L Mariposa, from the very first moment we spoke you have been nothing short of a miracle, I remember pre-book days all the information, literature and documents you sent my way to feast upon, thank you, love you too. Also, to Hope Babirye, this is a girl who has brighten up my days even more with her magical smile. May you continue to be a shining light in my life. Thank you, for entering into it.

To my friends: Patricia-Livingston Lee, thank you for taking the time to read parts of this book and giving feedback, and for always cooking the most scrumptious traditional West Indian food the way your mother taught you, my belly was always full when leaving yours, yummy. May I also add that you and Derick being the most loved up married couple I know, your strength together is amazing after going through so much over the years, you're a testament on how a man and his woman get over adversity and grow stronger. Nishika Hewitt-Nnabude, my Soulja Sister, not only are you a loving wife to your husband Chigozie Nnabude and a brilliant mother to three children, your activism work for our people is second to none. Keep fighting the good fight, my favourite Social Justice Warrior, you truly have been an inspiration from afar. To my oldest and wisest best friend Shailesh Jati, bro, thank you for everything, you truly are the best mate a man can have. Finally, to my brother from another mother Darren Gregg aka Isaiah "Nature" Bourne, there is not enough words in the English language to describe the person you are. Forget whether I know there is no one like you, FACT; there is literally not another human being like you. All I can say it's been an honour to stand by your side from back in the day and to still know you now, it's been the most amazing journey, completely out of this world. To another amazing and intelligent lady Nini Thompson;

your mind is an abundance of intelligence that is truly up there with some of the best scholars I know. Thanks for your assistance on Chapter 47 with the Deja character and helping me translate English into Brooklyn Hood slang, Respect x Last but not in the least there is a lady that speaks her mind without apology, she is best island gyal I know. Thanks for your post in helping me get the final piece to the novels ending; Chamaine Felix thank you Miss!

I also want to make a dedication to three other special women in my life. First up, Aundrea Minto; Well what can I say other than you're the most amazing and strongest lady I know, you have been through so much and yet you continue to smile for the world. I hope from here on in you truly get blessed and get all that you're fighting for, love ya to the max. Secondly, Candice Bowen, if I was to describe this girl in two words 'Fighter and Survivor' hit the mark. No matter what obstacles life throws at her. She always manages to find a way to come out on top, love you 2 x. Last but not in the least is Junie Daniels, a lady with whom I've come accustomed to call my mother, since my own mother's death. You stepped up and have blessed me as if I was one of your own. I love your no-nonsense attitude to life and how you keep fighting through your pain. All three of you are an inspiration to me in many ways and I love each one of you uniquely.

To everyone mentioned above and to the rest of you, thanks a million for all your moments of clarity, direction, knowledge and contributions in many different levels and ways. The endless chats about me going on about this character and that part. The hours of brainstorming with some of you was priceless.

To all those that read the introduction and prologue and there has been too many for me to mention by name, but you all know who you are. From the bottom of my heart thank you for giving me constructive feedback and criticism, your help has been gravely appreciated.

Also, as a pre-dedication, thank you to all those that will purchase a copy of this book in the future and for taking the time to read it, when you could've been doing something else.

Sincerely,

S.P. Micallef

SIMON P. MICALLEF

Introduction

"Psst, hey! Hello there? Yes, you? Not you over there. I'm calling you the person in front of the one I'm not trying to call. I'm talking to the person who is pointing their finger at their chest. Don't just walk away after running your greasy fingers up and down my spine and after the fish and chips, you just ate from next door."

"Are you seriously considering to continue to walk around this bookshop in search of a novel that will hopefully intrigue your curiosity enough to become engaged that you won't put it down after a few chapters?"

"It's just like the times when you did that with the last three novels you attempted to read but was failed miserably by the lacklustre plots and seemingly lifeless characters."

"Now, I've been watching you from up here on the six-tier of this bookshelf, and I had noticed that you have been walking around looking like you do not know what you want to read today. Am I right? If I am, then good!"

"Let's continue!"

"Since I've got your attention, I want to allude you to one or two things. Firstly, can you please wipe the grease off my spine? There you go, nice one. Secondly, I will you to read the media's statements on the back of this book about how wonderfully entertaining and educating this debut novel is."

"Just take a minute or two, digest, and I'll be waiting right here."

"Now that you have done all that. I want you to dust me down and carry me to the till once you have reached there, you will smile at the cashier while you pay the £11.99 or $14.99 price tags. When you have completed the transaction, you can pop me into a bag, and you will carry me to your next destination with extra due diligence where you will no doubt ably get stuck into reading this with a cup of your favourite drink."

"I know you're curious and baffled as into who or what has taken minutes out of your precious time. Then allow me to narrate."

"Now, you have opened this book, and when you get passed the credits and introductions, you will find me on the page entitled 'The Prologue', and this is where my story begins."

"So let's do the formal introductions and get it out of the way and allow me to re-introduce myself. My name is Erykah Gaines, and I'm a single black female with a hell of a story to tell, and It's my pleasure, finally, to meet your acquaintance."

STAND IN YOUR POWER

The Prologue

Hey, hello there again. As you have gathered by now, my name is Erykah Gaines. So let me tell you a little bit more about myself.

I'm a 27-year-old graduate with a degree in Sociology & Psychology. Though in this age, when fame is the altar at which most people worship, I am not sure why you should care who I am or that I exist. But in hindsight, I hope my story and the words I type may intrigue your curiosity enough to read on. So I shall begin.

The year was 1988 and in the UK, a woman, yes a woman, is the first female and longest-serving prime minister in the 20th century. Who would have thought? There was a national buzz around the pending results of the first-ever GCSE examinations that were sat by the nations glossy-eyed 16-year-olds. Then there was me. Erykah Gaines. I was born on August 17th, the only child of Mr and Mrs Howard and Harriet Gaines. I grew up in a neighbourhood where many people lived below the poverty line. A situation that several black people could relate to back then in many different ways.

Unfortunately, in poverty-stricken areas, most people know what went down. I'm ashamed to admit this, but you know the kinds of things I'm eluding to here. Anti-social behaviours such as residential drug dealing, vandalism, loud music, engines revving and offensive behaviour and language to name a few. I was exposed to many crimes my eyes and ears shouldn't have seen or been exposed to, especially as a lil pee-wee of a person, but that was life. Everyone had their struggles and hustles. We just had to get by.

Ultimately some of the lessons I've learned kept me alive, and others shaped the next 21years of my life in a bad way.

I was raised and still live in Princess Road near the notorious Alexandra Park Estate in Moss-side, South Manchester, and as much I as I am proud to live where I live. I've never much liked my accent. Not that I am mocking it. I felt it was not befitting of me and to a lot of people that may sound pompous and to be honest I don't care what anyone thinks about it, it's my life and I do as I please. It just is what it is. Worse things are going on in this world—no apology needed here then.

So, for the past five years, I've been taking lessons with an elocution school in my own time. It's expensive but well worth the money. I've learned how to speak the Queens English to a tee. Also, I've been self-teaching myself on how to talk in various London accents. I can mimic, anything from Street slang to an east end cockney accent. YouTube video's and Urban dictionary sites have been all that and then some.

And to quote an ancient Chinese proverb; A sharp tongue or pen can kill without a knife.

I'm really in my element when I study subjects I enjoy, and that will be beneficial to me in times ahead. My next conquest is to learn Ebonics, which is a linguistic phenomenon of African American English.

That may or not may sound realistic to a lot of you, and I can hear some of you saying as you read this, 'How will she completely get away from her Mancunian accent when she is mostly around other people that talk that way?'

Easy, I practice hard and continue to execute my new-found dialects no matter who I encounter.

The funny thing is, and this may sound a bit far-fetched, everyone in the Gaines family from the Northern parts of England has had the same elocution lessons as I have. The street dialects and patios they already had from back home in the Caribbean.

I felt it was a good thing. Because it became something that bonded us a family together even if it was only on the day of the lesson, you just can't have it all.

Also, I made some good friends with people that came to study in Manchester from London, and it was from them that I learned words and meanings the books and videos couldn't teach.

Auntie CeCe said when I will need to execute either dialect depending on who I was talking to, with the attitude and determination I possess, she feels it will work detrimentally in my favour for any situation that may arise in the future. I hope she is right.

Growing up as an only child wasn't always easy, but some occasions had its advantages at times like; getting extra presents on birthdays and at Christmas from relatives and when my Father could be bothered to remember.

But if it weren't for the love and heartfelt kindness from my Uncle Jeboniah and Aunt Celestine who coincidentally came to my rescue more times than I can remember. Then well, psssh, most of you can guess the rest, I hope.

So one day in the near and not so distant future I have vowed; I made a solid promise and told them, "Uncle, Aunt someday I will make you so proud of me, and I will repay you for all you had done for me over the years, especially when dad neglected me or forgot I was there." Sounds harsh, but that's the truth. All they wanted and said in return was; "Erykah; just be the best you can be, and that will make us proud." Damn, I'm about to buss a little tear right now; but I know I got's to keep it cool. I love them guys so much.

Anywho moving on, let's just say like millions of other young people who have ever been in situations similar, my life never started smoothly.

In my younger days, my life to say in the least was as up and down as a roller coaster ride, and there were always more downs then there were up's.

My first vague recollection of trauma happened when I was only six years old and paved the way for my bad behaviour.

My mother her name was; Harriet, she died in a car crash, and somehow my father survived with just a broken shoulder and a few crack ribs and only until recently, certain actions of that night have been brought to my attention of late, thus questioning my dad relentlessly about that day but to no avail and rejected based on his ongoing alcohol and misuse of any narcotic he could get his hands on and his reasoning for this continuing onslaught to his body; that the night in question was a painful reminder why he was so lucky to be alive and my mother wasn't.

That changes you. Makes you afraid of losing people. For the last four and a half months; I've had it up to the point where I feel like I'm going to get a brain tumour or something, not that I wish or am I mocking anyone with that horrific disease.

But in truth, I've just about had all I can take of my father's abuse to himself.

Over the years at least on four occasions after constant battling and planning when he agreed to rehab, each time my father attended he has never finished the course, and that has only driven a wedge further every time between our already cantankerous and unhinged relationship.

Lately, I've often been found daydreaming and going into myself. I guess you can say that I'm putting up barriers around me so that I can protect myself from what maybe again.

I know I have serious trust issues, and when you read on, you will see why!

Also, I'm finding myself thinking deeply a hell of a lot about my past and how my life might have been if my mother survived.

Of late, I'm seriously considering leaving home and embarking on new venture's; just when I can sort and iron out a few things first.

So back to my life story; when I reached my teen's life took on a different somewhat unexpected but not surprising turn. As far back as I could remember, my first crushes were; Marvin Gaye and Bob Marley. I damn well cried for days when I found out they were already dead.

I managed almost single handily to get kicked out of school just before my 16th birthday and wait for it, drum roll, please. "The award goes to for the most stupid pupil ever for sleeping with her Maths teacher, and you can just picture the scenario; shocked and disgusted looks on family and friends faces, not to mention the media, Miss Erykah Gaines".

There's no claps, just jeers and finger-pointing and the usual vile comments; slut, homewrecker, young floozy, ratchet, thot, bitch, the list is endless. All because I told Jocelyn Maynard my best friend at the time, that I had a silly schoolgirl crush on Mr Smith.

Yet not once did any outsiders ask if I was alright with any real heartfelt sympathy or asked for my side of the story. But now I see them for who they are, and I forgive, but I won't forget them, you feel a sista, hmmm...although in truth it's just damn right flawed across the board.

My counsellor, who helped me get through my trauma, told me that it was my lousy behaviour also that got me kicked out of school. She went on to say that my behaviour was a learnt behaviour from the lack of male love in my life. But regardless of my schoolgirl obsession, the responsibility lay's with the adult.

During the trial, child protection and social services put me into care while they investigated the case and my home life.

I was shamelessly taken from school to home and back to court. Everywhere I went paparazzi was out following me in force. They made my life a living hell. Looking back; I don't know how I coped with it all at that age.

On the last day of the trial when the judge read out his statement to the jury, at one point I swear down it seemed to me like he was accusing me of grooming Mr Smith. I was shocked and horrified at first; the judge's comments were cruel and untrue. He made me sound like a 16-year-old predator. But he groomed me.

In the end, I was glad members of the jury saw past the judge's slight fabrications if I had known better back then, you never know what back-handers might be going on under the table so to speak.

Anyway, the story became a national scandal; by the time the British media finished with the story, Mr Smith went down for ten years in custody, but with good behaviour and rehabilitation he only had to serve half his sentence.

I will never forget Smiths vile looking face when the judge handed down his sentence and read the final notes.

'I have never come across a more culpable and grave course of sexual criminality which has involved such a gross and grotesque breach and betrayal of your Hippocratic Oath. All this almost pales into significance set against the trauma, fear, and distress you have caused to your victim and her family.'

When he was released, Smith was put on the Sex offenders register for life, and a distraught and lonely me had gone through a lot of turmoil for those five years until my ex-teachers release from prison in 2009.

Upon that; Mr Smith left out of the country to a secluded location for his protection; gave an interview to the British media explaining the truth in his words and not that of the media's during the trial. He explained how he sought after me when I was just fourteen and groomed me from the age of eleven which now I know is so true and not the other way around as meekly suggested on internet forums. And I do mean the part when I was fourteen; not eleven okay.

But that bastard rightly got everything he deserved sentenced for sleeping with a minor. They should've thrown away the key and locked that paedo's sorry ass away for life or until he died in jail!

Anyway on his release; Smith went on to say "How he manipulated and took advantage of a young girl whose life lacks any moral guidance and structure". That is the truth, nothing but. Also that he fell victim to a weakness in him, (in whatever way he may have meant to himself) to me that sounds like I gave him the come-on jeez.

Only to the detriment and help from my Uncle and Aunt kept me steady from time to time. But in the long run; I was too much of a roughneck teen for them to handle most days and that's how my overzealous nature landed me in hot water more times than you could imagine, and yes I do blame my father for the most part and the rest of it on the environment he exposed me too.

I'm talking about the drinking, the drugs, the endless nights of gambling with men who I had to all call uncle out of respect, yet most of them were grotesque and stank to high heaven.

Please don't even let me get started on how many different women or skanks as I called them back then my father has bought into our not so humble abode. Just as soon as I got comfortable with someone, the next moment she was replaced by someone new and the process started all over again!

This behaviour seriously has doubted my trust in the opposite sex, and I can't afford anymore to get my heart broken or my mind polluted with unseeded corruption when it comes to matters of the heart.

Although in the last four years, finally now I'm old enough to bare the shit, though it still hurts a little, my father to be fair to him has tried more than he has ever shown the family and I have given him credit where credit is due. He has slowed down somewhat these days and how he bagged the lady whom I've become very fond off and call just until recently Mum.

It's a new and strange phenomenon to me, yet an overwhelming feeling to have a positive elder female in my life, although I could've done with Bernadette being in our lives a lot sooner; oh well better late than not at all.

To be honest though seriously, I don't know how Bernadette puts up with my father when he is having one of his episodes. But I do admire the way she takes charge of the situations. I've laughed out loud a few times when I see my father bow down to Bernadette like a dog that just chewed up on some expensive piece of furniture or something.

I very much take lessons and strength from her tolerance and patience. Her resistance to my father's escapades are strong, and I suppose she gains her strength from God almighty. Although I'm Agnostic by faith; Bernadette never misses an opportunity to tell me; "Child, You must fear God first and people second".

But now I know at the end of the day it was proper attention and unconditional love I was seeking and Mr Smith was a good teacher; he stepped up to the plate. He showed and told me things in school on how to better myself.

My head was definitely in awe and stuck in the clouds; that I was a fourteen-year-old schoolgirl who was so dumb, that I took Smiths kindness and generosity for love and affection in a teacher to pupil way and that's how he manipulated me to a bed, so he could pretend and get away with stating that he was my Step-Father and I was his Step-Daughter; so that he could get his wicked and sick way with me.

I must've been in a trance through the escapades because before I knew what was going on one day, I woke up from the madness that succumbed me and I realised what he had done, and that's when I blew the whistle on his ass.

I was frigging scared as hell that day, and this was a rare occasion, but pops were there for me when I needed him most, blessings to you father for that.

Anyway, after Smith's exerts; I was awarded reprieve from the presses hounding of myself and anyone associated with my family. Eventually, in another short case the court's awarded damages of £250,000 from five different national newspapers and I Erykah Gaines left the court a happy, yet a relieved woman in a financial sense; but an emotional wreck all the same.

By this period I was 21, and I had amassed a small fortune, though it was out of wretchedness; my bank account for once in my life was looking more than healthy for a girl my age and where I lived. Now I can build a new life for myself and boy, don't I deserve it?

But upbringing and lifestyle are impressionable when you still need to grow up a little more. I hadn't learnt all of life's early lessons yet.

During Smith's five-year stay at Her Majesty's Pleasure! The boyfriend before my last was an alcoholic and in many ways, reminded me of my dad, and that so-called relationship was cut short. Not a good start there then!

My last boyfriend Aaron was twice my age; oops I hear some of you say as you read this; "Hmmm, here she goes again," But something's take time to leave your way of thinking and feeling in a die-hard sense and as the saying goes; 'better late, than never' and honestly as I tell you this I'm over men twice my age, trust.

But wait; hear me out. Aaron in his twisted sense of the word told me that he loved me too much and that he's jealous and possessive nature suffocated and sucked out any goodness that was left in me and the relationship got worse the more I tried to rebel over time. Our relations became more about his insecure and violent ways which turned into; curfew's, lockdowns and daily beat downs over seven treacherous months.

If it weren't for the help of my twin brother and sister cousins Daniel and Danika; I knew either my ex or I would wind up dead eventually.

Moving on; when I finally got past my last relationship and the others, It took a whole year's worth of counselling before I could move on.

Now I was in a predicament where for the first time in my life, I had no idea what I wanted to do or direction I wanted to go in.

STAND IN YOUR POWER

The year now was 2010, and I was a 22-year-old, black female with no formal qualifications or experience to my credit, and I felt like I was staring down the barrel of a shotgun wanting to pull the trigger and die.

Since my father had cohered me into putting most of my newfound monies into an account where I had to sign and make him guarantor on my estate until I hit my 30th birthday, in the event I didn't make it; then father would become the beneficiary. So all I had to play with was £10,000; a lot of money to most; but when you have no job or prospects, and the social have you declaring here and there, things to say in the least were a bit tough on occasion.

The point in my life now was a day I will never forget for the rest of my life as it was such a time where the saying goes; this is your turning point.

It was October 6th, 2010, an overcast autumn's day, and on this Sunday it began like most days.

I would roll out of bed at 7 am sharp as always and began my daily ritual of having freshly squeezed orange juice from oranges that came from Spain only the best and a croissant for breakfast.

Then it was into the front room for a thirty-minute Zumba workout. Then after I had finished I would shower, get ready and wake up father when Bernadette wasn't in residence because that was Church day for her and afterwards as she does until the present day, she would pop by after so Father and her could go market, come back and make our kitchen look like one of those daytime cookery programmes.

So after getting ready it was a quick trip to the corner shop so I could get father's paper and anything else I needed. When I got back home I cooked him a hearty breakfast; which consisted of cornmeal porridge, ackee

11

and saltfish, fried dumpling, yam and orange juice. Yes, I'm not a useless chick.

Between Bernadette and Aunt CeCe, I got taught how to cook a variety of Caribbean dishes. A skill they said which was the way into a man's heart. Sounded all a bit theatrical to me; as far as I knew until I was told the way into a man's heart was to give him the goods whenever he wanted. Big mistake there then; because as quickly as the sentences I spat for them finished; that was my first real lesson on where I learnt Men are from Mars and women are from Venus! Case closed for now.

After father finished his breakfast; we had a quick catch up for 10 minutes. Afterwards, he excused himself and went to get ready for market. While dad was showering; I quickly washed and dried the few dishes and cups in the sink and then went to put them away.

This was Erykah's time now, so I phoned my two best friends in the whole world, Chantel Porter; my homegirl from school days and Nina Lawrence; whom I met at counselling. Chantel was Sweet, kind and thoughtful. A red-skinned beauty with a body to die for, she stood at 5'10 and was quickly snapped up by the best modelling agencies in Manchester.

She was telling me on the phone that day on how a top agency in London was after her services. Ah, I was so happy for her.

Nina, however, is a different prospect altogether. Like me, she had a turbulent start in life. Her father left her mother when Nina was only nine months old, so she never until this day knew or knows where he is even her mother doesn't anymore. Her mother did her best on Welfare and part-time jobs, but that meant Nina was shifted around different people's houses; mainly friends of the families.

STAND IN YOUR POWER

On one horrific day when Nina was just twelve years old, one of her mother's friend's nineteen-year-old son was in charge of Nina. The son raped and sexually abused Nina. It ended up Nina becoming pregnant and having to abort the baby, and the boy went to juvenile detention. That day was so devastating for me to go into too much detail, all I'm going to say it shaped the path of destruction Nina took.

After I finished with my phone calls, I took out my laptop and began going through my social media. I did a few posts and shared a few on Facebook. I tweeted and retweeted on Twitter, and then I went to read my new emails.

As I was scanning my emails I came across one that headlined the words; 'Want a new direction in life then why don't you check out over 1000 courses starting in September at the Manchester Metropolitan University.'

So that's what I did. Three years later, in July 2014, I graduated as the first-ever black person in my family with a (BA) honours in Psychology and Sociology and passed with first-class results.

Not bad so far for a girl who has had the kind of start in life that I have had. For the last year, I've furthered my studies in my own time by reading books on human nature and events. I have learnt about who is in control of our planet, slavery, history, and I took a one year masters degree in Philosophy, Politics and Economics.

Now that's me up until this moment. So I am kindly going to hand over the narration to the writer of this novel and the person in question is a Mr Simon Micallef; I will let him continue my story in his unique take on things and style of writing. You won't be disappointed that I can guarantee. So enjoy!

Chapter 1 – The Move

The only other time that I can remember feeling such a mixture of sad and happy emotions in one go; was the day when they sealed Mr Smith's fate though the feelings of that day were way too painful to endure for any young person that had been through that ordeal.

Today the feelings felt similar, not the same as then, just a little different. I felt sad because father had been sitting motionless; most of the morning in the living area, in his favourite red chair, and eyes glued to the TV.

He only managed a petulant 'Alright' this morning when we crossed paths, as I was exiting and he was entering the bathroom, and three hours later all he had managed to say to me still was nothing.

I was getting way too worried about him on what is supposed to be one of the happiest days of my life.

While I was getting ready and packing up any last things to load onto Uncle Jeb's van, all I could think about was to make sure father was going to be okay when I wasn't around.

It's not as if Bernadette, Uncle Jeb, Aunt CeCe and I hadn't discussed the case in detail; many a time already.

Sitting there, with father not saying a word all morning, I was beginning to have my doubts about leaving.

You see my father is old school and I guess I get my stubborn streak from him?

Neither one of us in a one to one situation pitted against each other would back down first.

So I guess on this occasion, I will have to submit to his stubbornness and allow him to have this battle, but in no way was he going to win the war before I leave.

STAND IN YOUR POWER

Aunt CeCe, on the other hand, would always remind me how beautiful my mother was, but it was from father's dashing good looks that I got my real beauty.

Father didn't have much in the way of grey hair, and as far back as I can remember, he always sported a goatee.

He stood at six-foot, three inches tall, and for a man of fifty years of age, he used to keep himself in peak physical shape. But after the years of drug-taking and alcohol abuse, it was beginning to take its toll on him, and this is the main reason why I was so worried to leave home.

I felt sad because he is the one person in the world that I love the most and I hated him being mad at me and for what I don't know yet?

I was staring at father for what seemed like ages and hadn't noticed Auntie coming up behind me, not until I felt her soft, warm hand on my shoulder.

"Are you alright, Erykah?" She whispered in my ear as not to let father overhear.

"I think so!" I murmured back at her.

I turned around sluggishly with my arms folded to meet her gaze, which was ever so soft and calming!

"What's the problem?" She said, sounding very apprehensive.

"To be honest Auntie, I don't feel a hundred per cent positive right now," I said, feeling very uneasy about the whole situation.

"About what?" She said with a caring nature.

"If I should go today or wait a few more days to make sure he is alright."

At the tender age of fifty-three Auntie carries herself like a woman half her years.

You see, my Aunt CeCe is a stunning lady. The ancestors have blessed her with the most fantastic melanin. Her dark-skin complexion and with a head of the most potent looking locks always gives her an air of authority when you're in her presence.

My Aunt is half Jamaican & half Grenadian, and she is the proud owner of a Youth Centre and Community Charity right here in Moss Side.

Her nephew and my cousin Daniel runs the London branch of the Community Charity. She has been married thirty years to Uncle Jeboniah, and they're both the proud parents of their only child Darius.

She is a strewed, powerful and no-nonsense businesswoman and is currently Manchester's Black Business Woman of the year 2014.

After several minutes I managed to calm myself down as soon as the last of her words escaped from her mouth.

Auntie immediately knew what to say to me in these situations.

"Erykah, come over here?" She said as she began walking away from my presence while motioning me with her arm to follow her into the kitchen. "Shut the door, please?" She continued to say. I did what she asked of me. "Here take this?" She instructed as she handed me a few tissues.

"Why are you giving me them for?" I quizzed with a puzzled look on my face.

"For what I'm about to say next Erykah." She whispered back.

"Okay," I said as I took the tissues from her grasp.

Silence fell between us for a minute as Auntie opened up the kitchen window and then took out a cigarette from its pack, lit it up, took a few puffs then laid it in the ashtray beside her. She turned back around to face me and then came her sermon.

"Erykah, listen to me and listen to me good. Ever since your mother passed away, Uncle Jeb and I have always been more fond of you over any of our other nephews and nieces. You're like the daughter that I've never had, and I know Jeboniah feels the same. We love you so much and have been through the many difficult times with your father and you. Now your father is on the road to recovery, I believe very much, and since Bernadette came into his life four years ago, he has made so much improvement."

I looked back at Auntie, she was right; as I nodded my head in agreement, I couldn't hold back the tears anymore. I began to cry and laugh nervously simultaneously as she continued to speak.

"So now it's your time, with everything you have been through in your young life. I want you to go forward to London and find yourself and experience what life has to offer and take strength in the fact that your father may not always show it. Still, deep down underneath that macho exterior, he loves you more than life itself, and to him, you will always be that six-year-old he held in his arms on that tragic night as he wept and you cried and screamed uncontrollably for your mummy until you feel asleep."

At that moment, I rushed towards Auntie and flopped myself onto her chest and held on tight for dear life and cried like I did when I was six years old.

"Your Father loves you so much Erykah, don't you ever forget that," she whispered in my ear while I was making a right mess of her beautiful summer dress, though it didn't seem or feel like a summer's day at all to me. "Howard is going to be alright! He has Bernadette, your Uncle and I and his legion of friends. So go with the knowledge and satisfaction that he will be okay." She finished off saying.

"I know Auntie, I know. It's just the first time father and I will be living apart," I said sadly.

"That is true, very true!" Auntie concurred with what I said and added. "But there comes a time in most children's lives; that when they grow up, they leave the nest, same goes in the animal kingdom, that's nature and the evolution of life. Now it's your time, and you must go with no pressure leaving here or with any preconceived feelings about where you're going. You have been planning this journey for months on end, and everything is falling into place nicely." She wrapped.

"I'm not going to argue with you about the latter on what you just said."

"That's good to know. You see your father, he will come around Erykah, you will see. Howard is just coming to terms with the changes as you are. But Bernadette will be here with him on most occasions. So don't worry yourself!" She finished off saying for the moment.

"You're right as per usual, Auntie!" I pointed out as I pulled away from our embrace. "Thank you."

"What for?" She said with a baffling look on her face.

"Not just for today, but everything and always." This time, it was me handing Auntie a tissue or two.

"You're most welcome my beautiful and gorgeous niece," she said as she wiped away the few tears that began to stream down her beautiful face. "Now, please, go finish off the packing, and I'll finish tidying up in here, and then I'll prepare the food for the journey."

She said as she ushered me out of the kitchen and watched me walk past father.

I glanced over in his direction; he must have felt me looking because my father, most of the time, had that knack of knowing when I was doing it.

It was just earlier on. I knew father knew I was staring at him. He just chose not to respond.

STAND IN YOUR POWER

Father looked up at me and managed half a smile then turned back towards the TV without saying a word.

At that point, I felt angry and upset.

All I could do was hurry away quickly as fast as my legs could carry me.

As I got nearer towards the front door, I picked up one of the boxes that were near the entrance.

As I went to exit out; that was the moment when I heard Auntie verbally attack Dad.

She must've seen fathers and mines exchange, or maybe it was the moment's silence between us that had sparked her onslaught.

Either way, it prompted her to curse him out about how selfish and unfair he was treating me today and though she understood why he was upset; this day wasn't just about his feelings.

His is a grown-ass man I heard her continue to say.

As I continued making my way out of the flat, all of a sudden out of nowhere, I felt an overwhelming feeling of good energy pour into me.

I know Aunt Ce-Ce will knock some sense into my father, and there is a big part of me that also understands how hard this is for him.

To watch and see his only child leave the roost, even if I am a grown woman of 27 years and embarking on new ventures without me around every day.

That would be hard for most people if they were in our situation.

I do also feel how he feels, but I got to do this; otherwise, I never will.

Everything I've ever worked for or been through has never come easy. So why should it now?

Better get my skates on, and it's like Auntie said back there; things will fall into place by the time I leave, she was adamant about that. I just hope for everyone's sake; she was right.

So on that note here it is; the day of reckoning has finally arrived. My big move to London that I've been planning and saving for months on end was just hours away from me being there live in person!

As I walked a few feet further and got to the top of the landing, I put the box down beside me momentarily.

As I stood there, I looked forward into the distance and focused on a large object. When I found my target, I sucked up a deep and meaningful breath, held it for a few moments and then let my breath come out in slow, short spurts. I repeated the process several times.

When I felt more relaxed, I picked up the last box marked miscellaneous and took it downstairs.

I felt funny thinking that and I don't know why as I proceeded my way down the thirty-two steps to the very grey looking scene of the street below and to outside where Uncle Jeb was neatly stacking my belongings one on top of each other inside his van.

As I walked across the green towards it; I noticed more than the usual amount of neighbours that were out in force on this Sunday.

To my knowledge, there weren't any local events happening, and there was me thinking I was going to leave quietly today. And I reckon, no I know father has told everyone the last time he went to play dominoes at the local social club with his friends.

A cheeky smile swept across my face, as I imagined the scenes father must've caused.

Plus after the massive leaving party, my family organised for me last Saturday night. I'm pretty glad, and it was quick thinking by me that I didn't decide to leave last Sunday.

STAND IN YOUR POWER

But I did tell everyone in my family to say to people I was going last week. I spent the last week in our flat. To not cause the mayhem on this day as I predicted, Oh well, that plan has gone out of the window, but it's nice to know that I'm loved and thought of by a lot of good people.

Some of my father's friends from the club have been living in my area for around the same time my father told me my mother, and he was.

Each time I've come downstairs to bring something out to the van; some neighbour or family friend has come up to me and wished me all the best.

It has been very touching and emotional thus far.

Winston; who was always repairing some part on his favourite pride and joy. A BMW X1. He is one of my father's best friends from when they were youngers and he also happens to be my one and only godfather.

Just before I got to the van, he greeted me and said how sad it was that I was leaving.

I told him I was going to miss him very much and could he please keep an eye on father.

Like always he said he would, and I know he won't let me down.

I swear down I saw a tear or two forming in his eyes when he pulled away from hugging me.

Ah, how sweet to see, I thought myself.

He nearly had me going again, and I've genuinely only ever seen Winston cry once in my life, and that was when he lost his mother to Sickle cell.

So sad! That day hit my father hard, too; after all, she had adopted the role and was like a second mother to my dad growing up.

You see Winston and my father are part of that second generation that got an education that wasn't indoctrinating and they're also the sons of Caribbean parents who came to be in the UK; what was known as Windrush in 1948. Other friends and their parent's came by aeroplane to.

After I left Winston to get back to his car, I eventually reached the foot of Uncle Jeb's van.

I stopped and marvelled momentarily on how much items I had consumed in my short existence.

A rush of emotions came over me as I slumped down and sat at the edge of the back of the van.

Uncle was a few feet away inside still shuffling and moving boxes to make sure there was enough room for everything.

At the age of fifty-four years old, Uncle Jeb was born in Camberwell, Greater London. For a living he works as a Carpenter, so he knows his way around anything that needs repairing.

He is the oldest of three siblings with father and Aunt Lola as his younger's.

My Uncle Jeb is a remarkably assured and confident individual. He is very down to earth and is up to the time with modern lifestyles and ways of the younger generation, mostly thanks to Darius.

With an abundance of intelligence at his disposal, it makes him a knowledgeable person.

I was very close to him, and we had a uniquely, quirky and jokey relationship. But one thing we always were, is that in certain situations we are very in tune and in sync with one another, almost telepathic?

I went to slide the box next to me to one side, but I got stopped in my tracks by Uncle; who made a comment that nearly had me falling out the van and onto the street below.

"Erykah," he said as he pointed to all the boxes and stuff behind him. "Ow ave yuh accumulated suh many t'ings inna yuh young life? Tell mi nah," he continued to say.

I laughed so much at Uncles over-exaggeration that I thought I was going to pee myself right there and then.

"Uncle," I said playfully. "You're so silly sometimes." I exited.

He looked down at me and was about to deliver of what looked like a sermon coming my way.

Immediately I looked up at him with my puppy dog smile, and to my relief, he winked back at me and got the joke. He was not too old for humour, yet I thought to myself.

As I slid the box next to me towards Uncle; to gather up, the lid suddenly flew open.

I grabbed the box and brought it back towards me and set it upon my lap. I asked Uncle if he had any brown tape left, he said he thinks he left it inside the flat.

"I'll go check for ya!" He smiled and said as he went past me to retrieve it.

As soon as Uncle was entirely out of my way for a bit, all of a sudden, my curiosity got the better of me. I was intrigued by what I had packed into the box marked miscellaneous.

I took in the deepest of breaths and then exhaled as I flipped the four lids back.

I marvelled at the contents inside, because I was glad it was these things I had packed in here.

I dipped my hand inside and one by one I skewered through old journals with the years 2002 and 2003 written on the front of them.

These were the last two years of school for me, and it was the beginning of the worst two years of my life that followed on.

I came across one more, and immediately the hairs on the back of my neck stood up to attention and a tingling sensation went through my spine too.

I took out the journal from the box; that had the year 2004 written on the front of it.

At first; I felt apprehensive and a bit reluctant to open it.

For several minutes, I stared at the journal like it was contaminated.

Inside of me, a world of emotions was going through my mind. I contemplated for a further few minutes whether I should or shouldn't open it.

I kept on telling myself. "Erykah get a grip. It's in the past. You had counselling. Smith is long gone. You have done so well thus far." I kept on repeating those phrases, shaking as I started to relieve the emotions.

I felt my breathing starting to become very shallow. My head began to feel heavy, and at the end of the day, I just can't bring myself to read what I had written inside.

I have to muster some courage from somewhere I kept on thinking to myself.

Several more minutes had passed, and I was feeling slightly better. So I decided to have a sneak peek anyway.

I opened the journal randomly to the page of the date of May 18th, 2004. That was the last day of the school year before we took our exams.

I flipped forward through some more pages, and as I did so, I started to feel out of sorts and was managing to get myself into a state of anxiety.

I stopped and stared at the page with the date of July 21st, 2004 staring right back at me.

As soon as I glanced at the date, my mind cast me back to that very day; which coincidentally was the first day of Mr Smith's trial.

I quickly shut the book tight as if it were to about to come to life.

I threw it back into the box, and then I folded the lids as I did so Uncle came back with the tape.

STAND IN YOUR POWER

He passed it to me, and I quickly wrapped the box up. I did it in a way as if to tell myself. 'Now you can put that part of your life all behind you Erykah and leave it in the past where it belongs.'

But sometimes; life, it has a funny knack of coming back to bite you when you least expect it. And I'm a living legend of that notion, believe me!

Afterwards, I passed it up to Uncle, who had his arms outstretched with a look on his face that told me to hurry up.

I turned around and got off the van and stepped onto the street below my dangling feet.

When my feet touched the ground, I took a few steps forward. As I did so, I heard a familiar female voice hail out my name like she was in imminent danger.

At first, I couldn't see who it was. The voice continued coming towards me, breathing hard with arms waving frantically and sweat dripping like they had run a marathon.

After a minute, Chantel stopped a few feet in front of me. She bent down to catch her breath for a few moments and then came up to hug me.

"Ewe Chantel; move from me girl with your stank self," I said as I pointed at her hairdo that was fraying around the edges.

"Hey Erykah; I thought I missed you already?" She said, finally recovering.

"Nah girl, I still got a few more things to pack yet." As soon as the words escaped my mouth, Uncle leant his head around the back of the van with a look of complacency etched on it.

"Wah yuh mean more t'ings?" He said, looking a bit stifled!

"Exactly that, Uncle!" I repeated.

"But didn't yuh just tell mi before dat box did di laas one?" He said, sounding exasperated.

"No, Uncle, that's what you thought," I said back at him, smiling. Uncle looked at me hard and kissed his teeth all the same and then disappeared out of view around the other side of the van.

I must've been daydreaming for a few moments because in the background I could hear Chantel hollering at me very loudly.

"Erykah," she continued to bellow at the top of her voice.

"Yes Chantel; what is it?" I came out of my trance and questioned back at her in my deplorable state.

"I've been calling you for ages girl. Where's your head at?" She said looking concerned all of a sudden.

"I'm right here Chantel. Where else do you think I am?" I answered back looking slightly perplexed.

"In body, you're yes. But in spirit, you seem far, far away."

I walked over to the bench, so I could take a rest before Uncle came back and started moaning. Chantel followed moments after and sat herself inches from me.

"Girl, I ain't letting you leave here smelling like you do," I let out a simmer of a smile. "You can use my shower before you go." I continued to say.

Suddenly, I started to feel sad. I didn't know what was coming over me, but tears began to form in the corner of my eyes.

I turned around and looked at Chantel for a few moments. I began to study her face and features like it was the first time I ever saw her. That's when the commotion spontaneously happened.

I began to feel my shoulders shake, and my legs tremble. I couldn't hold back the tears anymore; they came flooding down my face like a river flowing. My whole body shook like a red nose Pitbull.

I felt like I was having a seizure. I further panicked and was crying uncontrollably, and I couldn't stop it. Chantel held me and tried to calm me down.

"Erykah you're frightening me what's wrong?" Now she was staring at me looking more frantic than I was.

"In my pocket, in my pocket!"

"Which one?"

"In my pockets Chan," I snarled. "Look in both of them?" Chantel found a way into my pockets with me trembling like a bowl of jelly.

When she found it, she retrieved my inhaler and then passed it on to me. I took hold of the piece, but immediately I dropped it onto my lap because my hands were shaking violently now.

Chantel quickly scooped the inhaler up from my lap before it dropped onto the floor.

"Open your mouth Erykah?" Chantel grabbed my jaw as to stop my teeth from chattering and then squirted a few puffs into my mouth.

I breathed hard and fast, and all the same, I was trying to get my breathing down to a feasible level.

"Ahh," I bellowed out loudly. "I'm scared Chantel I can't breathe properly!" My heart was beating at a rate of what felt like a thousand beats per minute. I started to feel nauseous and dizzy as well.

Sometime later. I eventually woke up on my living room couch. Standing over me was Father, Uncle Jeb and Aunt CeCe, Winston and Chantel.

The last thing I remember before I blacked out; was Chantel doing my breathing for me and I heard Uncle Jeb run over, saying something in patios, but I couldn't grasp what he was trying to disclose before I passed out.

(Ten Minutes Later)

"Give her some room people," Father said worryingly. "Baby girl." He said in the softest of tones.

"Yes daddy," I mustered to say in my little girl's voice with my head still feeling foggy.

"You frightened us all for a minute back there,"

"I'm sorry dad!"

"I'll get her some water," Auntie said smiling away at me.

"Some food as well?" Uncle added.

"I'm not hungry," I said in protest. But to no avail, nobody listened. That's black folks for you. Always thinking they know what's best for you. But don't get me wrong. I do appreciate my family—more than life itself.

"You need to eat something Baby-girl. Keep your strength up. That's why you fainted!" Father added.

My throat felt groggy. Auntie came back with my glass of water.

"Thank you, Auntie," I said with half a smile as I tried to get up.

"You're welcome," she said back.

Father helped me to sit up and tucked a few pillows behind my back. Chantel came over with my favourite knitted blanket; it was one of the few things left I had of my mother.

I began to reminisce about the day mother finished making that for me. I also vaguely remember the smell of the cookies she baked.

As I came around from my thoughts, I felt myself beginning to well up. I was starting to feel emotional again. This day was becoming more and more overwhelming than I imagined. By the way, things were panning out. I don't think I was going to leave today now!

"Erykah what did you eat today?" Auntie said. "Because I ain't seen you eat since breakfast, and you only had a bowl of cereal then." She noted.

"I know Auntie, but I'm fine," I said back in protest. "I've probably overdone it a bit today and all week," I concluded.

"Overdone it, that's the understatement of the year Erykah if I ever heard one," father added his two pennies worth. "But you know Baby-girl." Father knelt and took my hand in his. He looked at me with a severe glare of his eyes. It was the look of a guilty man. I knew what was coming my way next.

"Father," I said at him with a bit more steel in my voice.

"Erykah," he sternly said back at me.

The atmosphere was tense. Everyone around us didn't know whether to stay put or leave. Father withdrew his hand away from mine and rubbed his goatee several times.

"It's okay everyone, stay!" I was beginning to feel better already as I sat up some more and took in a few deep breaths to muster what I've been waiting for all day so far.

"Erykah listen." Father looked me dead in the eyes and not for a second did they leave my gaze.

I could see all the pain and happiness all at once, and the vibe he was giving off was transferring over to me.

"Yes, father?" I said nervously, trying to anticipate what was about to be said.

"Baby-girl hear me out," funny how at my age he still calls me that. Inside I smiled all the same. "For the last twenty years, I haven't always been the best father," I interrupted him in mid-sentence.

"Ain't that the truth!"

"I exposed you to things that your little eyes and ears shouldn't have seen or heard!" I took father by the hand and rubbed his forehand gently. "My problems with drink and drugs, the home casino nights, different women were coming and going, and most of all, the neglect and lack of structure in your life since we lost your mother. Her death was the catalyst to all the drama in your life, and I'm truly sorry baby girl; I let you down too many times and failed you as a father and a role model. To be honest, the only explanation I've ever had for all this is that I blame myself for your mother's death."

Uncle and Aunt and the rest, including myself all turned towards father's direction with perplexed and puzzled looks on our faces.

"Father," I said back in shock horror.

"Let me finish," he said nonchalantly. "Like I said already, most of your life I haven't done right by you!"

There was a sudden hush of silence. Father looked at me momentarily then around at everyone else then back to me. Everyone was waiting in anticipation on father's next words. I instructed him to sit next to me; then I got myself a little more comfortable.

"Ever since we lost your mother, you know of all people how hard it hit us, and all I'm trying to say baby girl and what is obvious to you now is that I couldn't cope with the grief. My years of binging and gambling tripled with my arrogance and reluctance to avoid rehab kept me in denial and nearly cost me my life and your sanity. Because of me, you went through all the drama and nearly lost yours on more than one occasion."

Father paused for a moment. He took a sip of water then continued what he started.

STAND IN YOUR POWER

"I've often wondered what our lives would've been like if your mother had survived, but she didn't so you were stuck with me. Hell, I wish it was me dead instead of her."

I leant forward and gave him a big hug. I was thinking, though a part of me was glad he was self-punishing himself. My conscience was saying to give him a break.

"Father what you are saying is ludicrous, and I'm shocked even to think you've been carrying those thoughts and feeling for years in secret. Now I can see how that contributed to your demise. Why did you push me away? Why was I neglected time after time?" I said with a smidge of anger in my voice and a big part of it was lurking within me and was promising to come out like a tornado. Father grimaced then continued to speak.

"Why are you asking me that for the answers are simple?" His voice edged with sarcasm.

"It's important father. When I needed you, you weren't there, and you palmed me off to whoever could do the job you were supposed to do," I angrily said back at him.

"Babygirl, I couldn't cope. Which part in all of this you don't understand?" He said as if what I was saying was crazy.

"Father get real and take responsibility I've heard it all before I remind you of mother, and that's what makes it hard blah, blah, and blah. Of course, I look like her and things I do will remind you of her. But aren't I my mother's daughter?" I said, sounding exasperated.

"Yes, you're, and that's what made it hard," he said with a solemn look on his face.

"Fine Father! When you're ready. I know you will tell me eventually. All the same, it's about time you pay me a compliment and wrap this up for now." I said sternly.

"Erykah; since the trial and with the help of the family, I've watched you grow into an intelligent, beautiful black woman. I'm sad to say that I deserve no credit for your turnaround in fortunes." I tried interrupting him in mid-sentence, but he shut me down before I could begin.

"But father," he waved his hands in front of me so I could stop.

"Hush, don't say nothing baby girl. Let me wrap this up like you just said." I nodded my head in agreement with him out of respect this time.

"Twenty years of ups and downs and now in a blink of an eye you're leaving me as well," a tear began to form in the corner of my left then right eye. "I'm not saying you shouldn't go on the contrary. I'm just saying you are my life Erykah and it's going to be hard without you around every day." This time, when I interrupted, I stuck with it.

"Father hear me out for a moment," he shook his head in acknowledgement. "I've heard everything you said and understand now that it wasn't easy for you too." I paused for a moment so I could gather my thoughts together. I felt exhausted. Auntie put her arm around me and began rubbing my shoulder for support. In the next moment, we all turned towards the noise of the key in the front door. I instantly knew it was Bernadette and a cheeky smile quickly flashed across my face.

The door opened and in walked the love of father's life. Bernadette was carrying several bags of heavy shopping with her. Uncle quickly got up and went to her rescue. Father looked up at Bernadette and greeted her in his formidable fashion.

"Wha'ppen baby," father said in his deepest patios voice.

"Mi tired darling," she said, sounding exasperated. Bernadette walked over while she took off her coat to where the rest of us were. "What's going on here?" She continued to say, looking bewildered. Father got up from next to me and went to greet Bernadette.

"Erykah fainted outside." Bernadette looked over at me with a worried look on her face.

"Are you okay, mi dear?" She said, concerned for my welfare.

"I'm okay now, mum. A lil' hungry but I'm fine," I said reassuring her.

"Let me fix you something to eat!" She said back as she got up from the settee next to me and walked towards the kitchen. "I got some leftover chicken soup or curry goat and rice n peas," she hollered on her way.

"Chicken soup will suffice," I said, smiling back at her.

"Anyone else?" She said. There was a unanimous yes. One by one, everyone went to wash their hands. Chantel went to see if Bernadette needed some help. I wanted to finish off the conversation with father before we ate.

"Father!" I said gently to get his attention.

"Yes, baby girl, what is it?" He questioned back.

"Father, I want to finish off what I was saying," I said with urgency in my voice.

"Okay, go ahead." We walked over to the dining area and took a seat each at the table. Father sat where he always did at the head of the table. I took my place beside him.

"As I was saying before, I know life and dealing with mother's death wasn't easy for you too. But all I ever wanted to be was for you to protect and nurture me and show me the love a father should return to his child. Before Bernadette came along and since the age of twelve, I've taken care of you despite the madness that succumbed my upbringing. I shouldered your pain as well as my own, and it should've been the other way around. Don't you agree father?" I threw the ball in his court. If his answer weren't up to my expectation, things between us will get awkward, to say in the least.

"All I can say to you once and for all Erykah is that you deserve the truth," he surprisingly stated. He now looked like he was in deep thought. I shot him a look of suspicion as he clocked my stare. He stumbled a little before finally opening his mouth!

Fifteen minutes later, and I was somewhat satisfied with Father's explanation of the truth according to him.

At least that's what I hope it was because most of it made sense and I didn't want to leave Manchester in a 'what if' scenario.

But all the same, it was the best explanation I was going to get for a while.

So I decided it was perfectly fine to head to London.

Chapter 2 – Journey South

Uncle had driven a third of the way down the M6, and I was in dire need of a break. I got him to stop off at the next available services so I could gather myself and my thoughts together.

"Well, here we are," Uncle said as he finished parking the car.

"Finally," I said relieved to the fact I was bursting for the ladies.

I unlocked my door in a timely fashion and exited out the van as fast as I could. While Uncle locked up the van, I told him to find a café and meet me in there.

I continued to walk frantically towards the complex that housed many franchised businesses. When I reached the entrance, I stepped through the automatic sliding doors and in my desperation, I couldn't see the sign for the toilets.

I swivelled my head left to right several times, and at the same time, my body went left then right in sync with my head.

In my sudden state of panic, I eventually noticed across from me a burly, white security guard who was standing behind a podium.

Immediately, he spotted me staring at him.

As I walked towards him looking all flustered and a bit out of sorts, he eyed me back a death stare and I was getting an eerie feeling he was doing it like I was a criminal.

As I got nearer to the desk, the guard stood up to attention while holding his hands by his waist.

As I caught my breath and crossed my legs, I put my left hand onto the desk for elevation.

I looked down and saw on his security belt handcuffs and a gun. I was stunned by this for obvious reasons. After all, this is only a motorway services area, and in my mind, I didn't see the need for weapons of that magnitude.

"Excuse me," I said, desperately pitching my voice loudly over the noise of music coming from the record shop opposite.

"Yes, what is it?" The guard said back to me in a very unruly fashion.

"Yes, erm," I said frustratingly. "I'm looking for the ladies toilets?" I said gawking at him. Now I was feeling pissed.

All of a sudden he spoke into his radio, I overheard him summon another guard. At this moment, I was confused, I decided I had enough, so I began walking away from him.

I approached to ask an old lady where the toilets were, and as she pointed and told me where to go, I thanked her and started to proceed in the direction she instructed for me to follow.

I barely took two steps forward, and that's when I felt a heavy hand rest on my shoulder.

In my annoyance, I turned around only to see another burly, white security guard who was accompanied by his sidekick female counterpart.

I kissed my teeth and cursed under my breath, shot them both a repugnant look and continued to walk towards the toilet.

"Miss, can you stop please?" The male guard said in a robust voice. I ignored him again and carried on my way. "I said Miss, can you stop right now?" This time his voice went up a few octaves.

STAND IN YOUR POWER

I continued walking because, at this rate, I was going to pee myself.

"Young lady for the last time, stop right where you are!" He sounded way too serious this time. "Do not take another step further. I repeat. Do not take another step further, otherwise." Otherwise, what I thought.

Suddenly the atmosphere had changed, and the place went dead quiet. You could've heard a pin drop. I was judging by some of the expressions on some of the folk's faces, that my instincts were right. Now I had the clarification of what I initially first thought.

"Put your hands on your head and turn around very slowly." The male guard instructed.

A young man early twenties looking who to my right was about ten feet away in front of me bobbed his head at me and mouthed something.

I couldn't quite grasp what he was trying to tell me, but I got the distinct impression I should do as the guard said.

In the next instance, I put both my hands on my head, and as I slowly turned around in my shock horror only to find both guards had their guns pointing at me. I couldn't contain it any longer. I began to tremble like a bowl of jelly.

With that tears slowly started to trickle down my face and at the same time I peed myself right there on the spot!

"Get on the floor and your knees right now!" I did what he said.

Within seconds the female guard handcuffed me, while the male guard still had his gun pointed at my head.

"Why am I being detained?" I said clearly confused by this whole situation.

"You can tell everything to the police when they arrive." The male guard stressed.

"What do you mean the police are coming? I haven't done anything wrong."

"We will see about that!"

"What do you mean by your statement?"

"Miss like I said already, you will see why."

"This is so unfair!"

"Life is unfair. Unfortunately for you. This day isn't going to be a good one!"

"This is nothing more than social injustice and a violation of my human rights?" I bellowed out with an air of anxiety in my voice.

"Miss, miss," he kept on saying. I was beginning to think this either was a case of mistaken identity. Like us, black folk look all the damn same or and I didn't want to go down that road, but my intuition was still nagging at me that this has to be racially motivated. "Miss I'll advise you to keep your mouth shut until they arrive." As he lifted me to my feet.

"Ouch, you're hurting me!" As the female guard took over and began to march me to where I presumed was the room marked security that was situated just behind the podium.

"Be quiet you black bitch." I heard her say as she maltreated me and continued to frog march me towards the security room.

I can't believe what I just heard. I was right; this was racially motivated. Yet why the guns for little old me. Now my intuition was telling me something more sinister was going down here.

One or two onlookers shouted out some expletives towards guards. The guards shouted back at the crowd to move on. I spotted the mixed-race boy from earlier who was still filming the saga.

"Psst, yo gee," I hollered at him. He looked at me with a shocked look on his face. "Wait there for me by the seats behind you." I winked at him, and he nervously nodded his head, but he didn't move from his spot. He was good, I thought. Somehow I knew he would wait.

The female guard was frantically looking around to see whom I was talking too.

"Who is your correspondent?" She said like the bitch she was.

"I don't know what you're on about," I mocked back at her in the same tone she addressed me.

"Cocky little bitch aren't you?" She said, sounding humiliated.

"Takes one to know one." I wasn't going to let this bitch completely overpower me.

"You're funny, real funny," she said back through gritted teeth.

"Yeah, didn't you know. I'm the regular comedian around here. Full of laughs, that's me," I said, taking the piss.

"Oh really wow I didn't know. Maybe I can buy a ticket for your performance? Well, let's see who will be having the last laugh." She said in disgust. I looked at her name badge.

"Is it Miss or Mrs Gaiter or maybe you swing another way?" I sniggered back at her.

"Move it now!" As she grappled my wrists and yanked me by the handcuffs to move.

As I reached the foot of the door, something told me to turn around. As I did, I couldn't believe my eyes! They had Uncle too.

"Uncle Jeb!" I shouted out. As they frog marched him towards me. A tear began to stream down my face as I noticed they had put him in handcuffs too.

"Erykah are you alright?" Uncle said as the female guard pushed me quickly inside the security room and sat me down a little too ferociously for my liking. Then she moved to stand in the corner by the door of the room, and a fourth guard forcefully sat Uncle down.

"No, Uncle. That woman called me a black bitch, and she maltreated me too." Uncle kissed his teeth in defiance. He was not impressed.

"You two, shut up over there." The guard behind the desk said as he sneered at us. I quietly whispered to Uncle.

"What the hell is going on, Uncle? I don't quite understand why they've detained us." I said, feeling shook.

"Erykah don't panic. Be strong and let me handle this," he said, trying to reassure me.

Uncle leant slightly forward and opened his mouth. "My Niece and I would like to know why you have detained us?" Uncle questioned towards the guards.

"Bring them over here?" The head guard instructed the others to escort us nearer to his desk. "Before I tell you why you have been detained. I need to ask you a few questions." he relayed to us.

"What sort of questions?" Uncle quizzed.

"Just a few informal ones," the head guard said.

There was a knock on the door and in walked what looked like an undercover plainclothes officer. Judging by the gun and handcuffs, he was wearing around his waist.

"Sir," the undercover guard said.

"Mr Foster; how may I assist you?" The head guard asked.

"Just to inform you the estimated time of arrival for the police will be around ten to fifteen minutes." The undercover guard concluded.

"Noted Mr Foster; will that be all?" The head guard asked. Foster nodded yes back at him. "Right, where was I?" The guard said to himself.

He shuffled a few pieces of paper around and then clicked and unclicked the pen in his hand several times. Uncle and I looked at him in anticipation. We remained in silence until the questions came.

"I'm going to ask you two individually a few questions to establish who you are." Uncle and I looked at each other again and agreed telepathically to go with the flow for the meanwhile. We both said yes back at the guard.

"Okay, good. I'll start with you, young lady." I pulled a mini screwface at him to let him know I wasn't impressed by his actions, but I was ready. "Firstly, may I have your name, address, and date of birth," I complied.

"Miss Erykah Gaines I live at Flat 7, Bedford House, Princess Road, Moss Side, South Manchester M14 3NP and my date of birth is the seventeenth of the eighth, nineteen eighty-eight." I relayed.

"May I ask what you do for a living?" He asked. But I didn't want to respond. I was baffled on why he needed to know that. Uncle gave me that look so I told them.

"I'm a University Graduate," I said back at him with pride in my voice.

"Okay, so do you work now?" He nosily asked.

"I don't see why that's any of your business?" I angrily said. My voice now was edged with sarcasm.

"Erykah, please don't make things hard for yourself just tell dem nah." Uncle pleaded with me.

"Yes, Miss Gaines; I strongly suggest you take your uncle's advice," the head guard said like he owned us. Fucking bureaucrat I thought.

"I don't," I said, feeling exhausted now. All I wanted to do was to get the fuck out of here. These dudes were seriously derailing my journey to London.

"There you go. That wasn't so difficult, was it now, Miss Gaines?" He sarcastically said while continuing to devilishly smile at me.

"Whatever," I said dismissively.

"Sir, same questions apply to you," he said while sticking his nose in the air at Uncle.

"My name is Jeboniah Gaines, and I live at 348 Denison Road, Moss Side, South Manchester, M14 6SG and my date of birth is the twenty-ninth of the fourth, nineteen sixty-one," Uncle said in his best English accent. I had to laugh at the sheer bravery for a second.

But that was typical of Uncle always looking on the bright side. Wish I shared his confidence.

Uncle had seen many a day like this when he first came to England. This moment wasn't anything to him. But to me, I was a lot more scared of this situation then he was.

We yet don't know why we are being questioned, and in the back of my mind, I didn't need to kop a criminal record after the past I've had.

So much for a fresh start. I hope London fairs better and can finally give me the satisfaction and joy I crave in my life. Time will only tell.

"And what do you do for a living Mr Gaines?" The guard ordered for Uncle to say.

It felt so much like a military operation. Well, that's what my soul was telling me.

Everything seemed so covert. I started to get the feeling Uncle, and I wasn't going to reach the great capital today or tonight.

"I've been a carpenter for thirty years boss," Uncle said reverting to his usual patios tone.

"Okay." The Guard answered.

"I'm the proud owner of my own self-established business. Anything else you want to know?" Uncle looked more pissed off than me now.

"No, Mr Gaines, that will be all for the personal questions." the guard said then paused for a moment.

All of a sudden, he put on a severe face. In turn, he stared at uncle and me for around five seconds each.

"Right, now to the matter at hand," he said, sounding gleeful. What a prat, I thought. These people are jokers.

"Mr. and Miss Gaines; the reason why you in here, is that in this area and surrounding counties over the past month two other motorway services situated in Knutsford and Keele have been subject to armed robbery," I looked at Uncle and began to breathe awkwardly. Uncle noticed my sudden change in mood, and he quickly covered my hand with his. Immediately the warmth from his hand gave me a comforting feeling of safety. Uncle had that natural calming nature about him.

"So what has that got to do with us?" Uncle said, looking a bit mystified.

"Well, how can I put this delicately without seemingly offending you," the guard said precariously then continued. "I hope you can appreciate what I'm about to say. You must understand that in a town like you are in we don't get many people like yourselves around here." He concluded.

"Many people like us!" I had to bite my bottom lip hard as to stop myself from launching an attack at this son of a bitch.

I know I can't speak for Uncle. But what I do know he is as disgusted as I was at the sheer cockiness of what he just said to us.

At this point, I wanted to exercise my democratic right to excuse myself. But I knew if I tried to make a dash for it, I'd probably make myself look guilty as hell.

"Miss Gaines calm down please?" He had a nerve. "I'm merely stating a fact." He rudely concluded. These heinous acts of micro-aggression are making my blood boil. In turn it was promising to realise a wrath of anger that was warranted in this scenario. But I quickly changed my mind and decided it was time for a little less aggression and a lot more old-fashioned diplomacy.

"Listen, Mr," I leant forward a bit more so I could make out what was written on his black name tag. "Mr Donahue; I appreciate that you're doing your job. But what I don't like," I paused for a few seconds then I continued. "Is how you think, because as you've finely stated, people like us. I presume you mean black people!" Donahue shuffled nervously in his seat and cleared his throat from having to look away in embarrassment.

"Just because we are black, you automatically assume we are criminals. I only came in here to use the toilets and have a coffee. Now you got my Uncle and me in here and accusing us of armed robbery. I've never heard anything more absurd in all of my twenty-seven years of existence."

"Miss Gaines; let me reassure you and your Uncle that at this stage we are just following enquiries." He sounded off like he was enjoying scrutinising us. I looked at him, and back at uncle, then it came.

"Listen Mr Donahue; like I said I appreciate you're doing your job," I moved around to where he was and towered over him. "But you have no right to hold my Uncle and me here without any evidence or proof. So unless you're arresting us, I suggest you let my Uncle and I leave this room. I will then buy myself some new clothes, get cleaned up and changed. Then we are going to walk out of this

44

complex with no fuss, get in our vehicle and leave." I argued. Suddenly the expression on Donahue's deeply-lined face was one of instant irritation. He mumbled something unintelligible to himself and then came back at me with venom in his voice.

"Miss Gaines;" he bawled out. "My professional suggestion to you is that you remain calm from here on in until the police come." He said assertively.

"Erykah cool yuhself nuh an listen to di man," Uncle pleaded for me to stay calm. But I couldn't sit here any more than we had to. I was wet, stinky and hungry. I needed retribution and recuperation.

"No, Uncle, I can't do that." I looked at him like I had steel coming out of my eyes. Uncle knew by my look, I meant business and that I didn't give a flying fuck about what was going to happen to me next. That would've been cool if I was on my own. But I had Uncle to consider, and the last thing he needed was to get arrested. So I decided to hold it down for a minute, while I contemplated my next move.

The undercover guard that came in earlier came back into the room and whispered something into Donahue's ear. He looked frivolous. Donahue jiggled his head then gathered his papers together, put his pen in his shirt pocket and then addressed Uncle and me.

"Mr & Miss Gaines can you stand up please?" As soon as we did what Donahue said, in walked two Police officers.

"What the fuck?" I whispered to Uncle. I couldn't believe it they were serious about the Po-Po coming.

"Erykah Nuh worry yuhself dis a jus formality. Dem ave no evidence pan wi. But it dem job fi follow up enquires." He finished saying trying to reassure me.

"Alright Uncle, I'll take your word for it this time," I had enough of fighting for now. I felt dirty, and I wanted to get changed. I knew by Uncle's statement we were going to be arrested, so I requested an action before they arrested us. "Mr Donahue!" I shouted over everyone.

"Yes, Miss Gaines; can I help you with something?" This mother fucker being all polite and shit now because the police were present. I tittered inside and seized my opportunity to get what I needed.

"Thank you, Mr Donahue," I replied with the biggest grin I could muster. Maybe I was pushing my luck. But right now I didn't give a damn. "I was wondering if could ask you a favour," I said still grinning from ear to ear.

"What favour would that be Miss Gaines?" Donahue said through gritted teeth. His eyes lowered in stature, and he looked like he was about to spontaneously combust.

"I need a change of garments and some toiletries because of my little accident earlier." He had no choice. He was cornered. He had to agree otherwise refusing a request like mine would make Donahue and his whole crew look bad.

"Okay, Miss Gaines; due to the exceptional circumstance, I will grant your request. Two of my officers Mr Gadson and Mrs Weeks, will accompany you. But Miss Gaines, if you try anything funny you will make matters worse for yourself, understood?"

Judging by the look in his eyes, I knew he wasn't fucking with me. I picked myself up. As I walked past the guards, I reached the foot of the door and was about to step out when a third police officer grabbed me by my arm.

"You got fifteen minutes Miss Gaines," she quietly whispered in my ear. I bowed my head once back at her as to comply with what she just said.

As I finally stepped out of the room, I breathed a huge sigh of relief. Donahue told me they would keep Uncle as insurance in case I tried to escape. Dumb fucks! How could I, when Uncle was the one with the van keys?

I shook my head in disbelief at the amateur operation they had going. I mean who in the middle of being accused of something as serious as armed robbery and had guns pointed at me not too long ago, is allowed to go and recoup myself.

So while they held uncle in the security room until my arrival back I told the guards, I wanted to go two places. Clothes shop and a chemist! They said where I could go and began to lead me to the first place.

As I began my walk with the guards, I saw the boy who was waiting. Ah, I thought to myself. I had to try and find a way to get a moment with him.

As I got nearer to where he was standing, I gave him a wink and mouthed for him to follow us. Mrs Weeks looked at me like I was filth and began to shuffle me and told me to pick up my pace.

"This one," I said to Mrs Weeks. She waited by the entrance of the store, and I quickly walked inside the small boutique and immediately was greeted by a smiling blond lady, early thirties looking.

"Welcome to Prestige Fashions, how may I assist you?" Her friendly approach was reassuring in a town full of narcissistic individuals.

"Yes, I need a pair of jeans, underwear and a new top please," My voice dipped in tone as I realised why I was shopping for new clothes in the first place.

"Judging by your figure, I would say you're a size eight. Am I about right?" She questioned with that darn infectious smile again.

I was supposed to be staying mad, but she was so lovely and helpful, and her sunny disposition was rubbing off on me.

"Yes," I said, sounding surprised. "How did you guess?" I said, amazed by her professionalism.

"Oh, it's my job to know," she said as she began to guide me around the store. After she helped me pick out my clothes, I followed her to the till. On route, I clocked my boy walking into the shop with another female beside him. I saw Week's nose turn up when she spotted me looking in her direction, but I don't think she suspected a thing.

In the next instant, my boy handed me a piece of folded paper, stared at me for about five seconds and proceeded to walk around the store. I stuffed the paper down my bra top, paid for the clothes, said goodbye to the assistant and walked out the store where I was met by Mrs Weeks and Mr Gadson.

"How long have I got left?" I said a little nervously.

"About eight minutes more," Gadson responded in his dry, monotone voice.

"Okay, good to the chemist please," I said to the guards. So we proceeded in it's direction. Once I finished paying for my toiletries, I looked at my watch and saw I had about four minutes left.

With the guards, I quickly made my way to the ladies toilets. Once I was inside, and with Mrs Weeks closely guarding the entrance, I ripped the price tags off the jeans and top then I took out my underwear and toiletries. When I finished, I double-checked myself in the mirror.

"Damn girl, you're looking fine," I mumbled to myself. I had to try and lift my spirits some more because I knew when I reached back to the security room, the inevitable was going to happen. The guards and I made our way back with one minute to spare. When we reached, we entered the room.

Donahue clocked me in an instant, and as in doing so, he licked his lips like the cat that got the cream. Hmm maybe

48

after an hour in my presence he looked like he wanted a piece of my black ass. Oh well, this was one white man that had to suffice with that notion in his dreams.

Still, as I walked past him, I shot him a sexy look for his memory bank, and I swear down for a second he looked like he went weak at the knees. Inside of me, my thoughts and feelings had me in hysterics. I sat down and asked Uncle if he was okay. He motioned back to me yes and took my hand in his.

"Did they treat you alright?" Uncle asked. He was concerned for my welfare considering what happened to me back in Manchester earlier today.

"So, so Uncle Jeb; but I'll be fine. We, Gaines, are a strong bunch and we all have had graver times." Uncle looked at me and smiled because he knew I'd be fine in the long run.

We waited for a few moments and in came the officers. Donahue told Uncle and me to stand up, so we did as he instructed.

Considering my small outburst earlier, I evaluate that Uncle Jeb, and I have corresponded very well. We were ready to see what was about to go down next.

"Mr Jeboniah Gaines and Miss Erykah Gaines I am arresting you both on suspicion of armed robbery of this complex at Sandbach and two other complexes I mentioned before in Knutsford and Keele. You do not have to say anything, but it may harm your defence if you do not mention when questioned something which you later rely on in court. Anything you say may be given in evidence." Immediately I burst into tears and Uncle's face turned very sour.

As the officers handcuffed Uncle and myself, part of me wished I had held on longer and stopped off somewhere else. But I couldn't have predicted this in a month of Sunday's.

As we were shamelessly walked out of the complex, Uncle was told they were going to tow his van to the police station where we were heading to.

They were going to hold us for twenty-four hours while they investigate.

We were shoved into the back of a meat wagon like we were criminal masterminds of the twenty-first century.

The van sped off to its destination with Uncle and myself in it.

I felt angry as well as upset now. All I had to do was tell the truth because this is a blatant case of mistaken identity, and when Marcus, our family solicitor proves they have nothing on us. The police will wish they never messed with Uncle and me.

There is one piece of crucial evidence, and that is the video from the mobile.

I hope the boy was for real because I planned on suing the Cheshire police force at the first opportunity I get.

Chapter 3 – 24 Hours

Dear White People was a film I watched last week, and It's in America where they are still behind in race relations.

You wouldn't think in good old not so Great Britain these problems still exist. But they do. Not only do they do. The powers that be are very covert and mask their hidden agendas very neatly in many forms.

For example, things like equal opportunities! Ha, you don't want to see me get started on that bullshit. Trust me; I'm not in the mood.

Thinking about it, I remember a few years ago when I was listening to an online radio station broadcast and the presenter who is not around anymore. No, he is not dead. He just retired.

I remember distinctly him saying one time on his weekly talk show, that how the local council and private entities are trying to price out the existing black business tenant in Brixton, South London by charging them double the rent.

I mean how ludicrous is that and proof how evil these people are.

So what I'm trying to say is; when you're faced with difficult times, know that challenges are not sent to destroy you; they're sent to promote, increase and strengthen you. Know that knowledge is the pursuit of power, and manifesting power through struggle will give you the right kind of strength also.

As I remembered all that, I had to take heed of my own advice!

We finally arrived. Uncle and I were escorted inside Sandbach & Alsager Police Station. If I didn't think before we got arrested that this was happening, then reality struck and suddenly it dawned on me the varsity of what we were being accused of.

Though at this stage Uncle and I had to play the waiting game and that wasn't going to be an easy task either.

Inside the station's reception area, funny smells mixed with one guy constantly banging on his cell door was putting my head in a daze already.

I looked over at Uncle who was putting on a brave face for my benefit.

When we finally pulled up to the desk, the duty officer standing behind it began to check us in. He turned his attention to me first.

"Good Afternoon, my name is John Brown, and I'm the duty sergeant who will be conducting your formal interviews on this day of August, the ninth two thousand and fifteen. I will be going through with you a series of questions to establish your state of wellbeing, which is a formality. You will be searched and have to sign on this scratchpad to verify you've been questioned, and you have understood everything I've asked of you. Do you understand everything I've said to you both so far?"

Uncle and I shook our head's and said yes.

"Right you first," he said, looking down on me. "Can you empty your pockets please?"

I did what he commanded. I emptied my pockets and put the belongings onto the desk. The female officer that bought Uncle and me in searched me over.

Sergeant. Brown was itemising my things, and when he was done, another officer bagged them to store away.

"Do you want me to strip naked as well?" I disdainfully said to him. He scowled his face at me by surpassing what I said and continued.

He is quite the large man is officer Brown, but for an officer of the law he looked like a big softie. He reminded me of one of those gentle giants you see in movies. He had bits of hair down the both sides of his head and the rest of the few
strands of hair he had left, was combed neatly across his bolding head top.

"Erykah, behave yourself!" Uncle ordered me to settle down.

"I'm just getting warmed up." I reacted by rubbing my hands together. Uncle juddered his head from side to side with a disappointed look etched on his face.

"For the record, all I want you to give me at this stage is a yes or no answer. Do you understand?"

Sergeant Brown said, looking down at me like I was short.

"Yes, I understand," my throat felt dry. "May I have a glass of water, please?" Expectantly he granted my request.

Brown motioned to another officer who was standing a few feet away from him to fetch my water.

"John; what did your last slave die off?" He said back to Officer Brown.

I found his comment a bit comical, but he looked like he'd been around the block one too many times in his life.

He possessed the heinous of vibes and he had that look like he was member of the English Defence League. As he walked off, he gave me a look that made me feel he was a racist. I could sense it from the atmosphere he was giving off.

"Right, I shall continue," Sergeant Brown carried on where he began. "Like I said a yes or no answer please," I dipped my head back at him in compliance. "Are you Miss

Erykah Gaines of Flat 7, Bedford House, Princess Road, Moss Side, South Manchester M14 3NP?"

"Yes, I am."

"Your date of birth is the seventeenth of the eighth nineteen eighty-eight. You're a university graduate and are currently unemployed. Is this information correct?" He reiterated to me.

"Yes," sheepishly replying. Officer Brown then began to ask me a serious of personal questions. Something I personally love to hate. Auntie always told me it stemmed from the days of relentless questioning from the media.

Unless I know you very well, I tend to keep certain information about me private. Since my sexual abuse case back in 2004, coupled with the hounding of the press which was accompanied by their fabricated lies has made me this way.

Before all that I wasn't. I was as happy as certain days and life would permit me to be, and that wasn't many.

I would go as far as to tell you that only about five years out of my twenty-seven of existence have been genuinely remarkable.

To top it all up that is a lot, considering the upbringing and tribulations I have encountered throughout my younger days.

"Right," he said as he licked his lips and continued. "Miss Erykah Gaines I'm arresting you on suspicion of armed robbery by using and carrying a dangerous weapon. You have been accused of robbing and endangering the public of three motorway complexes in the county of Cheshire. To help us conduct our investigation under section 8 (1) of the theft act nineteen sixty-eight. When we obtain a warrant, we have the right to search your home property. If we need to Greater Manchester Police will be assisting us due to the distance of your home. What will happen now is that you will be taken to another room, where you will be photographed and fingerprinted. You'll also be asked if you want anything to eat or drink. You'll be seen by the police surgeon where he will take a DNA swab and check your state of health to determine whether you are physically and mentally able to be in our custody for twenty-four hours why we investigate these allegations against you. You will be supplied with a duty solicitor unless you have one of your own. If you have, you can tell us now so we can log their details and contact them for you. You're also permitted one personal phone call too."

"How very generous of you." I sarcastically replied.

"Okay, I'm now going to ask you some legal questions. Do you understand?"

"Yes, I do," I complied back. Now I was getting bored with Officer Brown.

"The first question, do you have a history of taking drugs?"

"No," I replied.

"Have you taken any drugs or consumed any alcohol in the last twenty-four hours?" He continued questioning.

"No."

"Have you ever had suicidal thoughts or tendencies?"

"Hell no!" I was getting mad as fuck now.

"Do you have a history of mental health, depression or epilepsy?" He asked.

"No, no, no." I fired back very quickly, feeling so frustrated with this whole line of questioning. I'm innocent for fuck sake. I kept telling myself to convince myself I was.

"What's your sexual orientation?"

"Do I have to answer that?"

"Yes its formality Miss Gaines, so answer the question please." He commanded.

I leant forward and cheekily whispered a short distance from his ear.

"I like my men big and strong like you sergeant. Does that answer your question?" I smirked as Officer Brown shuffled nervously in his seat and cleared his throat in embarrassment.

He didn't know where to look as he fondled around with his keyboard.

A few beads of sweat began to fall from his head, so he wiped it off. He tried to compose himself the best he could. He took a deep and meaningful breath and continued where he started, still shaking his head.

I swear down a little whimper of a smile formed in the corner of his mouth, but it was hard to tell. I laughed inside. It was nice even for a moment to feel in control of a bad situation.

"So I'll ask you the same question again. What's your sexual orientation?"

"I'm heterosexual, of course."

"Last question. What's your ethnicity?"

Inside I was laughing uncontrollably that it almost came up to the surface. Was Officer Brown serious? I know he is not blind.

"I'm Black British with Afro-Caribbean parents and African heritage."

"IC3 female okay." He nonchalantly replied. It was like he wanted me to say yes. So he could record on his little computer another black person with all kinds of issues.

"Right now can you take a seat over there and when we have finished processing your Uncle, you'll both be escorted to the photo room one by one." He concluded.

After they finished booking me in, they moved on to Uncle and put him through the same process.

"When will I get my phone call?" I quizzed.

"Miss Gaines; when we are finished here, and the surgeon has seen you." He certified.

Finally, after ages, the officer whose name wasn't prevalent to me yet came back with my cup of water.

He handed it to me but held on to the cup for a few seconds longer than he had to. I tried to wrestle it from him, but his grip was stronger than mine.

I looked up at him and shot him a stare that was saying what the fuck. He had a smirk a mile wide across his face that gave me the impression he done something nasty to it.

Eventually, he let the plastic cup go and walked away back through the door that took him back up through to the desk.

I looked down inside the cup, and my hunch was right. At the bottom swirling around, it looked like he'd spat in it.

In my disgust, I immediately threw the cup towards him, and the water went everywhere, even a bit caught Uncle's boot.

I screamed out loud, hollering at the top of my voice. I was fuming now.

"You fucking, dirty bastard." Instantly I got up from where I was seated and began hurtling towards the desk.

In my minute of anguish, I attempted to climb over the desk, and I succeeded. I jumped over and lunged myself onto Racist taking the bastard with me towards the floor below us.

"You pig, you low down scumbag." I started laying into him with a combination of lefts and rights to the face. He tried to fend me off by throwing his arms up in defence.

"Get off me you crazy bitch," he said between blows.

As I was about to go for it some more, from behind me, two strong arms lifted me off him kicking and screaming.

This time Office Brown; put me in handcuffs, marched me at a quick pace around the desk and stood me, so I was facing in front of him again.

The officer I decked was up and standing next to me. He was rubbing his head from where I punched him and spitting blood from the cut on his mouth.

"You stupid little girl," he angrily said to me as his face contorted in rage. It also looked like as if an atom bomb had exploded inside of him.

In the next instance, I turned my head towards him and whispered into his personal space.

"My, my you're a silly little man aren't you, your words do not affect me. You're a human that is intellectually circumcised and serves his existence with a mind that is limited by ignorance. Call yourself a copper! You act worse than a three-year-old child." Boom, sucker punch. I gave it to him good and proper. He looked like a little-lost lamb and had no comeback except the power of police brute force.

"Shut up," he said through a false smile and gritted teeth while grappling my left arm.

Uncle looked over at me, which I interpreted as if he was saying well done and stupid at the same time.

I couldn't be bothered with what anyone thought. I learnt a long time ago that I wasn't a person to be intimidated easily and kept in a box. My nature and my core being wouldn't allow it.

So if they were going to slap an extra charge on me, then so be it. Why? Because I know they have CCTV everywhere in here and when I point it out to them, I'm sure they will find out what I suspected.

"Miss Gaines; I know you're upset. But unprovoked you attacked one of our officers. An attack on an officer of the law is a serious offence, so we are going to be adding that to the list of charges against you already. Do you understand?" Officer Brown asked.

"But it wasn't unprovoked!" I said in protest.

"Oh, and how did you get to that conclusion Miss Gaines?" He said, looking at me like I was deluded.

"Your colleague spat in my cup. What you think I screamed out expletives for the fun of it? Considering the charges. Do you think I want to make matters worse for myself?" I anxiously said.

"Well, Miss Gaines, I don't know about all that. But what I do know is that I witnessed and our CCTV will back up your so-called unprovoked attack on a fellow officer of the law. There is no proof of your allegation and." Before Officer Brown could mutter another word, Uncle cut him off in mid-sentence.

"Sir, with all due respect, my niece would not lie about such a thing or attack this man without just cause. I'm not saying or condoning on how she handled it. I know my niece very well, and that's what I'm saying." Finally, Uncle came alive and on a level.

Injustice and police brutality was something he had grown up with back home and when he first came to this country.

It was something that eked at his very core being. So whenever it reared its ugly head. The disparity he always felt towards the police was with serious contempt. His anger magnified even greater, especially when it came to black folk and his family.

"Mr Gaines; regardless of what your niece has accused my colleague off, It doesn't look good from where I was standing, does it?" He repeated to Uncle in a very patronising manner.

"Listen if my niece said he spat in her drink then that's what happened. I'm going to make sure after this justice is served." Officer Brown looked at uncle in a very sceptical way.

He looked like he wasn't quite sure on how to take Uncles assertive comment. All he could do was to force his authority over him by side-tracking our plea and continuing with why we were brought in here in the first place.

"Okay, Mr Gaines; we will look into it." Uncle shook his head back imperturbably, but in a manner that was saying to himself, I don't believe you.

I sat back down, awaiting the inevitable.

"So now you're both booked. Like I said before you'll be in to have your photos and I.D taken and then on to see the police surgeon. Miss Gaines; my staff have got in contact with Mr Hudson, and he is on his way." A momentary smile swept across my face because I knew, once I told Marcus everything, I know he will find discrepancies and when Marcus does; by the time he will be finished with this lot. They're going to wish they never arrested Uncle and me in the first place.

When they finished questioning Uncle, I was instructed to get up by Racist. He grabbed my arm a little bit too vehemently for my liking.

As I turned around and shot him a screwface, he gripped my arm a bit harder.

"Ouch." He was hurting me as he compellingly began shoving me towards the fingerprint room opposite the booking desk.

Uncle was behind us and saw the whole thing.

"Mind yuhself nah man?"

"Oh, really, and what is that supposed to mean?" Racist said, questioning Uncle.

"I don't like the way you're handling my niece. She is complying, so is it necessary to rough her up in that way?" Uncle looked him square in the eyes. Racist got the female officer to hold on to me.

He walked right up to Uncle and stopped inches from his face.

I began fearing the worst for Uncle.

"Listen here, boy," he said, emphasising the word boy. "I don't take orders from an overgrown, jive-talking nigger like you. One more word and I'll make sure you're charged with obstructing police business."

Oh my gosh, Racist didn't just call Uncle a boy.

Racist remained glued to his spot, which was antagonising Uncle even more. That comment left Uncle sieving with anger. But uncle was better than him and showed solidarity that had me feeling proud.

"That's what I thought, nothing but an empty shell." Uncle frowned upon Racist, but no words came out of his mouth. If it were me, we all know what I'll do.

But Uncle has been through worse in his life, and he isn't about to let some scrubby little racist white cop get to him.

Still as much as Racist is a motherfucker he is just another cog, a puppet in a system that is corrupt and institutionally racist.

For a further minute, it went quiet. I figured Uncle decided to back down and not to say another word. He cut his eye and kissed his teeth at Racist and then looked over at me. He mouthed and asked if I was okay. I mouthed back that I was fine for the moment.

The pair proceeded to walk us into the fingerprint room. Racist and the female officer handed us over to a miserable, large looking, fifty-something lady.

By the look, that was planted on Misery's face. It seemed she hadn't been fucked in a long time. I knew from that, she was another cog in the machine.

As soon as a crazy thought of Racist and Misery getting together entered my mind as quickly as it came into it left all the same.

I let out a little whimper of a laugh to escape my mouth as I scanned Misery up and down.

She stood around five foot, five tall and looked like she weighed around a hundred and seventy pounds. Her hair was pulled back and tied in a neat bun. She wore glasses and reminded me of an old high school teacher.

"Afternoon," she said in a low, husky voice. "You know why you're in here, so shall we just get on with it?"

Her attitude was condescending and stank to high heaven. What was wrong with everyone around here, did they all get up on the wrong side of the bed this morning?

My hunch was telling me they were like this every day or when they arrested black folk or scum of the earth.

"Right young lady, can you come over here and sit in this chair?"

I suppose it was too much to expect a please from her as well.

I sat opposite as she was concentrating on the screen in front of her.

She began typing away on her keyboard, and every other moment she would glance up at me, hold her gaze for a few seconds and then proceeded to tap away again. Strange, I thought.

"Okay Miss Gaines, can you put your hands onto the purple hand pad in front of you?"

Yet again, I followed her orders. I was beginning to feel sick as thoughts of being incarcerated came flowing into my mind.

I mean everyone that knows me, knows I'm not a believer in God, but that doesn't stop me from believing in coincidences.

You see I'm a major Netflix fan and I've just about watched everything on there. The last thing I was watching was season three of 'Orange Is the New Black'. Most people reading this now will know what I'm talking about, but for those that don't, it's a U.S based drama series set around mainly a central character and a bunch of women doing time in prison.

So you see all this that is happening today is maybe more than a coincidence from watching that programme I believe. What if this is my destiny? Crazy, but the signs were there. I didn't see them coming.

At the end of the day was I supposed to?

I'm so stressed and confused right now, and all I can do is weigh out this process and hope Marcus will find the evidence Uncle, and I need to get off.

"Good, now can you go stand in front of the white screen behind you. Look straight into the camera in front of you and when I say turn left then right, then do so. Please, no smiling or funny faces. Nice and normal, okay?"

After Misery had taken my prints and photos, the female officer handcuffed me again and escorted me outside to the seats. Uncle went in after to go through the same procedure as I did.

A few minutes later, Racist led Uncle out to where I was seated.

"You two remain here quietly please until the Police surgeon is ready for you." Racist concluded.

"Are you alright Uncle?" By the look on Uncle's face, I was getting a little concerned for him.

Not because if he was feeling any fear. He is one of the bravest, toughest and smartest men I know. Nah I was worried more about his welfare.

I know he is strong, but he has been up from five a.m. getting my things ready, and all that driving so far must be taking a small toll on him.

"Yeah man, I'm a guh be alright yuh kno. I'm just a likkle hungry. But oddah dan dat mi gud. Ow, bout you?"

"To be honest Uncle Jeb, I'm scared as hell. My mind is going around and around in circles, trying to piece everything together. We both know we are innocent. I hope Marcus can come up trumps this time."

"Listen to mi gud?" He said.

Uncle shuffled himself a bit closer to me and whispered.

"With you being afraid is killing me softly. Remember nothing confuses a man or woman more than a kind gesture to his enemies when then renders him or her open to suggestion. Overstand?"

I bobbed my head back that I understood.

"Suh try an compose yuhself Erykah cuz mi cun tek yuh being fraid too. A likkle fear fine yuh human. Just kno seh ow di Babylon system a set up. An eff dem or Marcus cun find nuhting. Den wi inna deep trouble. But mi truss inna mi heart t' ings wi be fine. Mi might be an old optimistic fool, but mi nuh chupid. Suh nah worry yuhself?"

"Okay Uncle I'll try, thank you."

"No worries Erykah I got your back."

As I smiled a small weight began to lift off my shoulders.

A few moments later, Racist and the female officer came back.

In the next phase, they led Uncle and me through some double swing doors still handcuffed.

We proceeded down the long corridor with Racist and the female officer.

STAND IN YOUR POWER

When we all reached our destination, we had descended on a dark blue door. The plaque on the door, which was in line with my eyesight had the words police surgeon engraved in black lettering on a silver background.

Racist knocked on the door three times, and the voice from the other side said; 'Come on in'.

Once we stepped inside and sat down, Racist introduced us to Dr Heston.

Heston pleasantly greeted Uncle and me.

"Mr. and Miss. Gaines; relax please." Was he taking the piss?

I swear down I heard him say relax. That was an understatement if I ever heard one so far in this place.

I smiled with a bemused look on my face. Uncle looked at me precariously, and when he saw me smiling, he managed one of his own.

Racist looked over at Uncle and me in turn. He seemed a little perplexed but continued all the same in a surprisingly professional manner with no fuss.

"My name is Dr Heston, and I'm the police surgeon who will be conducting your DNA tests today. Also, I'll be conducting a basic health check. As I'm sure you know why we need to do this?"

Uncle and I simultaneously nodded our heads back at him in acknowledgement.

"Right, that's great," as he took a swab out of its pack. "Miss Gaines; I'll do yours first," he said as he shuffled his seat nearer to mine. "Open wide." He continued to speak.

A small grin began to appear on my face. Those words were very synonymous with things of a sexual nature, and I couldn't help or keep the laughter from rising in my belly.

"Are you okay Miss Gaines?" He asked quizzically.

"Yes, I'm fine, Dr," he continued to swab my mouth while looking at me over his specs with his beady eyes.

Uncle knew why I was laughing and saw the funny side as well. But it was only another front I was putting on because, to be honest, it was hiding the fact of how scared I was feeling.

"Okay, that's all finished," he confirmed. "Now I'm going to do a few more checks, and we will be all done."

He went through the motions, and before I knew it, I was out of the room.

Uncle remained inside to do his tests.

Racist led me to cell seven.

He told me to take off my shoes and anything else I could potentially harm myself with, and then he unlocked the door.

I slowly shuffled myself inside.

Racist told me to turn around and face the cell door as he shut and locked it. He opened up the hatch and told me to put my hands through it. Once he finished taking my handcuffs off, he told me what was going to happen next. I asked him how long that will be. He replied when they are ready as I'll be spending the next twenty-four hours in here and if they had no case Uncle and I would be released.

Over the next twenty-four hours minus eight for uninterrupted sleep Uncle and I were interviewed three times apiece, two times were together.

The second charge against me for attacking a police officer stuck. I had to surrender my passport and give them notification of where I'll be living.

They told me in due course I'll be sent a letter outlining a court date and time and in the end as I knew for the first charge of armed robbery they had no case.

Marcus, who has been our family solicitor since Smith's trial reiterated it was as I suspected a case of mistaken identity.

I mean, I was relieved. But at the same time these mother fuckers have wasted a whole day of our time and most of all they showed us how they are not so far behind the USA in how they deal with the black community.

Chapter 4 – On The Road Again

After Uncle and I retained his van from the police compound, we headed back towards the M6 and began our journey to London again.

"Erykah mi nah kno bout yuh, but I'm suh hungry mi cud nyam a horse," Uncle said like he hadn't eaten a good meal for time.

"So am I, Uncle Jeb, so am I," I said, feeling flustered and deflated.

"Wen mi si di next town I'm a guh drive dung there an find a likkle cafe or sup'm," he said reassuringly.

"That will be cool Uncle nice one," I said, trying to sound as happy as I could muster at this point. I needed uncle to cheer me up because I was feeling angry as fuck. One sad look his way, and that was enough to ignite the fire within him.

"Erykah what's up? Yuh luk like you're carrying di whole world inna yuh shouldas." Uncle had picked up very quickly on my sudden change of mood.

"I'm a lil' bit Uncle. But truly, I'm angrier than ever. I mean I can believe, because as a race; we have had to endure brutality and injustice from the police all over the world for centuries. So that's nothing new. What I'm pissed off most about, is the fact how under-developed and uneducated certain areas of this country are in the 21st century."

I was feeling aggrieved. The events over the last twenty-four hours had me thinking deeply about things I only lightly bothered about in the past. I felt as if I was getting pulled into a new direction. My instincts were telling to follow a path and see where it led. Universally willing, I will die hard trying to achieve the inevitable my life thus far has brought me too.

"What's the plan Erykah?" Uncle knew me very well and could see right through me. He could read me like a book, and he knew I wasn't going to rest on my laurels.

"First things first Uncle; food is the plan," my belly was now commencing to have a growling contest with the rest of my body. "After that, when we reach London. We unpack, settle for a bit. You leave and a day's rest later, I try and make contact with the youth from the Sandbach Complex." I said, and that was my plan so far.

"Sounds good to me, but don't forget to call your father when we reach Nina's flat?" Uncle said as he put a brand new CD into the car's sound system.

I tilted my seat and headrest back a little as I allowed myself to become immersed in the sounds of Beres Hammonds; 'Practice What You Preach' tune which came wafting through Uncles sub-bass speakers at the right time.

The melodic tune was a comforting backdrop to the minefield of madness that was ransacking through my mind. I closed my eyes and relaxed my body until we reached the next town.

(Half an hour later)

"Erykah wake up. Wake up, niece!" The sound of Uncles bassist voice came coursing through my ears and up into my head.

The panning rigorous noise had woke me up in an instant.

"What's all the panic about?" I said as I rubbed my eyes to disperse the fogginess in my head. I stretched my arms up above me and backed down again and then turned to face Uncle.

"I found us somewhere to eat," he said, sounding like an excited little kid.

Uncle turned off the engine, and I undid my seatbelt. I opened the van door and got out.

The street seemed very busy for this time of day. I suppose people were doing last-minute shopping and making the most of the end of summer sales.

"Erykah luk pon deyah! Cross di road." Uncle pointed out behind him. I couldn't believe my eyes, was I dreaming.

"No fucking way. Hang on, where are we, Uncle?" I said, sounding confused and elated at the same time.

Right across the road was a massive Afro-Caribbean Centre. Inside my heart was beating ten to the dozen, and my stomach was doing somersaults.

"The exit coming in said Hanley," Uncle said back to me.

"I can't believe this. It looks perfect. You're a star Uncle," I said, smiling at him.

I leaned forward and gave him the biggest hug I could muster. On impact as my head rested on his chest, the tears came flooding down my face as I let out all the emotions that had been pent up inside over the last two days.

Uncle held me tight as thoughts over the last forty-eight hours went through my mind.

"Come let's see what's inside?" Uncle let go of me and offered out his right hand to me. I took it as we proceeded the short walk together into the centre.

As we went through the automatic double doors, we were greeted by a beautiful thirties looking, black lady. For a receptionist; I noticed she was immaculately dressed from head to toe in a designer Versace woman's business suit.

Very plush for a place like this seeing where it's situated. But as I opened my eyes and looked further, I could tell by the décor and the artefacts that surrounded Uncle and I that we were in a place that not only appeared but smelt of richness.

With me being a person who needs to see and feel a lot to be impressed, this building had me in awe of it.

Uncle unbelievably was acting all cool, and he had a Sauvé spring in his step all of a sudden.

As we edged nearer to the reception desk, Uncle seemed like he was in a trance. His eyes were focused and transfixed, and he was drooling like a dog in heat.

When I spotted where he was looking, I gently nudged him in his side. He came out of his fixation quick fast and did what men his age do; act like nothing was wrong.

The lady behind the desk must've noticed Uncle's tongue hanging halfway out of his mouth. She managed a small chortle of laughter to escape her sexy frame. I mean, I felt what Uncle was doing. If I ever was to turn tricks that would be a female I would sort after, you feel me.

"Good afternoon and welcome to First Approach Afro-Caribbean & African Arts Centre here in Hanley, Stoke-on-Trent. I'm Caroline Arani; the owner of this fine establishment, seeing as my receptionist hasn't come back from her lunch break. How may I be of assistance to you?"

Her gentle approach greeted Uncle and myself and immediately had me feeling good inside.

"Hi, Miss Arani! My name is Erykah Gaines, and this is my overgrown Uncle, who is acting like a lovesick teenager; Mr Jeboniah Gaines. But in our family, we call him Uncle Jeb."

"Nice to meet your acquaintance, Miss Gaines," she offered out her hand to me. I took it and gave it a gentle shake. "Uncle Jeb," she said with a cheeky smile on her face. She offered out her hand in the same way as she did for me. But Uncle was old school. He took her hand in his and brought it up to his face. He bowed his head down towards her hand and kissed it in a way I've never seen him do. I know he loves the bones of Aunt CeCe. But I've never seen him kiss someone with such passion before. "Oh my, what a gentleman," she said in a theatrical tone. As soon the words left Miss Arani's Mouth, Uncle bought his head up very slowly and rolled his eyes upwards towards her with a brazen grin on his face.

"My pleasure mam," Uncle said with solidarity in his voice. "I was brought up in an era where manner's to the opposite sex was paramount. Not like the youth of today." He concluded.

This man had the audacity to attack my generation in front off a lady he hardly knew, so he could score some cheap points at my expense.

Such impudence I thought to myself.

But I decided quickly to react in a charmingly and chivalrous manner.

"Uncle." I playfully grabbed his face and mumbled a load of silly words. Uncle took my face in his hands and gave me a big smacker of a kiss on my forehead. I laughed out loud, and Uncle had a titter too.

Uncle and I were very close as Aunt Ce-Ce, and he played a big part in my upbringing.

Miss Arani stood behind us with her arms folded and smiled a smile a mile wide long at Uncles and mines antics.

"Well, your manners have been duly noted." As soon as she finished talking. Another lady came behind the desk and sat herself down on a seat. She took off the plastic card that was attached to a neck chain and slotted into the side of a keyboard. She proceeded to tap a few keys and then looked towards Caroline.

"Nice lunch break Miss Caulker?" Caroline said with an air of authority.

"Yes, thank you, Miss Arani." The receptionist replied as she looked over at Uncle and me.

"Okay good," Caroline said as she picked up a few papers and other items from the desk. "These people are exceptional guests of mine. See to it that they are treated to a VIP table in our restaurant Miss Caulker. Mr & Miss Gaines I presume you're both hungry?" She questioned.

"Yes, we are, " I said excitingly. Uncle just smiled.

"Okay, then." Caroline replied as she excused herself from our presence.

As she went to go, Uncle lightly grabbed her arm. What was he doing, I thought to myself? Caroline turned around a bit startled. When she realised it was Uncle, the expression on her face changed to one of sheer delight. I knew that Uncle and Aunt were having their problems of late. Still, on what I saw on observation I could see there was a mutual attraction between Miss Arani and Uncle, and I was getting the feeling that Uncle was going to put me in an inevitable position because he wasn't hiding the fact his lust for Miss Arani in front of me.

They exchanged a few words between themselves, and then Uncle motioned to me he was going to the restaurant with Miss Arani. I nodded back and signalled for him to go ahead.

I asked Miss Caulker where the ladies toilets were, and she duly pointed me in the right direction.

After I finished my lady business, I walked back through the large reception area and headed towards the restaurant. As soon as I got to the entrance, the smell of curry goat and jerk chicken wafted past me, prickling my senses and causing my belly to rumble.

As I sauntered my ass inside, I first spotted Uncle and Miss Arani seated in the VIP section that was situated over in the far left corner by some massive windows that were draped with blue velvet curtains. They looked quite content and deeply engrossed in conversation.

"Erykah over here." Amongst the busy restaurant clientele, When Caroline had sighted me she began waving her arms frantically in the air. The way she was shouting, you'd have thought we were at a football match.

When she noticed I clocked her, she sat back down and continued to converse with Uncle. Thirty seconds later, I reached their table.

I took off my coat and placed it on the back of my chair and then sat myself down. For about a minute, all of us just gawked at each other. Uncle looked guilty as hell and Caroline flicked her fingers through her shoulder-length hair a few times like she was an innocent teen who got caught masturbating with her knickers down.

"Hey Erykah; Miss Arani," Uncle said. Caroline quickly cut Uncle off in mid-sentence.

"No need to be so formal Jeboniah." I shook my head ever so slightly while trying not to make my smug smile so obvious. "Call me, Caroline, please?" She stated.

Oh my gosh, I don't know how much more of this flirting I can take.

"I have no problem calling you that." Uncle affirmed in response.

"You're welcome Jeboniah," she said in a deliberate sexy manner while fluttering her long eyelashes and maintaining to keep Uncle interested in her. These older folks are worse at keeping their emotions in check compared to us younger's when it comes to affairs of the heart. I thought it was supposed to be the other way around?

During my degree I learnt that the longer you stay in a relationship that is making you unhappy on the inside and years have passed since you haven't had the merriment of enjoyment you use to partake in before all the disputes and quarrels. So when someone better to your knowledge and perceptive crosses your path and shines a beacon of light in your direction, and you're awakened emotionally from it. You can't afford any longer to waste any more time hanging around, in calamitous defeat.

So in a sense, hidden beneath his calm and unruffled exterior I can understand to a point why Uncle was pursuing relations with Caroline. What I didn't know was the extent of Auntie and his marriage. It had to be pretty unscrupulous for him to do this and in front of me. Like he didn't care what I thought or cared if I disclosed this situation to Aunt CeCe.

I was beginning to feel sorry for her. She didn't deserve this. But at the end of the day, I had to find out the truth about their marriage once and for all.

"What were you trying to convey to me earlier, Uncle?" Caroline jumped in again before Uncle could answer. This woman was seriously vexing me now. I juddered my head a few times so I could gather myself together.

"Erykah sorry to interrupt sweetie." Now her tone of voice was irritating me too. "I took the liberty of ordering a few things from the menu. On the house of course," she said like we needed charity. Don't get me wrong. I was grateful for small mercies. But do I look like I'm in dire need of a hand-out? What a nerve she had, I deemed to myself.

"It's okay Miss Arani," I said as I re-adjusted myself in my seat. "I can cover whatever you have ordered. So no thank you, although your kindness is appreciated," I said eyeballing her.

"It's alright, keep your money. Your Uncle has informed me and it seems you're going to need all the money you got. He was adamant about that." That was it I had enough of this bitches undermining of me. I got up ferociously from my seat. I felt the steam coming out from my ears, and my nostrils flared up to double their size. I wanted so much to knock seven bells out of her. But I quickly remembered my police caution, and I nullified that idea out of my mind as soon as it entered.

"Uncle, may I have a word please, in private?" I said as I began to move away from the table.

He stared back at me; complacency has always been Uncles default mannerism. No matter how hard he tried to avoid it, it shadowed him like a bad nightmare. On this occasion, his luck ran out with me.

"A'right, Erykah; Caroline, can you excuse my presence for a moment. I'll be right back."

Uncle got up from the table, pushed his chair in, gave Miss Arani a peck on the cheek and followed behind me as I picked up my pace out of there.

As I continued to walk, Uncle yelled after me, but I kept on walking. As I neared the entrance, I waited for Uncle to catch up. When he did, I turned around to face him.

"We can either do this in here or go to your van. You choose?"

Uncle had a bemused look on his face. I gathered two things from it. Either he had no clue on why I was so vexed, or he was playing the stupid card. In my mind, the latter suited.

"Duh wah Erykah; wah mek yuh lef di restaurant suh vex? Yuh kno suh mi hungry a mi can't understand wah mek yuh a guh pan like dat." He thought I was stupid.

Uncle of all people knew me better not to assume that. I waited for him to recycle what he said and come properly.

"Come again?" I gave him the evils now. I wasn't playing anymore.

With all the drama over these last two days and the bullshit men, including my dad in there had span me all my life. Uncle of all people knew I wasn't anybody's fool no more. So why was he trying to play me like this?

"Nah Erykah! Wah gwaan wid yuh chile?" Uncle was seriously testing my patience.

"Give it up uncle. Stop playing. I know you know why I'm so annoyed." I moved closer to him with my arms folded and my eyes staring up at him.

"Wah mek yuh a guh pan like that?" I waited for him to be real. But he declined. So I went ahead and gave him instructions.

"Listen good, because it's like this," I said then I licked my lips and continued. "Uncle; one, go back on in there alone and I emphasise alone profusely and get me a takeaway of my favourite food and bring it out to me because I'll be waiting for you in the van. Or two; then you can either go back in there finish your meal, wrap up any dealings with Miss Arani, say goodbye because you're going to need your strength and come out to me. Or three; get a takeaway of food as well, sort your business and join me okay. So what's it going to be?" I wrapped.

"Let mi si," Uncle said as he stroked his neatly cut and styled beard.

For a man his age, he carried off a look of a man in his mid-thirties. Uncle sceptically looked at me as he contemplated my statement.

"Well!" I said, still waiting while tapping my right foot impatiently.

"A'right," he said as he looked up to the sky. Like he was in deep thought. "Here is what you are going to do first." Uncle seemed adamant, and he was eyeballing me seriously.

"What do you mean by what am I going to do first?" I said as I put my hands on my hips and gave Uncle one of my formidable I got a problem with what you're saying looks.

"Listen, ah mi. Mi nah cata tuh threats like dat, duh wah yuh wa fi duh." He finished saying and began to walk away from my presence.

"Uncle," I said, screaming at the top of my lungs. Uncle turned around and walked back towards me with a face like thunder.

"Listen Erykah like mi seh aready mi nah a guh bow dung to yuh demands. Suh ear wha mi a seh. Mi is a big man an I'm a guh duh wah mi wa fi duh, overstand?"

I've never seen Uncle this defiant with me before. I bowed my head as I walked past him and made my way back into the restaurant.

As I cursed under my breath, my mind had a flashback. I reckon I must've been around ten or eleven years old.

It was a Friday, and I was coming home from school. See for years since mother's death, Friday's have always been a tradition in our family. It was when in turn, we would eat at another family member's household and everyone returns the favour on another Friday. It must've been a lost memory in my subconscious, because for years until this very moment I remembered like it was yesterday.

All that day, I had an eerie feeling. Like something life-threatening was coming my way.

I remember vividly walking back home into the estate.

STAND IN YOUR POWER

It was its usual Friday afternoon hustle and bustle. The school run, the part-time workers, unemployed and the man dem coming out of the bookies.

As I got nearer to my block of flats, I sighted Winston and his apprentice at that time, Andrew; working on one of the cars outside his makeshift garage.

As I tried to slide neatly past them without saying hello, Winston clocked me and called me over. Reluctantly I went over to where the two guys were.

"Erykah ow things wid yuh young lady?"

Winston addressed me first in his usual manner.

"I'm fine Godfather. How are you?" I lied.

"Mi a'right baby girl! Mi cun complain. Bizniz gud a mi ave mi health," he said, smiling.

"That's good," I said sheepishly. "Hi Andrew," I said in an exaggerated and babyish voice.

He was a very tall, good looking and a very muscly boy for seventeen years of age. He was the first boy ever to give me pre-menstrual feelings in places I wasn't ready to discover yet. All the same, he was my first crush.

"Hi Erykah," he said in that deep, husky tone while winking at me.

"Listen up, though." Winston motioned for me to come closer to him! As he put his arm around my shoulders, he told Andrew to take a break. "Come, walk with me to my office." His rough-and-ready office was made up of a table, a chair and a dimly lit lamp, situated in the corner of his car garage. "A couple of minutes of your time?" He pleaded.

"Okay," I lethargically said in response.

"Yeah, a'right." Winston seemed a bit on edge all of a sudden.

"Are you feeling alright Godfather?" I leaned forward and placed my hand on his knee. "Winston." I continued shaking him.

He was beginning to worry me now. Something wasn't quite right with him. "Let me go get you some refreshment from the flat." I motioned, pointing towards the garage door.

"Nah I'll be a'right. Please jus' sekkle yuhself. Mi ave sum important news fi tell yuh." He ordered me to stay put, so I did.

"What kind of news?"

"Erykah you're young an yuh ave been threw ah hol' heap a t'ings inna yuh life." I looked at him like misery was my company. I knew the minute I heard words like that; my suspicion was terrible news.

"What's this about Winston because I need to get upstairs?" I had no patience as it was at my young age. So he better hurry up I thought to myself.

"For your age, your insight is impeccable." He looked at me fondly and then carried on.

"Thank you," I responded politely.

"Erykah, I will be as real with you and mindful as permitted." He conveyed.

"I'm not a baby, Winston." I forcefully said while giving him a disapproving stare.

"A'right, I'll bear that in mind." He thought he was smart. But already at my young age, I had grasped when an adult was trying to put one over me. So I let it slide this time because I wanted to get home. "Erykah I don't know how to say this," he looked down at me to see my reaction. I didn't say a word or move yet. "Nobody is at home. There has been an incident today," I remained silent

80

waiting for this serious news to come. "You know your Auntie Celestine is pregnant," I nodded my head and made an 'ah-ha' sound too. "Well your father and Uncle have gone
to North Manchester General in Crumpsall with her, and if you want, you can stay here with me, or I can get Andrew to drive you to the hospital. It's your call, Erykah?" He looked at me, waiting for my reply.

"I want to go to the hospital," I said trembling as one tear came then two and before I knew what was happening, a flood of them came streaming down my face and onto my coat and the floor.

"A'right baby girl," he said, putting an arm around me for comfort. "Let me call Andrew to come to take you." He took his mobile out of his pocket and phoned Andrew.

I moved away from Winston and went to stand by the door. As I leaned up against the frame, a few trickles of raindrops began to fall. I reached out my right hand to try and catch some. When I did, I studied it and then wiped my hand on my coat to dry it.

"Andrew, where are you?" Winston raised his voice, and his mood took on one of grave concern.

He once told me since I was born. That he said, not asked, but told my dad under no circumstance should he ask anyone else other than himself to be my godfather.

Father said he wouldn't dare ask anyone else and the rest is history.

Anyway, the rest of the day went not so smoothly. Auntie had lost the baby, and I remember for weeks after the strain on Uncle Jeb's and Auntie CeCe's marriage.

As my mind came back to the present day, I made a mental note to be nice to Uncle until we got to London.

It wasn't going to be easy to be cool, but I will try hard. Also, I was going to make sure before Uncle left for the next day, I was going to get him to tell me the truth. Just like I did with father!

STAND IN YOUR POWER

Chapter 5 – Introductions

We finally arrived at Nina's house in Brixton, South London shortly after nine pm. As I stepped out of the van, the cool summer night breeze hit my face like a refreshing morning shower.

"London; finally I'm here," I said to myself.

I couldn't wait to get inside and greet my best friend I haven't seen in ages.

As I got nearer to her door, it opened and out she came hurtling towards me like she was about to rugby tackle me.

"Erykah," she screamed my name as loud as she could, as she threw her arms around me and squeezed me ever so tightly. I swear down the whole street heard her. But the Nina I know wouldn't care about that one bit.

"Hey, Nina how are you, girl?" I said as I pulled away from her embrace.

"I'm cool Erykah; what's up with you?" She said, smiling through her perfect set of teeth.

"Ah girl, where do I start?" I said as we began to walk inside.

"Tell me about it," she said with a shrug of the shoulders.

"In good time girl."

"Oh okay, don't worry about that for now. Let's get inside and settled first." Nina put her arm through mine while we continued our walk.

"Yep, no problem," I said gingerly.

I guess I was feeling the pinch from the last twenty-four hours. Tiredness was finally succumbing me. All I was thinking about now was getting myself into a nice hot, bubble bath and a cosy, warm bed.

We got inside the house and took off our shoes and placed them on the neatest stacked shoe rack I've ever seen.

Nina escorted us inside the main living room.

"How are you, Mr Gaines?" Nina politely said to Uncle.

"Not too bad Nina; mi jus' a likkle tired yuh know. How are you, darling?" Uncle said, perking up a little.

"Can't complain at the moment, Mr Gaines." Uncle cut in.

"Call me Jeboniah or Jeb for short; no need to be so formal." Uncle pointed out to Nina.

"Mr Gaines; my upbringing was conducive of old fashioned values. As I was about to continue to say beforehand, I'm beginning to make money after a long time."

I already knew what she did for a living, so I let Nina bring Uncle Jeb up to speed.

"You hear that Erykah?" Uncle shouted. I could almost feel how proud he felt to hear those words.

"Yes, Uncle, I heard." He never missed an opportunity when it presented itself to remind me how some of us young people in the 21st century take life for granted.

I would always answer back as politely as I could muster and remind Uncle though I respect old fashion values. I clearly, have to stand up for the youth of today and remind him times have changed and the blame isn't all young people's fault.

"So how are you making this money, Nina; I'm intrigued?" Uncle quizzed.

"Well, Mr Gaines; after years of chasing dreams and coming up short nine times out of ten. That's when I had to go back to the drawing board and rediscover what I wanted to do." Nina first said to Uncle.

"Did you discover anything at that stage?" Uncle asked philosophically.

"No, not at first. It took the best part of a year of going to talks about save the community from this and that to find myself attending many fractions of different kinds of black religion's and believe me, Mr Gaines, there is plenty. I mean I've figured out that for every hundred black folk; seventy to eighty of us belong to a different religion or following from each other. Other races don't have that problem. Take Europeans or Asians; out of their every other hundred religious people they only got around four to five different ones. Why are our people so exclusive to this way of being so disconnected?"

Uncle and I laughed at the last part of Nina's speech. It was the way she delivered it in such a comical fashion. My belly hurt so much from laughter; I had to walk out of the room and come back. After about a minute or two, Nina continued.

"Girl, you always crack me up. I think you should become a comedian," I said, still laughing at her earlier antics.

"Nah I'm good. I'll leave that to other people. I'm too serious for that kind of thing," she said, smiling back.

"Please continue Nina," Uncle said while giving me a funny look like I interrupted something fundamental to him. Crazy man, I thought to myself.

"As I was saying Erykah," she said theatrically towards my vicinity while shaking her head as well.

"Oh whatever girl, just get on with it," I replied.

"Anyway, Mr Gaines; after I was rudely interrupted," this girl is a joker I thought to myself. I blew her a kiss and then she continued. "Yes so for another year I prodded along looking for my next adventure and then on one mild

autumn evening I went along to this talk at the
Community Hub right here in Brixton." Uncle cut in again.

"What was the talk about?" Uncle remarked.

"Are we Black verses are we African," Nina said.

"What do you mean?" I quizzed. I was baffled by what
she just said.

"Ain't that the same thing?" Uncle questioned looking as
lost as I was.

"Well, that's what I was taught to believe. But when I
went there, boy was I in for a culture shock." For a
moment, Nina fell silent. It was like she was reminiscing
about the night in question.

"Nina, are you alright?" I said, putting my hand on her
shoulder to give it a gentle rub.

"Yeah, I'm good," she said in response.

"Listen, Nina, since it's late and loads of my belongings
are in Uncles van, and it's going to take an age to get all the
boxes out tonight, would it be okay if Uncle stayed the
night so he can help me in the morning." I looked over at
her awaiting her reply.

"Yeah sure," she said, smiling. "I anticipated you were
coming late because one; you always are and two, this
time, it wasn't your fault. Between now and a little later,
Eric will be back home. I'll ask him if he can help you then.
Plus the curry goat has got another hour before it's ready.
So I'll prepare then; so in the meantime, you can help me
make up the spare bed either in your room or down here
whichever I'm easy. If you and your Uncle want to take a
shower each; I'll fetch you some fresh towels and some
shower gel if you like." She concluded.

"Ah, thanks, Nina; much appreciated," I said as I moved
closer to her.

Nina eyed me confusingly. I leaned over and whispered
into her ear. "Also I've got to have a real talk with Uncle

about some other shit that happened on the way," I said finishing as I moved away from her.

"Oh okay," she said, trying to act all cool.

"Plus," I said, still whispering. "I'll fill you in once Uncle goes on his way home," I concluded.

"So Nina, you were going to tell us about this debate you went to." Uncle was eager for Nina to finish her story. Come to think of it, so was I.

I always loved Nina's stories, good or bad. Just in the same way with her spoken word performing, Nina loves an audience and knows how to command the attention of a room. It was what she thrived on most. It was like validation of her existence.

Because growing up, Nina was treated like she was invisible most of the time by certain members in her family circle. All because no one except her younger brother Eric; believed for years that her stepfather abused her.

"Yes, I was," Nina took her place back in her seat and continued. "Well, Mr Gaines, I'll give you a brief breakdown! But first, I want to tell you something, and in my opinion, it plays an integral part of the topic and is iconic to human nature."

She got our attention as she always does.

"Did you know that scientifically, the black woman is the only organism that possesses the mitochondrial DNA that has all the variations possible for every different kind of human being on this earth (The African, The Albino, European and Middle Eastern etc.) When the DNA of a black woman mutates all other types of human beings come about. If you don't believe me guys, go and check the internet and research the Eve gene. It's only found in black women."

At this point, my jaw felt like it had dropped on the floor. Nina had Uncle, and I transfixed on her every word.

"Also, what if I told you that we are an unbounded conscious of intelligent life energy that can never be created or destroyed. We are an eternal and vibrational non-local field of awareness, forever connected to a source energy, some will say God others will not; curiously experiencing life in a mortal body for but a short time."

"Well blow me down," I said, sounding amazed and I was of what I just heard. "I can't believe that girl. I mean, is it true; you and I are manifestations of whatever source we were created from?" I was beginning to feel excited and a little powerful by the news.

"Yes, Erykah; like I said go and research it. The information is out there," she concluded.

Although, I'm delighted I didn't know this detrimental piece of information earlier when they had a gun pointed at the back of me. I don't know what or how I would've reacted if I had already known.

Nina carried on schooling us for the next half hour. She told Uncle that nowadays she taught a creative writing course at Brixton college for two full days and nights a week and in her spare time she was rising around the circuit as a brilliant spoken word artist.

After that, she helped me make up the spare bed for Uncle in my new room. Nina informed me, Eric, just finished painting the room last week and she also said at the weekend she would treat me to a new bed, carpet, curtains and a wardrobe and chest of drawers set as house warming gifts.

At first, I was like you can't. Nina hushed me by putting her finger over my lips. I smiled, cried and cuddled this beautiful and kind black woman who opened up her house for me until I found my feet, and I thanked her several times. I'm so glad she is a friend of mine. She said no problem you're my sister and my best friend for life, and we gotta stick together like glue through everything life throws at us.

After Uncle and I had our showers, Eric came home. It was so lovely to see him. He was looking more buff since the last time I saw him; he was almost unrecognisable. But it was nice to see him looking and doing well.

Over dinner, he was telling Uncle and myself about this new teaching gig he was going to start in September at a local secondary school.

After dinner, we all chilled for another hour, and I caught up properly with Nina and Eric, respectively.

I asked him how the teaching gig came about; because the last time I saw him which was around two years ago, he was still a student himself.

He informed us that he kind of cheated and done one of those new government initiatives that fast tracks the elite students with the highest marks on a six-week program. Well, I was astonished and proud of young Eric all the same.

At around eleven o clock everyone felt tired. We all said goodnight to each other, then Uncle followed me into my room.

After we both got settled into our beds, I took the opportunity to ask Uncle about his behaviour at the Caribbean centre and the real state of Auntie's and his marriage.

At first, he was reluctant. With a little persuasion he went on to tell me in short, many moons ago in the early years of their marriage and before Darius was born, Aunt Celestine had an affair for over two years and not only that she got pregnant by her lover and had a miscarriage. Well, that was what Uncle knew, because during those two years she had to go back to Jamaica for around ten months to look after her dying father. Uncle Jeb had no idea on who it was with.

Well, I was shocked. I always knew about Auntie losing one baby, but two that must've been trauma for her.

I suppose a vast relief came when Darius was born because for years she must've feared hard in trying to have more babies.

At that moment I took a lot of pity on Uncle and had nothing but admiration for Auntie.

I can see and feel now why things between them over the years were tough. But you would've never known by the united front they seemed to have always shown the world and to the many times, they both put others before themselves, effortlessly.

So I guess sometimes when you genuinely love someone nothing can break you apart completely. I hoped that notion applied to the both of them and that Auntie and Uncle could save their marriage. They were my heroes, and I promised Uncle I would do anything if needed to help with the repairs. On that note, I kissed him goodnight and went to sleep.

Chapter 6 – Propositions

I woke up early this morning with a banging headache. My head was pounding like I'd been hit with a frying pan and my whole body felt like it had gone twelve rounds with a heavyweight champion boxer.

The alcohol intake I had consumed last night; coupled with the stress of a pending court case looming over me, was beginning to take its toll.

Nobody was awake yet. When I got off the phone with my lawyer Marcus; it wasn't good news. He told me they had set a date for the preliminary hearing on September fifteenth.

He explained what would happen on that day. The prosecution and the defence would present its evidence to the criminal court judge before that preliminary date. On that day, the judge will inform both parties whether a case will go ahead at a later date.

I was being charged for the attack on that vile, racist police officer Charlie McCann who's name I became prevalent with while in custody. Marcus also informed me; that if I was found guilty, the statutory limitations and the maximum penalty is six months imprisonment.

Now that's what I call a kick in the teeth?

After I got off the phone to him, I went and sat at the breakfast table feeling gloomy about the situation with a glass of water and five-hundred milligrams of Magnesium.

When I had finished taking the meds, I made myself a light breakfast. Afterwards I showered, got dressed in my workout gear and left the house a little after nine am without waking anybody.

I wanted to join a gym and the night before Nina told me about the great facilities at a black-owned, value for money place in Gresham Road.

I decided I would jog slowly to the address, so I could begin to shake off my hangover and try not to think about my case, at least for a while.

On route, I passed through a newsagents and bought myself an isotonic drink. After I paid for the juice, I left the newsagents and began on my way to the gym.

According to my phone's map app, my destination was five minutes away.

When I reached to the top of the road I turned into it. As I walked a little further I looked up and spotted the gym. According to the app it was saying fifty yards away. A few minutes later, I had finally arrived. I noticed behind me opposite the gym there was a bookies and what looked like Brixton's most granular in full effect standing outside.

Just like in Manchester, most main cities looked the same to me.

As I got to the entrance of the gym, I heard a few wolf whistles and wha'ppen baby being thrown in my direction.

I turned my head around halfway and cut the man dem a cute smile. One of them called me over, so I went. It wasn't like there weren't other people around, so I briskly walked over.

When I reached, I quickly decided to play a lil' game with them. Before any of the guys realised I drew out my phone, stood in between them and said 'look up to the sky' as they all did looking baffled, I took a cheeky selfie and then ran back over to the gym.

As I walked through the entrance, I swivelled around and blew them all a theatrical kiss followed with laughter. They all threw their hands in the air towards me dismissively in a joking manner, and I acknowledged it by sticking out my booty and giving it a gentle slap, and then I went inside.

As I got in, I walked through the reception area and straight up to the desk. Upon arrival, I was greeted by a young man who had a body to die for. But by the time he opened up his mouth and finished talking, I felt like I wanted to walk the fuck out of there and join the man dem across the road. This dude was seriously talking some gibberish.

"Ryan Leslie." I threw a name at him. He looked mystified.

"What you on about?" He said, acting like the last convict that had just come out of prison.

"The tune gibberish by Ryan Leslie; don't you know it?" I said, sounding a bit smug. I knew this fool didn't know. I wanted to throw him off my scent.

"No I don't know babes, but you can give us your number. I mean sorry your address and contact details," he said, sounding all flustered now.

"My number, I bet you ask every pretty girl that walks through that door, don't you?" I said, putting him on the spot.

"Nah not really, I've been waiting for someone like you to walk in here." I shook my head in disbelief and asked him how I could join. But before I could utter another word, I could feel the warmth and smell the cologne of a next man approaching me from behind.

"Sorry is this rug rat hassling you miss?" The voice said as I turned around to greet the person who was diverting my attention.

"Nah he's good," I said in reply. As soon as I clapped eyes on the voice; I felt my knees tremble and my heart rate speed up. "He's a bit full of himself tho." I continued to say.

If the guy behind the desk was buff but dim, then this dude seemed the polar opposite.

He stood around six foot three or four inches tall, muscly but toned and ooh wee sexy in all the right places. The dude's hair was in cane rows, and it looked like he just had it done yesterday. His jaw was chiselled, and his eyes were almond-shaped and green in colour, a rare sight.

"Oh yeah, was he now? I've been thinking about this for some time, but I'm certified now. I'm going to make a trip to the pet shop, to buy JC here a dog leash." I suddenly burst out in hysterics. The voice had me in stitches from the jump.

I just met voice, and already I was feeling his personality, something that hasn't happened to me in a long time.

"If you do, you gonna make sure that you take me for regular walks?" JC said back, seemingly embarrassed by voices comment.

All the way through that exchange, I clocked him staring at me. Poor guy, I thought now. Voice had dented his confidence. He was no match for him.

"Sorry about all that. How may I help you, Miss?" Voice said as he stood glued to his spot while eyeballing me to tell him my name.

"Miss Gaines," I said, batting my eyelids like I was high. "Miss Erykah Gaines," I concluded, trying to catch my breath. This dude was seriously doing something to me, and it felt so good.

"Nice," he said back letting a chuckle of laughter escape out from his mouth.

"I'm sure you can assist me with anything," I lustfully said while biting on my bottom lip.

I stood standing still directly in front of him and crossed one leg over the other, awaiting his reply.

"I'm pretty sure I can Miss Gaines," he said back licking his lips. I felt his eyes pierce right through me like he could see me naked. It looked like he imagined taking off one garment at a time very methodically.

For a few instants, I got caught up day-dreaming about having hot and steamy sex with this fine specimen of a brother. I know I sound like a nymph, but it's been a long time since I had any D. Right now, all I wanted was him inside of me.

"Do you do tours of your facilities?" I asked, hoping he'd say yes.

"I can do better than that Miss Gaines," he said as he passed me one of their pamphlets.

"No, please call me Erykah." I quickly skimmed read it and came across something I liked.

"Okay Erykah; my name is Donte Williams, and I'm the manager of this fine establishment," he said, reaching out his hand so I could greet him.

I reached over and shook his hand, and as I did so, he gently rubbed the area between my thumb and forefinger. His touch sent shivers right through my body and that got my juices flowing. Donte was seriously turning me on big time, and now he had me horny as a motherfucker.

"I've seen something I like here," I said as I pointed out the one I wanted.

"Ah, good choice Erykah; the 30-minute free tour and taster session, that's a predominant one for people that will potentially join," he said as he smiled and went back over to the reception desk. He motioned for JC to pass him some paper and then he came back over to where he had left me.

"Is everything alright?" I asked as he hadn't said anything for a minute.

"Yeah," he boldly said. "JC; man the fort and I'll come to relieve you for a break in about an hour," he began walking away from us, so I followed behind him slowly. "Erykah come, we can go to the canteen area, and I'll explain the session in more detail for you in there if you like?" He concluded.

He was very assertive and assured in his nature. Two attributes I admire in real men, and so far, Donte Williams seemed like one. A few minutes later and we reached.

"Are you hungry or thirsty?" He asked politely.

"No, thank you; I'm good," I said, smiling back as we both took a seat and sat down at the table.

Donte convened into the chair opposite me. All I could do was stare and become hypnotised by his presence. He was eye candy alright and easy on the eye. I hoped he was as into me, even if it was for an intense quickie.

"Okay," he said shuffling about in his seat. When he looked comfortable, he began. "Before I can book you on a session, I just need to ask you a few lifestyle questions," he explained.

"Silly question maybe. But why would you need that kind of personal information at this stage?" I said back looking absent-minded.

"Well to determine if you're suited," he said, looking perplexed at my line of questioning.

"Fair enough, but I haven't said yes to joining yet." I pointed out.

"Very true, but I'm sure by the time you see our state of the art facilities, I have a feeling you might," he said sounding like he was the king of the world.

"You're very assured of yourself, but I like," I said as I leaned back in my chair. I eyed Donte some more, giving him the head to toe stare down. I wanted him, and I wanted him right now.

"Well, how would you like me to answer that?" He said back putting me immediately on the spot.

"Maybe somewhere else from here, somewhere a little more private, where we can be alone." I gave him a stone-faced look that suggested I was serious, and I was. I wanted Donte Williams and most females in my position right now would feel the same.

I don't care how many chicks he has had in there. I'm not looking for a boyfriend right now or anything serious. I just want some good old fashioned dick. Preferably thick, long and hard!

"My kind of girl," he said as he walked around the table. Within seconds of him standing in front of me, he unexpectantly scooped me up by my legs and began carrying me towards some double doors. He managed expertly to free one hand and punch in. I counted a four-digit code. The doors unlocked, and Donte continued carrying me towards the end of the corridor like he had rescued me from a dire situation.

But for a girl like me who doesn't have much in the way of worldly possessions, my imagination was running wild and it had me thinking that in this present moment, I was in mid-scene on a movie set.

"Where are you taking me?" As if I didn't know. I was playing the role and into his hands, allowing him to take control. As strong as a woman I am, in other matters when it came to those of the bedroom kind. I like a man who is equally as dominant as me.

"To my office Erykah; we won't be disturbed in there," he said as he gave me a gentle slap on my bum.

I let out a nervous giggle as he opened the door to his office. He took a few more steps with me still cradled in his arms. When he stopped; he put me down, and I looked up at him, and within seconds I was slowly and sensually planting kisses all over Donte's face, neck, and mouth. Donte gave in to my tender touches. The strong smell of his cologne lingered over me like a tidal wave and brought a sense of euphoria to my whole body for a few flashes.

I stood up and clutched Donte by the hand and led him to the L-shaped sofa that was situated at the far end of his office. I pulled Donte from around the back of me. He turned around, standing with his whole body to the back of the sofa. Suddenly, he grabbed my face with both hands and French kissed me.

After about a minute, I pulled away from his embrace and went for his belt, I unpinned and tossed it to the other side of the sofa, letting his trousers fall by the wayside. Then I went for the prize I had been waiting for all morning. I took my right hand and guided it into his boxers. I pulled out his cock and began to stroke it gently. Donte let out a moan of delight, as he slowly, guided me backwards. We both simultaneously slumped onto the sofa together and began to kiss again with a little more vigour. I sat in front of his member. With both hands, in one swiping motion, I took off my top and threw it carelessly onto the floor.

By the expression on his face, I could see he was pleased with the sight of my breasts. That brought him to dribble like a lovesick puppy. I came back at him, and for a brief moment, I stared attentively into his sexy big green eyes and melted away.

As he ran his hands over my firm breasts, Donte copped himself a good feel then he continued the motion by sliding his fingers until he reached my back, unhooking my bra.

My troubles began to take a backseat in the theatre of my mind. As his nature rose firm and fast, my journey away from life's difficulties was only just beginning.

STAND IN YOUR POWER

He began to run his lips over the curves of my chest and the simmering surface of my smooth stomach. With two fingers, he pulled aside my panties; he reached a little further down when his fingers found their target, he began to stroke the entrance to my already wet and obliging pussy. I let out a shallow moan like I almost couldn't breathe.

Donte's fingers began to build up speed as he played with my clitoris and every other second slipping them into my hole. He continued the process several times. After a few minutes, I wanted to switch position. I got off him now like a woman possessed and was ready for the nasty.

Donte got up, standing there in all his nakedness, my eyes locked onto the sight of his huge cock hanging like a baseball bat between his legs. That was when I went weak at the knees, and my legs gave way. Donte quickly noticed and supported me.

"You okay girl?" He said with a caring temperament in his voice.

"I'll be fine." I just about managed to say breathing hard through my mouth and nostrils. I was seemingly embarrassed as Donte lifted me with ease, he laid me gently onto the sofa, still panting, gasping and moaning all nine and a half stone of me. He grabbed my long legs, climbed on top and slowly entered my already pulsating and throbbing pussy. As he moved into place, our eyes locked, I noticed a bead of sweat break out from his forehead. He began to mount me like a stallion as I scream for God. He thrust back and forth, and I pumped up to meet him. I could've sworn he was getting bigger inside of me. I pulled at his shoulders, begging him to make me come. Donte obliged as only he could. I shuddered with the after-effects of an orgasm that must've been heard around the gym. I hoped any other staff was far away and otherwise engaged. But at the moment of breathlessness, I didn't care. The treatment had run its course. As we lay on the sofa, Donte began to trace a line down my body with his finger, from my neck to my breasts and down to my belly button. I raised myself on my elbows and looked him dead in the eyes.

"Is there anything else?" I said, gasping, still trying to catch my breath.

"No, not right now. But if I think of something you'll be the first to know."

"You think there's going to be a next time?" I said, questioning him with a cute smile that suddenly swept across my face.

"Oh, I'm sure of that, you better believe it, girl." As I rose from my position with a big broad grin etched on my face, I began slowly moving off the sofa. Donte's eyes kept on following me as I went around the office, picking up my clothes.

"Stop looking at me like that?" I said, feeling shy all of a sudden.

"Why are you getting bothered by that?" He asked while cheekily grinning at me.

"Never mind." I nonchalantly replied.

"Okay, then all good," he concluded.

"May I use your shower please?" I politely asked.

"Yeah sure," he answered with a bemused look on his face. "Straight through that door." he continued saying.

I left Donte laying there as I embarrassingly rushed into the en-suite shower room. Ten minutes went by when I heard Donte walking in.

My attitude completely changed the moment I feasted my eyes on his six-pack.

"Hey, Mr Sexy. Did you miss me?" I asked in a deliberate sexy tone.

"Hell yeah, but I think he missed you more." Donte grabbed his dick and began stroking it. I smiled, already well aware of what he was capable of doing with it.

Erykah turned her head away from me and stepped into the shower. I watched her perfect frame turn on the shower and water rained all over her body. She put her hands on the wall and let the water run down her back. It slowly ran between the crack of her ass. She turned around, grabbed the shampoo, and washed her hair. I admired her perky erect breasts staring back at me. Her dark brown skin was flawless. The bubbles from shampooing her hair ran between her breasts, continuing across her pussy and down her legs. I continued to watch her bathe herself.

"Damn girl, you're one fine woman." I stood there, stroking my dick. I wanted to make sure it was wide-awake once I stepped foot into the shower.

I entered the shower then walked right up on her. She opened her eyes with a shocked look on her face that I was right next to her.

"I'm almost done. I will be right out of your way." I stated as I tried getting the last of the soap off my body.

"You ain't going anywhere."

I looked down and was like damn.

Donte smiled. "What's up?"

"Your dick. I swear down, it looks bigger than before." I quizzed as I admired the sheer beauty of his manhood.

"Don't worry about him, he's harmless," he said, moving towards me.

"Shit, I can't tell. Twenty minutes ago, your dick looked and felt more than harmless." Donte put his strong arm around my back then placed his mouth on my right nipple, and began to suck gently.

"Oooh, Doooonnteeee..." His name rang out loud in my head, but it wouldn't allow itself to leave my lips. This nigger was paralysing the fuck out of me again, and I was weak to his touch.

The water rained down on us and gave me chills all over my body. Jodeci's classic tune 'Freak n'you' was playing in the background on the radio.

'And tonight baaabyyy I wanna get freaky wid ya.'

Donte zoomed in to give the other breast the same treatment. This time, he grabbed my leg and brought it up to his waist so he could slide his dick back and forth starting at my clit and bringing it all the way back. Donte continued to kiss my lips, then back to my shoulders and then on to my breasts. He put me up against the wall so that now I was up in the air and had full control. Donte began kissing me passionately and roughly at the same time, giving me that kinda thug love feeling. He turned and walked me over to the shower bench, 'stand on here' he commanded.

I did just that. I was standing there with my hands on Donte's shoulders, not knowing what he was going to do to me next.

I took the time to stare at her body, and her perfectly shaved pussy staring right in my face.

In one move, he put his arms under my legs, lifting me and placing one part on each one of his shoulders, positioning my pussy right in his face. He took another minute to gaze at it. The lips were pretty and glistening, so my clit was calling, so a nigger had to answer.

"Is there anything else you want to know because you're going to be speechless for a while?" He didn't wait for a response; he was now sucking on my clit just right, sending electrical waves up my spine. He put his hands on the small of my back; he moved over a little to position me under the showerhead as he began giving me that diesel tongue.

"Aaaaaahhhh...," I arched my back and put my head against the wall. He grabbed my hips then stiffened his long tongue and slid it in and out of my pussy like a dick.

"Oh, my god! What the fuck?" I didn't know what to do with myself.

Donte knew he had my ass. I was now screaming. I've never had an orgasm in my life like this before.

After a few minutes, I begged him to stop. "Wait! Wait! I have to get out; I need to pee?"

As soon as the words escaped from my mouth, the phone from the office rang out loudly. The phone continued to ring, but Donte was reluctant to get it. He tried to continue where he started, but I pulled back from him.

He had no choice now he had to go. He gave me a look that said 'what the fuck'.

I smiled falsely and tilted my head to one side and stared long and hard at him.

That was his signal, so he quickly backed up from me and skeeted into his office. He answered the call in the nick of time as I was walking back through into the office as well. I saw him put the phone on loudspeaker and then the voice on the other end came through.

"Yes, JC; what is it now?" Donte questioned. I could see he was annoyed at the untimely interruption.

"Boss, sorry to disturb you! But you better come quickly to reception." JC sounded well in a panic.

Whatever was making him act like that, a crisis if it was, couldn't have come at a worse time. I decided to get dressed as Donte continued with the call.

"What's the matter JC?" Donte said as he slid his trousers up.

"There's a lady, a member who is claiming she was assaulted in the changing room." JC reiterated.

"Okay, I'll be there in a minute." With that, Donte quickly got dressed and darted out of the office without saying a thing.

"Donte," I called out loudly, but he didn't answer. "Donte; why are you going so fast, slow down?" I said, calling out again while running after him half-dressed myself.

He didn't slow down or say a thing. I got dressed as I walked. When I finished, I went through the double doors he had carried me through earlier. I passed through the side of the main gym and came out eventually into the reception area.

"JC; who is the customer in question?" I heard and saw Donte ask.

"Over there, sitting down. The lady with the blue Nike top and black cycling shorts." JC pointed out.

"Bless, JC." I watched as Donte began walking towards the woman in question.

As he passed me, he had a look of terror etched across his face. At that moment, I suddenly felt for him. I gave back a knowing look of support his way. He duly noted and grimaced back at me. I walked over and went and stood by the reception desk.

"JC; pass me an application form to fill-in?" I demanded in a hurry. "I wanna look busy." He passed me a form, but his eyes were transfixed on Donte and the lady. "A pen too please," I said with my right hand outstretched. JC reached into a drawer. When he finished fumbling around, he eventually found one and gave it to me.

"Hi, miss. I'm Mr Williams; the manager of this gym, my colleague has informed me of your allegation. Do you wanna follow...?"

But before Donte could finish his sentence, the lady interrupted him.

"Excuse me, allegation. Are you for real?" She shouted back at him. The lady was angry and upset that Donte merely suggested she was lying.

"I'm sorry miss; I didn't mean to upset you!" Donte was acting a bit weird. He seemed a lil confused on what to do next. So I stepped in.

"JC; I'm gonna try and get the ladies details," I said as I began walking towards them. I took over the situation with immediate effect.

"Miss, would you like to come over here?" I said as I reached out my hand to comfort her. She came towards me and walked over with me back to where JC was.

"What's your name madam?"

"Siobhan Ryder; miss!" As she said her name, JC; pulled her details from the database.

"Here we are, I found you!" When JC had successfully got her details up, he printed off a copy and handed it to me. I walked over to Donte and gave him the piece of paper.

"Here, Donte." As I handed the details over.

"Yeahhhhh," he said, looking like he was in deep thought. He rubbed his chin repeatedly. All of a sudden, he went white as a sheep, if that was possible.

"Mr Williams; are you feeling alright?" With that, he looked down at me, then over to the lady, turned around and walked away from us and back through the doors to the gym.

I thought he was acting a bit peculiar and also leaving the woman stranded. I apologised to the lady and instructed JC to keep her safe and to get another member of staff to help.

When I sorted things, I followed after Donte. When I caught up with him, I found him sitting near the treadmills with his head buried deep in his hands.

I walked over to where he was and sat down next to him.

After a few minutes of him doing the same, all I could do was rub his back and wait in patience.

Another five minutes had passed, and still, he said nothing. I heard the doors behind me open. I turned around to see JC with his head popped through. I waved him away almost instantly and mouthed in a whisper that I had this. He nodded his head back in approval and went away.

"Donte; come on Hun, talk to me?" I said as I kissed him on the back of his head.

After another minute, he finally came up.

"Erykah; I'm okay. I need a minute to get my head around this," he said. He was looking a bit peaky, and his eyes went red from the tears he had shed.

"You don't look okay," I said as I moved slightly away from him and took his hand in mine.

"Nah, it's cool. I'll be fine. I'm the manager. I got this. You have done enough for someone I've only known a few hours. So thank you Erykah, but don't let me hold you up any longer." That was it. He seemed fine now.

"Alright, only if you're sure, Donte?" I asked, still concerned. I felt there was more to this than meets the eye. But I've just met him and have no idea of his history.

"Yeah, yeah. You go along." With that Donte stood up and so did I. He pulled me nearer to him and gave me his best French kiss so far.

"Mm, what was that for lover boy?" I said back cheekily smiling up at him. I was misty-eyed for a for while. When I came back into focus, he was staring at me like he found the most precious jewel ever.

"So, am I going to have the pleasure of being in your presence again?" He asked like the daddy he was.

"Well, that depends on," I said, surveying him up and down.

"On what?" He asked, still smiling that sexy smile for me.

"Ima make you a proposition," I said, licking my lips. Donte crossed his eyes, waiting on what I was going to come out of my mouth. "On whether I get free membership." I put it to him assured he was going to say yes.

"Mm," he said, looking up towards the ceiling and rubbing his chin at the same time.

"Well?" I said, waiting in anticipation.

"How 'bout I can do better than that." All of a sudden, he sounded excited — a quick turnaround from ten minutes ago.

"Go on; I'm listening," I said back with my arms folded.

"Look, I'm in desperate need of a deputy manager, and I want to offer you a job here." Well, I was gobsmacked. I never saw that coming.

"Wow, you like me that much, huh?" I said still in disbelief.

"You know, I do. Look what we have just done." Donte relayed.

"But that's just sex. You haven't known me long enough to like all of me yet."

"Well, I wanna get to know all of you in time. But what I've seen so far. That's certifiable in my book."

"Okay, I concur."

"Good and truly how you handled that lady and me moments ago tells me you're perfect for the job. I can see you're a people's person and a likeable character. I will train you personally on all aspects of the business from accounts to banking to how membership operates and how the gym works. In no time, you'll be a competent worker. I can offer you a starting salary of £19,000 with a review of pay grade every annum. I took the assumption that you're without employment as you just arrived in London. If you answer, yes, come and see me Monday after lunch so I can sort out a contract for you and we can have an interview too. So what do you think about that?" He concluded and awaited my reply.

"Well that all sounds amazing Donte, and a girl has got to start somewhere. So if that means I get to see your sexy ass every day, then I'm in. You got yourself a deal." He shook my hand first like the professional he is. I grabbed it and pulled him into me this time and kissed him hard until I couldn't anymore.

Chapter 7 – No News Is Good News

On my way back from the gym, I was feeling thrilled with emotion, and I couldn't contain it any longer. I let out the biggest yay ever, as I jumped and skipped down Brixton high road.

Never in a million years would I have dreamt I would bag a boyfriend and job in one go, amazing if I do say so myself.

People were staring at me. Some had perplexed looks on their faces, probably thinking look at the crazy woman. Others saw and could feel my aura beaming from my apparent elated state of happiness and smiled back at me. That connection lifted my spirits further.

It was a far cry from recent revelations, and I must not forget a possible court case that could muddle everything up that I've worked so hard to get.

But that's why I had Marcus; I was always optimistic that I had him in my corner and he was rapidly gaining the reputation of becoming one of the country's best defence lawyers.

As I came to a sudden halt, I took a few moments to take a breather. I patted around in my bag, looking for my mobile. When I located it, I took it out and decided to call father.

On the third ring, I heard the phone crackle and a rusty voice coming through.

"Hello." The sound of someone who had just woken up answered.

"Dad, is that you?" I said, sounding a bit cautious.

"Erykah; yes, it's your father?" He said, straining his voice.

"Dad, have you been drinking again?" I was beginning to feel a little disappointed and angry all the same.

"What you take me for? I haven't touched a drop in weeks, and you damn well know that." Dad sounded well pissed that I suggested he was drunk.

"Alright, Dad, I didn't phone you to get into an argument. What I phoned for was to tell you how I am and what's going on and also to see how you and everyone else is!" I said, trying to dead that chat before it escalated.

"I mean. Why is it that you always look for the worst in me, instead of greatness." Father threw back at me. I'm like damn. Why did he have to go there? I decided to handle his statement with kid gloves.

"Okay, you got a point. A tiny, minute one but a point altogether and the reason I say this is only obvious to everyone that knows and has known you, dear daddy." I was hoping he was going to accept my statement of calming intent and move on.

"Fine baby girl, let's leave it there. So tell me your news?" He asked.

"Well, where shall I start?" I said as I struggled on where to begin.

"The good news first baby girl, the good news," Father said, sounding a bit chipper all of a sudden. I reckoned Bernadette has just come through the front door. She always guaranteed to put a smile on Fathers' face.

"Well, guess who got themselves a job?" I said, sounding like I just won the lottery and to me it did. This good news was a long time coming for him to hear, and I hoped it would have a profound impact on pops.

"Babygirl, well done. Bernie, you hear that? Your step-daughter has already got herself a job." Dad sounded like he was bouncing around the room in sheer ecstasy. In the background in Father's excitement, I heard Bernie telling dad to pass her the phone.

"Well done Erykah; I knew you would land on your feet quickly." I could feel the proudness accentuating from her voice. It made her sound like she was in her twenties.

"Thank you, Bernie. I love you." Ah, I thought to myself I'm glad someone like her is in our lives. Over the last four years, she has stepped up to the mark. Not only as a step-mother to me but as a wonderful girlfriend to Dad, she has exceeded and excelled all of our expectations and more. She truly is as she would put it. 'I'm just an ordinary woman who can do extraordinary things when called upon or when I'm needed.'

"Ah, child, in Jesus's name there is no need for that. You did this all by yourself. Your steely attitude and sheer determination to never give up no matter the odds has got you where you are right now. All the best in your new role Miss Gaines; God bless and I love you too." She concluded.

Damn that woman almost had me in emotional meltdown. Had to keep my cool on road. So my mind had a quick exchange of words with my soul and decided to neutralise any tears coming out.

"Again, thank you, Bernie. Father, thank you too." It was always good for my preservation of solace and peace of mind to especially be getting Father's thanks and statements of approval.

"You're most welcome baby girl." I got a sense from his response that he was still grinning from ear to ear.

"So how are you, father?"

"I'm doing a'right, but I'm missing you like crazy Erykah; especially your Sunday morning breakfasts." As soon as he had said that, I began to reminisce about

111

Sunday morning's past and our traditional Friday night Gaines family dinners. Days like those I'm going to miss like crazy at first that I know. I will be feeling very emotional about it all from time to time.

"Ah Dad, before you know it I'll be back up there cooking you some more," I said, carrying delight within my voice.

"I can't wait, baby girl," he said with an air of excitement.

"So how's Godfather?" I asked as I was turning into Nina's road.

"He is fine Erykah; Winston is popping around later for dominoes night. I'll get him to give you a call when he arrives."

"Ah that would be cool, and I'm glad everyone is doing great."

"So what's the bad news baby girl?" Father said, changing the conversation.

"I've reached home, Dad, and I'm famished. I'll text you the news a lil later alright," I said as I put the key in the front door.

"A'right, Erykah; be good baby girl. I love you." He concluded.

"Yes, Father, take care; I love you too. Bye Bernie; I love you as well."

"Bye Erykah; walk good, God bless."

"Speak to you both soon." I finished saying as I ended the call and slotted the phone back into my bag.

I turned the key and opened the front door and walked into the kitchen. I laid my bag over a chair and then I went to turn on the kettle.

When I did that, I walked over to the door that led into the garden and opened it up.

STAND IN YOUR POWER

As I rested my body against the door frame, I couldn't help on thinking of what has happened to me since I left Manchester.

Things like the motorway services saga. What was sad about that is that black people are a long way off from ever being seen or treated as equal humans to white people. The more I thought about it, the more pissed off I got.

Then there is the Police station business. I mean was I over the top when I jumped over the counter and punched the Po-Po in the face. Well, maybe I was, but how I felt at the time and why I did what I did, it was a little justification for me. The bitch part about it was how I copped a charge.

Then there is last night, Nina; offering to buy me furniture. I love that girl so much. Now today so far, well, enough said there then.

After I had finished making a cup of tea, I sat down at the kitchen table and pondered over my immediate future. From where I was at present, only one obstacle was standing in my way.

If things go my way, I hope I'll end up with just a caution or some hours doing community work seeing this is my first offence.

As I came out from my thoughts, I heard the key in the door. In walked Nina with music blaring as she headed towards the kitchen, she still had her headphones on and was singing to herself.

"Nina," I called out to her. But she still couldn't hear me. When she entered, she put her handbag onto the table and then gave me a wave and one of her formidable smiles.

"Hey girl, what's good?" She said as she took off her headphones and turned the volume down.

"I'm alright, sup wid you?"

"I'm all good, a little tired but I'm cool."

"That's great. How was your day?" I said as I got up to reheat the kettle.

"My day was pretty exhilarating, to say the least."

"Would you like a tea or coffee?"

"Mm, decaf, black with one sugar, the brown stuff," she instructed.

"So, what was that you were listening too?"

"Ah, that. Just catching up on talk show from the weekend."

"Wow. What kind of talk show has music blaring throughout?"

"Erykah; you're so crazy at times." She pointed out.

"What?" While laughing, I threw my arms out innocently.

"Never mind. The show, well, it's called 'The Community Show', on Resistance 89.6FM and its host is none other than the man himself, and he happens to be a personal friend of mine a Mr Calvin Felix." She highlighted.

"Well, well, look at you. Rubbing shoulders with the need to know people of Brixton." I was seemingly impressed.

"Well, you know, that's how I roll," she said to me laughing.

"Alright, maybe you can give me a low down about it all later," I said as I took another sip of my tea.

"Yes. I wanted to ask you if you had any plans this evening."

"Erm, no. What you got in mind?"

"Well Eric and I were chatting this morning, and we both thought it would be a lovely idea if you allowed us to take you to dinner and a place of your choosing."

"Yeah, that sounds great. But what is it all in aid off?"

"Nothing major, just Eric and mines way of welcoming you to our home and family and our city."

"Okay, I'm down. I fancy some great Mexican food, and I don't mean Nando's either." I said back licking my lips at the thought of eating a substantial mouth-watering burrito.

"Yummy Erykah, that's right up my street. Now you're talking, and I know just the perfect place situated up in central London." She said, looking all excited like a kid in a candy shop.

"Ah girl, look at you," I exemplified. "It's so lovely and endearing to see you have found your smile again and I'm delighted you're doing so well these days. I don't know how you did it, but it's working. I hope some of your luck can rub off on me. Bring it in!"

I motioned with my arms outstretched. With that, I gave Nina a massive hug, and on impact, the tears from her eyes soaked up my top. I didn't mind. Like me, this girl has been through the mill and then some. She deserved everything she worked so hard for and more. Hashtag: Girl power.

"Thank you Erykah; your words mean a lot to me, and I can say the same for you, Hun," she said with a smile so radiant showing her perfect set of teeth.

I smiled back. "You're most welcome girl."

All of a sudden Nina changed the subject.

"So what did you get up to today young lady?"

"Oh my gosh, you won't believe me if I tell you," I said as I took a few more mouthfuls of tea.

"Try me."

I sensed she knew something juicy was going to come out of my mouth.

"Alright, you've asked for it." As I got up from where I was seated, Nina laid both her legs on the seat I vacated.

"Go ahead, girl and don't miss anything out." She smiled and leant forward, stopping six or so inches from me. She was pulling off the demeaner of an expectant reporter waiting for the exclusive of the week.

"I'll cut a long story short. I had the wickedest sex this morning and bagged myself a job too. Plus I possibly helped my new boss from a lot of trouble." I said very quickly then paused for a moment awaiting Nina's response.

Immediately Nina stood up and hovered over me with one hand perfectly poised on her right hip and the left waving and pointing down in my face.

"Excuse me Erykah; who, what, when and where Missy?"

"Laugh out loud, Nina; you're acting like, you know."

"Like what? You've only been in London a hot minute, and already you're the one who's acting ratchet."

She uncontrollably laughed at me. At first, I couldn't tell whether she was acting real or not. It was when she put her hand on my shoulder I realised she was taking the piss.

"Well, his name is Donte Williams, and he is the manager of the gym you instructed me to attend." As soon as I said his name, Nina, went crazy like a wily coyote.

"Oh my gosh Erykah, I can't believe it, really, Donte, oh my gosh, wow." Nina looked flabbergasted. She said those words like she was stumbling on everyone I mentioned with difficulty. "All I can say is that you are one lucky lady." She wrapped.

"Yeah I think so too," I said giggling my way through that sentence. Nina eyed me with smiley eyes. But by the way, she was eyeballing me up; I got the distinct impression she had something else to say to me.

"Donte is a special guy Erykah," she said seriously enough like I was going to do him something one day. But in hindsight, you never know what the future holds, do you?

"So this specialness you say he possesses. Do you know this from personal experience?" I asked.

"No, he is like a brother to me. We go way back from school days. He is a fellow Mancunian if you didn't detect already. But he relocated to London like five years before Eric and me. That is why his accent is waning."

"Oh, I see." I was surprised all the same.

"You're in good hands there girl. Donte; he is one the good guys. A real twenty-first-century classic man." She wrapped.

"All good there then." As I went to get up, I heard a key being turned in the front door.

"That must be the guys?" All of a sudden, I felt happy.

"Oh, I forgot to tell you. When you went out earlier, Eric helped your Uncle unload your belongings into your room."

"Oh, cool. Saves me the job and to be honest I wasn't looking forward to doing it."

I clocked Eric first walking down the hallway and then I saw Uncle lagging his old ass behind him. Eric entered the kitchen first.

"Sis, Erykah. How are you ladies doing?" He questioned. We both nodded our heads at him without uttering a word. Uncle arrived shortly after.

"Wha'ppen niece, hey Nina?" Uncle came in as his usual chirpy self. But he did seem a little more than usual and from what I witnessed the other day at the centre. I wouldn't put it past him that Uncle Jeb has been to see an old flame or to converse with Caroline. He thought I didn't notice her writing her details on the back of a company brochure and handing it to him.

When we got back into the van that day, I asked him if I could have a look. He handed me another, and that was the moment I knew.

"I'm good, Mr Gaines; how are you?" Nina asked.

"Mi gud yuh kno Nina, real gud," Uncle replied.

"Glad to hear that Mr Gaines."

"So Uncle, where have you been all this time?" I sternly questioned him to see if he dared try to lie to me.

"Why are you questioning me like I'm guilty of doing something wrong?" He answered back in a manner that suggested to me who the fuck do you think you are?

"Well did you?" I said very seriously with my arms folded and my head cocked to one side.

"Did I what Erykah?" Uncle took a serious tone to me. "What are you trying to accuse me off? He sounded well pissed as he kissed his teeth in utter defiance.

"I'm not accusing you of anything Uncle. I'm merely asking where you been that's all," I said a bit more relaxed.

"Cha Erykah;" he shook his head at me as he laid his bag onto a chair. "I've been to your Aunt Lola's salon in Kensington," he concluded.

I searched his eyes for any sign he was trying to pull the wool over my eyes. He damn well knows what I've been through in my life and one major thing I hate is goddamn liars.

"Okay, how is she?" All of a sudden, I felt like a fool. I kept on telling myself to give Uncle a break.

"Why don't you go visit her and see for yourself? She was asking why I didn't bring you."

"I'll text her right now." I got up again from where I was seated and moved to head out of the kitchen. Uncle followed behind me and almost banged straight into the back of me.

"Erykah watch yuhself Nah?" I kissed my teeth and crossed my eyes at him as he shuffled his large frame past me.

For the first time today, he was beginning to irritate me. The quicker he sorted himself out, the quicker he could leave.

I decided to give him a helping hand to speed up the process. When Uncle is finally gone, I can begin the next chapter in my life without his sermons.

All I need to do now for today was to have a nice soak in the bath and book myself a hair and nail appointment.

During the melee with Uncle, Nina asked if I wanted to invite Donte; I immediately said yes.

So as soon as Uncle is gone, I was going to ring him and see if he wants to come and also to email the young man with the footage.

All that remained between now and Monday was unpacking and ordering my furniture with Nina's credit card of course.

As of Monday, it was contract talks with Donte and then a short visit to see Aunt Lola.

So new life here I come. I have no idea what it may bring. But whatever it is, at the position I'm in right now. I will grab every opportunity that comes my way with positivity and a hint of caution.

Chapter 8 – A Lesson Learned

"You're coming to London when?" I had to ask Chantel twice because of the noise coming from inside the hairdressers. I was already approaching being here for three hours. Now my hair was done, my nails were almost too.

"I'm coming down on the weekend of the twelfth of September until the thirtieth." She relayed.

"Cool, that's great Chan. What's happening for you then?"

"Well, I thought I'll get there early. I wanna support my girl. You didn't think I was going to leave you to perish on your own?"

"Ah, Chan; that's so sweet of you. But I don't want you to put yourself out for me."

"Girl, hush your mouth, allow all that extra fearless shit and let us be there for you! I'm presuming Nina is coming along too?"

"Yeah, she is."

"All good then. The three divas back together in force."

"That will be cool Chantel; I can't wait to see you."

"Me too Erykah; and after when you get off with some community work. We're going to celebrate and everything is going to be lit." And she was serious too.

One thing with Chantel, she was ever more the optimistic one of us all. Bless her, one day she will realise life isn't always peaches and cream.

Her metaphors are misguided and come from working in the fickle, airy industry she does. Basically, at the moment it can't be helped.

"Okay, Miss Porter; as long as you're paying?"

"No doubt," she concurred. "Plus you have got to get off; I need Nina and you there for my modelling show taking place at the Savoy hotel. We can go couture shopping, lunch and have a glorious day out altogether, all on me of course!"

"Virtuoso. I can't wait, and as of my case; I wish I had your credence and optimism." I had shared my real feelings with Chantel. It wasn't easy either at the worthiest of times when it came to personal ones. I preferred to keep them private. But she was one of my best friends and if I couldn't confide in her then who.

"Erykah; I understand you're worried. But remember you have Marcus fighting your corner, who is one of the best defence lawyer's money can buy and if anyone can find a loophole, a way out, he can. Enough said sister."

"I'm not worried Chantel; combatting in the legal field is something Marcus is adept at. My issue is, is that I'm struggling with the notion that the system want's me to accept this like I'm some second class citizen."

"I feel you on that, girl and its such a kick to the soul that even the slightest sound of a cop car gets you jumping like someone is jacking a thousand volts up your ass?"

"Too many black folk on a daily basis are struggling with mental health issues, because they have no faith in a system that was never designed to include us in a fair and unprejudiced capacity. Personally, I'm aggrieved by the whole situation and I don't know how much more of this I can take?"

"I've always stated that in our communities we need better resources and facilities to combat mental health. Initially, I use to think that could only come from local government initiatives? But if we as a people can find ways to build and fund our own facilities, then we Miss

Gaines will never have to rely on the white man for handouts."

"Easier said then done, but in the realms of possibilities its possible?"

"But before we can do that, our community needs to face up to the facts of mental health amongst us and put a stop to sweeping it under the carpet like bygone years ago?"

"That is so true. But how does one go about getting a whole generation out of the realms of their own stubbornness?"

"By bringing back good old-fashioned awareness. The narrative needs upgrading and a changing of the guard quick fast?"

"A heinous task indeed. Leaders in our communities need to pull their resources and start braining storming as a collective. Who is going to initiate the idea of getting a lot of our folk on board?"

"Erykah, you'll be surprised of the turnouts to a workshop, a debate or even a play that spreads a message like this, that times need a changing?"

"Look at you sounding like a politician. I didn't know you was so passionate about Mental Health?"

"I'm was invested into it by my upbringing. When you have members of your own family that have suffered from the atrocities and only to get diagnosed with a condition that has no relevance to their current. You get to learn a great deal when its in your face most of the time?"

"I didn't know that about you?"

"Well, of course you didn't? It's not something that has ever come up in conversation between us before, until now?"

"Who was it? The family member."

"My Aunt Claudia on my father's side of the fam. She suffered from Schizophrenia, Severe anxiety and PTSD from her time serving in the armed forces."

"Wow, that's a lot of shit to deal with right there."

"That's why it's ever more prevalent to get the message out there, before folks get to that stage where help is beyond them, just like my Aunt Claudia?"

"Like I said I'm aggrieved by the whole situation."

"I know babes. But you can't let all that bother you. Otherwise, you'll give yourself a hernia as my mother used to tell me when I didn't know when to slow down."

"Chantel; you're the only person I know who can find the light in a bad situation."

"Ah, Erykah; that's such a nice compliment," with that she gave me a theatrical kiss down the phone. "You're my best friend too, and I love you, girl. Anything positive I can do for your case, all the better for you Hun." She concluded.

"No doubt girl, that's why I love you so much. You're always leaving me feeling good when we part conversation or company."

"Girl, you do alright too," with that she said her goodbyes. "Well, I'm off. Got things to sort for my trip. So the next time I'll be seeing y'all is when I come to London. Adios chicka."

"Later's Chan; take care Hun, bye."

"You too, girl; be cool and stay safe."

"I'll try." She cut off the line dead.

It was now five pm, and the day seemed to drag on a bit. After Uncle had left at four, my conversation with Chantel took an hour out of my time. I had approximately two hours left to get ready in between Eric and Nina before the cab came. Nina said she had reserved us a table at

Chiteritos; one of my favourite places to dine as they had franchises all around the UK.

As I got off my bed, I grabbed a towel and my wash bits from one of the packed boxes and proceeded the short walk towards the bathroom.

When I reached, I went to grab the door handle. I was about to turn it when the door flew open and a hella lot of steam too.

The bathroom resembled the Amazon jungle as my eyes squelched for a few seconds. I tried to brush the fumes away from my face. But to no avail that notion seemed fruitless. I then took two steps nearer when amidst the heat, Eric walked through. I nearly had a heart attack, when all he was wearing was the minutest white towel I've ever seen barely covering his never regions.

The sudden sight of his muscly, wet six pack almost had me weak at the knees. I had to compose myself and remember who he was.

"Eric;" I said slightly embarrassed.

"Erykah;" he repeated sexily as he brushed past me.

I licked my lips as he carried on walking.

You see a few years back before Nina and Eric moved to London; we had a little thing going on and behind Nina's back as well. I always felt guilty every time Eric and I had sex because if she had ever found out, I don't know how she would've taken it and on this occasion, it was proving difficult to resist this chocolate man.

"How long have we got?" I said, trying to change the subject.

"As long as we need," he motioned with his head to follow him into his room.

At first, I was reluctant, but my curiosity was getting the better of me.

Me being my nosey self, I told myself a quick sneak peek around his bedroom and out.

I stepped inside and procured to the middle of the room with my back turned, I heard the door behind me shut quickly.

As I turned around and to my shock horror, Eric; was standing there fully naked brandishing his dick in his hand, while stroking it gently.

I shook my head at him a couple of times; then I proceeded to walk towards him. My aim was to get out with minimal fuss.

As I went to turn the handle, it wouldn't open.

"Eric, please unlock the door?"

"Stay, please?" He said in a sexual tone.

"No Eric; what you think you're playing at?"

"Ah come on Erykah; indulge manz for old time's sake."

"Eric, I said no. Now move out of the way, otherwise."

"Otherwise, what?" He sniggered back at me. Was he thinking I was playing?

"Otherwise I'll punch you straight in your face," I replied as I grimaced back at him.

I stepped forward and shoved him out of the way. When he began to laugh back at me, I decided to do something more devious. I grabbed hold of his dick and balls and slowly began twisting them.

"Ouch Erykah, that fucking hurts?"

The pain on his face suggested he was submitting to me.

"I was just playing with you; please let go, girl."

"Playing or not. You never again do what you just tried to do to me, understand nigger?"

"Understood!" At that point, I let go of his tackle. Eric tried to hide his tears and embarrassment as he bowed his head in shame and went and sat on the bed.

For a brief while I felt sorry for him.

"Are you okay?" I asked with grave concern.

"I'll be fine, don't know about my ego, though." He looked up at me, awaiting my reply. I went and sat next to him and put my arm around him for comfort.

"You're so silly, ain't ya?" He acquiesced in agreement. "Look listen up. What we had a few years ago was a bit of fun. We agreed back then never to repeat it. What we did then was great in a sexual sense, and you're an attentive lover—always putting the female's feelings before your own. You're a good man Eric Lawrence and one day in the future you're going to make some lucky lady and children, and I emphasise the word lucky, a fabulous husband and father. Trust me. What you did just now was a bitch move by your standards. That isn't you, acting like you some pimp. Please stay as you usually are otherwise you will never get noticed by the kind of women you're supposed to end up with." I concluded.

"I'm sorry, Erykah; I hear ya. I don't know what came over me. Please accept my apology."

"You idiot, of course, I'll accept it. Let's pretend this didn't just happen and next time check yourself, okay."

"Agreed." I gave him a hug and a peck on the cheek and left him to get ready.

Before I left the room, I clocked the time on the wall clock; it said five thirty-five pm. I had approximately eighty-five minutes before the cab came.

I shut the door behind me and went to get ready. As I got into the bathroom Donte text saying to meet him at his house—something about running late at work.

Oh well if he comes I know he is serious about us. If not, then it's boss and employee status, and that's how it will remain, believe me.

STAND IN YOUR POWER

Chapter 9 – Opening Up

As I stepped out of the cab and onto the street below, on the journey up here, I kept on telling myself that having fun was paramount tonight.

I wanted to at least for one night, to try and forget about my recent predicaments. It wasn't going to be easy. But with Nina; Eric and Donte by my side they would go to great lengths in making sure I won't fall apart too early.

"It's alright I got it, guys." I heard Nina say.

I turned around and bent down so I could lean into the car and peer in on them.

"Sis, I can't let you pay for the whole fare." Eric insisted.

I kept on watching and laughing to myself at the two of them arguing with each other on who should pay.

The driver suddenly shouted over everyone. But there was no response from the siblings.

"Testi, Emo ko bikita ti o sanwo bi enyan ba saaju ki ale ale to jade." By the way that outburst sounded, the cab driver looked pissed.

"Bredrin, what did you just say?" Donte asked looking baffled by the driver's statement.

"It's my native Yoruba tongue," the driver relayed back to us. "What I said was; listen, I don't care who pays as long as someone does before the night is out." I looked over at Donte and signalled for him to pay.

"How much will that be boss?" Donte said as he reached into his shirt pocket.

"That will be twenty-five pounds, sir?" The African cab driver said.

Donte opened his wallet and gave the driver thirty pounds. As he received his change, he exited the car.

Nina and Eric hadn't noticed because they were still arguing. Donte slid next to me as we both and the driver watched on in amusement.

A few minutes later, I shouted down to them.

"Hey you two, get out of the car already?"

As soon as those words had escaped my mouth, Nina and Eric look around simultaneously at each other than to the back of the cab and realised Donte, and I wasn't vacating it no more.

"Erykah, what's going on?" Nina asked, looking surprised.

"I've already paid for the cab Nina," Donte answered.

She looked a little perplexed now as she began getting out of the car.

A few moments later.

"Oh my days, how shameful," she said back.

"Girl, what was that all about?"

"You know what Erykah; I don't even know what to tell you!"

"Donte; let me give you the money you paid for the cab?" Eric was insistent in his proposal.

"Keep your money, man I got y'all. You know we go way back. So don't sweat it bruh."

Donte turned around to face me and offered out his arm for me to take.

Eric and Nina said no more as the four of us strolled into the restaurant in unison.

Upon entry, we were all greeted by a young Spanish or Portuguese sounding lady at reception. Nina progressed up to the desk first.

"Good evening and welcome to Chiteritos, South Kensington. Do you have a reservation?" For a foreign girl, her pronunciation of the English language sounded better than mine.

"Yes, I do," she responded excitingly. "It's Nina Lawrence."

"Ah yes, here you are. Miss Lawrence plus three guests. Okay very well," as she tapped away on her laptop. "I see here you haven't filled out your online specifications form?"

"Honestly, I completely forgot. I'm a very busy person."

"That's Okay Miss Lawrence; you can tell me right now if you want."

"It's my friend here, Erykah." Nina put her hand on my shoulder. "I'm doing this meal for her. So you can ask what she wants instead?"

"Ah thank you, Ni. Are you sure?"

"Yes, I'm sure. It's your night after all."

"Okay, Miss Erykah, would you like a table near the window or inside?" The receptionist questioned.

"I'm sorry I don't know you, so please address me as Miss Gaines?" Everyone was looking at me like I was overly rude.

"Erykah;" everyone said together.

"What?" I said back exemplifying the word.

Nina shook her head at me.

"Never mind boo."

"Come on Erykah I'm starving man," Eric added his two penny's worth.

"Where do guys want to sit?"

"Erykah, we want whatever you choose. It's is all about you, Hun." Nina pointed out.

"Okay, black people, thank you. Err by the window please."

"Thank you, Miss Gaines," the receptionist pressed a button on her desk, and within a minute a waiter arrived by her side. "Xavi here will escort you all to table forty-two." She concluded.

"Okay, thank you." When the receptionist was finished with us, we followed the waiter and proceeded the short walk to our table.

One by one, we all took our seats respectively. Xavi; handed us all a menu each and then walked away from the table.

"Bredrin; how's t'ings going down pon di gym these days?" Eric asked Donte.

"I can't complain bro. T'ings are going real good."

"That's what I like to hear. Brothers doing well."

"It's so lovely too see black men in support of one another?" Nina specified.

"Bless, Nina," Donte replied.

"Good looking out Sis," was Eric's response.

"Besides Eric; it's been a hot minute since I've seen you there, man. You need to come down and renew your membership bruh. We got some great offers on at the moment." Donte further explained.

"Yeah, for sure. I've been busy with interviews and preparations for this new job."

"How's all that going?"

"So far, bredrin, everything is copasetic."

"Great. Glad to hear it."

"Mm, so much choice to choose from," I said with my face firmly planted two inches from the menu.

"What do you fancy eating Erykah?" Nina asked all excited.

"I don't know. I'm so hungry; I could eat a horse right now." I contemplated as I scanned the menu extensively.

Nina turned her attention to the guys as the waiter came back.

"Are you ready to order?" Xavi stood waiting with a tablet in his hands. He was tapping his foot nervously and looking a bit more flustered than before. By the look on his face, he might have had an argument maybe with a chef or his supervisor.

"Eric, Donte; what do you guys want to eat?" Nina eyeballed both of them to get a move on.

"I'm going to have the spicy chicken fajitas with extra salsa and guacamole, Mexican rice, black beans and chips." Donte wrapped.

"I'll have what Don is having," Eric whispered.

"Erykah are you ready?"

"Yes, em, I'll have a meat flour burrito filled with fajita veggies, salsa, guacamole and sour cream. Also, can I get some Mexican rice extra spicy and chips? Plus a salad with romaine lettuce, sofritas, beans, salsa, guacamole, cheese and chipotle honey vinaigrette."

"What would you like madam?" He said in his sexy-sounding accent as he turned his attention to Nina.

From where I was sitting, his pupils became dilated, and a few beads of sweat began breaking out from his forehead. I was getting a sense he fancied Nina and why not she's a great catch and Xavi is a good looking foreigner; not usually Nina's type, but with the luck, she has had with men over the years maybe this dude would be a refreshing change to the standards before.

"I would like," she exemplified while gazing through the menu. "I want some soft corn tacos with sofritas, salsa, guacamole, cheese and romaine lettuce. Plus some chips, Mexican rice, and the same salad as my best friend here." She concluded saying as she tapped me on my left shoulder.

After he finished selecting the last of our orders, Xavi gave another cute glance towards Nina's direction, but she didn't see it because she was obliviously chatting to Donte.

The waiter took the menus and walked away. As soon as Xavi was gone, I nudged Nina in her side to get her attention. She didn't respond straight away, so I prodded a little harder.

"Erykah, why do you keep poking me like that?" As she turned around abruptly and questioned me looking a little too aggravated for my liking.

"Girl time, toilets, now!" I rapidly got up from my seat and kissed Donte on the cheek, then I took Nina's arm in mine as I rushed her away.

"Be back in minute guys." Nina barked.

"What's up wid them two gee?"

"I don't know Donte. Woman are the strangest creatures at the best of times, beats me."

"Erykah what's going on? You're acting real peculiar."

"Shh, don't make a scene, Nina; just get your ass in here," I instructed her to follow me into the ladies toilets.

"What's with the amateur dramatics girl?"

"Be quiet for a second. I want to ask you something important."

"Okay," Nina responded. The look on her face was one of a bewildered woman.

"Listen, do you think I should ask him?"

"Ask who?"

"Donte; silly."

"What do you want to ask him?"

Suddenly I felt overwhelmingly shy in front of her, and I didn't know exactly why. All I knew is since the moment I first clapped eyes on Donte I got all up in my feels; a kinda rush that I've never experienced before for a guy. One time I thought I was in love with Darren Grey, but that relationship proved to be nothing of the sort. So what was holding me back from asking? I needed homegirl to help a sister out.

"Nina, I need your help badly. I can't decide."

"Girl spit it out. What could be so problematic, it's making you clam up like this?"

As I was about to tell her, I began feeling nauseous, and I was also getting butterflies in the pit of my stomach.

"Erykah are you alright?"

"Oh, I don't know. You see since I met Donte," I said, trembling with excitement. "You see since I first ever laid eyes on him. All I knew in that precise moment of our paths crossing for the first time, in that meeting, I felt vibes from him that no other man has been able to give me, ever."

"You is definitely in love, girl?"

"The hell I am. Am I? I can't be Nina; I just, I err no." I was in a state of emergency again. Feeling like I did the day I was leaving home when I was with Chantel.

"Erykah what's up?" She began to panic between my rapid, heavy breathing. "What shall I do?" She continued to say as I fell to my knees, I squeezed her hand tight.

"Quick in my bag," I said as the pain intensified. "Get my inhaler out."

"Which one," she said, sounding more frantic than I was. I think this is the first time she has seen me have a severe attack.

"The brown one." I pointed out as she reached her long arms into the jungle of what was my bag.

"I got it; I got it." As she handed the inhaler to me, I took it off her and did my usual routine when I was able to do it in these situations.

After a few minutes, my breathing subsided to a steady pace. I could feel myself getting back to normal.

Nina had simmered herself too, and I noticed the sudden smile of relief etched on her face, which was also the perfect welcoming vibe I always needed in these dilemmas.

But on the contrary, she handled my attack about right for a first-timer.

"Thank you," I said, exemplifying my gratitude.

"No need for thanks, girl. What was all that about?" She further questioned.

"Nothing, I'm alright now." I lied. I didn't want to worry Nina any more than I needed.

"That didn't look like nothing Erykah!"

"I'm fine. I'm fine. It was a minor asthma attack."

"I thought you grew out of all that?"

"Not yet, girl."

"Well if you're saying that's all it is. Then I'll have to take your word for it."

"Girl stop playing. You already know my word is bond." Nina raised an eyebrow at me and had a look of doubt in her eyes. To be honest, she can believe what she wants right now.

"Come on, Erykah; the guys are going to be wondering where we are."

"Let them worry. It isn't gonna kill them."

"Well, I'm going back because I'm starving." Nina started heading back into the restaurant.

"Wait!" I said as I grabbed her arm lightly.

"Girl, which part of I'm starving, didn't you quite understand?"

"Every part."

"Good, so let me go."

"Nina; I need to know if I should?"

"Listen, you do whatever your heart tells you. But if your head says something else, like, raises any seed of doubt. Make your conscience decide, indefinitely."

"I suppose," I said as I prepared to escort myself back to where the guys were. "Thank you for the advice, Nina. I know most of what you told me I'm gonna use. Bless up, serious t'ings."

"No worries," she said. Her smile was so radiant, but her eyes seemed to betray that gorgeous smile of hers. Although it seems her life has taken a turn for the better in some aspects since she came to London. I'm getting the distinct impression she is hiding something deep within her.

"Wait, hang on a minute?" I grabbed her by the shoulder lightly. She turned around to face me, and as she did so, the look on her was one of those 'what the fuck now' looks.

"Erykah; seriously, I need to eat, right now before I pass out?"

"Come on then. We can walk and talk."

"Thank you."

"No problem."

"So what's up now?"

"What do you think about the dude?" I inquisitively asked.

"Which dude?" She said, sounding a bit confused. "You mean the waiter Xavi?" She finished of saying towards me then back to him and all I could see is that she was giving him a good old fashioned head to toe stare down.

"Yes."

"Hm, he's kinda cute. Not my usual type, but handsome all the same. Right now, though, I'm not looking to share my life again with anyone."

"Ah come on, girl! Who else am I going to go on double dates with?"

"I feel you Erykah, but right now it's not feasible for me. I have other types of plans for the forcible future, and a relationship is not on the agenda girl."

"Alright, fine ima leave it there for now."

"Hmm, I think it will be in your best interest if you leave it altogether," she said, laughing as we got nearer to our table. I clocked Xavi bringing out our orders from the kitchen.

"What have you two been doing all this time?" Donte asked.

"All this time please, we were only ten minutes, so stop exaggerating," I answered.

"Babe, ten minutes is a long time when you're waiting on someone. Especially in a restaurant full of people staring at you."

"Why would people be staring at you?"

"Because."

"Cha Donte; why you acting like there's a problem?"

"Sit down Erykah; you're making a scene?"

"Wait! You for real?"

"Yeah, I'm for real! You think I'm playing wid you?"

"Excuse me! But I think you're overstepping your remit?"

"What do you mean?"

"Word of warning. Erykah is one girl you can't tell what to do ever?" Nina warned.

"Is that right?" Donte barked.

I gently leaned to his left side and whispered into his ear.

"The only time you can ever tell me what to do is when I'm submissive in the bedroom department. You feel me?" I concluded.

Suddenly a big, broad grin swept across Donte's face. I though he might like that one. I suspected that statement was probably making in his head was one of sheer ecstasy.

"A'right, a'right, mi overstand. Every'ting bless."

"I hope so for your sake."

"Yes, yes everything is cool babe. Let's all eat now."

"Good," I said as Xavi began serving out our food from left to right.

"Mine looks very appetising," Nina added.

"Tastes wicked," Donte said with a mouth full of food.

"You pig!"

"Ah, leave him alone, Erykah; he is enjoying himself."

"Enjoying himself a bit too much. Before allowing us ladies to go first."

"Excuse me?" Donte was trying to adjust what I was saying about him.

"Excuse you what?"

"Since when is it stated a man must wait for a woman to go first before he can eat?"

Everyone went silent. Even a few onlookers from other tables were now engrossed in our little melee. Donte threw the question at me like I was the rudest bitch of the century so far. He was making me look like a bully.

"Since it was customary to be a gentleman."

"Well, one thing you're going to learn very quickly about me is that I'm no gentlemen. I'm far from it."

"Is that so? Okay, I'll remember that for when you don't want me to be a bitch." I said back giving him a false smile look of disgust.

He held my gaze, and then I stuck out my tongue playfully at him, and he returned it with a wink and a theatrical kiss.

"You know what?" Nina interjected. "You two are perfect for each other."

Donte and I looked at Nina in a jovial manner and then at each other. He took his hand in mine and looked tentatively into my eyes. I returned his gaze with a knowing smile. If I was questioning or had any doubts about the sincerity of my feelings for him before, then this exchange of vibes between us was now confirming what I wanted to ask him earlier.

"Donte," I said nervously as I took hold of his hand and gave it a gentle rub.

"Erykah," he said back sternly.

"I want to ask you something?" I stated by saying, and then the nerves suddenly took over at a heavier rate. Nina sensed my anxiety and intervened.

"Take your time?" She said as she lightly held my forearm.

I took a couple of deep breaths, and I decided to go for it.

"Come on Erykah; the way you're acting you'd think you were preparing to propose."

"Shut up, Eric; you're not helping?" Nina barked at him.

"Ah Sis, I'm just playing." Nina gave him a condescending look like she didn't believe him.

"You like playing around a lot, don't you, Eric?" I asked, grimacing at him.

Straight away, he slightly lowered his head and shoulders and sank back into his seat without uttering another word.

I took Donte's hand in mine, and I didn't have a care in the world on who was watching now.

"So, what is it you wanted to ask me?"

"Wait, wait, wait,?" Eric shouted at the top of his lungs.

"Eric," I annoyingly said at his untimely intrusion.

"What you playing at Eric?" He was also getting Nina mad as hell now.

"Hold up, Sis! I'm feeling a moment here. I gotta film this."

"Whatever turns you on, Eric?" I nonchalantly replied.

"Eric put the phone away! Can't you see she is having a hard enough time already?"

"Whatever Sis."

"Eric; I'd appreciate if you didn't," Donte asked serenely and politely.

But now Eric seemed he'd had enough of being told what to do. I could see it beginning to fester from the back of his eyes.

"Ah, what's up with everyone? I'm having a bit of fun."

"Yeah, well not on our account," I said as I began to feel angry with him.

"Man, you lot are acting like a bunch of old people. Whinging and moaning. I'm going outside for a cigarette, since my food ain't here yet, jeez."

"Thank God for that," Nina replied.

"Now, where was I?" I said, questioning myself.

"You was about to say after you said, I want to ask you something."

"Yes I did, didn't I?" I repeated through gritted teeth.

"So, what is it that you want to say to me with such a huge build-up?"

By the loudness of our voices and general dramatics, we had managed to attract half of the other tables to watch, and it was as if they were listening to a TV drama.

"Wait, this ain't easy for me. I don't normally ask a guy to be my official boyfriend every day."

Donte peculiarly looked at me as he withdrew his hand from mine. He looked out at Nina respectively, and then he focused his gaze back on me.

"What do you guys think?" He said out loud.

What a cheek I thought as I humorously hit him on the arm.

Eric came back from outside. He must've been in earshot because he was the first one to answer.

"Err, I don't know. What are you asking Donte, are you asking if she is a reputable person or is relationship material?"

"Eric; behave. Don't say silly things like that?"

"Why not sis? He asked, and I delivered."

"He was asking hypothetically dear brother."

"Ah, whatever."

"Erykah don't worry babes. I got a mind of my own."

"Glad to hear it. But before you give me your answer. I feel you need to know what kinda person you're getting involved with."

"Why you're not a murderer or worse still a serial killer, ooh the suspense it's killing me. You get it, guys, killing me yeah. Okay, no one is laughing, joke over. Continue babe."

"No, don't be silly," I said chuckling.

"Go ahead then, tell me?"

"You sure you want to know?" I asked, searching his eyes for any signs of him lying.

"Yeah, babe. Do your thing."

But before I was going to bare my life story, we all decided to finish off our meals prospectively first.

It was a tense half-hour of small talk, mainly consisting of all of them chatting about their careers.

When we were all finished, Nina suggested we should all retire to the upstairs lounge. I concurred, and so did the guys. So we followed Xavi as he directed us to a beautiful area that was situated by an old fashioned log fire.

As we all took a seat on the most beautiful leather sofa I've ever had the privilege to sit my bum on, Xavi asked if we would like some deserts. We all passed except Donte of course who ordered himself a slice of cheesecake.

When Xavi went away, I couldn't help but get engrossed with the décor. The building looked very old and had some interesting artefacts scattered around the equal-sized massive lounge as the downstairs restaurant.

As I settled myself and the others got comfortable too, I decided to go for it and carry on where I left off.

"Babe, you still want to tell us?"

"I'm not a hundred per cent, but I'll give it a go all the same."

"If you're sure babes then cool. But anytime you need or want to have a breather or completely stop just say the word!"

"Thank you, sweetie."

"No problem."

"Well, here goes everything," I said as I took in a deep breath and then exhaled. Donte, Eric and Nina continued to get settled while maintaining their attention on me constantly. I gave Nina a 'am I doing' the right thing kind of looks, as I didn't want to appear too vulnerable and exposed.

She sensed my anticipation to tell and gave me back a look of confidence. So I proceeded. But before I could open my mouth and utter another word, Donte touched my hand and smiled at me.

"Babe I want to know everything. So don't hold back?" That gave me a further boost. So I went for it.

"Well, way back as far as I can remember and my memory is very vague about this. I must've been around three years old, and all I remember is being told off by my mother for sneaking into her bedroom and painting half my face with her bright red lipstick. I must've looked like a clown because my father was laughing his head off in a hysterical manner. I also remember mother shouting at him to stop while she took me into the bathroom to scrub the makeup off. To me, that was one of the good memories. A bad memory was when I was six years old; was the day I was told in the most diplomatic way a family member could put it to me. My Aunt Celestine, bless her, I can't wait for you to meet her Donte, she said that my mummy had to leave this planet and go live in heaven with other family and friends who have gone there to and that although she was never coming back to earth, she said one day in heaven I'll get to see her again. Years later, I found out she died in a car crash after having a serious argument with my dad, and the result was he survived, and she didn't. Shall I continue?"

"Yes, continue Erykah;" he said with a solemn look on his face. Both Eric and Nina became engrossed on my every word.

"Okay," I said, feeling the energy and love from all three of them.

"It's alright girl; you don't have to do this. Does she Donte?" Nina tried to contain my chat, but she fiercely questioned Donte.

"It's up to her Nina."

"Erykah," Nina said, looking me straight dead in the eye.

"It's fine, Nina."

"Okay, I suppose it's better now than when it might be too late."

"I concur, sis," Eric added.

"Well, I was saying after the crash that sent my father into a complete meltdown, and my father he began a path of destruction. Inevitably it was the usual suspects, heavy drinking, drugs and gambling. Subsequently, that had an adverse effect on my well-being. I was neglected and on most occasions had to find food for myself. I would end up shipped around neighbours and family friends in fear of social services getting wind of my unfortunate situation."

"That is so sad babe. What happened next?"

"Well, after a year of shenanigans, I found myself in a unique position. There was an intervention, and my Aunt Celestine and Uncle Jeboniah stepped in and took over where father couldn't. For the following three years, until I was nearly ten years old, they became my surrogate parents and did everything for me. They fed, clothed and kept me safe and warm. They even helped me with all my secondary school applications and right up to when I was enrolled and had done my first two months. Father had been to rehab on two occasions. Everyone agreed after four years of not living with him that he was on the mend and I should go back and live with him. Well, the first year was alright and going at a good tempo. Then one day near Christmas he had a relapse and things for us became more and more strained, and as a result, our relationship grounded to a halt. By now, I was twelve years old and capable of looking after myself in the coming months of my father's misfortunes. I took myself to school and back and all the rest. From time to time, Auntie and Uncle looked in on us. Those were the day's father made sure he was looking well, to fool them into believing everything was alright and submitting me into being quiet about it all. Over time, fathers escapades got worse. He became a full-fledged alcoholic and narcotics user and for the next ten years until I reached twenty-two that's when I saw my father sober and drug-free again. But before my twenty-second birthday, let me take you back to my high school years. I started at Manchester high school for girls in September 1999. My first day was like most other students starting a new chapter in their life. As I walked through the main gates and looked around, I felt such a nervousness from within, and straight away, I felt like I wanted to walk back out."

"Well did you babe?"

"No, I didn't. I managed to muster some courage from somewhere after Aunt CeCe gave me some formal encouragement."

"So, what happened next?"

"Nothing that major baby. Just a nervous and slightly crazy first day. Over time I made a few key friends. But my best friend throughout high school was a girl called Jocelyn Maynard. She went through all my highs and lows in those five years. But most notable was the sexual relations I had with my maths teacher Mr Smith."

Everyone looked flabbergasted at what I revealed. Donte immediately stood up and came at sat beside me on the arm of my chair. He looked down at me as I looked up to him. He put his right arm around the back of my shoulders while stroking my left arm with his left hand.

"Oh shit," Eric responded, looking like he couldn't fathom what I expressed. Nina started to cry slowly. By the look on her face, I could see it was opening up old wounds for her.

"Nina; you alright?"

"Erykah;" she said as she began to tremble with confusion.

"I don't have to carry on if you don't want me to?" I asked her.

"Sis, is it the thing, you know?" Eric asked.

Nina didn't say a word other than get up from her chair. She began walking towards the top of the stairs.

"Where you going girl?" I anxiously asked.

"I'm sorry Erykah to interrupt your story," she said as a heavy stream of tears began to fall from her puffy looking

144

eyes. "But if I don't get some fresh air, I feel like my head is going to explode."

Immediately we all stood up together, grabbed our belongings and headed towards her. When I reached her, I put my arm around her for comfort as all four of us strode downstairs into the restaurant in sheer silence. Nina and I accessed the foot of the stairs first. As we took a few steps, we descended upon the payment area. Nina was too tearful to do anything, so I asked Eric and Donte to cover it as Nina, and I walked a bit further to retrieve our jackets from the cloakroom.

Xavi came over and kindly helped us with positioning them on.

As I was adjusting mine into the right feeling position, Xavi slowly and attentively began putting Nina's coat on without taking his eyes off her. The look in his eyes was of utmost care. But what I witnessed next was so touching, and the moment I knew Nina's life was going to change forever.

As I stood there in awe, time seemed to slow down, and everything in front of me was being played out like it was in an ultra-slow DVD speed.

I watched Xavi put the jacket over her shoulders.

In the next moment unexpectedly Nina lightly touched Xavi's left hand with her right and then stroked it gently a few times. By now Eric and Donte were both at either side of me, watching on in amazement. In the next instance, Nina turned around to face Xavi and flopped her body onto him, and on impact, she cried uncontrollably, shaking and gripping onto his waistcoat like her life depended on it.

Xavi looked over at us all for assurance to see if it was cool for him to give her solidarity. We all gave him the thumbs up as he continued to stroke the back of her head

145

for a further two minutes until she stopped and realised what she was doing. She looked up to Xavi's 6′ 2″ frame with sorrow lurking from her eyes and a considerable chunk of embarrassment as well.

"Are you okay now, Miss Lawrence?" He said to her with so much empathy.

"Erm, I'm so sorry. What must you think of me?" Nina shyly answered as she tried desperately to wipe away her tears.

"No problem Miss Lawrence. Anything for you." And there It was, the moment those words escaped Xavi's mouth something miraculous almost magical happened between them.

Their auras were beaming out a bright beacon of light from their heads which was lighting up the temperature in the place.

"If you're sure? Then I won't be bothering you anymore." As she began walking away after she thanked him by giving him a peck on the cheek.

"Wait?" Xavi hailed.

Straight away, Nina stopped dead in her tracks and looked at all of us. She squelched her eyes, and then a little smile started to formulate from the corners of her mouth.

"You forgot something." Xavi blurted out.

By now most of the staff and customers, including us three watched on like it was the last scene in the final episode of the most talked-about drama series in years.

In seconds he was up in Nina's face. He grabbed her face softly with both his hands and brought it up nearer to him while he was lowering his.

For thirty or so seconds, they stared at each other like it was their last moments on earth.

Xavi homed in as Nina closed her eyes, and then their lips met, and he began kissing her in the most sought after, sexy and passionate kiss I've ever witnessed in reality.

The whole restaurant clapped and jeered as I was overcome with emotion.

"Go on, girl you get it!" I screamed and cried out aloud as they continued obliviously locked in a dreamy embrace.

"I can't believe it?" Eric looked so shocked. But I did see a tear or two coming from his usual unemotional persona.

I looked up at Donte and gave him a big smacker on the lips of my own. He looked back at me and smiled.

"I love you, Donte Williams. Do you want to know the rest?"

All he did was hold out his hand for me to take. I Signalled to Eric to get Nina when she was finished and meet us both outside.

As we reached outside and waited for the other two, Donte took out his pack of cigarettes from the inside of his jacket. He pulled one out and lit it up. He took a few drags and blew the grey smoke up towards the sky. As the smoke descended on its journey; Donte turned around to face me.

He stood there staring, and I felt like he was examining me. I didn't know what to make of his sudden idiosyncratic behaviour, but it was beginning to freak the fuck out of me.

"Donte; what is it. Why are you flexing like that?"

"Shush," he commanded.

"Baby, please." I was desperate now. I hoped me telling how I felt weren't putting him off.

"Miss Erykah Gaines; wid your funky self and cuckoo behaviour at times, in the little time, I've known you. You have grown on me in ways I can't comprehend yet. But what I do know already is that I don't want to go a day without either speaking to ya or seeing you. So, missy, I think, no, I know. I love you too. There I said it."

"Ah," at that moment, I felt so happy and secure. Nina and Eric must've heard Donte's speech because Eric was congratulating him and Nina myself.

Opening up felt relieving and comforting to my well-being. I yearned nothing was going to spoil this one precious thing I had going in my life so far.

STAND IN YOUR POWER

Chapter 10 – Turning Point

Uncompromising, unforgiving and disenfranchised is what a lot of folks have said about my family and me over the years as I grew up. Yet was it my fault I turned out the way I did?

So excuse me for a while, while I continue to procrastinate here because I feel I have to if I want to get to the level of pleasure that Nina has reached.

I suppose those labels that had stuck with me throughout my inconsolable and harrowing childhood came from getting involved with street gangs back in the day and being involved was a must not a given.

Simply if you weren't part of them, then you were against them, and with all the turmoil I had in my life around them times being part of a family that wanted and needed me even though it was dangerous was way healthier than what I had at home.

But like most families that occupy the earth and the very air we breathe they equally have their share of problems too. Our particular unit had a fixation on authority and the lack of respect for it.

Most of us that grew up on the Alexandra Park estate in Moss Side came from meagre and poor homes. You think my father's position was the worst hell nah. The friends I acquired from my click, their families were worse off.

When I reached eleven years of age at the time, I didn't realise that I'd been groomed for sexual relations by Mr Smith and by the time I had reached thirteen I became a sought after street hustler. I earned the reputation for not being seen, and that's how I obtained the nickname 'Shadow'.

My exerts didn't go unnoticed and by the time I reached fourteen and a half years old I'd been approached by a couple of street soldiers who were from the biggest firm in the whole of South Manchester and these guys became my road family for life.

They were notoriously known as the Lime Close gang. They took me under their leadership and treated me like their little sister. In a short space of time I had built up and ascertained the reputation of someone to not fuck with and I earned the total respect and admiration from every other member even until this very day.

They were even there for me throughout all my sexual abuse case, and I hold a special place in my heart for all of them even if they are criminals.

I remember one day when I was online, and I typed in about gangs in Manchester. As I was scrolling through the page, I saw an article that was published on the sixth of April 2013 in the Daily Bugle, and this is what part of it had said; 'The Lime Close gang, Moss Side, South Manchester. The gang was formed in 1989 and instantly became bitter rivals to the Codrington gang resulting in a turf war that saw 32 people die and 235 wounded in four years of shootings. Leaders Carlos Ramos and Terrence Joyner, former hitmen, ran a drug network making up to £7,000 a day and mercilessly sought to wipe out rival gang members, owning an array of weapons including submachine guns and sawn-off shotguns. The arrest of the gang's leaders in 2008 along with nine fellow Lime Close members led to a 94 per cent drop in shootings and not a single gang murder in a year.

After I read all this, I was saddened. It brought me back to the day the police had expertly raided all their homes and arrested those mentioned and how I got away with everything was a mystery at first until I realised why they called me 'Shadow' and the rest is history.

So as I briefly mentioned in my dialogue in the prologue. I was exposed to things my lil pee wee self shouldn't have been exposed to, and now you all know why I don't trust any mother fucker that poses a threat to myself, my family or my livelihood.

So on the way to our next destination, I also managed to disclose the rest of my life story to Donte, Nina and Eric.

Half an hour later the four of us had arrived outside the Rich Mix club in Bethnal Green. A popular venue for all Spoken Word lovers and this was the place Nina was performing at tonight. I think the punters are in for a special treat after what took place between her and Xavi at the restaurant earlier. She was definitely in high spirits and one away from the mood she had been in when she said she wanted some fresh air, and her positive vibes were also beginning to rub off on me.

"Well, this is it," Nina said all excited as she jumped out of the cab.

"Looks good from the outside," I stated.

"Wait till you get inside."

"Why Sis is it decked out with twenty-four-carat gold interior?" Eric said mocking his sister's elation.

Nina ignored him. She wasn't going to let her brother spoil her temperament.

She continued towards the venue, and we all followed suit. As we got nearer to the entrance, we were stopped by two tonk, security guards who happened to be brotha's. The first one who resembled something out of terminator was eyeballing Donte hard for some reason.

"As-Salam-u-Alaikum, Jonas?" Nina said as she greeted the superior of the two guards.

"As-Salam-u-Alaikum wa-rahmatullahi wa-barakatuh, Nina?"

"Thank you."

"So what's good with you, Nina."

"Same old, same old. Dogmatic lifestyle."

"I see and how are you feeling about your performance tonight?"

"Ah, you know me, I'm excited to get on that stage as always. What's good with you?"

"Ah, you know me I'm not one to complain."

"Why what's up?"

"Nothing major. Just a few work issues, nothing I can't resolve soon enough."

"Oh, okay. Holler at your girl if you need to talk?"

"Sure thing."

"Cool."

"Who your peoples?"

"Thought you never ask. Well this handsome gentleman you know already," Nina remonstrated as she put her hand on Eric's shoulder. "These two are my friends, and they are a couple. Mr Donte Williams and Miss Erykah Gaines, respectively."

"Safe bruh, safe," he said as he touched fists with Eric and Donte followed by giving me a peck on the cheek.

"Yo Jonas; what's wrong with your boy?"

"Donte don't." Nina pleaded with him to not start anything.

"Leave him be Nina? You know he never backs down."

"Yeah, sis besides. My man over there been giving us the green-eyed monster stare down like we some punks up in this bish."

"I know, I know all that. I ain't blind. I see what he doing. He motherfucking jealous because we roll up here with you two."

"How long he be working in this joint and this motherfucker doesn't know you, sis?"

"That's some straight-up bullshit right there," Donte added.

"Guys, seriously."

"We are serious, Nina."

"No, listen. You got to be smarter. I don't want no one to get hurt."

"Ain't no one getting hurt around here sis believe me."

"Stop being so melodramatic Nina," I added.

Jonas ushered us with his hands to come closer to him, and then he whispered.

"Guys don't worry about him; he just received some bad news not long ago."

"Well if it's bad. Then why is he still working, especially with that attitude?"

Nina inquisitively asked.

"Better he is here than wherever he got that attitude from in the first place."

"Okay no worries boss," Eric concluded.

"Wait! That isn't right. If he carries on like that, the next person he does that to may not be so cool."

"I'm head doorman! I got this."

"Just make sure you keep him away from Donte and me," I whispered into Jonas's ear as we all passed him and entered into the venue.

As we all stepped inside and began moving towards the reception, Donte lightly grabbed hold of my arm and pulled me back towards him.

"What were you whispering to Jonas?"

"I just gave him a friendly warning about his boy."

"Babe, you're so ghetto, but I likes it."

"That's what's up. I'm a ride or die kinda chick. You swear down you do right by me and I'll have your back always."

"Now that's what's up!" He exemplified with a few hand movements followed by that gorgeous to die for smile.

As we continued moving forward when we finally reached inside the main arena voluptuous applause welcomed us for the act that had just finished their set, Nina to was excitingly cheering her ass off by jumping up and down and clapping ferociously.

It was so good to see her happy again. I hoped, this time, Xavi was the real deal.

"Wow, this place is heaving with people." I expressed in astonishment.

"Every Saturday night is like this!" A voice said coming from behind me. I turned around to glimpse the face of who the beautiful tone belonged to.

"Kyndra you made it?" As thrilled as Nina was to see her. I was taken aback by the sheer glow of this dark skin beauty. She had the most gorgeous oval-shaped eyes, plump full lips and round hips that suited her facial features.

She had breasts the size of melons and an ass befitting of an African Queen. I also noticed she was carrying a large bump in her belly and looked around five or six months pregnant.

Her head was covered in a multi-coloured wrap and to compliment it, she wore the most elegant looking dashiki dress.

"Sister Nina; how are you?"

"I'm very well, thanks," she replied with a sneaky little grin.

"Greetings black people," she said bowing as she addressed the rest of us.

"Hi," was all I managed to say. I was still blown away by Kyndra's spirit.

The aura that was projecting from her head was having a profound effect on my soul, and when this happened, it meant only one thing.

That somehow I knew upon first impressions of Kyndra; that she was going to be a pivotal person in my development and growth as a strong black woman.

"Greetings sister Kyndra?" Eric remarked.

"Sup," was all Donte offered with a slight shake of his head.

"Sister Kyndra; I gotta say you're looking remarkably well."

"Thank you sister Nina;" she duly acknowledged.

"Loving your Dashiki outfit. Can I ask where you bought it from?" I asked.

"Thank you, sister," she said, elongating her words.

"Oh," I said. "Where're my manners. It's Erykah; Miss Erykah Gaines, and it's a pleasure to meet you." I said as I extended out my left arm and offering my hand for her to shake.

"Greetings; it's nice to meet you." She reciprocated by accepting my handshake.

"So, what time are you performing Nina?" Donte asked.

"My slot is around quarter to ten," she replied.

"Cool! I got time to get us some drinks and find a spot." Donte gave me a peck on the cheek and proceeded to the bar with Eric in tow.

"Well, it's Nine twenty-five. So I'm going to get myself prepared. See you guys after."

I leant forward and hugged Nina.

"Good luck."

"Thank you, girl," she said as she embraced me and gave me a peck on the cheek.

"All the best sister Nina."

"Thank you, sister Kyndra." Nina was off to get ready for her set. The guys were still at the bar. So I took this opportunity to probe Kyndra for a bit.

"So, how did you meet my best friend then?" I questioned like an excited kid. For some strange reason, I was drawn to her aura. Her energy was infectious. I literally couldn't keep my focus off her.

"Well, strangely enough now you ask. It was at a Resistance Movement meeting in Brixton last October."

"Who and what is the Resistance Movement?" I asked.

To be honest, it all sounded like a political organisation to me.

"Well, when you put it like that. The resistance movement was set up some ten years ago. It's owned and run by our radio station called Resistance 89.6fm."

"What's the movement's purpose?"

"The purpose of the movement was initially set up to combat the negatives and ill's we are faced within the black community. To give a platform, a voice, to the people so we can purposely come together and build a blueprint for success. That will enable us to execute our plans accordingly after we have found concrete solutions."

"Wow, it all sounds amazing. I could've done with you guys a few days ago."

"Why, what happened?"

"Well, I've only been in London a few days so far, and I'm staying with Nina and Eric respectively."

"How are you finding the upheaval and settling process?"

"The upheaval part. I'll get onto that in a minute. The settling in part has been wonderful. Nina and Eric have been great! They both chipped in and completely bought all new furniture, curtains, and carpet for my bedroom—Donte who you just met. We were bizarrely acquainted when the day after I arrived I went to the local gym from Nina's house. It happened to be that he owns and runs the place."

"Well, from what I witnessed, you two seem very close."

"I'm in love with him."

"Wow, that can happen. That's alright. Besides, you seem to have a certain glow about you. Excuse my manners. But you wouldn't happen to be pregnant?"

"No, not unless Donte is a magician."

"Oh okay," she said chuckling to herself.

"What I meant is that I'm on the pill."

"I see."

"So what about you?"

"What about me?"

"How far gone are you?"

"I'm seven months."

"Do you know what you're having?"

"A boy."

"Ah, how cute."

"Thank you."

"You're welcome."

As soon as I finished saying that Donte was up in my face hovering a drink in front of me.

"What's good, babe?" He said as he handed me my favourite drink in the whole world—a white rum and coke.

"Thank you, darling," I said as I took the drink from him.

"I believe this is yours," Donte said as he handed Kyndra her mineral water.

"Thank you, brother. Most kind of you."

"So what time is Nina's set?"

"Oh wow, five minutes from now," I said, looking down at my watch.

"Okay."

"Where's Eric?"

"Over there," he said, pointing to the back of the club.

Eric acknowledged by giving us the thumbs up, and that big ass grin on his face was prevalent for everyone to see.

"Ladies after you," Donte said as he made way for Kyndra and me to pass.

When the three of us embarked onto the table, Donte kindly pulled out our chairs and especially helped Kyndra push her seat.

"What was that you said earlier about you not being a gentleman?" I whispered silently into Dante's ear.

"Behave yourself?"

"Just a couple of minutes now." I was so excited as I rocked slightly back and forth in my chair. I couldn't wait to see my friend perform for the first time. The anticipation was unreal.

"Erykah; you didn't get to finish what you were saying earlier?" Kyndra reminded me.

"Yes," I said, coming out of my daydream. "Where was I?"

"I believe you were about to tell me about the upheaval part of your move to London."

"Yes I was, weren't I?"

"You certainly was."

"Where do you live if you don't mind me asking?"

"I don't mind. I live in Peckham, South London."

"Oh, good. Do you drive?"

"Yes, I do why?" She said, beginning to look a little confused.

"I got a proposal for you."

"Alright, I'm listening."

"Donte and Eric have to leave straight after Nina's performance, and I want to stay to the end. I thought if you're not pressed for time. May I suggest, Nina; you and I stay longer and have some drinks, and I can tell you all about the upheaval part? Also, I can give you some funds for petrol. So what do you think?"

"I think that sounds like a fabulous idea. You seem like you have a bit to tell me?"

"Yeah, I do indeed." Suddenly the lights dimmed low except for a spotlight that was focused on the centre of the stage.

The room went quiet for a few moments. Erykah Badu's Bag Lady tune wafted out of the speakers and circulated around the arena. In the next moment, a male MC walked out, and everyone in the building stood up and gave him a raptures round of applause. He started to speak once the music was lowered to an appropriate volume enough for him to start.

"Good evening, ladies and gentlemen and welcome back to Literary Geniuses part two. Let's make some noise," people cheered, wolf-whistled, clapped and jeered on response to the MC's request. When everyone finished, he continued. "Now, have I got a special treat in store for you guys? She is a resident of Literary Geniuses and has peaked in her performances I would just about say at the right time. I think you all know who I'm talking about and if you don't know, then by the end of her performance you'll be talking about her at your workplaces, Universities, etc., etc. So please be upstanding and give a warm welcome, to one of our resident poet's Miss Nina Lawrence."

"Thank you! Trevor, thanks for the beautiful introduction. How is everyone doing on this wonderful evening? Good, good. Okay, I'm going to read you a few pieces for my e-book Vol.1 they're a bit on the dark side. But I hope y'all enjoy all the same. Okay here goes."

"Go on, Nina," I shouted out.

"Thank you. Well here goes my first contribution hope y'all like it. It's entitled 'You don't speak for me.' Enough! You don't speak for me! Vulgar and disrespectful Rap does not makeup enough of a cross-section to represent the black demographic. One small, albeit loud, percentage of rap holding women in low regard; referring to other blacks as niggers; while vocalising little if any respect for others and their style Enough! You don't speak for me. How dare you fix your lips to say nigger isn't disrespectful as long as a Black man says it? Hiding behind freedom of expression no less than the slave tyrants who formed this nation under less than equal opportunities? How could you speak for me? You're too ignorant even to know you're a plant! Who do you represent? Surely not the Sojourner Truths! Surely not the Benjamin Banneker's! Surely not the Martin Luther King's and Malcolm X's who had more respect holding up a middle finger than you do in your entire monologue. Were the trials and tribulations of our people lost on you? Did you miss that piece of history where people fought and died so you and I could share water fountains and bus seats?! Or are you so unappreciative and ignorant to think you earned your bling, bling, on your own?! Silly rabbit, tricks are for kids, and you have proven you never grew up and will probably die 200 pounds foolish and 60 years mentally enslaved because that freedom you think is dressed in all that money. Ain't nothing' but a giant cage and you never even left the plantation!"

STAND IN YOUR POWER

As soon Nina's last word dropped from her mouth, I was about to stand up and explode into a frenzy of applause. Just as well I didn't because as she stood there smiling and watching the crowd, every individual clicked their fingers back in response to the beautiful piece she just read. The shame I suddenly felt when I replayed in my mind the embarrassing scenario I would've caused. Oh well nobody told me at the door that was the thing to do. You learn something new every day. Donte and Eric were staring and smirking at me, and it was beginning to freak me out a lil bit.

"Why you two watching me like that?" I said as I kissed my teeth and cut my eyes at them. They continued in the same manner, and now it was beginning to piss me off.

"Watching like what?" Donte asked.

"Da fuck is wrong with you two. Quit bugging me out." I commanded.

"We were just wondering what the fuck you were just doing?" Eric added.

"What do you mean?"

"Babe, the fucking way you half stood up and in mid-flow you looked like you were gonna do something and realised nah so you changed your mind."

"Well if you knew that already, then why the fuck you asking me stupid ass questions?"

"We're fucking with you."

"Ha, ha, ha, da fuck you think I look like?"

"My future wife."

"Donte."

"Yes, baby."

"Stop fucking with me!" I said, sounding like a baby, while I gently banged my fist on the table.

Kyndra grabbed my arm gently. Immediately I calmed down. She must have sensed my confusion and quickly came to my aid.

"Gentleman, I think we could all do with another round of drinks here." Kyndra took hold of my hand and instructed the guys to leave.

Immediately Donte and Eric clocked my mood had changed to a more vulnerable state and hurriedly left the table.

"Are you Alright, Erykah?" Kyndra kindly asked.

"Kind of."

"What seems to be the matter?"

"Where do you want me to start?"

"Whatever works for you."

All I could do was sigh and put my hand over my face to hold my head up. Kyndra looked at me and had an ambiguous expression etched on her face.

"Sister your face tells the picture of your life story and girl I see a lot of pain from it."

"You don't know the half of it, and I'm sorry for acting the way that I did."

"Erykah; never apologise for showing feelings. When you do so, you apologise for the truth."

"That's a great analogy Kyndra; I've never thought of it like that."

All of a sudden, a smile began to creep from the corners of my mouth. This woman was one serious vibes adjuster, and for the better, it seemed.

"Look, don't hang with people who make you justify your vibe, black holes don't give the light back."

"Kyndra; I want somebody worth me quitting the games I've been playing and the games that have been played on me."

"Do you think Donte is that person to do that?"

"So far, so good! I can't complain. You see, when I first laid eyes on him, I gave a voice to a thought, and he does seem the type of man you instantly want to add their last name to your first."

"Erykah; this feeling of convulsion that rush to conform. Don't be too quick to adjust your personality to please."

"Never doing that. Growing up, I learned that lesson the hard way when I was around the gang culture lifestyle."

"In the long run, what I'm trying to say is that take time, build on your foundations by working on your friendship, and you do that by always communicating and keeping things interesting. When you've accomplished that and solidified, that's when you take it to the next level."

"But we have had sex already. Doesn't that compromise with what you just said?"

"No my sister it doesn't. Sex is nothing but a mere feeling of heightened emotions amongst many others. If you're trying to compare."

"Okay, I think I can deal with that."

"Erykah understand this. Don't let your loyalty become your slavery. If he doesn't appreciate what you bring to the table, let him eat alone."

"I feel what you are saying Kyndra, and I hear you loud and crystal clear."

In the next moment, Nina began on her second piece.

"Thank you and for my second piece its entitled Soft Small Frame."

"Soft Small Frame! Raindrops fall, splattering as they hit the ground masking the sound of quickly moving feet. A faster-moving heartbeat, pulsating, vibrating a small frame body as it presses against an alley wall catching a breath, pausing for a quick rest thunder sounds, lightning strikes high, splitting the night sky heaven cries, sorrowful tears indeed looking at her hands, water rolling from face to

cheek meets salty drops young black seeds in hard earth
soil grow solid like stone homegrown to be hard as
diamonds, but many with a soul soft like cotton touched
by God at conception, and kissed by the devil at birth earth
is in its last days. They are in a maze of confusion.
Delusions of love are passed over for lust and sex. Regrets
are made in the throngs of passion. Passion draped all over
the hands of one young woman standing in the rain.
Looking at hands that had just come from caressing soft
brown skin. But not knowing though his body was within
hers. His love was only between her thighs; her eyes regret
the day they first saw him and try as they may, they
couldn't wash away the memory flashbacks and visions of
all she had seen off and in him. These things proceed and
all of a sudden the rain gives way to sunny days of
happiness picnics, six months of indulgence in a world
that was not hers lured in by his charm, holding on to his
arm everywhere they went seemed like a sign outwardly
of his inward content. Still, content is sometimes only
contempt in wait as he played her with Veronica, Suzanne,
Elizabeth, Shawna and Grace from massage to manage,
from discrete circumstance to desecrate indulgence his
fingerprints on their bathroom mirrors punctuated his
deeds, tendencies are ironies in wait because as was his
practice, as was his fate she had left in a commotion as
Grace came to confront him seeds that he had let grow
inside her, how could he have lied to her. Her fingers on
prints of pictures taken with a camera phone of a friend
when he was showing outward content in the arms of
Suzanne perhaps one could have been seen as a
confrontation of short will versus high heeled
determination, but now, prints clutched in her fingers, him
inside this young girl when nightmares hit the real world,
you get stab wounds to the tune of 143, the rain fell

violently, a relentlessly hard picture caught in a soft small frame."

Everyone in the place erupted, and I was especially happy.

I couldn't contain my joy any longer as I ran full pelt towards Nina. As I jumped up onto the stage, two security guys quickly grabbed me and pulled me down. Nina immediately saw and on the mic told them to leave me alone. So they did and apologised profusely to Nina and me.

But being me, I had to do something back when I felt injustice occurred.

As I stuck my tongue out at both of them, they shot me back a look that told me I was lucky Nina had my back. Fuck em, I thought to myself.

"Erykah; I don't know whether you're a badass chick or a crazy one girl?"

"I'm most definitely somewhere in-between," I concluded as we both laughed out loud together.

But on a serious note. Being in them modes had its advantages as well as disadvantages. I had to learn when to use the right mentality at the right time for the right fights.

"But on a real Nina; your poetry is dope as fuck. Where do you get the inspiration for your creativity?" I said as we began walking back to where Kyndra and the guys were.

"Past experiences, like relationships with a significant other and from friendships of all different types. Many people have different mechanics to their personality. The key to writing successful poetry is to keep it as real to the subject you're rhyming about when you're blessed with the creativity to conjure up ideas for writing that in itself is inexplicably inspiring. However, inspiration is all around us, what resonates with your soul and moves you, whether it be political, socially or emotionally. Writing and then being able to perform and convey your story, your take on how you view a particular subject and how the masses perceive it. That's the key to success and writing as a whole. So I think that should answer your question and any theories you may have."

"Yes, thank you, Nina; great explanation."

"You're welcome anytime."

She said as we continued on our walk. When we both had gotten to the table where the others were, Donte pulled out my chair as I went to sit down, he leaned over my shoulder and whispered something into my ear.

"Babe, I'm sorry if what I said earlier wound you up."

"Forget about it for now," I said as I lightly stroked his hand with mine.

"Yeah, no problem. Whatever you want!"

"Look Donte let me tell you a lil something about me for your peace of mind."

"Go ahead," as he sat back. He began to stroke his beard resembling some old wise Chinese man. To look at, it was quite funny. Donte was a comical guy, alright. But it took a particular type of personality to get the kind of humour he was dishing out.

"Donte understand this. Money doesn't impress me; gifts don't excite me. You want to know what impresses me and makes me happy? The shit that doesn't have a price tag on it. Like consistency, loyalty, real love, things that can't be bought. Do you want to impress me? Then be what the other niggas aren't, and in return, I'll be your medicine, not your headache. Coz baby even on my worst day, I kill it. I belong to no-one, no-one owns me. I'm a grown-ass woman, and I can take care of myself. I know my worth, and I won't be controlled anymore. If I give you my time, it's a privilege, not an obligation okay. I'm done,"

"Wow, ain't you something. So do you feel you're in a position to command those statements?"

"Err yeah. Otherwise, I wouldn't have said what I believe in the first place."

"Okay I gotcha, I believe you, baby." He and Eric excused themselves, said their goodbyes to everyone and left the club peacefully.

"Are you sure he is the one?" Kyndra asked, looking a bit concerned that what I said earlier was true.

"Well if he isn't time will tell."

"And if he ain't?"

"Then it's on to the next one."

"Alright, Erykah; you're giving me so much joke."

"I'm glad you're feeling entertained."

"Sister Nina, has your set finished?"

"Yes, Sister Kyndra why?"

"Okay good. Well, Erykah suggested we stay on longer and get to know each other a bit more."

"That's a great idea. I think it's my round anyway. Back in a few!"

As Nina left the table, Kyndra suggested I finish off telling her my misadventures and escapades on route to London.

In return, when Nina got back, they both filled me in on their adventures within the Resistance Movement and invited me to their next monthly meeting. I obliged their offer and thanked them both.

Two hours later, approaching nearly one am, I was exhausted. It had been a long and insightful day. For the first time in years, I began to feel alive again.

We all finally left the club as the last punters and eventually headed back to South London and got home in one piece.

As I said goodnight to Nina and began going upstairs my phone pinged. I looked down and saw I had a message from Eric.

As I put in my password and got to my messages, I opened up What's app and scrolled to his name.

As I opened it; it read 'Donte's been stabbed and we are at St. Thomas's hospital.'

As an array of bizarre emotions went through me at once, the tears came flooding out of me a few seconds later. I went numb in my mind and weak at the knees. As I dropped down to half my height, my first thought was what the fuck as I trembled with rage and sadness.

My first instinct was to phone Marcus. As I did so, Nina heard me talking to him frantically as my words came out all jumbled and in an erratic manner.

Nina immediately came upstairs to comfort me.

When I finished, Nina said she would come.

As we left all I kept thinking about was how bad my luck was and if this man I already loved and cared for was going to live.

I seriously began to think I'll never be happy, and just when I thought I had my turning point today. The universe slaps me back down to reality and makes me see how precious life is and how easily a situation, a moment can change your life for the better or, the worse.

Chapter 11 - Feet Firmly On The Ground

Nina and I shortly arrived at the hospital a little after three am. As we rolled up to the entrance and stepped inside I frantically scanned the signs for a department that sounded like it treated stab wounds.

However Nina, calmly went up to reception and asked politely.

"Excuse me; I'm looking for my brother that was bought in here last night?"

"What's his name dear?" A young woman I say in her late twenties with the biggest weave ever I've seen on a white girl asked.

"His name is Donte Williams, and he is my boyfriend, so hurry up please," I said as I began to get infuriated while pacing up and down at the same time.

"Yes, I have him here, and I believe you will find he will be taken onto Nightingale ward after he comes out of surgery."

"Surgery! What you mean surgery?" I frantically asked as I leant over the counter and eyeballed her square in the face.

"Mam, that's all I know. You'll have to go to Nightingales reception. They will tell you more there." She said in a smug sounding voice like she didn't give two shits.

"Bitch, I should fuck you up right now!"

"Excuse me? There's no need to take that tone of language with me."

"Erykah fall back," as Nina put her arm around my mid-section. "Look I'm sorry for my friend's obscenities, but

I'm sure you can understand her loved one is hurt and she has no idea why this has happened."

"Yes I can sympathise mam, but we have a zero-tolerance policy operating in this hospital, and any form of abuse or violence against members of staff is not permitted and can result in dire consequences. But under the circumstances, I will let it slide."

"You'll let it what?" I said standing a little distance away from where Nina had moved me. Though as I was talking, I felt myself inching forward to where the blond bitch was seated with clenched fists and gritted teeth.

"Okay, thank you," Nina concluded. As she came towards me looking me dead straight in the eyes while grappling my arm and pulling me with her.

"Erykah; you gotta calm the heck down?"

"Why! Didn't you see how patronising she was? Fucking looking down her nose at me."

"Yes, I did girl. But you can't react to every bad or small situation in that manner all the time."

"You tryna say I got anger issues?" I said as we entered by the lift doors and stopped in front of them.

"Well, you said it. Think about how you're reacting to even over-reacting to even the most trivial things. You respond and jump from frustration to violence straight, and you miss out anger and aggression in between."

"Do I?"

"Come on, Erykah; you damn well know the answer to that?"

"I don't! That's why I'm asking."

"Well, I'm telling you. You do."

"Oh my gosh. I didn't realise. How can you tell?"

"You know what happened to me when I was younger? So I triple, no quadruple know that your ends don't justify your means boo."

"Fair point Nina. So what do you suggest I do?"

"I suggest sooner rather than later that you get some professional help. I know an outstanding counsellor. She helped me out once or twice. I'll hook you up after we've seen Donte."

"That will be cool. I appreciate the gesture. Thanks."

"You're welcome. Just get that temper sorted before you end up hurting someone real bad."

"I will, and thanks again."

"For what?"

"Just being you."

"No problem."

When the lift arrived, the doors opened and out stepped a few people before we could enter.

When they all did, we stepped inside and within ten seconds the doors closed. I still hated confined spaces, but I had talked myself into trying to conquer my fear head on.

I gripped Nina's hand tight as she looked at me and smiled. Instantly It brought a little comfort to my already frail state.

When the lift reached the third floor, we both stepped out and followed the signs to our left. A minute later, we were upon Nightingale wards reception only to be greeted by a kind-looking middle-aged black woman of Caribbean descent.

When she opened her mouth to speak, I could tell straight away she wasn't Jamaican. My guess she was either Trinidadian or Bajan.

"Hello, how may I be off assistance?" She greeted Nina and me with a warm smile. I was still too emotional to be courteous. So Nina answered for me.

"Yes, we were told by the receptionist in the main foyer to come up here."

"A'right, are you here to see someone?"

"Yes, we are."

"What's their name, young lady?"

"Donte Williams."

"Okay, let me have a look," as she tried to look over her low cut spectacles, she scanned her finger down a piece of paper until it stopped. "Here we go, Mr Donte Williams. He's due out of the theatre in around half an hour. In the meantime, you can go and wait in the room opposite if you like. Down the end of the hall, there is a vending machine. When he comes out and has settled, firstly, the police will want to ask him some questions, and after they have finished, a nurse will come and get you alright?"

"Yes, that'll be fine," Nina answered, as we both shuffled our butts into the waiting room.

As Nina got settled, that was when my emotions got the better of me again.

"Why, Nina, why him?" I said, as I threw my arms up in the air in protest.

"I don't know Hun. If I knew the answer to that, I would be a wealthy woman."

"I mean, we had a good evening. Eric and Donte left and a few hours later, now all this. Something doesn't quite add up Nina."

"Oh no; you got that look in your eyes you do when you have a hunch, or you know something no one else does."

"Hear me out? Tell me if I'm mad."

"Go on," she said, leaning forward, looking straight at me the whole time with anticipation written all over her face.

"Remember when we pulled up to Rich Mix?"

"Yeah I do. What about it?"

"My man. Green eye. The security with issues."

"What about him?"

"Oh, my gosh, Nina. I thought you were the smart one girl."

"Hm. Wait! Oh no, you ain't Erykah. That's plain ludicrous. Scratch that idea completely from your mind right now?"

"Listen! You ain't listening to me!"

"Of course, I am."

"Then understand this. How long have you known me?"

"For year's."

"And in that time, when have I ever been wrong about a hunch? Go on, how many?"

"Never!"

"Exactly! A hundred per cent record so far. So give me the respect I've earned and hear me out. It's the only thing I got right now to stop me going skits."

"Sorry, Hun. You carry on."

"Look, this is my theory. Ima put it out there. Remember the whole screwface shit?"

"Yeah, I do."

"My hunch is that when the guys left—knowing Eric. My bet is they confronted green eyes and asked him why he was doing that to them. My man got hostile back, and probably some heat started between the three of them. It got defused quicker than it started but enough to ramp up the friction levels then the guys left. But this is where I think it got interesting. When Donte came back from the first round of drinks he bought, you were already into your first performance at that moment. He told me some guys at the bar struck up a conversation with them. Which seemed pretty normal because of what they were talking about, he said."

"What did he say they said?"

"About what brought them there. The spoken word. The girls and other small but unharmful chat?"

"That all sounds normal to me."

"Wait up. It's not that part that was alarming. It's what was said afterwards."

"What happened?"

"They all of a sudden switched on him and started aggressively asking him personal questions. He said they became hostile and stood closer all up in their personal spaces. Donte was like what the fuck. Eric furthered the obscenities. The other guys tried to grab them and walk them out. But they stood up to them and tried to walk off. That was when one of the men opened up his jacket and brandished a gun."

"Oh, my Erykah, what happened next?"

"Nothing at that point obviously, otherwise they wouldn't have come back to where we were."

"Why you only telling me this now?"

"Because one, you were performing. Two and I know it sounds cliché, but I didn't want to worry you at the time."

"Thanks for your concern. But I'm a grown-ass woman, and I can handle a bit of drama. So what happened next?"

"Easy girl. Well, Donte said he could handle it. I asked how? The same way he came in peacefully he said. I was like you're a genius, taking the piss obviously and that's what he and Eric did they left quietly. My suspicions after that green eyes got them guys from the bar and probably a few more carloads to follow them and the rest is history."

"Fucking hell Erykah. We should go to the police?"

"No, no, no. The Police are coming to interview Donte. We will see what happens then. It's not our call to make Nina."

"Fine, we'll do it that way."

"Yeah, because we don't have the luxury of choosing."

In the next moment, we embraced each other and had a long, much-needed hug.

As we finished a few moments later, a nurse came into the waiting room.

"Miss Lawrence; if you're ready, you can go and see him now?"

"Has the police already been in to see him?" Nina asked.

"Yes, they have. So it's okay to go in. Just don't overdo it and remember Mr Williams is still in recovery."

"Thanks' nurse. Are you ready, Erykah?"

"I have to be," my confidence was taking a beating. This whole saga was reminding me of my gang banging days, and unlike then, I was feeling insecure and things at this moment in time were so unpredictable.

One minute I'm getting arrested for robbery and then I've been arrested and charged for assaulting a police officer, court case pending to getting a job and a new man, who is now in hospital.

I mean what more bad luck could happen next. Time will tell I suppose. But I needed some balance and stability in my life real quick.

As we got nearer to Donte's room, I noticed two guys lurking around the entrance. I had that sinking feeling like I've seen them somewhere before. But on a real, they didn't look or feel like they should be there to me.

When they clocked Nina and me getting nearer to them, they immediately started walking slightly towards us.

As I caught a glimpse of one of the guys looking at me, I immediately went into fight or flight mode. It was the same two guys that had approached Donte and Eric at the bar in Rich Mix.

As they passed us, I called out to them.

"Hey, da fuck you doing here Nigga?"

"What the fuck!" The first one said. "Bitch, who you calling a nigga?"

"You, fucking dumbass bitch."

"Yo G," the second one said to the first one. "That must be my man's girl?"

"Yeah, yeah, yeah I think you're right, you know." The first one concurred.

The second one came at me first. But before the thug could launch any kind of attack. I was already two steps ahead of him and boy he didn't see this coming.

I caught him square on the jaw, hard, with a neat, right jab and to my surprise I knocked him cleanout.

As I stood there admiring my handy work, with my hand throbbing, all I heard was Nina shouting 'Watch out'. But it was too late.

The first one had grabbed me by the throat, lifted me off my feet and threw me back against the wall still in his grip.

In his next move, all I could remember as things around me were getting darker was him punching me in the face and Nina telling him to let go of me.

(Moments later)

"Mam, mam, can you hear me. Can you tell me your name?"

As I came round, I could hear the echoing sounds of a man shuddering my ears with his high pitched voice.

As the blurriness began to disperse from my eyes and the fogginess in my head, I made out a large figure of a white man in a white overcoat.

"What happened to me? Where am I?"

"Miss Gaines; you were involved in an incident. My name is Dr Price, and I'm the senior consultant assigned to Mr Williams case. You're on Nightingale ward in St. Thomas's hospital."

"Where's my friend?"

"Erykah; I'm here. How you feeling?"

"Like someone hit me with a baseball bat."

"Miss Gaines; we're going to run a few tests to make sure everything is in order."

"I'm thirsty."

"I'll pour you some water, Hun." Nina said.

"Why does my throat and neck hurt so much?"

"Miss Gaines; according to your friend. You managed to single handily knock out a six-foot-plus male with one blow."

Was this fucker trying to be sarcastic? It was as if he was declaring a woman doesn't have the strength or capability to do that.

"I asked why does my neck hurt?"

"Miss Gaines; you were also ferociously picked up by your neck, taken off your feet and slammed against a wall."

"I need to see Donte, Nina; have you seen him?"

"No, not yet. I've been with you the whole time."

"Please, go check on him for me. Tell him what happened! But not to worry coz I feel alright."

"I will do as soon as I know you're."

"Nina please?"

"Okay, okay. Keep your weave on."

"Funny, ha-ha. I'm all na-tu-rail Hun."

"Whatever."

"Miss Gaines I'll be back in ten minutes. Nurse Lee; can you prep her for a CT scan?"

"Wait. What! Why a CT scan? I feel fine, besides my neck and throat."

"I know Miss Gaines, but it's routine to eliminate any possibilities?"

"Whatever you say Doc. You know, what's best."

"Thank you for your co-operation Miss Gaines; I'll be back shortly."

"Right, see Nina; the doctor has everything under control. So will you please go and check on him for me?"

"Yes, okay."

"Finally, thank you."

As Nina departed the room, some extra nurses came in to help Nurse Lee prep me for my scan.

A small part of me was starting to get agitated because, to be honest, I was beginning to feel better. I was anxious because inside of me I felt there was no need.

Seven minutes later, I was looking up towards a big light. I was told not to move as the machine I was laying on begun to descend backwards. A bright red laser came up across my body in a criss-cross shape and finished up resting on my face.

"Right Miss Gaines; are you ready and comfortable?" The Doc said over the tannoy.

"I'm a little scared." I started feeling myself beginning to hyperventilate.

"Miss Gaines there's no need to panic. It will be over in a couple of minutes."

"Okay, Doc, I trust whatever you say." Well, I had to. It was the only bit of assurance I had.

As I calmed my breathing down, the laser began to move up and down my head and face. Like the Doc said it was over in a few minutes.

When the overhead see-through casing opened up in the middle and separated beyond either side of my arms, I was gently helped up by Nurse Lee; then she helped me onto a wheelchair.

A few minutes later, I was back on the same ward as Donte was. Just at the other end instead.

I took a few moments to shake the perplexities out of my head. Once I had checked my bearings, I noticed a tall, dark and handsome man walking towards me in what could be described as a Zimmer frame. But wait, it was an old peoples Zimmer.

When I searched my eyes and blinked a few times, I could see it was Donte looking like he'd been a casualty on the front line of a war.

"Baby, I finally found you. What the fuck happened to you?"

"Donte; I'm fine. How are you feeling boo?"

"I've seen better days. But I'm thankful I'm here chatting with you."

"I was so worried that I might've lost you," I said as tears came flooding out of me.

"Nah, no way," as he put one arm around me. "You're not getting rid of me that easily."

"I don't ever wanna get rid of you?"

"Is that a promise?" As he leant over my bed and gave me a sensual kiss on the lips.

"Yes, it is?" I said as I kissed him back.

"So wah' gwaan wid you?"

"No, baby, you first."

"Me?" Mine is just a stab wound in the leg and arm. Doc said I got to stay in for a few days. For observation and t'ing."

"Well, our t'ing is that Nina and I were a few feet away from entering your room. Then suddenly I noticed two guys up ahead trying to get into where you were."

"Damn, probably the same man dem or other men of that crew coming to finish what they started."

"Motherfuckers! How da fuck did they know where to find you?"

"Good question, babe. That's something I would like to know."

"Me too! Them the same niggers, the ones that put me in here."

"Is that right babe. Well, that will be the last time they ever touch a woman like that again. Trust me."

"I do baby."

"So you gon' tell me what them niggers did to ya?"

"Like I was saying before. Nina and I were on our way to your room when we noticed the two guys trying to get in there. Straight away, I panicked. I do that a lot. But when the adrenaline kicked in, I challenged the bastards and asked who they were and what did they think they were doing. My hunch to challenge them was justified cause from the jump they wasted no time trying to eliminate me. The last thing I remember before I blacked out was that the main dude, had me in a chokehold up against the wall and at least a foot off the floor and Nina was pleading with him to let go of me."

"Son of a bitch. I swear down them niggers are dust. Nobody messes with my livelihood, my family or friends and especially my girl."

"So, what now, babe?"

"We need a plan of action, trust me, baby, I will seek revenge in time, but revenge all the same."

"But how?"

"Every dog has its day. I'll know when my time comes."

"Okay. Have you seen Nina?"

As soon her name escaped my mouth, she was there standing by my side like she'd been there the whole time.

"Erykah; how are you feeling girl?"

"I'm fine."

"Donte, what are you doing out of bed?"

"Shush, Nina."

"No Donte, you have been stabbed and through a traumatic experience. Now get your ass back into bed otherwise I'll tell a nurse."

"Nina, I will go in a bit. I need to wrap up a few things with you two."

"Fine! But after that, I'm carting you back there myself if you don't comply."

"Laugh out loud Nina give him a break?"

"Alright cool."

"Anyway, missy. Where did you get to?"

"I was taken to a consultant's office to give a witness statement. Then the Police kindly for a change repurchased me here."

"What did you tell them, Nina?" Donte asked, concerned.

"Just exactly as probably Erykah has told you!"

"Bless, I know it's the same. One thing about you, Nina; you're a very astute person."

"Why thank you, kind sir?" Nina said, taking the piss out of Donte's remark.

"So what you got to tell us about babe?"

"We need to be extra vigilant for a while until these guys are caught. I don't feel these guys are big time. Rather than a security guard with an inflated ego and a few heavy's he knows."

"I hope you're right, babe?"

"What makes you so certain Donte?"

"Nina; I know the type!"

"Oh yeah! Enlighten me?"

"I know because I wouldn't be sitting here talking to you two."

"That could've been a warning projectile?"

"Like I said. Trust me; I know the type?"

With that, Nina and I both fell silent. She looked at me with the most shocked look on her face I've ever seen.

Me, I touched my neck lightly, holding my hand around it like a chokehold and thinking about the severity of what Donte had said.

He wrapped things up by telling me to go and see JC and get my contract signed and for him to show me the ropes and work with JC until he came back.

All I could think about now was how unsafe and unlucky we all were.

My confidence had hit an all-time low again, and it will take a lot of love, support and assurance from friends and loved ones for me to get back to where I was before this nightmare started.

STAND IN YOUR POWER

Chapter 12 – Reprieve

From the first moment I woke up today, I decided I wanted some much-needed reprieve. My confidence was low, but one thing that rarely evaded me was my self-esteem.

After breakfast I departed for the gym. Once inside I had an impromptu meeting with JC about my position and starting date. In our exchange he handed me my first day duties list and I had signed my first ever working contract. JC also informed me that Donte said I could start as soon as tomorrow.

I took an hour out of my time to see Donte. His health was improving at a steady rate, but the consultant said he had to stay in for further observation until the end of the week.

After I had left the hospital, I grabbed myself an early lunch then I made my way to Aunt Lola's hair care centre.

Today was all about me and preserving my sanity. With everything going on in my life at present I needed this day to go well.

As the train pulled up to South Kensington tube station, I got up from my seat and went to stand by the doors.

When the train stopped, the doors opened. As I went to exit out of the carriage, I felt my bottom touched.

In my sudden change of mood, I turned around to sight a mixture of black, white and some other race of youths standing there making all sorts of sexual hand signals.

In my disgust, I felt the need to jump back on the train and either give them all a hard slap across the face each or to educate them on etiquette on how to treat a woman.

To stop myself from doing anything to them I had to ride my repulsion, jiggle my head, smile and then walk off. Easier said than done. But in my pre-eminent position it was in my safest interest for today to do so.

A few minutes later, as I exited out of the station. My phone sat nav app told me to turn right and walk around seventy-five yards straight ahead.

When I got to that point, it told me to take a left into Exhibition road. As I kept on walking, It felt like the temperature had gone up a few degrees or maybe it was myself feeling the heat from my encounter on the train. Either way, I decided to take my time and stroll while I took in my newfound surroundings.

There was an air of affluence in the area. The streets smelt of money and the businesses, they're vacated by middle-lower upper class occupancy.

As I neared my destination, I noticed I was on the opposite side of the road from the centre. Auntie's business looked tremendous from the outside. It was decorated with a posh looking design and with the word's Lola's beauty therapy and hair care centre written in a calligraphy typestyle in black on a white background.

I proceeded to walk across the road as I did so from out of nowhere a car came speeding towards me and stopped with a screech of tyres inches from my feet.

"Get out of the road you crazy black bitch?"

I don't know if it was because she was in her area or surrounded by mostly her people that this bluefoot blond-bitch was so brazen in a semi-crowded street and in the middle of the day that immediately I was incensed and didn't give a fuck.

Horror-struck from the core of my being. I was in complete and utter shock. I sauntered to the driver's side of her car, opened the door, grabbed the posh-looking bimbo by her hair and dragged her out of the vehicle.

In one move, I had her laid flat across the bonnet of her car. I began to rough her up, and in between slaps, I was asking her questions.

"Get off me you psycho?" She pleaded. But her attempt to free herself came to no avail.

"Who da fuck are you calling a black bitch? It's people like you that make a person like me very angry."

"I'm sorry. I didn't mean it. I'm, I'm having a lousy day." She started panicking for her life.

"So fucking what! Ain't we all?"

"I'm soooo sorry. Please don't hurt me?" She begged this time.

"Pooki; what the hell you doing?"

I looked up only to see Aunt Lola standing in the doorway of her premises, waving a pair of scissors in one hand and a small towel in the other.

"Auntie; how nice to see you," I said, through gritted teeth.

"Why are you holding that girl like that?"

"She nearly ran me over, and she insulted me too."

"Alright, give her a little slap from me. Then let her be and come inside real quick." She instructed.

"And that's why you're my favourite Aunt in the whole world."

"Yeah, yeah. Just get your black ass inside before the police come?" She said in her middle-upper class accent.

Funny to think someone in our family talked like Aunty did. But what a boring world it would be if we all sounded the same.

As I looked the woman in her eyes, I gave her a grave lesson on her errand ways. For extra security, I asked her to provide me with her driving licence so I could take a photo of it. After a few minutes, I let her go and sent her on her way. I also warned her if any police were to come sniffing around Aunt's salon then she would be a dead man walking or woman in her case as I reminded her I had her address.

Petrified as hell, she left with no fuss and with a promise that nothing of the sort would happen. This little saga never took place case closed.

As I gathered myself together, I began to walk in the direction of Aunt's salon. When I reached, Aunty gave me one of them knowing looks. You know the kind that is double-barrelled with a mixture of well-represented and why did you go and do a dumb-ass move like that for? And then threw her arms out for me to reintegrate.

"Erykah; where trouble goes. You're always right there to follow." Aunty indicated.

"What can I say? Other than I'm never the provoker." I answered.

"You haven't changed one eye iota," she said cackling to herself.

I found it funny as hell. Aunty always had that knack of doing that. Plus what is more amusing is when she busses into her patois and at the same time with her posh tone of voice. So when she talks, that's when she kills it.

"It's so good to see you, Aunty; you're looking very well," I said with a synonymous action.

"Why thank you, Pooki; although I can't say the same about you," she said looking me up and down with a disapproving stare. "What have you got yourself into now?"

"Well, firstly I...," but before I could finish my sentence, Aunty interrupted me.

"Let's get you inside first, and you can tell me all about it over a nice cup of tea that you'll be making." She stated.

"Fair enough," I finished saying as I went to engage my arm around Aunty. As she took her arm in mine, we continued our walk into her premises. As soon as we entered every person in the place stopped what they were doing and focused their attention on Aunty and me.

At first, I felt a bit awkward. Aunty sensed my slight insecurity. She took my hand in hers and gave me a reassuring look. A look that told me everything is going to be alright.

"Everyone since you all seem fascinated, especially you Monique; I see you there so behave yourself, young lady." Aunty hasn't changed either when it comes to her family and her livelihood. I guess you can say that for most of the Gaines clan.

Suddenly she leaned onto me and whispered into my ear.

"By the way Erykah; that one is partial to a bit of you know?"

"I got you, Aunty. It's all good," I said, smiling back.

"This here everybody is my Brother Howard's daughter Erykah?" Aunty said as she patted my back.

"Hello, hello, hi everyone," I said in my shy little girly voice.

"Over there in the far corner is my deputy, Marcia?"

"Hi," I said, nodding my head.

"The handsome young man cutting the ladies hair is Damari."

"Heyyyy," he said in the most camp voice I've ever heard. Okay then. The first impression of him he seemed a very genuine person.

"To your right in the other far corner is Cherri. And last but not least nearer to us is Monique."

As soon as Aunty finished introducing me to all of the staff. We began walking away.

As Aunty guided me towards the back of the shop, she couldn't resist telling me about my recent behaviour.

"Look Erykah; it's taken me a long time to build a reputable reputation around here. Folks in these parts don't take too kindly to a young Negro causing trouble. Especially one that did what you just done." she outlined with sincere effort on her part.

"But, but Aunt Lola," I said stuttering to get my point across to her.

"Sorry no if's and but's here," she said informingly.

"I get what you are saying, Aunty. But people like that make me sick."

"People like that Erykah; have been doing things like that and are still doing things like that and worse to people like us for centuries!"

"So then it's ever more paramount they get dealt with in a certain way."

"I feel you on that, but what are you going to do every time someone does that to you?"

"Punch them in the face of course!"

"No, no, no, no Erykah; hell no. You're going to end up in prison if you go around doing things like that all the time."

"Only if I get caught."

"Erykah, please. I know you ain't dumb, but please refrain from playing the fool in front of me?"

"But Aunty what am I to do instead?"

"Deal with it in another way."

"How?"

"You got to rise above it and show them you are the better person. Firstly, you step outside the situation and analyse it in your mind. You do this by thinking of the scenario as if you were watching yourself on television. Secondly, take stock of your situation by using your morality and think of the best solution on how to deal with it. I understand at first that it will be hard because your emotions will drive your adrenaline, and the emotional side will trigger the last two stages of anger, and that is aggression and violence. The way to calm down your eminent frustration is to use the rational side of your brain. It will make you in seconds, assess the outcome should you act violently. Your rational will make you think of the dire consequences. At that stage, you will imminently calm down and act accordingly and save yourself getting arrested. That's how you deal with anger, and it won't happen straight away. But the more situations similar you find yourself in, the more experienced you will get and in time you will be adept to using your mouth more constructively than your fists."

"Wow, that's some insight right there. Thank you, Aunty. I appreciate your sound advice, and I will try to implement it straight away into putting it into practice."

"Don't just try Erykah; do it. The quicker you practice these ethical ways of dealing with anger, the less chance you have of being anywhere inside a police cell or prison."

"Alright Aunty, I got you. No problem."

"Good, good. Now let me give you the grand tour of the building," she said, sounding prominent.

As we both walked through to the back of the shop, I turned the corner first. As I made another step forward, I nearly crashed into my cousin Danika.

"Erykah; when did you get here?" She said sounding startled.

"About half an hour ago!"

"Mother, you didn't mention she was coming?"

"Danika; I don't have to run everything I do past you do I?"

"No mother, you don't. But something as important as my favourite cousin in the whole world coming to see us. Then yes, you do."

"Oh, I see. I'll remember that for the next time," Aunty said with a shrug of her shoulders and a pretty mean-mugging looking screwface. I couldn't help it. I couldn't keep my laughter locked inside any longer.

"You two, what are you like?"

"Oh ignore my mother Erykah; she's been on one all day."

Aunty kissed her teeth and went to walk past us.

"I'm going upstairs for my break. Danika show your cousin around, please?"

"Yes, mother," Danika said, mocking her mother's command. "Cuz, come here and bring it in?"

With that, I threw my arms out as I walked towards her; I embraced her for a few minutes without wanting to let go. I haven't seen my cousin apart from skype, in the flesh going on nearly two years.

"So, what's going on with you? Uncle Jeb came by here last week and filled us all in about the motorway saga."

"Ah cuz, it was so dreadful. Here's me trying to start a new chapter in my life, and already, trouble seems to follow me."

"Well, you're looking healthy, after what happened to you in the hospital?"

"Healthy, I'm fucking lucky to be alive Danika!"

"I know," she said and then Danika paused for a few moments. I got the sense from her staring at me like she was, she was going through some drama of her own.

"How is Terrence these days?"

"He's good. Working too much as per usual," Danika said frowning.

"You say it like it's a bad thing?"

190

"It's neither good nor bad."

"So why the long face for then?"

"Well, one. I hardly get to see Terrance apart from facetime or what's app calls. So never seeing him physically in the flesh that often contributes to once in a while of not having any alone time together."

"Alright well, I feel you cuz. But my limited relationship advice to you is to tell Terrance how you feel. Talk to him. Let him know things need to change between you two?"

"Erykah; don't you think I've tried all that so many times before?"

"Try harder?"

"Maybe! I'm tired of it all, to be honest."

"Never mind," I said back with half a smile on my face.

"Anyway, what about you?"

"What about me?"

"How's your love life going?"

"Well," I said with a big broad grin swept across my face this time. "My love life is going pretty good. You know what I mean?"

"I got you cuz. So what's his name?"

"What makes you think it's a man?"

"Are you serious?"

"Nah, I'm just fucking wid you."

"Erykah you're forever the joker."

"His name is Donte Williams," I said as I took out my phone from my jacket pocket. "Here that's him."

As I passed my phone over to her, she took one look at Donte's picture.

"Seriously, this is your boyfriend?"

"And why not Danika?"

"Because he is frigging gorgeous. Oh my gosh! Does he have a twin brother?" She said sounding exasperated, without taking her eyes off my phone.

"Well, he doesn't have a twin brother." As she handed the phone back to me.

"Oh, not fair."

"Wait! He does have a handsome younger brother, two years his junior and he is single and ready to mingle, and I think, no I know he would love the skin of you."

As I passed my phone back to her and she clasped her excited self over Trae's photo. Danika's eyes lit up like a Christmas tree.

"Pass me back my phone and stop drooling over it. You nasty girl?"

"Erykah his brother is to die for. Please make something happen. I want to meet him, like now?" She said sounding like she'd never seen a good looking man in her life before.

"What about Terrence?"

"Who?" She wasn't joking either.

"It's like that is it?"

"Yeah, it's like that. I think it's time for a change. A girl like me needs to be happy, and my boyfriend hasn't been able to do that in a long time."

"Alright let me see what I can do. Let me take a photo, and I'll send a caption to Trae and then wait."

"Hang on! Let me fix myself up first?"

"Okay, hurry up I wanna see the rest of the building?"

After a few minutes, Danika came back looking real plush.

"Wow, you want to make a good first impression, don't you?"

"Of course. It's all about how you market yourself."

"You're making it sound like your trying to secure a business deal?"

"Erykah; everything in this life is about dealings and relations. The way you seal a deal depends on how well you implement and execute your plan."

"I suppose you're are right since you're the mechanism that keeps this ship sturdy."

"That I am cuz."

"Okay, are you ready for this photo. Because I require the ladies toilet?"

"Wait let me get into position?" She said like she was a model posing for a fashion shoot.

"Look at you!" I said as I took several photos. Before I sent them I typed a few words to entice Trae to reply and then I showed Danika before I did.

"I like them. You can send."

"Good."

"Can't wait to see what Trae thinks?" Danika was getting all worked up like she sensed something good was going to happen, and she wasn't wrong. On my way to the toilet, Trae phoned.

"Erykah; who is that?" He said, sounding as excited as Danika was a few moments ago.

"That's my cousin Danika."

"Damn, no disrespect. But Danika is one sexy ass looking, lady. What she saying?"

"She saying you are to die for."

"Ah, man. You gon' get a nigger blushing over here."

"Trae let me tell you one thing?"

"Ite, what's up?"

"Danika is an extraordinary girl, and I love her to the bone, and I would do anything to protect her. You feel me?"

"Erykah; if we kick it off well and depending on how things pan out over time. Let me assure you from that first moment we FaceTime or whatever I will treat her with the utmost respect. You have my word on that, and my word is bond truss' me."

"You're Donte's brother. Of course, I trust you. I wouldn't be trying to hook you guys up if I didn't feel you two wouldn't be a match. I'm just letting you know where I stand on this should things get a lil' messy, okay?"

"No worries, girl. It's all good."

"Cool, since you're interested. Niks told me she wants to meet you."

"Ah, no doubt. That can happen. Give Danika my number!"

"That's great. Niks is going to be stoked."

"Thank you Erykah; I need this. You dun' know the drama I had last time out?"

"Yeah, I do. So I'm very confident things are going to work out this time, just like your brother and myself."

"For real. Ite, ima shoot off. Got some business to sort out."

"Ite bad boy. Take it easy."

"You too, Sis."

"You joker. Peace."

"Bless Erykah; take care," Trae cut the line dead. I went to finish my lady business, and then I went upstairs to find Danika sitting in the kitchen.

"Wow, that smell's divine cuz. What are you cooking?"

"Ah, it's nothing much. It's spaghetti Bolognese my style,"

"What are you mixing in there?"

"Some mushrooms, cumin, scallions, red, yellow and green peppers and a little bit of paprika."

"Sounds exotic?"

"I don't know about that. But what I do know it will leave a lasting taste in your mouth,"

"Soon you'll be applying to appear on master chef ta rass."

"In my wildest dreams, maybe."

194

"Never say never, Danika."

"True."

"Anyway, Trae phoned back."

"Oh my gosh, that was quick."

"Well, he doesn't play when he likes what he sees."

"That's because I'm easy on the eye when men or women are looking at me."

"You sure are Danika."

"And look at you too. You got gorgeous eyes and tantalising lips Erykah. Donte is one lucky brother."

"And don't he know it," I said, letting out a little chuckle of laughter.

"So what else did Trae say?" She asked with more anticipation in her voice than earlier.

"I'll let him tell you himself. He told me to give you his number, and you can call him whenever you're ready."

"Damn girl. What am I going to do about Terrance?"

"Danika hear me out. What I'm about to say is very important?"

"Okay, I'm listening."

"First take time, slow your row. My advice while chatting and getting to know Trae, you need to ask Terrance about making more time for you. Depending on how he responds and acts, that's when you will be able to decide and make a decision on who you want."

"But isn't that cheating?"

"Technically it ain't. In another sense, it is. All depends on how you view it. As long as you're only chatting to Trae until you decide what you want Danika."

"Oh, ok. That sounds alright to me. I can deal with it like that."

"All good then."

As I handed her Trae's number, after a couple more hours of seeing the rest of the complex, including the training centre, which was very impressive, I took some time out in getting to know the staff and catching some joke on the way.

After business, Aunt Lola, Danika and I headed back to their house where I caught up with Uncle Sebastian who is Aunt Lola's husband. Daniel who wasn't there is Danika's twin brother.

Throughout the evening, we enjoyed a stupendous, mouth-watering Caribbean meal. Which was prepared and cooked by Aunt and Uncles catering staff?

I couldn't believe it when I was introduced to James, the butler who coincidentally opened up the door for all of us. The Briscoe's have moved up in the world.

After filling in Uncle Sebastian about my recent troubles, we all caught up on everyone's life until the present. Uncle said his company was on the verge of a multi-million-pound deal. He said, in a nutshell, everyone in the family will be taken care of.

Ah, that was a grand gesture to the extreme. Being Uncle Sebastian's favourite niece, I wouldn't have to worry about money anymore.

I said back I got money, I only needed my sanity back without the tampering. At the end of the day, I got the reprieve I came for.

After Uncle dropped me home at around eleven pm, he gave me some advice that was going to prove valuable in the coming days.

All I had to do was to stick to a good plan of salvation and not to let it falter.

STAND IN YOUR POWER

Chapter 13 – Trouble In Paradise

 After yesterdays antics, I woke up to a barrage of texts and missed calls.

As I got my ass up out of bed, I did my usual stretching routine and sat up in the lotus position; I rubbed my eyes, stood up and reached for my phone. I opened the phone and checked all my messages. Most of them were from Danika saying I must call her urgently.

As I dialled her number, it rang out three times.

"Erykah; oh my days. You won't believe what has happened. I swear down I'm being punished."

"Danika calm down. What's going on?"

"It's Terrance; he's been in an accident."

"What the heck, is he okay?"

"I have no idea! His mother just phoned me, and all she said he'd been taken to the Chelsea and Westminster hospital."

"Did she say what ward he was in?"

"Yeah, yeah! I got all that info."

"So what's making you think you're being punished?"

"After you and dad departed. I phoned Trae."

"How did that conversation go?"

"It went too well. In an instant, Trae knew how I wanted to be spoken to. He catered to everything I put his way, and he never swore or had anything negative to say. I sat and talked and listened to him and vice-versa for two hours because he had my pulse racing and my head in a daze. It felt like I was a teenager again and talking to a boy for the first time."

"That's all gravy Danika, but you haven't answered my question."

"What question?"

"The one about you saying you're being punished."

"Well yeah, I am."

"Why Danika; why do you keep saying this?"

"It's obvious. It's because I spoke to another in ways I shouldn't have."

"Yeah, but nothing happened to you personally. What happened to Terrance is an unfortunate disaster and it has nothing to do with your conversation with Trae, alright cuz?"

"That's your belief. But God is punishing me."

"So what's your next move now?"

"I'll go to the hospital. If I don't, it's going to look suspicious."

"It sure will."

"Yep."

"So cuz, it seems like to me that you have come to a decision?"

"Right now I can't think about that!"

"But if I was a betting woman. I would tell people to put their money on Trae."

"Then you'll end up a wealthy girl."

"I knew it, I knew it. Those William brothers have a certain Je ne sai quis about them. Wouldn't you agree?"

"I do agree with you Erykah, but right now I have to check on Terrence. I can't be thinking about Trae right now as hard as that is going to be!"

"Danika I know. I was trying to lighten the mood."

"I know you were and I thank you for that. But I'll be alright."

"Only if you're sure?"

"I'm sure, Erykah. There's no need to worry about me. I've inherited my mother's steely disposition when it comes to dealing with emotional trauma; however, big or small."

"That I can concur. You have Auntie's trait on things like that."

"Listen Erykah; you take care of yourself cuz, and I'll let you know what's up with Terrence."

"No worries, make sure you pass on my best wishes to him."

"I will. See you soon."

"Peace," I cut the line dead.

As I finished with Danika's business, I went through the rest of my notifications. I came across a few from father, who was saying that at his weekly alcohol meetings, he was making great strides into achieving his goal on the twelve-step program. That was music to my ears. I hoped he could keep it up and get to the end this time as a new, improved alcohol-free non-dependent man.

I flicked through a few more and stopped at one from Kyndra. I opened it, and it was information and details about the Resistance Movement Event entitled 'The War on Blacks'. It seemed like a grave subject and definitely, one that needs a lot of support and awareness within the wider black communities around the world.

I decided I would go after work and see what this Resistance Movement had to say for themselves.

After the way, Kyndra and Nina talked up the t'ing a few weeks ago. My choice became a bit easier.

Besides, after I finished my degree, I did take a year out to study world politics and black history in my own time for personal gain.

I also made a big decision of late. While I'd be working at the gym, I could finally study for my masters. I planned to do it with the likes of Open University. It seemed a good deal when I saw their tuition fees were almost four thousand pounds cheaper per annum.

As I put on my nightgown and headed towards the bathroom, I remembered I had a driving lesson after work. Shit, I wouldn't be able to get my hour lesson in and something to eat before the event.

I rang JC and told him I'd have to leave at five pm, and he said he would be happy to cover my hour as long as he got double pay for it. Blooming cheek, he had some front asking after the few small favours I did for him. But in hindsight, he did deserve it after all his support with mine and Donte's attacks. So I agreed to the extra pay and since the event was at 7 pm that should be ample time to eat and make my way across Brixton in time for it.

After I had finished showering and getting dressed, I went downstairs and made myself some cornmeal porridge, a croissant, and some grapefruit juice.

When I had finished eating; I brushed my teeth and left the house at precisely 08:40 am. On my way, I made a quick stop at a local coffee bar and then I proceeded to the gym.

It was going to be weird not having Donte around. Another two weeks recovery for him and we'll be side by side working together again.

As I rolled up to the entrance at around 08:52 am the usual man dem from across the bookies called out to me. But this time instead of giving them the bum shot. I just gave them a pleasant wave hello.

When I reached inside, there was JC too greet me in his usual jubilant manner.

"Good morning Erykah;" he said through his cheeky looking laugh.

"Hey JC; sup wid you?"

"I'm good. Can't complain."

"Oh, I see. Don't tell me! That's your typical reaction of when you just got some girl's number?"

"Maybe! Why you want to know?"

"JC; I hope you're not harassing our female clientele too much?"

"Who me? Nah, that isn't how I roll. I keeps it professional. You need to get your facts straight."

"Ha, ha! So what your tryna say it's them?"

"You said it. Not me!"

"You're crazy JC; I think you qualify for the award of 'Male Slag of the Year'."

"You joker."

"I ain't joking."

"Whatever."

"Anyway is there any mail?"

"Here you go!" As he handed me a thick bunch of letters.

"Thank you. If you need me, I'll be in the office for the next hour."

"Cool."

As I left JC to his duties, I made my way to the office. As I passed the gym, a few of the regulars waved hello, and I equally greeted them back. It was good to see the gym being used in full effect.

When I got to the entrance of the office I entered and first walked up to the coat rack and placed my jacket on it.

I then sauntered over to the desk and when I reached, I plunked myself heavily into the chair and the letters onto the desk.

As I settled, I turned on the computer and then I began shuffling through the priority letters, meaning the bills and shit.

It was the usual three monthly demands, and a few about new supplement products and others were about state of the art equipment.

Once I read through all the letters, I had a quick check over my emails.

Over the next hour, I also went through the accounts and ordered some supplements we were low on.

When I was finished, I turned off the computer and left the office, locking the door on my way out.

As I casually strolled down the corridor and got to the entrance of the gym as I went to carry on walking, out came a male member so quickly that he almost bumped into me.

Luckily for me, I saw him before he saw me.

"I'm sorry, Miss, I didn't see you there. Are you alright?"

"I'm fine, try and slow down a bit. Health and safety and all."

"Yeah, I'm sorry again. But actually, I had an ulterior motive."

"Oh, did you now, Mr?" I asked suspiciously waiting on his reply.

"Denton, Miles Denton Miss!" He reiterated as he extended out his arm for me to shake his hand.

"Well, Mr Denton."

"Call me Miles please, I insist?"

"I insist not. I don't know you like that."

"Okay."

"As I was about to reply. If your motive is directed at me, I'm telling you now you're wasting your time."

"How am I doing that?"

"Mr Denton here at Body Active gym's we value every person's membership. But you're very deluded if you think you have a chance with me."

"Well, I don't give up that easily."

"Mr Denton; let me make one thing clear to you. Staff under any circumstances are forbidden to fraternise with any of the gym's members and guests."

"Is that so?"

"Fine Mr Denton. You have yourself a nice day. Goodbye." As I went to walk away from his presence. He grabbed my arm and swung me around towards him.

As I crashed into his hard chest, he put his sweaty hand over my mouth and with the other arm he held both of mines in a flying armbar hold which hyperextended my elbows, restricting my upper body movement. Then he frogged marched me through the double doors and down the corridor until we reached outside to the entrance of the office.

I immediately began to panic, as I struggled to wriggle out of his hold over me. He was so strong that the more I attempted to set myself free, the more he tightened his grip on my wrists.

The searing pain that was beginning to course through my arms had me starting to go weak at the knees.

I could feel from within my bones an anxiety attack ready to surface itself. I couldn't believe nobody wasn't around yet.

JC must either be on his break or otherwise engaged. I swear down if he is trying to chirps another chick while I'm about to die up in this bish! Then his ass is grass.

But right now, to be honest, he could be forgiven for not seeing this on the camera if he came to my rescue.

As Denton continued to drag me towards the office, in my anguish and near state of anxiety, all I could think of was that I defiantly needed some courage from somewhere.

In that exact moment I was thinking about it I trod down on his foot with so much force he immediately shouted out in pain.

"You fucking bitch!"

I then smashed my butt with all my strength into his groin area. That forced him to fall back from me, which gave me enough time to pull away, turn around and crack my fist into his jaw and when he went to feel his face I seized my opportunity to kick him in the groin again, and this time he fell to the floor in so much agony that he started to wince like a girl.

I began to chortle as I continued to land deadly kicks into his head and torso area. In my mind, all I saw was red and the disturbing images of him raping or even killing me.

This thinking further fuelled my state of anger as I pummelled him into tomorrow.

That last blow I landed was a 180-degree nutcracker onto the top of his skull. It instantly knocked him out.

As I stood there not knowing whether to marvel at my handy work; I spotted JC from the corner of my eyes coming through the double doors. Better late, then never I thought.

"Erykah; what the fuck happened here?" He asked, looking around in astonishment.

As I looked into his eyes and followed where he was looking, I couldn't believe what I was witnessing. There was blood everywhere. On the walls, on the floor. Even on myself. I left a trail that could have me banged up for twenty.

"Shit JC;" I said as I began to panic. "Is he alive?" I questioned as a stream of tears started to fall from my eyes.

"I don't know," he said, looking bamboozled.

"Go check him, please, JC, please check him?" I pleaded.

"I can't touch him. What if he is dead already? Because I don't see him breathing. Do you?"

"No, I don't JC; please see if he is alright," I said as tears from my eyes kept on falling.

"Ah Erykah; why did you do this brother that way?"

"Because he tried to drag me into the office with one of his hands over my mouth and the other had my arms restricted too."

"Then fuck this nigger man. He deserves to die." As soon as he said those harsh words, JC launched a powerful sidekick to the abdomen area of Miles.

Denton groaned; which assured us he was alive. But to what detriment. I couldn't afford to be in any more hot water right now.

As I turned away from Denton; I noticed I had conjured up quite an audience. I immediately asked JC to usher the members away from the scene.

While he was doing that I slowly walked over to where Denton was and proceeded to turn his heavy body over with my foot. It was a bit of a struggle, so I reached my arms down to finish the job.

To my ostensible horror, he looked fucked up. I really couldn't believe what I had done. As I continued to stare at his face that was swelling up quick fast, all I could think about was how bad my anger could get.

To be fair, I was panicking about my life being over again. But the retaliation outweighed the crime. Even if it was a man, I had no choice but at the same time no excuse to take it to that extreme.

I was still staring at him looking half dead when JC came back and took over the situation.

"Look Erykah; first let's get him into the office. Do you think you could manage that?"

205

"No, I can't," I replied, feeling depressed.

"Ite, let me get Ricky and Bobby to close the gym and then we can deal with this."

"If this dude dies on me JC, then that's it. You might as well say my life is over. The law would make an example out of me." I began to sob and feel sorry for myself at the mere thought.

"Well if you don't want that to happen then listen to me."

"Okay, I'm listening."

"First things first. You get a mop and bucket and some bleach to clean up Denton's blood. The guys and I will take the body into the office and find out who he is."

"Yeah, cool," I said through bated breath. "I can do that." I continued saying still acting a bit frantic.

"Erykah; you gotta try and keep it together. You better scrub yourself up real quick before you get the cleaning materials. Also, speak to Alvin about getting the security tape and changing it. He'll know what to do!"

"What do you mean he'll know what to do, has shit like this happened before?"

JC eyeballed me hard without saying a word. I left immediately without getting a vocal answer and straight on to do what he asked of me.

As I approached the reception area, straight away, I asked Jeanine to cover Keisha on reception. I instructed Keisha to go and clear up the blood. She did so without hesitation. What brilliant employees Donte possessed.

Me, myself, I headed behind the reception desk and into the security room.

Inside was Alvin our head of security and on duty with him today was Tristan.

"Hi guys," I said nonchalantly.

"It's been taken care of boss. You got no need to worry." Alvin answered, trying to reassure me.

"That's good to know. Thanks."

"You're welcome, boss. Anything for you." Tristan said.

"Are you guys, alright?"

"We're good boss. How are you feeling?"

"I'm still a bit shaken up. But I'm going to be fine!"

"Cool boss, that's good to hear."

"I'm going to head back to the office and help JC out."

"No, you're not! Tristan accompany Miss Gaines back."

"That's alright, Alvin. I think I can manage to get there by myself."

"Pardon me, Miss Gaines, but it's not alright. Look what just happened?"

"Exactly, I handled things."

"Please Miss Gaines; for my peace of mind. Don't make things more difficult than they are already."

"No problem, Alvin; you win. You're not going to get anymore resistance from me."

"A'right."

"Cool. Come on Tristan let's go?" With that, the two of us walked out of the security room together.

As we continued our walk through the gym within two minutes, Tristan and I were at the door of the office.

"Thank you for walking me here. You can go back to the security room now," As I said that I gently opened the door and walked into more madness. I could hear, but not see JC yet tearing into Denton.

"Coz I'm telling you right now, there ain't no member called Miles Denton here or on any of the other gyms databases?"

"What the fuck are you saying, JC?"

He had tied Denton up to the chair on the other side of the desk. Denton tried with all his might to wriggle out of his hold, but his efforts came to no avail.

"This motherfucker right here doesn't check out?" JC said, getting all worked up. The beads of sweat that were perspiring from his forehead began to fall and trace a slow line running down until they were soaked up into his eyebrows.

"What do you mean he doesn't check out. Has his membership expired?"

"No Erykah; he ain't a member full stop."

"Then who the fuck is he?" I said as my mind began thinking a hundred and one things all at once.

"That's what I've been trying to get out of him for the last ten minutes."

"Goddamn JC; you think he is part of the firm that has been coming at us?"

"Yo, pussy bwoy, wah shi seh. Ansah di fucking question?"

"No comment," Denton answered.

"Wah yuh mean no comment? This ain't no court of law." JC asked while giving him a few punches to the face.

Denton spat back out the blood towards us, narrowly missing us and then he began to snigger out a sinister laugh that gave me the creeps.

Suddenly in the next movement, I felt a gust of wind. As I turned around, Tristan had passed me in a rush, and within seconds he was right on top of Denton; grappling his tracksuit top and all up in his face.

"Listen and hear what I'm saying. I don't play games. So it's like this. You simply got two options."

"And what's that then?" Denton replied, still spitting blood out from his busted-up mouth.

208

"One, you tell us your real name and who you work for. Two if you don't we hand you over to the police who if I were to take an educated guess, they would be very interested in someone like you. Am I about right?"

"Fuck you; I am not telling you shit!"

"Okay big man, have it your way," Tristan said.

"Erykah; call the Po-Po?" JC ordered.

"No wait, let me call Donte first!"

"Fine, but make it quick because I'm running out of patience with this piece of garbage."

I took out my mobile from my tracksuit bottoms pocket and quickly searched his number and rang him.

After ringing out for 18 seconds, the phone was finally answered.

"Hello, Erykah, is that you?" A woman's voice came through. At first, I was startled; I nearly went from 0-60 in seconds. But a few moments later it dawned on me who she was.

"Mrs Williams I almost didn't recognise your voice. How are you doing?"

"I'm fine, my dear. How are you holding up?"

"I could be better thank you for asking Mrs Williams."

"What's troubling you, my dear?"

"Long story Mrs Williams; I'll explain later when I see you!"

"No problem."

"Anyway is he there. What's he doing?

"Yes, he is. He just came out of the bath, and I've just made him lunch. Then he is going to take his medication and take a nap too."

"Lucky I've caught him on time. Can I speak to him?"

"Yes, mi dear. Let me go pass di phone to him."

As Meredith went to get Donte, I mouthed to Tristan to go tell Alvin and himself to go help Ricky and Bobby close down the gym as smoothly as possible.

As he went to leave, I told Tristan to tell Keisha she must reimburse anyone who hadn't finished their session yet. I instructed JC to hold the fort with me.

"Donte; your baby is on the phone?" I heard Mrs Williams say. It managed to bring the slightest smile to my face for a few seconds.

"Thank you, mother. I'll be down for lunch soon."

"A'right, son. See you in a bit downstairs."

"Hey, sexy girl, what's up? Is everything alright?"

"You sound better baby. Those meds are doing the business for you."

"I haven't touched the one's the hospital gave me."

"So, how are you getting better?"

"Nothing but pure holistic natural remedies from one Rass I know."

"Well, whatever he is giving you. It seems to be working."

"For sure. I'm feeling a lot better. Feel stronger too."

"That's the best news I've heard in a while. But I hope you're sitting down right now?"

"You sound anxious babe. Why do I need to be sitting down? Are you breaking up with me?"

"No, baby, no! I love you more than anything."

"Phew, that's good. My heart was jumping out of my chest for a second there."

"Listen, Donte; you got a big decision to make."

"This sounds crucial. I'm listening?"

"It's vital that you do? Now don't interrupt me until I've finished giving you the whole picture?"

"Go ahead, babes."

STAND IN YOUR POWER

"When I finished doing all the paperwork etc., this morning. I left the office to check on reception and do the rounds. As I got through the double doors out came this man very quickly from the weights room. I asked him to slow down in future, but he turned around and said he had an ulterior motive. I asked, and he obliged by trying to get with me. I tried humbling him by telling him he had no chance and to be on his way. He then turned around and cheekily said 'He ain't giving up that easily' I laughed inside, said goodbye to the deluded fool and proceeded to walk away from his presence and that is when the mother-fucker whose only name we have at present is Miles Denton. Still, we now know that isn't his real name, but I'll get onto that later. He grabbed me tightly by the arm and swung me around 180 degrees until I crashed into his chest. He then put me in some sort of professional hold, while he covered my mouth with his free hand. He began forcefully shifting me towards the office and baby that's when I thought he was either trying to rape me, perish the thought or kill me because the look in his eyes was eviler than the devil could handle. I was also praying someone was watching the monitor. I was so scared and petrified for my life that when he paused for a moment, I seized the opportunity to do what I had to do. Next thing I knew JC was there, and there was blood everywhere, and Denton was out cold on the floor. At first, I thought JC had done it. But when I noticed he had no blood on his hands and I did, and he eluded me to it; I knew it was me. By this time Tristan had reached the scene and took with JC; Denton into the office I went back to reception and ordered Keisha to clean up the blood. Alvin has made the tape disappear. Right now between JC and Tristan, they have been interrogating further, but Denton isn't letting up. We've already established he isn't who he says he is. There's no record of him on any of the chains databases. He won't tell us his name or who he works for; I suspect that he must be from the crew that has hurt us already. Tristan; bless him gave him two options. One to give up who he is and who he works for, or we call and hand him over to the Po-Po. I told the guys I'd ring you first so you can decide baby. That's it so far. So what are you saying?"

"Holy fucking crap Erykah; first things are you alright?"

"I'll admit I wasn't before I rang you. I thought I'd killed Denton. I was shitting myself for real. But I'm a lot calmer since speaking to you. I'm just anxious about how we all play this out."

"Ite let me think, two secs." A few minutes had passed by, and Donte hadn't answered yet.

"Baby are you still there?"

"Yes, I'm still thinking. A'right, I got it!"

"Then tell me?" My patience was beginning to wear thin with him now.

"Right, where is Denton right now?"

"He is heavily strapped into a chair and out for the count."

"Okay good! Take JC and yourself into the secret room and put me on loud there?"

"Yes, darling give me a few minutes, hold the line."

"Go ahead. I'm going nowhere."

"JC, Tristan; come here a minute," the guys came over real fast. "Right, listen up, this what is going to happen first. Tristan call Alvin; once the gym is all shut down and secured, make sure you both guard Denton. Call all the staff one large cab and put it on company expenses. You know how to do that right?"

"Yeah, boss, I do. Consider things done!"

"Wicked, cool. Text me when you have finished all that?"

"Sure thing, boss."

"JC follow me?" A few minutes later, we were inside the secret room. I then put Donte on loudspeaker.

"JC; you good?"

"Yeah D; I'm fine all in a day's work. Nah I mean?"

"Only you JC can find light in a bad situation, and I wanna personally thank you for going above and beyond your duties and helping Erykah out."

"No problem, man. I got you guys anytime."

"I won't forget this. When I get back ima sort you out that pay rise you've been hassling me for, fa time."

"For real? One love bredrin!"

"Ain't no thing JC, it's a forgone conclusion."

"Ite boss. I gotcha. Bless up."

"Back at ya, player."

"Yuh dun know."

"Cool. Erykah, JC listen carefully. This is what is going to happen next. I got some people that can take care of Denton no end."

"But baby! What about the evidence?"

"Erykah, listen to me. There's something I need to tell you. You're not going to like it. Hey, you may wanna leave and take the first train back to Manchester."

"You're frightening me now Donte; what you got yourself mixed up in?"

"Baby, I promise I'll tell you later."

"No Donte; you can't do this to me. You don't get to leave me hanging. I want to know right now."

"Are you sure. You think you're ready for my truth?"

"I gotta be Donte; otherwise, how do I know if I need to move forward with you since you just said what you said."

"Ite, I'll tell ya. But not here. When you come to mine after the resistance event."

"Donte after this you think I can muster going to that event?"

"You have to baby. Keep things normal for a few hours, while the boys sort out the mess. I know you're confused. But you've got to keep it together for now."

"Donte I'm not going to the meeting. I can go fresh to the one on Saturday!"

"Alright baby, leave JC and the security to wait on them, and you get to mine as soon as."

"I'll be in the company cab. See you soon. I love you."

"I love you too. JC, you know what to do. I'll catch you at mine later."

"Yeah D, catch you later!"

Fifteen minutes later from Donte's estranged phone call. On my way to the cab with all the staff, I saw a white van pull up outside the front and out jumped two men with massive briefcases.

At that moment a lot of things slayed my mind. But I was tired, weary and starving.

Like a good girl, I would just have to wait until Donte told me the truth in his words on who he was.

Whatever he tells me, either way, it's most likely from how he sounded on the phone that many things between us would change for the better or worse.

I hoped no matter what he had to say, that our love for each other remains strong that nothing or no one could come between that. Time would have to tell.

Chapter 14 – Seeking Solace

In the aftermath of the gym saga, I spent the next 48 hours at Donte's house.

I was almost on the verge of having a nervous breakdown, and I couldn't tell whether I was coming or going anymore.

Since leaving Manchester a few weeks ago; I'm not 100% sure if this new chapter in my life is working out at all for me.

But as quickly as those thoughts were circling in my head, between the both of them they pulled off a near miracle, when I received a specific amount of that old-school, Caribbean, motherly, steely disposition, yet strategic words of wisdom from Donte's mother Meredith and plentiful uplifting statements of intent from my boo. These synonymous counts of action soon dispersed any negative vibes I had about going back to Manchester.

This is what he had said to me; Guilt can be a good thing. It's the soul's cold action. The indication that something is wrong. The only way to rid your heart of it is to correct your mistakes and keep going. Until the mends are made, I don't know what you didn't do or should've done. But the guilt, the guilt, means your work is not yet finished.

As I took heed to what Donte had relayed to me, the impact of his statement had me thinking about the mess my life was in and that of my family.

For starters, there was the impending court against Racist. Also, my pursuit of trying to sue The Cheshire Police force.

Then there was father's relapses and struggles with alcohol and drugs plus the years of self-inflicted abuse to himself and the effects on myself.

215

Aunt CeCe's and Uncle Jeb's ostensibly rocky marriage, cousin Danika's situation with Terrance's untimely though not any fault of his own of an accident and I say untimely lightly because of the conversations she has had with Trae.

Dilemmas, dilemma's, well, at least there was some salvation in the form of Aunt Lola and Uncle Sebastian saying they were going to take care of all the family's financial problems for the next year.

I wished they also had a remedy to vanish away all our problems in one go.

Donte also went on to tell me the real truth about who he was. At first, when he told me I nearly passed out. But he reassured me, and in the end, I got the impression of feeling more protected around him.

He had declared, back home, his family is one of the most notorious and respected in the whole of Jamaica.

As he further explained about our attacks, it all made sense now. The gang that had stabbed him and attacked me were bitter rivals of his family.

They managed somehow to track and locate where Donte was working and had followed his movements over the last few weeks.

When I had left the gym with all the staff, the white van I saw parking up and the two guys with massive black cases, dressed in white overalls and white facemasks got out and went into Body Active, was none other than a private company that was on Donte's family's books. I'm talking the kind that deals with certain awkward situations away from the eyes and ears of the law.

Donte stated that one of the guys was his Uncle Mike.

Uncle Mike and his Associate disembowelled any evidence that was left behind. They also did a proficient make-up job on Denton. Then they escorted and dropped him off at Brixton Police Station.

He also managed to find out that Denton was a known and wanted man for the past three years. His real name was Robert Green, and in that time he was arrested and charged with the actual rape on nine women and fourteen sexual assaults the police were aware of.

He had no connection to the crew that attacked Donte and me in the hospital.

Donte also found out that Green was the one that assaulted Miss Ryder. He had contacted and spoken to her and offered her a year's free membership. She duly accepted and told him she would pursue charges of her own. Donte reckoned my swift approach to the drama made her take his offer with ease. He concurred.

At least that was one situation we don't have to deal with, unless, we are called as witnesses, and something tells me we will.

I hoped it wouldn't conflict with my case because I would love nothing more than to see that evil bastard Green behind bars.

Then there was the little matter of how Green got into the gym in the first place.

He had told the Police he was looking after a friend's place for a month and that he was on a long-distance business trip. While Green was occupying Mr Kenner's bachelor pad, he'd stolen his membership pass.

Lastly, Donte had informed me that the gym was getting a makeover. The refurbishment was going to take up to at least three months until the end of November.

But the good news was that everyone was going to be paid while being off work.

Customers would be told they can use either the Croydon or Balham branches in the meantime.

When he'd finished updating me, we had a five-minute kiss and cuddle session while in between passing back and forth gentle reminders about personal things.

After I said my goodbyes to Mrs Williams and left Donte to get some rest, I said I'll come back after the event and stay the night with him again.

If my plans changed, I would let him know. He said he was cool with that and at 10:05 am I left the house and made my way to Brixton Tube Station.

Seven minutes later, I was standing outside the station. The surrounding area was flowing neatly in its usual busy and vibrant state.

As I stood there, galvanising, trying, to gather my thoughts. I suddenly had an overwhelming peckish for a chocolate muffin and a cup of coffee.

Rarely, I eat poorly, but now and then I treat myself, so I was going to indulge.

Besides working in a gym has its perks and my figure was proof that Donte had no complaints either.

As I thought about where to get one, I scanned around and right across the road from where I was standing was a Costa Coffee Shop. Perfect, I thought.

Besides, I had time to kill as I didn't need to meet Aunt Lola until midday.

I made my way across the road towards the shop. When I reached, as I went to step inside, I'd say a late twenties to early thirties looking light-skinned brother was coming through in the opposite direction.

When he had clocked me, a cheeky grin swept across his face as he held the door open for me. I thought to myself he seemed the consummate gentleman.

As I passed him, the smell of his cologne wafted pass me prickling my senses.

He stood around 6'3" to 4" tall, and I could tell under his shirt he was hench. He had a very distinguished look about him, and he oozed sexiness all over.

"Thank you very much?" I said, smiling back at him.

"You're very welcome. Have yourself a lovely day." As he began to walk off, I called out to him.

"Mr Wait! Hold up?" He immediately stopped dead in his tracks and turned back around to face me. He then squinted his eyes as they lowered in stature.

"Excuse me! Do I know you?" He said, looking at me cautiously.

"No, you don't know me. But I know someone who would dig the style of you?"

"Is that so, and why would a complete beautiful stranger want to do such a favour for someone you barely know?" Dude look at me with a careful eye.

"I don't know why? I acted on impulse. To be honest, I liked the look of you at first, but I get the distinct impression that you are a nice person, and I feel kind of safe in your presence."

"Why thank you for the kind words. Means a lot in this day and age for a brother to hear that from a sister."

"For real, for real."

"So this person that will dig the style of me, who are they?"

"You're intrigued then?"

"I might be. Depends on what you present."

"Mm," I said, scouring his eyes for realness.

"What's with the mm? You're the one that stopped me."

"Nothing." I lied.

"Okay, then."

"Listen if it's cool with you can I ask you a few questions, if you got the time?"

"Sure, why not. What do you want to ask me?"

"Do you or would you date a black woman?"

"Why, who's asking?"

"Just answer the question?"

"Yes, I do. Why are you asking?"

"Mr., you're cute, but I'm happily in love."

"Fine, then I'll be on my way!"

"No, don't go?" As I pulled my phone out from my bag. "Feast your eyes on this beauty."

"Whoa, who is the stunner?" He said almost drooling all over my phone.

"Her name is Syreena;" as I snatched my phone back from his grasp. "She is the younger sister of my boyfriend, and I know she would love to meet you."

If I was feeling Mr Cool on one level, then Syreena would most definitely feel this dude on another. I'm sure of that.

"So what's next? You trying to hook a brother up?"

"I'm hooking; I'm hooking. But before I slapdash Syreena's number out. Let me get a few pics of ya, and if everything is on fleek, then it's all systems go. You cool wit dat?"

"I'm fine with that."

"Alright, strike a few poses darling?" As dude assumed a few sharp positions. "That's good, like that. Thank you," as I finished snapping away, I sorted out the pictures by filtering and cropping them before I sent them on.

While I was waiting, I asked if he didn't mind escorting me inside to wait for Syreena's reply. He duly accepted like I knew he would.

So we proceeded to make our way.

As we both took ourselves inside and made our orders when we finished paying, we took a table near the middle of the shop.

I went to sit down and before I could the dude kindly pulled out a chair for me and then pushed it back in as I sat on it. Then he took himself to his seat and sat opposite me.

I decided I would launch into the questions.

"So what's your background? Where are your parents from?"

"I'm mixed raced. Half Jamaican and half French."

"Wow, that's a beautiful combination."

"My mother is French, and my father is from Jamaica."

"So what do you do for a living if you don't mind me asking?"

"I don't mind."

"That's good."

"Would you believe me If I said under this big ass frame of mine it's in my nature to protect people?"

"I do believe you. You seem to possess a very caring nature. I can tell by the way you have carried yourself since we met."

"I'm a bodyguard."

"I knew there was something safe about you."

"Ha, ha, ha, you're so funny.

"Why thank you very much kind, sir."

"Sir, I feel privileged."

"So are you a fully-fledged bodyguard?"

"If you mean do I carry a licenced gun, then the answer to your question is yes."

"Can I see it?"

"Not in here! I don't think it will be appropriate."

"Oh, go on. Just a quick sneak peek, please?"

"You're a very persistent person?"

"That I am."

"Okay! Since you're hooking me up. Just a quick flash, yeah?"

"Yeah, cool! Just show mi nah?"

"Cool, you ready?"

"Yep."

"There you go."

As he promised, he delivered.

"Oh, wow. So you must be all trained to kill and shit?"

"Yes, I am!"

"So what kind of people do you guard?"

"Mostly, celebrities and politicians. Although I do get the odd, eccentric wealthy person occasionally."

"Oh really, that's impressive! So have you ever received any benefits from clients?"

"One or two that I'm not at liberty to say right now."

"Keeping it close to your chest. Who are you trying to protect?"

"I work for a private organisation, so I'm bound under contract. If I told you, I'd have to kill you."

"It's like that, hey?"

"Unfortunately, yes."

"Oh, you doing me like that?" I said with so much attitude.

"Wow, sister. You going there?"

"Yeah, I'm going there. You got a problem with that?" I said as I stood up and begun stepping towards him, stopping inches from his face even though I had to creek my neck upwards to meet it.

"What do you mean?"

"Ah-hah, I'm fucking wid ya!"

"Phew, you had me going there for a hot minute."

"Your face. What a picture?"

"Cool! So what's your name?"

"Erykah and yourself?"

"The names Simeon," as he held out his hand, inviting me to shake it.

"Nice to meet you, Simeon," I said, returning his greeting.

"The pleasure's all mine."

"Great," Simeon said with such swagger in his voice. His cool, calm and collected demeanour was having a profound effect on me. Without him even knowing it, he was slowly soothing any left-over anxieties away since I left Donte's house.

"Oh, Syreena has texted back."

"Has she! What's the verdict?"

"The jury is in, and they have come to a unanimous decision."

Simeon kept his focus on me like he was a bird of prey.

"You can chill. Syreena is feeling your pictures."

"Oh, cool. Bless."

"It's no problem. You made it easy."

"So what did she say exactly?"

"She said in her own words; 'Who the fuck is that?' He is buff and so frigging gorgeous. I told her. Now she's texted back again and said; 'If you're feeling him so far, that's good enough for me. By all means, give him my goddamn number girl', and that's what I'm going to do," Simeon looked at me unbelievably as if he was thinking again why would a stranger do such an immediate favour to someone she hardly knows. "Give us your phone?" As he unlocked it, he handed it over to me across the table. I punched in Syreena's digits and gave it to him back. Simeon took his phone, leant back sinking low into his chair as he stared at her number with a smile that lighted up the whole shop. He seemed very happy and smug with himself, yet he remained cool, calm and collected all the same.

"Thanks for everything."

"It's no big thing!"

"Well, to me, it is. Especially that I've only known you for a minute."

"Well, it was easy. Look at you? Also, the fact that you got a decent personality to match your good looks."

Simeon just smiled brightly in my direction and came towards me, holding out both his arms. Even though I hate people touching me usually, on this occasion, I obliged by doing the same back, and so we embraced for a few moments and then let go.

"Well I'll be seeing ya Erykah; thanks once again and take good care of yourself too."

"It was my pleasure. Maybe I'll see you very soon?"

"Well, fingers crossed, hey."

"You'll be fine, you see. Make sure you treat her, right?"

"I will."

"Oh, one sec. I nearly forgot?" I said as I pulled out a business card from my bag. "Here you go." I continued as I handed it to him.

"What's this, Body Active gyms?"

"It's my place of work. I'm the deputy manager there."

"Nice, I might come check it out one day next week."

"Listen, my number is on the card. Give me a ring in advance, and I'll personally look after you."

"I'll do that. Listen, once again, it was nice to meet you and thank you for the hook-up."

"Like I said, it was easy."

"Cool, I'll see you around. Take care."

"You to Simeon, bless."

As we departed from each other's company and went our separate ways, I made my back across the road, heading towards Brixton tube station.

I continued down the stairs passing hustlers playing music for money.

As I walked a little further, some white guy who was wearing a blue Nike baseball cap, army jeans, and a blue Regatta puffer jacket was trying to offer me a travel card.

"How much for it?"

"To you lovely miss," he said in a proper Cockney accent. "Give us a pound?"

"Done deal." As I handed him the money.

"Here, you go gorgeous." As he handed me the card and left his hand hanging for me to shake, I politely declined and tapped my elbow onto it and went on my way again. I don't know where these fuckers hands have been.

I continued my walk through the barriers and down the escalators until I reached platform one.

As I moved along the platform about fifty yards and came to a stop, the electronic announcement board said three minutes for the next train going to Walthamstow.

My first stop on the Victoria line was Victoria station and then a change onto the circle or district to South Kensington, and that's where Aunt Lola's hair care centre was situated.

I also told myself to not forget where I was going this time and how I should behave. On this occasion, I would concur because it was in my best interests to do so for today.

Three minutes had passed by quickly as the train came hurtling at quick speed down the track.

When it finally stopped, and the doors opened, hundreds of people offloaded. I sat back, waiting on the bench for the crowd to disperse before I would board.

When the rush was over, I got up and walked onto the carriage. I passed through until I found a seat I felt comfortable to sit on.

Immediately I looked around and noticed an old Asian man who was sitting opposite from myself. I got the eerie feeling he was staring at me like I was contaminated. Every time I glared back, he didn't even flinch or be too bothered to look away when I gave him the evils back.

I couldn't be assed to get into anything. All I did was stand up in silence, kiss my teeth in defiance without taking my eyes off him.

I got away from him by heading towards the end of the same carriage. When I found a spot, I sat down, pulled out my headphones from my bag, put them on and began listening to my tunes.

Seven minutes later, I was walking onto the platform of the famous Victoria station. I took my time to embellish the surroundings and smells of the underground.

I made the switch to the circle and district lines. Another four minutes later, and I arrived at South Kensington.

When the train halted, I got off and made my way down the platform.

As I cut through onto the adjacent platform I made my way to the escalators; as I began to ascend, I must have dozed off in a daydream because all I heard in the background was one of my nicknames being called out. When I finally came out of my daze, I looked up and noticed what appeared to be my cousin coming down as I was making my way up.

"Daniel; oh my days. Where are you going?" As his escalator took him down opposite me.

"Wait at the top?" He said. "I'll come back up."

As I reached the top and got off, I waited on Daniel to make his way back up. Thirty or so seconds later, he had reached. He managed to get off as I hurtled towards him and threw my arms around him and hugged him real tight.

"Daniel; shit, it's you?" I said as I instantly became emotional. Soon after the tears as per usual came flooding out of me.

"Yes, it's me. Who else hollers at you like that?" He relayed as he took a handkerchief from his bag and handed it to me.

"You and Aunt Lola are the only two people even until this very day that calls me Pooki still," I answered his question in between blowing my nose and wiping my tears away.

I pulled a small hand mirror out of my bag and double-checked myself. When I was satisfied with how I looked again, I put it back away.

"Well, old habits die hard." He made a point in reminding me.

"Damn cuz look at you, all hench and shit." As I felt on his biceps.

"Yeah, been working out the last 18 months and I'm enjoying it."

"I can tell you do. Since the amount, you use to smoke and drink. Danika tells me it's been nearly two years since you gave up smoking and cut down on the alcohol?"

"That's right, I have. The gym has been keeping me honest."

"I bet."

"Danika told me you came up the other week. I was pissed; I missed you. But I'm glad to see your ass now."

"Ah, Daniel, that's sweet. You know Nika and yourself are my fav cousins in the whole world. I will never forget the times you two have saved my butt. I owe you guys everything."

"You don't owe us anything. That's what family is about, being there in times of desperation and need."

"Appreciate it cuz, real talk."

"I know, and you're always welcome."

"So, Mr Briscoe; where were you going in such a hurry all suited and booted?" I said with a slight smirk on my face.

"I just had lunch with Danika and mother, and now I'm going back to the shop."

"Oh damn yeah, I forgot you're the manager of the London franchise of Aunt CeCe's community and charity shop."

"Yep, you remembered," he said, mocking me as he laughed his head off.

"Don't mock me?" I said in a babyish voice as I hit him playfully on the arm.

"Cool, cool Miss Sensitive."

"Am not," I said protesting this time in the same babyish voice.

"Fine, you're not. Come, give us another hug I got to get going?"

"Ah already? Okay, Daniel, see you soon, cuz." As I embraced him again.

"Listen, mother is going to tell you, but anyway we were discussing and this Sunday if you're free she is going to cook a family dinner, and she said you could bring Donte, as it will be good to meet him."

"Them two wasted no time in telling you?"

"Why are you acting all surprised? You know the Briscoe women have a tendency in finding it hard to keep their mouths shut from gossiping for no longer than five minutes when they're in each other's presence."

"Yep, this is the kinda thing that makes me glad I'm not a Briscoe. No disrespect cuz."

"None took. I understand."

"Cool. You off now?"

"Yeah, you should pop by the shop sometime soon. I'll text you the address. It's easy to find."

"Will do cuz, take care."

"You too!"

"Oh, I wanted to ask you. Are you still with Kira?"

"Sure am. Going on five years strong and I'm more in love with her now than ever before."

"Ah, Daniel; that's so sweet. She's a lucky girl to have you."

"No Erykah; I'm the lucky one, trust me!"

"I'll take your word for it."

"Listen, it's good you're in London. We're getting engaged on the 3rd of October. Hence the big dinner. So everyone can meet everyone. Plus Nika has got some great news for you; I'll let her explain, as it's her thing to tell you?"

"Ite Daniel; I better get over there quick fast then. See you on Sunday and congratulations. Pass my love to Kira as well."

"Will do cuz. Take care. Bye."

"Later's Daniel; love you cuz."

"Love you too Erykah; be safe."

As I made my way out of the station, the sun hit me straight in the face. The weather had changed for the better since the rain this morning. Only in the UK can you get four seasons in a day.

I pulled out my shades from my bag and put them on as I did so, a couple of guys walking past wolf-whistled at me. I smiled back and continued on my journey.

I got the vibe that today was going to be a good one and damned as hell I needed it to be. A good day that has been a long time coming and if anything or anyone tried to fuck that up. I'm not sure where it will end up this time. Perish the thought.

Chapter 15 – A Different World

Everything that was numb in my body came back to life. Aunt Lola is the type of person that can meet you at the heart and make a difference.

Four hours later, after I had left her side, I was back in Brixton. I was externally glammed up; all I needed now was to have my soul replenished. I hoped at the function tonight I might learn something new that has been missing in my life so far.

I began to make my walk home. On route, I was feeling a certain cool vibe in the air. Brixton was bubbling today more than usual.

As I continued my walk home, I heard my phone ping. I took it out of my bag and checked it. It was a What's app message from Nina; it said the format of the Resistance event had been changed and the new subject was something called #BlackGirlMagic and that it was a ladies-only event for sisters of colour.

By the time I got home and stepped through the front door, I barely got my coat off when Nina greeted me in an excitable manner. To be honest, the way Nina broke it down it sounded like something I needed to hear. Hey, the way she was waxing lyrical about it, it had me more elated hence when I walked in.

By the time she had finished her exerts, I felt it was the right tonic I needed in this moment.

"So how's your day been so far?" Nina asked while bouncing around and doing a hundred and one things at once.

"It's been eventful."

"Why, what happened?" She answered back as she slowed down her roe.

"Ah, girl. I don't know where to frigging start?"

"From anywhere! Just tell me the main parts."

"Ite, I'll give you a brief breakdown."

"Go on. I'm listening."

"Let me ask you a question first?"

"What is it?"

"How well do you know Donte?"

"I would say I know him enough to trust him. Why, you ask?"

"Well, you already know what happened at the gym and everything about Denton; I mean Robert Green."

"I do! But what's that got to do with Donte?"

"Green has nothing to do with Donte personally. It's the small matter of the clean-up."

"What about it?"

"The private company that Donte used is headed up by none other than his father's brother."

"Wait! No way! Don't tell me. Do you mean his Uncle Mike?"

"Yes, Nina, yes."

"Holy crap Erykah; that's some weird stuff you're telling me, his Uncle Mike? I can't believe it, girl! Mike is such a nice guy and all."

"He probably is away from his work. But I don't know him. So what the heck I know?"

"I don't know. It's ludicrous."

"Tell me about it?"

"Oh, lord. Ima pray for him still."

"You do what you think is best?"

"So what don't I know about Donte?"

"Well, when he told me, at first, I nearly had a heart attack. Then when I eventually managed to process the information, I slowly warmed up to the idea of who he was. In the next moments, I made a conscious decision that if I wanted to move forward with him, I had to either tolerate or accept his position and carry on. So I did accept it, and here I am telling you."

"That couldn't have been an easy decision to make?"

"It wasn't! I huffed and puffed, contemplated and contemplated for ages. I didn't decide so easily!"

"You forget, I know what you're like when it comes to making hard decisions."

"So you do."

"You lock yourself away from the world for a few days. Your mobile is switched off, and wherever you're residing with people, you tell them, they ain't seen you!"

"You're right, I do!"

"Why do you do it that way?"

"It stems from my childhood after I lost my mother. My father, who was dealing with his grief in ways you're aware of already completely tried to isolate myself because I became a highly strung emotional child and any little trigger would set me off. All I did from the ages of six to eleven was fight, cry and be made to apologise every time. I guess you can say I'm still a lot like that now and I know I need to get help for my anger issues,"

"Now you're an adult, yes you do; otherwise there are dire consequences, and I don't need to tell you that. Although it's immensely understandable why you're the way you are."

"Nina, how did you deal with your atrocities?"

"You never get over it because it's a strong memory that in your everyday life, you see and hear things that take you back and remind you that you were a victim and still are. After years of counselling and therapy, there were two things that I learnt that stood out for me the most."

"What two things were that?"

"You learn it wasn't your fault, and you learn to live with that."

"That's it. That's all it takes."

"Well, for me, in the end, yes."

"Wow, well if you say so then I will leave it like that!"

"Listen, I'll let you go get ready first."

"Thanks', Hun."

"No worries."

After getting ready for the best part of an hour, I checked myself in the mirror one last time. Then I made my way downstairs where Nina and Eric were waiting for me.

"You ready girl?" Nina asked me.

"Sure am. Can't wait to get there either."

"Ite, let's go!" Eric commanded.

As we all began to make our way out of the door, my phone rang, and it was Donte. I told the other two to go ahead as I said I'll catch them up.

"Hey babe, what's up?"

"Nothing much! I just wanted to see if you were feeling any better from earlier."

"Oh yeah, much better. Thanks', Hun."

"I weren't sure if you were after this morning."

"I'll admit, I was a bit shaken up this morning, but really, I'm alright now!"

"If you're sure? Then that's good enough for me."

"Baby I'm fine! There's no need to worry about me. How are you though?"

"I'm getting there slowly, babe; went to the doctors earlier to get my stitches out and change the dressings."

"Did he say how much longer before you can be mobile again?"

"He reckons another two to three weeks."

"That's great news honey, I've missed you in more ways than you can imagine."

"Oh get out of here! You were by my side this morning?"

"That doesn't' mean I don't miss you when I'm not with you."

"Everyone misses me when they are not around me!"

"And who would that be?"

"Babe, stop playing."

"I'm not playing. I'm serious!"

"You for real?"

"What you think? Yeah, I'm for real."

"Wait, wait, wait, wait! You must be fucking wit me, coz I know you ain't saying you don't trust this nigger right here?"

"Ha, I got you. I'm just fucking wit ya!"

"Damn straight, you are!"

"Donte; I gotta go. Eric and Nina are waiting for me."

"Ite, enjoy yourself."

"I'll try babe, love you."

"Love you too, laters."

With that, the call ended. I made my way outside and up to the top of the street where surprisingly, Eric and Nina were still waiting for me.

"Erykah; come on, you're cutting it, fine young lady!"

"I'm coming; I'm coming. Keep your hair on!"

As I caught up with them, the three of us looking very stylish made our way to the centre.

As we continued our walk through the Brixton streets, we couldn't avoid bumping into neighbours and other people we knew.

A few minutes later, we reached the o2 Brixton Academy in Stockwell Road.

Quite a queue had formed outside, and there were ladies of all shapes and sizes anticipating to get inside.

The three of us moved up to the front of the queue. Nina stepped forward to a lady who was holding a small tablet in her hand.

"Hi, there ladies and gentleman. May I take your names please?"

"You sure can," Nina replied. "We have Eric Lawrence, Erykah Gaines and myself, Nina Lawrence."

"Let me take a look," the lady replied as she scrolled through her guest list. "Here we go. Says here Mr Lawrence is helping behind the scenes and should collect his pass from reception. Here's your green ticket Mr Lawrence to collect your pass with," the way she handed Eric the ticket you could've heard her heart beating as far as Brixton Town hall. Eric being Eric quickly noticed the lady had the hot's for him and stepped up his flirting game to another level.

"Sweet," Eric said as I watched him seductively take the ticket from her hand, making sure he lightly brushed his against it.

"You're welcome, Mr Lawrence," she said, sounding breathless while looking all misty-eyed.

"No need to be so formal. Just call me Eric, I insist."

"Okay, Eric;" as she pulled her hand away from his.

"And what shall I call your lovely self?" Eric asked probably hoping she would tell him. In the next move, the lady pulled out a business card from her jacket and handed it to Eric.

"Regina; cute name!" He repeated silently but enough for me to hear him. As we all proceeded into the Academy, Eric put the card into his jacket pocket and said nothing else about it.

As I observed him trying to hide his emotional gaze in his hour of conquest coyly, I couldn't help myself, but I had to do it. I kind of half jumped on Eric's back, teasing him about what just happened.

"Ahh, check you out, playboy."

"Well, you know how I roll," he answered back as his cheeks became flatulent with his smile.

"Oh dear brother," Nina said, shaking her head with a disapproving stare. She seemed disgusted by his reply, while her eyes rolled around in their sockets in contempt of his answer.

"So, you mad?"

"I'm not angry, Eric. It's the way you carry on with the females. You roll through us like we are an appendage to your sexual conquests!"

"What she is trying to say bruh! You ain't bout that life."

"I ain't stupid! I know what she is trying to say."

"Well if you know that then what I'm trying to say is why you carry on like you want to remain hood?"

"Because I am from the hood! Why are you trying to forget where we were born?"

"I'm not trying to forget other than better myself. You have a responsibility to your profession to keep yourself in check inside and outside of work."

"My personal life has nothing to do with my work. I do an outstanding job, and you aren't my boss, nor do you pay my wages."

"You two come on! You're making a scene." I added my piece, trying to calm down the embarrassment they were displaying.

"Fine, you remember that the next time you need a favour or a shoulder to cry on."

"See Erykah; see how my big sister is trying to manipulate and control my life as per usual?"

236

"Am not. How dare you little brother suggest so?"

"Listen, I don't fucking care what you think. Just allow me for a minute. My love life is my business. I'm not the one, truss me! So please once and for all, keep you nosey asses outta my business and get your kicks elsewhere. Right now, myself, I got a job to handle inside."

But before Nina and I could utter another word, Eric had dashed inside as fast as he gave off that last sermon.

As I stood there in abstract disbelief shaking my head, I looked over at Nina, and she had the look of someone who got told good and proper.

"You know your brother didn't mean it?"

"Oh yes, he did and to be honest he is right."

"What possible lame-ass excuse does he have to talk to us like that?"

"Listen Erykah; long before you came on the scene Eric's choice in the opposite sex, let's put it another way when it comes to the ladies and the pretty ones at that. My brother has the perception of a jumped-up, over-zealous fifteen-year-old boy when selecting suitable women to date."

"I think you're wrong and being very unfair, Nina."

"Oh, and how am I doing that? More to the point, how do you know he hasn't been acting like that?"

"Nothing, I don't know. I'm presuming Eric is."

All of a sudden Nina took on the disposition of a hunter about to kill its prey. She grabbed me by the arm, slightly hurting me in the process and aggressively began moving me away from the crowd. I got the sense she deeply wanted to tell me something significant. I kind of had this eerie feeling she has been dying to get something off her chest since the day when Uncle Jeb left to go back to Manchester. It seemed the moment had come, and by the crazy look in her eyes, I wasn't going to like it one bit.

"Listen, I know about my brother and you back in the day," she said, clenching her fists. I was shell shocked. I couldn't believe those words were coming out of her mouth.

"So why you never say something?"

"So you do not deny it?"

"Why should I? What's the point?"

"Well, at least you have the decency to be truthful. I've never said anything because I was waiting in vain for you or my brother to own up."

"Look Nina for what it's worth I'm not sorry or have any regrets with sleeping with Eric. I am sorry though for never saying anything I genuinely am."

"Fine, apology accepted. But if this little drama with Eric today didn't happen. Would you have ever told me?"

"To be honest, probably not."

"Why not Erykah?"

"I was hoping one day maybe Eric got drunk as I know when he does, he likes to confess certain truths without him wittingly knowing it until the next day."

"That's such a cowardly way of thinking, and I must say I'm in the least very disappointed in you, dear friend. But for this event, I'm not going to let it get in the way of our friendship for now. But you, Eric and I need to talk about this sooner rather than later."

"Thanks' girl, I appreciate it."

"Come on, let's get inside and get ourselves a good seat."

"Wow already! The event starts in ten minutes."

"Then let's go and get us some magic."

"Yes, let's do it!"

As we both finally made our way into the venue. We walked a few steps and got to the entrance of the hall where a kind looking security guard took our tickets and stamped our hands. He instructed us in case we needed to go outside and come back in. We both smiled at him and continued our journey inside. We didn't even get much further when we were surrounded by a six-foot-something, hench of a man blocking our path and what appeared to be Kyndra slowly coming up behind him.

"Brother Calvin; you startled me," Nina said, trying to regain her composure. "It's been a while. How's life been treating you these days?"

"Life's good Sister Nina. Can't say the same for some of our people in other parts of the world. But as part of the black nation in the UK, all we can do is our bit and make it count."

"That's right, brother Calvin."

"So is this the lovely young lady Sister Kyndra has been waxing lyrical about?"

"Yes, Brother Calvin; let me introduce you to my best friend, Miss Erykah Gaines." I blushed as he extended out his hand for me to shake.

"Miss Gaines; it's finally nice to meet you in person."

"The pleasure is all mine Mr Felix; I've heard quite a bit about you too."

"Well, all good, I hope?"

"Almost," I said, laughing.

Calvin saw the joke and laughed with me. From the off, I was building a good rapport with him, and I liked his personality too.

"Well, it was good meeting you, Miss Gaines."

"Please, call me Erykah; if you're a great friend to my friend, then that makes us friends too."

"That's cool, Erykah; will do. I'll be seeing you around, I got to get backstage and prepare for my speech, so take care of yourself."

"Thanks', Mr Felix; you too."

As he departed his way from us to the side of the stage, Kyndra popped her head around from the back. When she spotted us, she blew us a kiss, and we politely acknowledged and threw a couple back of our own.

When we were done, we vacated two seats in the front row and got ourselves settled. Within another five minutes, the whole place was packed to the rafters. There were ladies, even standing around the sides. The only men in the place were the security and anyone working for the Resistance Movement.

As the lights turn down low, the talking amongst the ladies sounding all excited suddenly became whispers as Calvin walked onto the stage with a mic in his hand looking ready to address the crowd. When everyone spotted him, there was an almighty roar, followed by claps and even some wolf whistles. After about a thirty or so seconds, the other ladies became silent until Calvin spoke.

"Wow, what a reception. Please give yourselves another round of applause."

The crowd responded to his command. Calvin possessed an air of authority about him. He hadn't said much yet, but already he had these ladies in awe of him. I guess he was the man around these parts according to Nina.

"First off. I want to thank every one of you who have come out this evening when you could've been doing something else to support this event and the ones before. You're valuable followers of the Resistance Movement, and from all the staff and myself we thank you sincerely for your continues fire. Okay, I'm not going to ramble on much longer. I'm just going to tell you wah gwaan over the next three hours. From seven-thirty to eight-thirty we got a special guest speaker to give all you lovely ladies the lowdown on this new phenomenon called BlackGirlMagic.

In the second hour, we got another guest speaker to talk to you all about something deeper #BlackLivesMatter. At the end of each talk which will last half an hour per speaker, the other half-hour of their set will be open to the floor where you can question the speakers about their subjects, and some of you will be asked if selected to come on stage and share a story relating tonight's topics. In the last hour, we have some light entertainment in the form of some spoken word from our resident poet Miss Nina Lawrence who is sitting in the front row here. We also have a local singer in the form of Nadia Clark and to leave you feeling nice a comedian who goes by the name of David Koontz. In the end, we have some light refreshments and literature on sale about tonight's talks. So for my first guest. She has been affiliated with our movement when she saw one of our events online and fell in love. When we received her call saying she wanted to be part of an event over here. We obliged and made her dream and our joy come true. She hails from North Carolina and is a seasoned motivational speaker across many black women movements and organisations spanning a twenty-two-year career. So without further ado, it's the Resistances pleasure and my pleasure to be welcoming to the stage Mrs Olivia Stone."

The whole place erupted into massive applause. It was like they all knew who she was, as Mrs Stone came out from the back, she was escorted to the stage by security. Once on, she casually and calmly took to the centre. When she reached, Calvin handed her the mic, and off he went too.

"Thank you, Mr Felix, for the wonderful introduction and to all you lovely ladies tonight looking beautiful and smelling sweet, give yourselves another round of applause." So we all did. After a minute, it stopped, and Olivia began her much-anticipated talk.

"First off, I want to briefly mention how delighted I've been treated since I arrived in the UK. Things have changed a lot in London since I was here last in 2005. I can see it's become more diverse than ever. Yet I struggle to see how many key black businesses are being given the mainstream promotion it deserves. But what I'm here to do is to educate you all about this new phenomena as Mr Felix mentioned called #BlackGirlMagic. So that's what I'm going to do right now," as she took a few moments to settle her papers on the podium I quickly ran over to the bar and purchased a couple of orange juices for Nina and I and promptly settled back into my seat. When I did, that's when Mrs Stone began.

"BlackGirlMagic, BlackGirlMagic; what is this sudden phenomenon and how it may or may not affect you as a black woman. Well, one thing I can say is don't bother trying to look up 'BlackGirlMagic' in the dictionary because it isn't there – well at least not yet. But I'm sure you've seen or heard the phrase plenty of times over the past year and are wondering what it means. If I had to nail down a definition, I'd say: Black Girl Magic is a term used to illustrate the universal awesomeness of Black women. It's about celebrating anything we deem particularly dope, inspiring, or mind-blowing about ourselves. It's a way we as black women express our solidarity with each other, and that's just the start. As black women in general, our essence, style and spirit are hard to define. Some might call us mysterious, but we're most certainly magic. Its current incarnation may live mostly online, but it is an embodiment of something many black women have been doing for years in real life: forming communities of support based around our mutual disenfranchisement. We, as Black women use it in different ways – there are no rules. It might be used to caption Instagram pictures on graduations, on Pinterest boards of fabulous hair or status updates proclaiming a love of black female role models such as Asia forth. She, in 2012, became the first black female director to receive an Oscar nomination. We deem each other, or ourselves, "magical" as a way of expressing our strength, beauty and success. Rayne Buchanan calls it part of the "secret language between us black girls. Its origins are ambiguous, but Laila Stonebridge, a feminist writer from the US, claims to have been the first person to others to use the term in 2013. Stonebridge says that it aims to "counteract the negativity" that society places on black women, but the phrase goes beyond that. It not only tackles the dangers of our culture that recognise few achievements by us. It's our collective stand against the stereotyping, colourism, misogynous and outright racism that a lot of us face daily – the kinds of treatment that are causing such high rates of depression and anxiety among black women. If you need further proof as to why the phrase is so important, look at mainstream magazines – black women are rarely represented or appreciated as being beautiful. The token exceptions, such as Makena Otieno – who, as writer Akinyi Simiyu puts it, is "an Ivy League graduate, [who] …comes from Kenya's globally recognised political class" and therefore falls into the category of "acceptable blackness" – are not enough. Here in the UK, women such as Rain On Me actress Catrina Parks and Make It Happen star Megan Johnson has spoken out about prejudice in TV and the music industry. Hollywood actress Sakina Brin puts it well when she says Black Girl Magic is empowering in comparison with the images of black women often shown in the media, "being tough, with a cap on, with graffiti behind them", "struggling", or "being a nurse In a period drama". Of course, not all black women buy into it. We have our sceptics."

"Black girls aren't magic. We're human," argues Gloria Fuller in Essence Magazine, saying that the superhuman connotations remind her of the "strong, independent woman" trope that black women are so tired of hearing. But Stephanie Major, who plays Liza in the Perception Deception trilogy and whose video about cultural appropriation, Appropriate that? Went viral in 2011, has been a big champion of the idea – even donning a sweatshirt with the term emblazed on it. In a recent interview with Smith in Teen Style, Major compared it to "shine theory", a phrase initially coined by New York magazine journalist Nichelle Lowman. "[It] says that when you become friends with other powerful, like-minded people, you all just shine brighter," said Major. Black Girl Magic works as a virtual way of practising shine theory, connecting women through the use of three simple words and lifting them to be respected and admired."

Olivia carried on for another half hour, and then the floor opened. Same in hour two and at the end after the comedian, I was introduced to a couple more of the Movements members, and I came across some very knowledgeable and educated brothers and sisters.

After I bought myself a couple of books, one was called My Blackness and Me, and the other was a recommendation from Nina about the history of spoken word. Nina and I caught up with Kyndra; it wasn't until 11:30 pm before we left the Academy when Eric, Nina and I got home.

After having a cup of tea, I said goodnight to the guys and went to get ready for bed, when I finished showering and creaming my body, I quickly phoned Donte to say goodnight.

After we exchanged our undying love for each other, I let him go and got myself into bed.

As I laid there mulling over today's and tonight's events I was feeling inspired. I guess I got what I needed to get out of the event as I contemplated this shift in direction I was being pulled too. It felt good, but I sensed tough times ahead as I had to make provisions and time for the new changes coming my way.

Chantel was coming to London tomorrow, and I had the job of picking her up.

But what this event gave me tonight was hopefully the strength of character to see myself through my court case and off to sleep I go—Goodnight world.

Chapter 16 – Best Friends

I woke up a few minutes past 08:00 am after having a beautiful night of uninterrupted sleep. As I began to fully awake, I rubbed my eyes, sat up and did my usual stretching routine.

Today was the day that my other best friend in the whole universe was coming to London, and I had the pleasure of picking her up and getting her settled.

Chantel was coming down a week earlier than she originally scheduled. As soon as she heard about my court case, nothing or no-one was going to stop her from getting here to support me.

After about five minutes, I got myself out of bed and headed straight to the bathroom. As I ran myself a shower, I took a few minutes to do my lady business. When I finished, I got up and washed my hands.

I left the shower running to warm up the bathroom as I was one black woman that hated the slightest bit of cold. You see, I'm one of many people in the world that suffers from anaemia. It's a condition in which red cells are deficient or of haemoglobin in the blood, resulting in pallor and weariness. That's why in the summer if there is any cold parts of the day I've got the heating on full blast to the dismay of anyone visiting or living with me. So if you love me enough, it's something that you must tolerate or suffer with, and I wouldn't want it to be the latter.

I made my way downstairs for a minute to check on things and to see if I had any mail. I did. When I opened the first of many letters and began to read, it was instructions from Marcus going over strategies for my court case. He further laid down more details about who the presiding judge is going to be, plus also the names of the prosecution team and some small information about Racist, which could come in handy. In my mind, I thanked him so much and then I transferred that love to a text. He was our families very own earth angel and had got us out of hot water more times than I can remember.

As I stood there reminiscing, I do recall a time and a funny one at that. When father in not one of his finest moments ever was coming back from one of his domino nights. According to him when he had to shed light on how he ended up spending the night sleeping inside a local furniture store, was that father couldn't remember due to the excessive amount of alcohol and how high he had got.

That was kind of a funny yet sad time for obvious reasons. I get why father did some of the things he needed to do to get through his grief, yet he didn't want to accept the remedies that could make him better. It was as though he was self-punishing himself and anytime a member of the family tried their hardest to get him to rehab or therapy or even just a doctor, he would put up such a resistance that even had him threatening to call the police on us.

I'm glad these days he is getting better, and I'm always ever so thankful for Bernadette coming into his life. Just when he was about to give up on himself, along came this miracle of a black woman and saved his sorry ass from further tragedy. Bernie has been father's salvation and in my eyes she is defiantly my father's saviour. She reassures me that father will be looked after and cured. If she can do that, then I'll be the happiest and proudest daughter in the world.

I looked around all of downstairs, where I eventually found a note leaning against the fruit bowl on the kitchen table with my name on it. As I grabbed it, I opened it up and could see it was from Nina, saying she popped into Brixton to buy some bits to make Chantel comfortable for when she comes to stay for a few nights. After she'd spent time with us, Chantel planned to head back to the London Hilton hotel.

When I was completed, I took myself back upstairs into the bathroom and locked the door. The first thing I did was to take off my dressing gown, and then I stepped into the shower.

I reached over to the handrail and retrieved a cap for my head. As I let the water hit my skin, I felt my whole body come alive. I stood there letting the water rain down on me as I thought of the prospect of seeing Chantel again. I knew it was going to be a crazy couple of weeks. But I also understood to have her around was going to lift my spirits massively and everyone else who will come into contact with her.

I also remembered the last time I saw her. It was the day when I was leaving for London. It was bare funny as I tried to make out at first on who was running up that hill like a dangerous dog was chasing them.

Only Chantel with her ditzy self could think I was leaving at midday. When the night before, we all went to bed late after the bender we all went on when herself and her boyfriend Dominique, plus my cousin Darius and that was the shock of the night because him being on the verge of signing for Manchester City's Elite squad, I didn't think he'd be able to make it. But make he did, and the rest is history.

STAND IN YOUR POWER

After I finished my shower, I dried myself off and headed back to my bedroom. I took another half an hour to cream my body, apply my makeup and finish getting dressed.

When achieved, I gathered up my keys, purse and phone and then I made my way downstairs. I double-checked everything was locked, and that the gas was turned off.

As I was about to vacate the premises, in walked Nina sounding and looking very chipper with herself.

"Why do you look like a cat that had a taste of the sweetest cream ever?" I asked, acting as excited as she looked.

"I just got off the phone to Xavi," she replied as she side-stepped around me and went to put the bags in her hands into the kitchen.

I followed her back in there to help her with them.

"So, how is Mr Lover boy these days?"

"He is doing well; thank you for asking. He was just telling me his good news."

"What good news is that then?"

"He got a promotion at the restaurant. The company have made him the chief waiter, and he said it was an extra £200 a month in wages."

"Oh wow, Nina; that means more gifts and presents for you then! Coz, you know how he spoils you already."

"Not this time babe we're saving for a holiday. We're going back to visit his native Brazil. He wants to introduce me to his family and his people's."

"No shit girl. I'm fucking jealous. I need me a holiday after all the crap I've been through lately."

"Then why don't you come? Ask Donte too! I know Xavi won't mind."

"Don't be fucking with me, Nina; are you serious?"

"Yes, I'm for real. Look as long as you two can cover your airfare; you can stay with us. Xavi's parents own a mansion near the beach of Sao Paulo."

"Ah, shit. I can't wait to tell Donte; ima call him on my way to pick up Chantel."

"You do that! I'm going to stay here and get the house in order."

"But I thought you were accompanying me."

"Erykah; what's the point of two of us going?"

"So we can both great our best friend!"

"It's better you go alone. You know where to go, right?"

"Yeah, I do! But that's beside the point. I promised Chantel we were both going to be there."

"Fine, give us ten minutes to sort out a few things and get freshened up."

"Yes, good, ima make a drink. You want one?"

"No, thank you, Hun!"

I made myself a blueberry frozen smoothie so that I could bring with me on the journey. Eight minutes later and Nina was making her way back downstairs. I looked up at her and smiled. As soon as she saw me, she returned my greeting with a smile of her own.

"You ready girl?"

"Yep, let's go get her!"

With our arms locked together, we proceeded to walk out of the house. Nina unlocked her car with her electronic key. As I got inside, I shut my door. Nina got in and started the car, and that's when I was able to whine down my window. I put on my Ray-bans, while Nina selected the music.

As she began to manoeuvre the vehicle out of the drive, the sounds of Nao's Fool to love tune came wafting through the speakers. We both nodded our heads back and forth in sync, as the sun came shining into the car.

STAND IN YOUR POWER

The melodic beat went through us like an ocean wave, as we both simultaneously sang out the lyrics and then we began making our way down Dalberg road.

It was another beautiful Sunny day in South London, as we drove through Brixton road, smiling, waving or even hailing at people that I knew or Nina knew, or we both knew.

For the first time in a long time, I felt contempt with myself. I was looking forward to the possibility of spending a month in Brazil, as soon as I told Donte that is.

The BlackGirlMagic event inspired me to change. Instead of going around dealing with threats of violence with my fists, it would enhance my chances of a rational outcome if I could learn a way to implement strategies and coping mechanisms that would distinguish my anger concisely.

Easier said than done, but I had to find a way sooner rather than later. Kyndra had suggested I take up Yoga. Donte said he would pay for me to go to anger management as he felt worried he'd ever dare say something that could spark my frustration towards him. I told him I love you too much for that to take place. Just keep treating me right, and there won't be any problems. Lastly, Nina insisted that I brush up on some Self-defence classes. She knows I can take care of myself; she just needed me to learn the discipline that goes hand in hand with it. So after all those instructions to sort me out. I decided I would enquire about all of them and take the lead from there.

After I had phoned Donte on route and told him about Brazil, he agreed to go and said I wouldn't have to spend a penny. He said he would cover everything. I didn't argue with him. So Brazil here we come. My man, what a fellow he is.

Forty minutes later and we were driving around the back and into the car park of the London Hilton hotel that overlooked Hyde Park.

The cost per night for one of the simpler rooms was extortionate; I can't imagine what Chantel was paying for the Penthouse Suite. Even though she had expensive taste, she could afford it.

Since she signed to this London agency, Chantel has been working in America and across a few countries around Europe. Soon she'd be rubbing shoulders with the likes of the world's top models; as she informed me on the phone yesterday, the agency was going to upgrade her contract to Supermodel status. No matter what job she takes on from here on in, Chantel will receive £193 per step she takes on a catwalk.

She informed me that within six months to a year, she would become so famous, she'd probably need a bodyguard or two when making public appearances.

Both Nina and I were so elated and ecstatic for her. Above a lot of people, I know she deserves it, after all, the sacrifice, lost friendships and even some family members when in her early days she did a few spreads in some mainstream men's magazines.

But it's a testament to her willpower that she got through the non-figurative horrors she'd had to deal with, coming up the ranks. For women like us, we have to do double the work, twice the advertising and promotion to get a sniff of the pie, let alone have a bite.

Chantel could finally now say to all the doubters, haters and non-believers she has made it, and I as her best friend couldn't be more proud of her, and that's why I'm so animated to see her.

When we made our way from the car park, we walked through the back entrance and continued until we reached the reception area.

When Nina and I walked up to the desk, a beautiful young lady with brunette hair and a pleasant smile greeted us.

"Good afternoon and welcome to the London Hilton hotel. How may I be of assistance to you?"

"Hi, yes," Nina said. "We have a dear friend of ours staying here. But we're not sure what room she is staying in."

"Okay, let me have a look," the receptionist said as she turned her attention to the PC situated in front of her. "What is the name of your friend?" She asked.

"Her name is Chantel Porter," I commented.

"Thank you, ma'am," she said back as she began tapping away on her keyboard. "I found her, Miss Chantel Porter. Would you like me to ring her room and inform her you're waiting down here?"

"We would prefer to go upstairs. If you just give us Miss Porter's room number so we can go there." I asked.

"I'm sorry ma'am, for security reasons we have to call the customers first."

"We understand miss! My friend is getting a little ahead of herself,"

"It's okay ma'am! Is it your first time visiting?" she asked as she rang Chantel's room.

"Yes, it is."

"That's okay then!"

As the receptionist proceeded to call Chantel's room, Nina and I got involved in some small talk of our own.

"Miss Porter said she'll be down in a few minutes. You can take a seat opposite if you like or if you prefer there's a bar further on. I will inform her you're there if you decide to go."

"Thank you," Nina said. "Let her know we will be waiting in the bar, ready, with her favourite drink."

"I will certainly do that; take care now."

Nina and I proceeded to make our way to the bar. On the way, I told her I needed the ladies toilets and that I would catch her up.

Five minutes later, I caught up with her. She was sitting at the bar, engaging in what looked like some heavy chatter with the barman, followed by laughter.

As I got nearer to where she was seated, Nina spotted me and ushered me to move real quick to where she was.

"Erykah; come, come my friend, I want you to meet someone very dear," she said as she tried to Marshall me to speed up my walk by raising her voice a few octaves and waving her left arm frantically. In my mind, I thought why the considerable urgency.

"I'm coming; I'm coming," I said back as I picked up my pace.

"Come, girl, take a seat, settle yourself," she said. It was almost like she was mothering me.

"What's with all the frenetic behaviour, Nina?" I questioned.

"Erykah; I want you to meet a very dear friend of mine." As she pointed and looked towards the barman.

"Greetings Miss Gaines," the barman said as his eyes lit up and his smile was one of a courteous nature.

"Hi, nice to meet you," as I extended my hand to meet his. As he came to meet mine, he took hold for around ten seconds, not letting go as he held my gaze for longer. I could feel him; it was like he was scanning me all over, not in a sexual way, but more like he was pouring wholesome energy into me. It felt quite magical and refreshing.

By the time he let go of my hand, I sat down next to Nina; I began to feel euphoric and a bit light-headed but in a good way.

"Erykah; this is Troy; he is Calvin's younger cousin and also works as an Events Promoter for the Resistance movement. Troy, this is Erykah Gaines, my best friend from Manchester."

"Greetings, once again, Miss Gaines."

"Same to you Troy," he stood around 6' 2" tall, was muscular in stature and had a flock of locks just past his neckline. He spoke with an accent that I couldn't pinpoint straight away.

"So, Troy, what's going on with you? Why are you doing this job?"

"Being smart Nina."

"Oh, and how's that coming along?"

"It's simple! I got a job here so I could butter up the Events Co-ordinator to do future Resistance events."

"Good thinking. It's so prodigious of you that you're trying to push the movement into new directions."

"Sister Nina; it's not just about the continuation of black awareness; it's also about letting the enemy within see we are consciously waking up."

"Troy I've known you for some time now, and I know you don't do things half-cut."

"Ain't that the truth? So, how you been keeping Sister Nina?"

"I'm doing well. The creative writing classes are going well, and my Spoken Word gigs are too."

"So, you're getting paid?"

"That's a misconception. But I'm doing alright, thank you for asking."

"Good! So Miss Erykah what brings you to our wonderful cosmopolitan capital?" He said while clearing his throat loudly.

"How well do you know this brother Nina?" I asked as he looked at me then Nina with a bemused look on his face.

"He is good people. You can tell him anything."

"How much time you got?" I asked sternly.

"As long as you want. My shift finishes at 5 pm,"

"Well Troy; unfortunately for you, I don't have that luxury right now, because we are waiting for our dear friend."

"No problem! Maybe another time."

"I'll tell you what! I can give the bite-size version if you like?"

"That'll be cool! Go ahead."

"First things first Troy; how about a round of drinks?" Nina said, pitching in.

"What would you ladies like?"

"Mm…I, fancy, something outlandish! Do you have a cocktail menu?"

"I got the perfect drink for you, ladies. I'll make three of them right now. You won't be disappointed!"

While Troy began fixing our drinks, within a few moments, Chantel hysterically came crashing into the bar. By her startling me which at first nearly had me jumping out of my skin if that's possible.

"Erykah; Nina," she said first as she hurtled at some speed to where we were seated.

"Chantel," I screamed out loud in the highest pitched voice I could muster. Within seconds I was hugging my other best friend in the world, and instantly I felt a surge of good energy pour into me again.

Chantel was grinning and crying tears of joy. I held on until I couldn't anymore.

"Oh my gosh, Erykah; look at you. You're looking fly, girl."

"Erm look at you, 'LOOK AT YOU', Miss I'm a soon to be Celebrity Supermodel!"

"Well, what can I say? You either got it, or you haven't," she said with the most confident look on her face. "Nah, I'm just fucking wit y'all."

"Check you out! Talking all American and shit! What state does that accent hail from?"

"Los Angeles, baby!"

"Ite, I got ya!"

"So what's all this, cocktails at noon?"

"Don't blame me! That's Nina's fault."

"Excuse me; I don't think so!"

"Yes, teacher, watch you now!"

"Erykah; leave her be."

"It's all good. Chantel."

"So, what's good with you, Erykah?"

"Today I'm feeling fine only because you're here, Hun!"

"Ah babe, that's so sweet of you. So, Nina, how are you babes?"

"I'm fine, Chantel; how have you been yourself?"

"Well, as you can see, life is pretty good for me at the moment. But on the flip side, I'm gravely concerned about what is happening to our people over in the states, especially our young black men."

As Nina was about to open her mouth, Troy interjected and tried to take over the conversation.

"Ladies, may I contribute some valuable information to your conversation?" As he handed over our cocktails, we took residence on the bar stools.

"Yes, go ahead, Troy," Nina replied.

"Life in the 21st century isn't always easy to survive in. We live in an age of fear. Fear of what's happened in the past, fear of what's to come and fear of the unknown. In today's society which is governed by a group of elite families that misdirect us from our true paths, they do this by selling us propaganda that brainwashes and pollutes our minds. Someone like Calvin and myself exist because of this. But within the black community, we co-exist because of the tribulations that are affecting our people daily. Like, for example, our fellow black men getting killed and caught up in the police brutality cycle that is sanctioned by the bosses of a country's government. This is known in conspiracy circles as 'The Rise of the Police state' which entails in giving more authority and power to their institution. They do this because everything they have thrown at us, we rise from, for example, the biggest being slavery. So their biggest fear is us finding a way to take power and control back and do to them what they have been doing to us for centuries. But as easy that would be to do, as a nation, overall, we ain't built lie that. We don't seek revenge! All we want is redemption, freedom, retribution and our lands and riches back. We call that reparations? But last and at not least we want one humungous apology."

"Personally, I don't think every black person, young or old. Would except any attempt of an apology, ever!"

"You may be right there, Sister Nina."

"That, Troy. Is a forgone conclusion."

When Troy had finished educating the three of us twenty minutes later. We finished up our drinks and left the hotel at around 14:23 pm.

For the rest of the afternoon, Chantel took Nina and me couture shopping. After we had finished, we ate dinner at an elegant looking Italian restaurant called Camano's.

STAND IN YOUR POWER

Later that evening, I decided I would step up my activism work in getting involved in priority projects within the black community. My first port of call will be protests and marches, but, I would quadruple my pursuit in joining the Resistance movement.

Chapter 17 – Blast from The Past

When I was younger, my father told me that Sunday's were a day of rest. No shops were open, except for the Asian man's sweet shop. I remember questioning 'Why', and he said some mumbo jumbo to me, it was something to do with the beginning of creation. Well, in my life at present, Sunday's have become a day of celebration in many forms.

Today was the day I was taking Donte to meet my extended family.

As I sat on the edge of my bed, I couldn't help but contemplate on how I thought everyone would perceive him. I know Uncle Sebastian will like him for making a success of his business ventures. That was a male egotistical thing.

Aunt Lola would probably like him for being a family man and the twins, well, just because I love him. Also with Danika; because he is Trae's brother.

I also got the approval to invite Donte's sister Syreena; I told her if she wanted it was cool to ask Simeon if he wanted to come along too.

As I got up from my bed, I walked towards my bedroom door and grabbed my nightgown of it.

As I began making my way downstairs, I spotted Nina coming out of her room.

"Morning, Nina."

"Morning."

"Heavy night was it?"

"Not heavy. I got in late. I was having a lengthy discussion with Calvin, Troy and Kyndra about the next resistance event."

"What's it going to be about?"

"Oh, the big matter of importance about the War on Blacks!"

"Serious t'ings, Nina!"

"Yeah, very serious!"

"Cool."

"So how are you? What you up to today?"

"Family meal at Aunt Lola's house."

"Ah, that's nice. Is Donte going?"

"Sure is!"

"Okay."

"So what about yourself?"

"I'm having a lazy day today."

"Why! Are you not performing tonight?"

"Yes, I am! I thought I'd take it easy until this afternoon. Then I'll probably go for a run, grab a snack on the way to the venue, and after that, I'm going for a meal with Kyndra."

"Ah, how is she these days? Baby should be dropping any day now."

"She's good. I think Kyndra has got four weeks to go."

"That's good to hear. Tell Kyndra I said hi and I'll link-up with her soon."

"Will do! What time is Donte picking you up?"

"Around midday," I said as I looked down at my phone. "Oh, my days is that the time already; 10:55 pm and I haven't even eaten breakfast yet."

"Tell you what! You go shower and get ready, and I'll make you your favourite."

"Are you sure, Nina? I don't wanna put you out."

"It's fine babes. You go, and I'll have it ready for you when you come back down."

"Bless you. Love you," I said as I began to make my way back upstairs.

"Love you too, Pooki," I heard her shout out.

Forty-five minutes later, and I was ready to go. Donte hadn't reached yet. So I decided to give him a call.

"Where are you, baby?"

"I'm two minutes from you."

"Ite, see you in a bit. Love you."

"Love you too gorgeous."

I said my goodbyes to both Nina and Eric and wished them both a good day and then I went to wait for Donte outside of the house.

A few moments later and Donte pulled up in his brand new Mercedes S-Class S63.

"Hey, hey, look at you," Donte said to me as he was getting out of his car.

I didn't move from my spot because Donte was all up in my personal space before I could.

"Hey, baby," I said.

"Hello my Nubian Princess," he said, sounding very chipper as he softly grappled my waist. I smiled so hard, and then I leant forward to meet his lips with mine.

We kissed and caressed each other for a few minutes and then we made our way into the car.

As I got myself into the passenger side and sat myself down, I began to make myself a little more comfortable. I opened up the mirror so I could adjust my hair and touch up my make-up.

Donte got in the car a few moments after me.

"You ready to go?" He questioned.

"Yes, babe," I answered as he put the key in the ignition and turned it.

As the car came into life, Donte looked over at me and smiled. He held his gaze for around ten seconds then, after he took his eyes off me and began to pull away.

Our first stop was back to Donte's house, where Trae, Syreena, and Simeon were waiting.

Five minutes later, we were pulling up outside his house. Donte beeped his horn several times, and within twenty seconds, the three of them all came out chatting and laughing together as they came towards the car.

"Yes, yes," Trae said first as he manoeuvred his tall frame into the car and sat in the seat behind Donte.

"Morning Trae, how's you?" I asked back.

"Man's bless. What you saying?"

"Feeling fine," I said in a dream-like tone.

"That's what I'm talking about."

"Hey girl," I said to Syreena who had the biggest smile ever, her teeth, glistening, off the sun's reflection.

"Hey Erykah," she said, exemplifying the words. As she leaned over through the seats, I turned to meet her hug and kisses with my own.

"Sup Donte, Erykah?" Simeon reiterated.

"I'm good," I said back.

"Yes, mi bredda," Donte added.

"Everybody ready?" I asked.

"Yes, yes, yes," I got a unanimous thumbs up from all three. So we were good to go. As we began our journey to Chelsea, I couldn't help but think how things were slowly turning around in my favour and believe me I'm going to cherish every moment that brings me joy. I needed all the support I could get at the moment because tomorrow was the first day of my court case against Racist. A big part of me didn't want to face that motherfucker, but a small part wanted to see what he had to say.

Donte got from Brixton to Chelsea Bridge in less than fifteen minutes. We went over the bridge and crossed onto the other side with minimal fuss.

We drove on furthermore passing famous historical monuments such as The State Rooms and The London Wall Walk to the more modern types like Altissima House.

I asked Donte to stop at the next available convenience store so I could get us some snacks and sweets.

When we located a spot, Donte parked up outside. We had ended up on Fulham Broadway. I got out with a list of things I needed to get in my head. As I quickly marched towards the entrance of the store, a brother, who looked around thirty-something dressed in an expensive-looking Adidas tracksuit was coming through in the opposite direction.

For a few moments it looked like he was trying to stall me from getting inside and I didn't know why? I inched a few steps closer, but the guy stood his ground. Immediately I felt myself getting angry, but I quickly remembered Aunt Lola's pep talk, so I calmed myself down as fast as I became irate.

"Excuse me please," I said, sounding polite and respectful. "But you're in my way," I said, looking up at him. He stood around 6' 3 or 4 inches tall, and he had a relaxed demeanour about his nature, but that doesn't excuse his lack of respect for me.

"I think you'll find I have the right of way. So technically you're in my way," he said so boldly and brashly with the cockiest smile I've ever seen.

"Okay, Mr I'm trying to keep my cool here. But you're trying my patience now."

"Still the same old feisty Erykah. You haven't changed one bit."

STAND IN YOUR POWER

All of a sudden, I felt a cold vibe go through me. I felt my right-hand ball up into a fist, ready, to launch into this motherfucker. As I was about to, it dawned on me on what he just said as he sidestepped out of my way. As I continued to walk inside, I turned around and met him still gazing and smiling hard at me, but with his arms folded this time.

"What the fuck. How you know my name?"

Shaking his head he continued to say, "You tell mi seh yuh nah recognise your first ever crush?"

"Andrew!" I said in disbelief. "Is that you?" I continued to speak. My heart was pounding in time with the frenzied lunacy that had suddenly succumbed in my mind.

"Yes, it's me!" He said, putting one hand on my shoulder.

"Oh my gosh, you gotta be kidding me. Da fuck you doing here?" I said in astonishment. I leant forward and gave him an immense hug.

"I relocated to London around six years ago."

"No kidding? You are the last person I'd ever thought who would leave Manchester behind."

"I can say the same about you. What you doing in London?"

"Many reasons. But the main one is that I needed a new direction and some purpose to my life."

"I feel you. Was kind of the same for me."

"So what do you do for living?"

"I run my chain of vehicle maintenance garages. I got around four in operation at the moment and three more in the pipeline opening within the next six months to a year."

"No, shit! What's your business called?"

"Nothing fancy kept it simple. I called it Drew's Auto Repair Centre."

"Oh wow, Drew, that's you? Come to think of it. On my travels, I've seen one around in Streatham. I'd never known or guessed in a million years you owned it, damn!"

"Why would you have? It's been around fifteen years since we last saw each other."

"Really? That long, hey!"

"Yep, I'm afraid so."

"Wow."

"Anyway, how's Winston these days?"

"He's doing well. But he is still working out of the same garage."

"No, shit? I can believe that. Winston is the tightest and most workaholic boss I've ever had."

"Isn't that the truth? Godfather use to come up with a measly £20 for my birthday and Christmas presents."

"I hope you mean £20 on both occasions?"

"Nah Drew; £20 shared, for both!"

"Damn, some people never change."

"I know, right. Anyway where you heading off to now?"

"I'm going home. I've got my accountant coming over later to mine to crunch numbers."

"Before you head off, come meet my boyfriend and his siblings. First, let me get the bits I came in here for. Follow me in."

"Okay, Pooki."

"Oh, gosh, you remembered?"

"For sure. I'll never forget!"

"It's so good to see you tho Drew. I must get your number."

"I still got the same number."

"Really? I kept transferring your number every time I brought a new phone just in case and here you are."

"Here I am."

"I still can't believe it. What are the odds?"

"I don't know. Maybe I'll ask my accountant later."

"You joker, still bussing them as you use too."

"Well, what can I say? You either got it, or you haven't."

"Ha, ha, yep, you should've been a comedian instead."

"Funny you should say that."

"Why?"

"I'm going to apply to next year's BGT,"

"For real?"

"I'm not joking. I'm deadly serious!"

"Shit! So you are. I remember that face from when we were young."

"Then you dun know?"

"Oh yeah, I dun know!"

"It's so good to see you. I must say you're looking healthy."

"Thanks'. You're looking well too. Do you work out? I said as I picked out the last of the refreshments.

"Yes, religiously. Maybe two to three times a week."

"That's great. Here, take this!" As I handed him my business card.

"What's this? You're a deputy manager."

"Yeah Drew; my boyfriend is the owner of the place. Come let's go meet them," I said as we walked out the store together. As we continued our walk back towards the car, we engaged in some small talk about the past that had me laughing my head off. At the same time, I clocked Donte staring at me with a screwface to boot. I quickly blew him a kiss and gave him the signal that we had between us that told him he had nothing to worry about. Soon as the screw came to be on his face, it turned back into a smile. That was the moment I breathed a huge sigh of relief. Drew walked with me and said no more. As we both reached the car, Donte signalled for me to go around to where he was.

"Hey babe," I said with the most innocent of looks when I reached to his side. Donte wound down his window and looked up at me with a perplexed look on his face.

"What's going on, who's the dude?"

"That's Andrew; he is a childhood friend of mine from Manchester. He relocated to London around six years ago to open a vehicle maintenance garage. He was telling me at the moment he owns and runs four of them and has another three in the pipeline he'll be opening within the next six months to a year. He's a cool brother, business-minded like you and I know you two will get on."

"Ite babe, don't leave a brother standing there looking lost. Go to him, and I'll follow you in a minute."

"Alright honey," I said as I leant into the car and kissed him on the lips.

After I finished with the smooches, I walked back over to where Drew was waiting patiently. All of a sudden, my belly began to pang. My energy levels were starting to wane. I needed some food real quick.

"Yo, Drew, where can a girl get some decent grub around here?"

"I was on my way to get some lunch myself,"

"Oh, good."

"I sometimes go to the Oyster rooms further down the road from here."

"Then Oyster rooms it is. Lemme see if the others are up for it."

But before I could say anything else, Donte and the others got out the car and came to where Drew and I were standing.

"Everybody, this is Andrew."

"Hey, everyone."

"Drew this is my boyfriend, Donte."

"Sup Gee?" Donte said as he grabbed Drew's hand and pulled him in for a shoulder to shoulder greeting bump.

"These two gorgeous people are Trae and Syreena. They are Donte's younger siblings and last, but not least this is Simeon who is Syreena's boyfriend."

"Yes, fam," Trae said while giving him a fist bump.

"Nice to meet you, Andrew!" Syreena said politely.

"Greetings," Simeon said with only a nod of the head.

"It's a pleasure to meet you all."

"So, Drew, lead the way bro," Donte said.

"Follow me then."

Five minutes later and we were all standing at the main bar of the Oyster rooms. Syreena vacated to the ladies room, while Trae and Simeon went to find a table for us to order food.

After a little while, Trae texted saying they were seated at table thirty-four and with their orders too.

While we were ordering the drinks, Syreena came back and immediately picked up a menu and began scanning it thoroughly.

"Erykah; can you order me the Californian burger with buttermilk chicken and a double Southern Comfort and lemonade with ice and a slice of lemon."

"Alright, Syreena the guys are at table thirty-four."

"Cool, see you over there," as she took out some money from her purse. She went to hand over £30. But before she could give it to me, Donte stepped in and stopped her.

"Sis put your money back in your purse. I got this."

"Are you sure, Bro?"

"I'm sure, Syreena. Your good!"

"Ah, thank you so much, D," she said as she leant in and gave him a hug and a peck on the cheek. "Love you."

"Love you too lil' Sis. I always got you. Now get over there to your man."

"Deuces Donte," she wrapped up saying as she took her ass over to where the other guys were.

It was so sweet the love the Williams family showed each other. But I especially know how protective Donte is over Syreena.

You see when they were younger, Donte told me one time when he was twenty-two, and Syreena just turned sixteen. How like usual on a Friday he would go over to his parent's house for dinner. At that time and still to this day Syreena and Trae still vacate there. He came on over this particular Friday only to find three guys had followed Syreena home from the supermarket and forced her to let them all into the family home. At first, Syreena was reluctant, but when one of them branded a U.S made spring-powered ballistic knife. She had no option but to keep her mouth shut and comply. When Donte got there, he immediately sensed something was up. At first, he could hear the muffled sounds of male voices coming from upstairs. Straight away Donte thought it was Trae and a couple of his bredrin's. But same way he went to investigate on a hunch and when he got upstairs and checked on Trae's room and realised his brother wasn't home. Donte knew it was Syreena's room and boy wasn't she in for hiding if he caught her with a boy in the house when his mother weren't home yet. When Donte got to the foot of her door with a baseball bat at hand that he grabbed from Trae's room, he could hear different voices. Immediately Donte went into a mission-ready mode. Firstly he began knocking on the door; there was no answer. He then called out, and on doing so, Syreena screamed and cried out as loud as she could for her brother to help her. Donte didn't need a second reply. Her door was locked so he kicked it off its hinges. When he got into the room, he sighted three youths around 19-20 years old—hovering around her bed. As they turned to face him, Donte, unexpectedly he didn't recognise any of the youths. When they moved out of the way, Syreena was lying on her back completely naked. The guy that was standing nearest to her had calmly put his dick back in his brief, as they all stood there nonchalantly in their brief like everything was cool. When Syreena cried out again, he wasted no time and didn't hesitate. He went for the guy standing over his sister first. The guy immediately pulled out his knife from the jacket he had on the bed and began waving it around in the air as it made swish noises which got Donte vexed. The second and third guy held a struggling Syreena down as they continued to rape her in front of him and that was the point when Donte woke up only to find the three guys were all knocked out around him. There was a lot of blood coming from underneath the first guy. The other two were lying out cold at the far end of the room. Donte didn't either bother checking on them; he left them as they were. Somehow he single-handily managed to take out Syreena's attackers. They both sat there cradling each other for about half an hour until Donte's Mother Meredith and Trae came home only to find a distraught Syreena crying in her brother's arms, still naked, other than her quilt to cover her body. Donte was numb with nothing else other than a expressionless gaze on his face with three bodies bleeding out on the floor around them.

So that was their family secret that has never been told outside their circle apart from pretty little me. From whence I was told, I was immediately entrusted with the information after I swore never to tell a soul and that gave me a helluva lot of confidence when it came to my relations with Donte and the rest of the Williams clan and most recently the gym saga and the cover-up. Nuff said.

"Ah, you two are too adorable," I concluded on that point.

"Cool, baby, appreciate the love."

"So the boys and Syreena have made their orders. What are you two guys having?"

"What did the boy's order babe?"

"They both ordered the same thing. It was the 14oz Aberdeen Angus steak."

"I'll have the same and a pint of grapefruit juice."

"Okay! What about you Drew?"

"Erm, em, I don't want to get what I religiously have. That would be boring."

"What's that then?"

"Oh, I usually get the Peri-Peri chicken breast with pepper skewers."

"Mm, that sounds tasty?" I think that's what I'm going to have."

"I recommend it. It's juicy and filling."

"Cool, I like the sound of how it feels. I'm sold. So what about you, finally?"

"I will have a Flaming dragon curry please and take this." as Drew handed me £100.

"It's alright bruh, hold on to your peas!"

"Seriously, it's no problem. I want to."

"I tell you what guys after you leave you egos over there. Why don't you both satisfy them and go 50/50 on it, okay."

"I'm cool with that," Donte stated.

"Me too," as they both handed me 50 pounds each.

"What drink are you having with yours Drew?"

"Get me a double dark rum and black!" Drew concluded saying as Donte, and he walked back to the table where the others were engrossed in deep conversation.

STAND IN YOUR POWER

It was nice to see someone positive from my past get on with someone special in my present.

After I finished making the orders and paying for them, over the next hour and a half, all six of us enjoyed our meals, and we all had the most mixed and frank conversations about our lives and what's happening to our black men in the States and in the UK.

By the end of it all, we all concluded we could help ourselves by living life as positively as permitted and to spread great vibrations as much as we can wherever we all go and end up.

Chapter 18 – Family

We pulled into Aunt Lola's and Uncle Sebastian's mansion courtyard at around 2:25 pm.

I was still feeling full from lunch, but Aunt Lola texted me on the way saying dinner was to be served at around 4:30 pm sharp. To my relief, that sounded gravy to me.

We left Andrew at the Oyster rooms at around 1:50 pm. I made a promise to him that we will link up soon and do something fun with Donte and the gang as well.

As I moved out of the car, the rest followed suit. Trae was already upon the door, banging it down, and while he was waiting, he was doing his own little jig. I nudged Donte gently in his side, and when he caught my attention, I gave him the eyes and a smirk to look over in Trae's direction.

Instantaneously Donte and I began laughing together under our breaths. But the more Trae jigged, the louder our hysterics became.

At the peak of our giggle-fest, our infectious laughter caught on to Syreena and Simeon. Within seconds, the four of us were either crying or guffawing so hard that I had to sit back down in the car so I could catch myself for a minute.

As I tried, Trae turned around and asked what we all found so amusing.

"Yo, where's the joke people?"

"You're the joke bro." Syreena relayed.

"What the heck you talking about sis?" Trae said, sounding off seriously.

"Bro, take it easy," Donte added. "We're just laughing at your antics."

"Ite, okay, I knew that," Trae replied, looking like he'd been caught doing something he shouldn't be.

A little time later and someone opened the door. As we began to descend on the mansion, out came an ecstatic Danika as she flew and jumped on to Trae. Luckily for her, Trae was alert. She began kissing him all over his face and head and squeezing him real tight.

Trae was still holding her like a baby. When Nika finished with the smooches, she gently rested her head on Trae's shoulder. Instantly a few tears flowed from her eyes as a bemused Trae continued to hold and comfort her.

"Damn shorty, you acting like you ain't seen a nigger in a minute."

"You know I haven't and stop referring yourself to the N-word," she said seriously hitting him on the arm.

"Bae it's only been a week."

"Exactly and a long one at that," she said as she released herself from his grip. Trae said no more to Nika's actions. As we all finished watching in awe, we continued our walk to the main door. Donte took hold of my hand, while Syreena and Simeon were close behind us.

"Whoa, your cousin is a bit full-on baby?"

"That's Danika for you. When she loves a man, she loves hard. She's an intelligent sister and pulls no punches. Trae's in good company, trust me."

"Ite babe, if you say so. That's cool wid me."

"It better be," I said, giggling back at him. He gave me one of his formidable smiles which told me thing's between us was copasetic.

When we arrived to the foot of the door, Danika quickly turned her attention onto Donte and me.

"Erykah," she said, screaming my name out loud as she threw out her arms for me to embrace.

"Hey, Nika; what's good cuz?" I said back as I leaned forward and met her greeting.

"I'm chill. So this must be the infamous Donte; it's finally nice to meet you, sir?"

"Sup, it's good to meet you too," Donte offered out his hand for Nika to shake. But she wasn't having any of that. Danika bypassed Donte's offering of a greeting and threw herself onto him and embraced him, hard. As she did, more tears came streaming out of her eyes.

Danika was acting very peculiar towards someone she just met. It was a far cry for her usual staunch, steady and robust personality. Straightaway Donte could sense something was up. He pulled back from her and held onto her upper arms with a bewildered look on his face. Trae and the others looked mystified and me, myself, I was as baffled as all their responses.

"Nika what's up? Why are you crying, love?"

"Because it's the way," she said in between sniffles. "He has treated and loved you so far. The example he sets his siblings, and most of all, is a self-made man."

"Damn cuz, is that how are you going on?"

"Bless Danika; that's a strong complement for someone you hardly know!"

"Yeah, cuz it is and chillax you, pessimists. I'm just giving your man his dues."

"Well thanks' again, Danika. I better make sure I don't falter then. I wouldn't wanna get on the wrong side of you?" Donte said with a smirk etched on his face.

"That's right, Donte; don't be fooled by this pretty face and cool demeanour," she said back half in a joke like way and the other half-seriously.

If there is one thing, I've learned about men over the years. Is that they need more nurturing than we women do.

"Are you all going to hot up my porch or are you coming in today?" There it was, the voice of reason. My beautiful Aunt Lola, looking amazing, stood a few inches inside the doorway and commanded us to hurriedly get our black asses inside.

"We're coming right now, Auntie." Right behind, Aunt Lola stood Uncle Sebastian.

"Hi, Erykah," he said as he sidestepped around Auntie and grabbed me into him.

"Uncle Sebastian, it's so good to see you."

"It's great you all came. So this is, 'Mr I never stop mentioning about him all the time, Williams?'"

"Mr Briscoe," Donte said as he outstretched his hand for Uncle to shake.

"No need to be so formal son, I insist you call me Sebastian," Uncle said while returning Donte's greeting.

"No problem, Sebastian," Donte said, chuckling.

"Auntie, Uncle, these other beautiful people are Syreena who is Donte and Trae's baby sister and Simeon who is Syreena's boyfriend." Simeon handed over a bunch of mixed flowers to Aunt Lola. Which instantly put a smile on her face.

"What a lovely young gentleman you are Simeon? Look at this Sebastian a modern-day young man upholding chivalry on his own."

Aunty fondly said as she smelt the flowers, Simeon gave her.

"I can see Lola, and it's just wonderful," Uncle said, responding to Aunties statement.

"You're welcome, Mrs Briscoe, that's just how I roll. You only have to ask Syreena that."

"He's been the best boyfriend I've ever had so far," Syreena said backing up Simeon's statement.

Aunt and Uncle both smiled and then turned to go inside. We all followed suit, walking in our respective pairs, all looking buoyant and content.

When we reached further inside by a double staircase that reared in a half-circular motion from left to right, we were all greeted by a butler. He called himself Jameson and was a lot older looking than Aunt and Uncle.

He was black and stood around 5'10" and was of stocky build. His nature and the directness of his voice gave off the impression he'd been a soldier or higher ranked officer in the armed forces.

After he took our coats, Uncle lead us into what I could only describe as the largest living room I've ever had the privilege to step foot in. It was at least a quarter of the size of a standard football pitch.

Aunt Lola said she was going into the kitchen to check on the state of dinner. Danika asked to be excused until dinner while she and Trae went disappearing upstairs.

"Come on in everyone, make yourselves at home." Uncle Sebastian offered up.

While Syreena and Simeon had an amble around, Donte and I chilled with Uncle Sebastian when Aunt Lola came back with Jameson, who was holding a tray of champagne and orange juice.

"Dinner will be served in forty-five minutes people," Auntie said as she settled herself down on a luxurious leather three-seater sofa. "Erykah, come sit next to your Auntie. Let me see you?" As I did, Donte took a seat on an armchair, while Uncle sat in his favourite black velvet chair. Uncle pulled out of what I could only describe as the most enormous Cuban cigar I've ever comprehended. I probably was going to see a lot of them when I get to Brazil. Jameson handed out the champagne. Only Donte, took, an orange juice as he was driving. "So, niece, what's going on in your life since I last saw you?"

"Well, quite a lot Aunt Lola. I got my court case starting tomorrow."

"Oh, yes, of course, you have. Well, not to worry. At least one of us every day until it's over will be there to support you."

"Ah, that's great Auntie! With you lot and Donte's lot, I'll have a united front of support behind me."

"Oh, Erykah, before I forget. I've arranged for Marcus to come over after dinner. He told me he was going to meet you an hour before the court case and he probably still will. But I advised him he'd do you better justice if he came and prepared you from tonight. Is that cool?"

"Uncle Sebastian you didn't have to do that," I said as I got up and he followed suit. I walked over to him and Auntie respectfully and embraced these beautiful people I had the fortune to have in my life.

"You're welcome Erykah, also if you will accept this." Uncle reached his right hand into the left inside of his jacket pocket and pulled out two pieces of paper. He took them both in his hands and unfolded them one by one, and then he handed both of them over to me.

As I opened up the first, it was a cheque for £10,000 payable to Marcus. The other one was for £60,000 and was payable to me. Immediately I was flabbergasted as I showed Donte too. His eyes lit up with bemusement as I tried to wrap my head around it.

At that precise moment, Syreena and Simeon sauntered back into the living room.

"Uncle, I, I, I don't understand," I said, still standing there in disbelief. Syreena came over and put her left hand on my right shoulder for comfort. Simeon went and stood next to Donte.

"Well, the first one is obvious. It's for Marcus's fees for the court case and the arrest. Your father told your Aunt and me last week that your money is tied up in a fund until your thirtieth birthday. Marcus needs paying, so your Aunt and I have got that covered for you if you accept that?"

"What do you think, Uncle? Yes, I gladly accept."

"Good, that's settled." As he sat back down in his chair and had a couple of tugs from his cigar.

"Has anyone got a cigarette please?" I said in dire need of one. My nerves needed calming down as I was feeling overwhelmed with happiness inside.

"Baby, what are you doing?"

"Please, Donte, I just want one."

"Erykah, here, take one of mine." Auntie handed me her box and a lighter. I took one out, light it up, took a pull and exhaled, and after a moment I gave them back to her.

"Wow Erykah, your family is amazing," Syreena said, whispering in my ear.

"Thank you." I murmured back.

"So, Uncle, what's the second one for?"

"Let me answer that love?" Auntie said to Uncle.

"Sure, go ahead, honey."

"Erykah, do you remember what you said to me when you first came to see me when you got to London?"

"I said a lot of things, Auntie. Was it something significant?"

"Well, to you it was very substantial and something you want to do when you get your money, but you said you're too impatient to wait."

"Oh, you ain't frigging serious right now? Donte are they serious?"

"Are you guys serious?" He repeated for me.

"Erykah, honey that money is for you to put a down payment on a mortgage for a flat like you wanted. Your Uncle will help you find the best value for money mortgage brokers and area you want to live in. The extra £10,000 is to help kit out your crib as you young ones say."

"By the time you reach thirty years of age in three years. My advice is that you can choose to buy your place outright or sell it and make a huge profit. Who knows by then, Donte and yourself will have a comfortable nest egg to help buy your own house and get married. After all, these were the things you told your Aunt what you guys wanted. We're helping you with the first steps on getting on that property ladder."

"Uncle Sebastian, Aunt Lola, I don't know what to say other than, thank you, from the bottom of my heart. I don't know what I've done to deserve this, but once again guy's thank you so much, this means the world to me."

"Erykah, it's well documented around the family the rough start you've endured in your young life. But since the day you obtained your degree, everyone was proud of you and from then on you've done nothing else other than trying to better yourself and have tried a credulous amount of times to get yourself out of the slumbers that have consumed your existence. Since you have been in London, you have bettered circumstances for yourself! I'm not going to list what's obvious already. But you, young lady, have earned the right to be given a chance to become whatever you want to be. Because as your favourite Uncle."

"And Aunt."

"Yes, honey and Aunty. Erykah, the both of us have faith in your aspirations and most importantly, we believe in you."

"Uncle, Aunty. Well what can I say to that? I love you both so much, thanks for the endorsement and your kind generosity."

On that note, I said no more and went on to enjoy the evening. At around 4:40 pm, we all settled down to eat dinner and engaged in small talk and deeper discussions. We were also joined by Daniel and Kira, who had announced the date of their engagement party. It was taking place on Saturday 3rd October 2015.

Shortly after dinner, Marcus came over, and we went through my final preparations for the case. If I weren't ready now, then I'd better be in the morning.

When everyone retired to another lounge that overlooked a massive garden that had a swimming pool and two tennis courts, Uncle and Donte got to talking about the restorations on the gym and the possibility in the future of opening up another one in central London, and that's where Donte's family were looking for investors. Uncle said he was interested in investing and had arranged a date to link up with Donte and his family to take the discussions further.

Daniel, Simeon, and Trae went off into the depths of the grounds until we couldn't see them anymore, probably to have a smoke in peace.

That left Aunt Lola, Kira, Danika, Syreena and I to discuss Daniel's and Kira's forthcoming party and a little bit more about my case. They all said seeing it was my first day; they all wanted to be there to support me.

I was thankful and blessed for that, and it gave me great mental strength. But on the inside, I was petrified as hell, but as a Gaines woman, I wasn't going to let them or the world, see me as someone, who is weak. That isn't our family's style.

STAND IN YOUR POWER

Chapter 19 – Judgement Day

When I woke up this morning, I felt inspired and apprehensive at the same time. Today would mark the day of the beginning to the end of my civil liberties and freedom if I were found guilty.

Then what would become of me in prison? A pretty thing like me would be prime juicy substance for all those sex-thirsty lesbians, and that isn't me. I don't divulge in such acts but nor am I against those that wish to practice it.

I never had parents to encourage me to do well and exceed their standards. That's why I turned out the way I have. I was shown no love, and I had no damn guidance. Well, that would completely be a lie, Uncle Jeb and Aunt CeCe was there for me when they thought I needed them, but they weren't there when I wanted them.

So, for a young black girl growing up how I did, in the hood, it wasn't good that I had to grind or beg for something beneficial to happen for me. That shit should be standard, but in most cases, it isn't.

As I sat on the edge of my bed, staring around my room, I took a few moments to evaluate where my life was heading at present.

On the positive side, I have an amazing man and career. I also have a blessed family and friends plus new acquaintances. I have a new interest I'm being pulled into and although all the things I've mentioned so far have been tainted with danger at some point. It seems the whole enchilada is getting back on track.

Yesterday, at Aunt and Uncles place, undeniably it was the best day of my life so far. I couldn't believe what they were doing for me?

As I got up from my bed and strode over to my chest of drawers, I pulled open the top drawer and stretched my hand inside. I took out the cheque that Uncle Sebastian had given me and began to marvel at this piece of paper as if it were magical in some form.

£60,000 is a lot of money for a girl like me, and I was so thankful for the start and faith they had in me, that boosted my confidence no end.

On the negative side, I have this damn court case against Racist aka Detective Charlie McCann, who epitomises the very essence of police brutality. For my sake, I hope they throw the book at him, but it's more than likely I'll be the one made to suffer.

Anyway, it was time to get a wriggle on and get my ass into gear. I had to be at court for 09:00 am and the time now was 06:07 am.

After I had my shower, I got dressed, when I finished the time was precisely 06:30 am.

I made my way downstairs to the distinctive ambiences of an English fry-up. I caught Nina laying the table, and at the same time, it sounded like she was reciting a new piece of poetry only because I've never heard it before.

"Good morning Nina."

"Hey! How are you feeling this morning?"

"Nervous, apprehensive, nervous."

"You said nervous twice. You really must be?"

"I am, I have no idea how things are gonna play out and besides you know how t'ings mostly go in situations like this. They will make a mockery of proceedings and make an example out of me while they're at it."

"Ain't that the truth. Amen to that."

"I know, right?"

"So, who is accompanying you to court?"

"Erm," I said. As I tried to think of who, while I was demolishing the contents of this bowl of cereal Nina had made for me. "Well, today, it's the girls coming. Those that have confirmed are my cousin Danika, Kyndra, Syreena and Kira and yourself if you can make it."

"You try and stop me?"

"I wouldn't dream of it," I finished saying as I leant my arm across the table and bumped fists with her.

"Right, I'm going to freshen up."

Ten minutes later and Nina came back.

"What time did you want to leave?"

"Are you driving?"

"Yes, I am."

"Okay, good. Let's say about 07:30 am."

"That'll be cool. See you in a bit."

"Okay, and thank you."

"No thanks needed, I'm here for you in any capacity you need me to be."

"I know girl, I know," I said with a lump in my throat. As I looked over at her, all of a sudden, I began to feel very emotional, again.

I felt the emotive lump beginning to swell, and my eyes began to fill with water. As I stood up, I remained glued to my spot. Before I knew it, Nina was upon me and had cradled me into her chest. Upon impact, I cried, and I cried until I was all cried out. Nina continued to comfort me by either patting my back or stroking my hair gently as you do to a baby and because I was feeling like one.

This singular moment was all the pent up emotions I had suppressed inside of me and every unscrupulous experience I had been through since I left Moss Side, was emerging out all in one go.

"Listen, don't worry. I got a feeling things are going to work out in your favour."

"Do you think so?"

"Yes, I do. So stop stressing, clear your head and when we get there, you walk into that court today as a young, proud, black woman that has nothing to fear okay."

"Okay!"

"That's the attitude. Now go get your black ass ready so we can get the hell out of here."

"I'm on it."

I emerged from the bathroom ten minutes later feeling rejuvenated and rearing to go in the best fashion I could muster. I looked at my phone and saw that the time was 07:23 pm. I quickly grabbed up my keys from the dresser and my coat from the back of my door and began to make my way downstairs.

As I began to descend, my phone pinged. I opened the phone and saw I had a text message from Donte; it read; 'Good luck baby...remember who and what you are and don't let them fool ya. I'll be thinking about you and there with you in spirit. I love you. Call me later.'

Ah, that was so sweet of him. I felt so lucky to have him as my man. Although more than often not, he would let me know, it was he who was the lucky one. I asked Donte how do you figure that one out, and he had said in time, I would see what he was saying is the truth. My response, I would shrug my shoulders and act like it wasn't that important to me. But secretly deep down it was.

Nina already was ready and was waiting for me by the front door.

I was ready as I could ever be. I took one last look and surveyed the house, from the roof to the floor.

When I finished, Nina and I walked the few metres to her car. Just as I was about to open the door, I remembered I left my lucky charm on my dresser. "Nina, give me two seconds. I just remembered I left Slinky in my room.

Start the car, and I'll be back quickly," Slinky was a small toy lion that could fit on a key ring.

I quickly ran back inside and upstairs. Slinky was where I thought he was, on my dresser. I grabbed the toy and was in and out of the house in less than a minute.

Nina was waiting for me in her car as I put my bag into the back of her boot.

"Did you manage to get your lucky charm then?" She asked clearly amused by my sudden moment of madness.

"Yes I did thanks, and I hope it will serve me in good stead."

"I'm sure it will. I feel it in the air."

"Yet again, as per usual. You're way more optimistic than I am."

"Well, someone has to be? We can't all be like you Erykah."

"What a damn right mess."

"No darling, someone who hasn't realised the massive potential they are."

"That's your teacher mode talking. Saying what I need to hear."

"It may be. But as your best friend who else is going to tell you the truth."

"You think I got what it takes to be someone great?"

"No! I think you got the swag to define greatness, period."

"Fuck out of here, Nina! Now I know you're chatting shit. Respect and all, but you ain't thinking straight."

"Alright Erykah; I know you don't believe, but God has a plan for you and trust me. I can feel something remarkable happening in your end game."

"Believing or not. I want to get through my first day with minimal retribution on my health and my sanity sister."

"Cool, let's get going." As Nina put her car into first gear and took off towards the direction of Southwark Crown Court where we will be meeting all the girls outside first.

A few minutes later and we were driving down Brixton-road. I decided I would map our journey, in case on other days I had to come on my own. Eight minutes after we first turned into Cranmer Rd. As we continued down Cranmer-road, we turned into Bolton Crescent and then swiftly into St Agnes place and then towards Kennington Park place. Nina turned right onto Kennington Park Place and then quickly onto Doddington Grove through to Manor Place then we turned left onto Walworth-road, followed through to Browning Street, Wadding Street and right onto Rodney road. After, we continued onto Catesby Street. A few moments later, we took Congreve street right through to Old Kent Road. Two minutes later and we were upon Tower Bridge road and drove to Bermondsey Street as we drove along we turned left onto Tooley Street we continued onto Battle Bridge Lane and drove the last stint and parked up by the Courthouse in English grounds.

As I exited the vehicle, I spotted my girls all huddled close together, waiting, outside of the archway of Southwark Crown court.

Danika was the first to sight us as Nina, and I strolled towards them.

As we rolled up upon them, she was the first to greet me.

"Hey, cuz, how you doing?"

"Hey Nik's, I could be better. But you know how it goes!"

"Don't I just," what she was referring to was a time in her teens when she was going through her rebellious stage. All the money in the world couldn't stop the temptation to see if she could steal some expensive makeup from a high-end West end store. She almost got away with it; if it weren't for the guy on the same counter as her befriending her by pretending to be buying perfume for his fiancé, instead he was a plainclothes security officer. Danika ended up doing community service as it was her first offence.

"Anyway ain't you suppose to be inside helping Marcus with the preparations?" I asked her.

"Yes! I wanted to catch you first and wish you the best of luck?"

"Ah, thanks cuz. I appreciate the work you've put into my case."

"It's my job. Marcus and I have built a great defence for you. I'm not an optimist. But in my professional opinion, I feel you'll only get a caution or community service."

"Well, let's hope you're right."

"You'll see. Right, ladies, I'm off. See you all inside. Erykah, love you cuz."

"Love you too."

"In a bit."

"Sister Kyndra, I'm so grateful you've made it. Please, any words of liberation right now would be most welcome," I said in all one mouthful without pausing. As I took a breath and then exhaled, I looked attentively into her eyes, awaiting her revelation to me.

"Erykah, Do you know what real progress is?"

"No."

" Progress is being at peace with all that makes you happy. Progress is respecting and still loving somebody based on their character and integrity even though they are different. It is not about focusing on our similarities and dismissing our individuality; it's about embracing what makes us who we are and being united and at peace with one another in that knowledge. Look, I love being black, and I embrace everything that comes with it: the pride, the culture and the struggles. I wouldn't want to be anybody else. Since when is difference so wrong? Why can't we fully love everything about a person? Why do we have to ignore something as significant as the core of our beings to be untied? All decent people have the right to be proud of who they are no matter what colour."

"Aww, I loved that Sister Kyndra, thanks."

"You do yourself right, Erykah. Remember, in the words of the late, great musical Icon that was Robert Nesta Marley. Him seh "Emancipate yourself from mental slavery."

"Bless you."

After I had greeted Syreena and Kira respectively, all of us made our way inside. As we walked around fifty feet from the front door, I spotted Marcus talking to what I can only describe as another lawyer.

Everyone has met Marcus already, so all the girls went inside the courtroom to take their seats.

I was ever so thankful for small mercies, as I analysed my surroundings. After a few moments when Marcus was finishing conversing with the unknown lady to me, he walked the few metres towards where I was sitting and patiently waiting.

"Erykah, how are you?" He said as he took the seat next to me.

"Well, I feel a lot better than I did this morning."

"Why, what has changed?"

"A beautiful remember who I am text from Donte and two great pep talks with Kyndra and Nina."

"That's good. It's great you got Kindred people around you to keep your spirits up."

"Sure is."

"Right it's time for your briefing. I got a room down the hall. So let's go. Follow me."

As I followed Marcus to the room, on my journey there, I spotted a family outside court three looking very upset.

"That's going to be our lot in a few hours." I pointed out.

"I don't think so Erykah. They look like their whole world has caved in."

"That's a damn shame," I said, shaking my head.

"Come on, stop staring and let's go."

We moved away from the scene as I took Marcus's arm in mine.

"How's Nicci and Tiffany?" I said, trying to deflect my attention away from my immediate crisis.

"Nicci received a promotion at work. She is now the Senior Vice-President of the logistics division and Tiff, she has one more year left at private school and says she is delighted. But with the youth of today, you never know? So that's why I make sure she gets the best nurturing I can muster. Nicci and I, we are looking at colleges from now. So they were both good the last time I checked."

"Ah, that's great news, Marcus! You must be proud?"

"I am. Now let's go and make you even more proud of me when I get you off," Marcus said as he opened the door to the room. Danika was already inside with her laptop open and a file of notes next to her as I followed behind him and walked towards the table and two empty chairs in the middle of the room.

I took my seat opposite Marcus and Danika. I couldn't help on getting this eerie feeling of criminality from the room. As quickly as I shook the feeling away, I instantly focused my attention on Marcus.

"Now, first things first. To prepare you, primarily I'm going to explain what to expect when you enter the courtroom. Secondly, I will go over the evidence and your version of events and based on your testament; I will form what I feel you should plea. Then on top of that, I will go through the charges, etc., okay?"

"Okay," I said as I shuffled a little nervously in my seat.

"Erykah, please don't worry. I promise in a few hours we will be laughing, and detective McCann will be facing charges, believe me."

"If that happens Marcus, I will forever be in your debt."

"Don't be silly. I'm your family's lawyer. I've helped many of your clan over the years. Plus I'm being paid handsomely for it. So it's all good. Now I need you to concentrate and follow everything I say and do from here on, understand?"

"Understood!"

"Good, I will now proceed."

As he took a few moments to gather his papers together, I started to think about mother Harriet. I was having a flashback and a clear one at that. I was remembering very well because it was 1992 and it was also my 4th birthday.

I was having a birthday party. I could see Uncle Jeb doing the music. Mother was nonchalantly drifting around always with a drink in one hand and a cigarette in the other. Kids were playing, dancing, laughing and making a general mess.

As I walked around with my blanket for comfort, I saw other adults, mainly family and friends of fathers and mother's who were mostly the children's parents.

After every other person either grab my cheeks or touched my hair and wished me a happy birthday, I got up off Godfather because I was thirsty and I wanted a drink.

As I got nearer to the kitchen, I could hear my dad talking in patios, but I didn't know who too.

As I turned the corner, I spotted Aunt CeCe as well. She seemed like she'd been crying because dad was consoling her by rubbing her arms every other second.

Then came the shock. Father began to kiss her, and it wasn't a friendly one, but a deep and meaningful one.

As soon as they saw me, father let go of Auntie, and I stood there in disbelief, not knowing what to make of the whole episode. Father came hurtling towards me, and all I said that I was thirsty. They did the entire pretence entity like everything was alright, gave me my drink and ushered me back to the party.

"Right are you ready Erykah?" Marcus said as I came out of my daydream.

"Yes, go ahead, Marcus!"

"I've been over the paperwork several times and so has Danika and we've seen all the evidence, and I think it's in your best interest to plead guilty."

"Marcus, why am I going to do that? McCann is the one who should be."

"Am I not the award-winning best criminal defence lawyer in the country?"

"Yes, you are."

"Then trust me when I tell you, it's in your best interest to do so."

"Alright Marcus, you know, best. I believe in you."

"Good, now what will happen first, is that I will tell the court you will be pleading guilty and then they will arrange for a sentencing hearing. Don't be alarmed I'll tell you in a minute what I feel you will be charged with. At sentencing, the judge will decide if you will be released, and the conditions of your release. Is that alright so far for you?"

"Yes, sounds daunting. But I feel good with you in my corner!"

"So, for today after I hand in your plea. We can leave here until a sentencing date."

"Right,"

"Also I'm going to give you some information to take with you?"

"Thank you."

"Right, let go do this. Should be no more than half an hour. Then I'll take all you girls for lunch."

"That'll be great," as I got up from my seat, I turned to Marcus and looked him dead in the eyes. For a few seconds, our eyes locked as I moved forward right upon him. As he looked down on me, he instantly knew what I was seeking from him. He laid down his briefcase on the table and reached out his arms for me to embrace, and so I did. Upon impact, I rested my head on his chest as he gently stroked my head to keep me calm. He instructed me to take a few deep breaths, afterwards we proceeded to court seven.

Inside all the girls were sitting together situated behind the defence desk. I sat next to Marcus at the desk. Danika was on my left-hand side.

A few minutes later, the judge called him and the prosecution team over to his stand.

As I looked around the Courtroom, I spotted Racist sitting at the prosecution desk, looking all smug and shit. When he sighted me, he glanced over my direction and gave me the evilest stare down, like he wanted to kill my black ass. Nothing new there then.

After a few more moments, the judge told me to stand up.

"Miss Gaines, you have been charged with the assault of a police officer a one detective Charlie McCann on the day of August the ninth 2015 at Sandbach & Alsager Police Station in the county of Cheshire. How do you plead?"

"Guilty, your honour," as soon as I said that there was an almighty gasp from behind me. I turned around and saw Syreena and Nina almost in tears. The other two had perplexed looks on their faces. I instantly smiled at them and threw out a signal to them, which told them everything would be fine. That immediately calmed them all and returned smiles to their faces.

"Miss Gaines you have pleaded guilty to the charge, and the first day of sentencing will begin on Monday 21st September 2015. We shall be reconvening then. I'll see you, Miss Gaines and your team at 9 am sharp on that day. Failure to attend court without a valid reason, Miss Gaines may result in issuing a warrant for your arrest. Do you understand everything I've said?"

"Yes, your honour."

"Good," as I was allowed to go. I thanked Marcus and Danika. Then all the other girls rushed me at once as we got together in a group hug and exchanged some words of solidarity amongst ourselves.

After we left the court, as promised, Marcus took us all to lunch. Being Marcus, he took us to some swanky joint up in Central London.

After lunch, we all said our goodbyes to Danika and Kira. I thanked them personally for their support today. Marcus offered to give them lifts home as he lived near Danika's house, and Kira was going there to see Daniel.

So it was reassuring in the knowledge that they would both get home safely. Nina, Syreena, Kyndra and I were Southside chicks. So we all linked our arms together and made the short walk to Nina's car.

As we all settled inside of the car, Nina began the drive back to Brixton. The girls were talking amongst themselves, so I took the opportunity to read the information Marcus gave me earlier.

'Assault on Police (NI) Act 1998 66. (1) Any person who assaults a constable in the execution of his duty, or a person assisting a constable in the execution of his duty, shall be guilty of an offence. You don't have previous convictions for violence. Also, you cannot hide from the fact that the court will not like an assault on a police officer. They get very excited about assaults upon people acting in the course of their duty. Also, it was a few punches, and it's helpful mitigation to make the point that you didn't know he was an officer. I will state that you're willing to offer a letter of apology, which is always very helpful. In fairness, he didn't suffer the worst injury. If the courts say what Nature of Offence then your Starting Point to Sentencing Range to what I feel the police will charge you with is Assault where no injury or where injury is minor and non-permanent (e.g. bruising.) Your sentence will be a Community Order + Compensation Order or Fine to Community Order + Compensation Order which a community is time spent doing some community work to their digression i.e. – picking up litter etc. Compensation is paying back money to the victim if found guilty. Of course, you don't have previous convictions, but you are pleading guilty, so probably they cancel each other out, and you are in the position of the man the sentencing guidelines envisaged. The court will arrange a sentencing appearance so that the judge can sentence you. At sentencing, the judge will decide if you will be released, and the conditions of your release. I would expect a medium level community order. They will probably adjourn off for presentence reports to consider all of your issues. Probation may find that you were victimised and racially abused as an issue against McCann if they cannot find any other problems though probably you are facing either a curfew or an unpaid work order. Given the fact that this is violence, seemingly unprovoked a curfew may be preferred as it has a nexus to the offence. You may also have to pay compensation and court costs of £85.

As I finished reading the information, I folded the piece of paper and placed it back into my jacket.

As a chilled, soulful tune came on the radio, I leant my head back onto the rest, closed my eyes and drifted off into a deep sleep until I got home.

Chapter 20 – Time for Friends

After I procured from court this morning, everything that Marcus had rationalised to me in the information he gave two weeks ago was correct.

For the assault on Detective Charlie McCann aka Racist, I received a 12 month suspended community resolution order only because it was my first offence.

How lucky was I? On my way home, Marcus received a call from the court. I mean that was efficiently quick. They stated that Racist would be charged with aggregating behaviour and improper handling of a suspect and asked if I wished to proceed with the charge. I mean, wow. Talk about a turnaround of affairs. I wasted no time in saying yes. Marcus said he'll take care of business and would be in touch soon to the courts.

Besides, Marcus explained that my opening statement to the court might have tipped the jury in my favour, and this is what I had said. 'I had to embellish a wrath of anger that was reminiscent of demonic treatment. Uncle had endured the ridicule of his character and his status. They poked and prodded, testing our will, our patience almost wearing thin. I did what I did because inside I felt wronged for no apparent reason other than I'm a suspect. McCann's eyes betrayed his actions. I'm no fool I saw from the second we were frog-marched into the station, that he detested us with a callous vibe from the point of activity'.

Now that I was glad it was all over, I was looking forward to a fulfilling day ahead. Tonight was all about one of my best friends in the whole world, Chantel Porter. It was the night of her first modelling show in London, and it was taking place at the world-famous Savoy Hotel.

So, before I get my hair and nails done this afternoon, this morning I was meeting up with Uncle Sebastian to view some properties he had located for me.

I left the court a little after 10 am with Marcus. After he made a statement to the media, we made the short walk across the road to where his car was parked. He was giving me a lift to my Uncle's business address.

As I got inside and settled myself, Marcus was about to put the key into the ignition when I shouted for him to stop.

"Wait, Marcus!"

"Is everything alright?"

"Yes, I wanna say something to you before I forget."

"No problem. What is it?"

"I want to thank you for everything you've done for me these past months."

"It's fine. I was doing my job."

"No, Marcus, it's more than that. The way you've helped my family and myself over the years is parallel to nothing short of magnificent. Your discretion is undeniably overwhelming. I feel you would've put the same effort in, even if you were paid less. Thank you so much, Marcus, and for all that I love you."

"Love you too Erykah, thank you for your kind endorsement."

"I do, mean, every word," I said between the tears and the emotions that were threatening to spill over as per usual.

"I know you do and I believe you."

"Thank you," I said while drying my tears with a handkerchief.

"Are you alright now?"

"Yes."

"Are you ready to go?"

"For sure. Let's get out of this forsaken area."

"Say no more," Marcus conveyed as he put the car into gear, did his checks. When all was clear, we took off in the direction of Chelsea.

As we drove through the traffic, every time we came to a standstill, I took a picture of something cool I liked.

Since I came to London, I started a Vlog. It's about my journey of self-discovery. I set it up in the actuality I become someone famous. Then, I would have a collection of videos to mark my steps and to remind me if I ever got too big for my boots, then I would go back and peek at my Vlog so that I could bring myself back down to earth.

The kind of preoccupations I document apart from the factors that have happened so far is my personal feelings. I'm beginning to learn how to love, motivate and appreciate myself for the first time in my life, through the support of friends and family.

The one person that has and continues to be the most influential is Kyndra. Her intelligence, guile and strength to help me has been the pinnacle of my recovery from fighting like the whole world has a conspiracy against me.

Her simple advice that if she were a professional, you would have to pay big money for it. So in many ways, I felt blessed in that sense.

But no matter the weather or if she is going through some shit of her own. She finds space and time to hear you out and help if she can.

After a twenty minute drive through London traffic, we finally reached Uncle Sebastian's business address at around 10:35 am.

As Marcus pulled up outside, Uncle Sebastian was already at my side of the car. I wound my window down to let Uncle lean in.

"Hi Erykah," he said with a serious-looking stare as he kissed me on the cheek.

"Hey, Uncle Sebastian."

"Marcus."

"Sebastian," they both did that mutual man respect thing with their greeting. You know, when the voice gets real intense, almost tinkering on a sexual element. I found it a turn on when Donte does it with the manz dem.

To me, it's a sign of being in control of your destiny, and here I was in the company of two of the most powerful, influential, black men in the whole country in their respective careers. Both, are at the zenith of their profession's.

One happens to be the best criminal defence lawyer in the land and the other the top property agent in the whole of London. They are both older men I love and respect very much and look up to the max.

"So, how did the court case go?"

"You know me well enough Sebastian to know that your niece wouldn't be sitting here if she was sentenced today."

"Great job Marcus, that is money well spent. So what was the proclamation of events?"

"They didn't have enough to charge her. There was a video of Mr McCann which showed him spitting into a cup which after he gave to Erykah. Plus the fact you could see the distress this caused her and coupled with the other acts of brutality against her and Jeboniah and it being her first offence. Well, you tell him, Erykah."

"I got off Uncle with only a 12-month community resolution order."

"Oh, that's marvellous news Erykah. For a minute there, I got a little worried, but Marcus came through for you."

"Well, she is a tad lucky. Considering the motorway services debacle. I think it's a stupendous result all around."

"Touché lawyer man. Care for a quick refreshment before you depart?"

"I'll have to take a rain check. I got a new client I'm meeting in half-an-hour back at the office. So I'll catch up with you soon."

"I'll hold you to that, Marcus."

"Erykah, a word to the wise. Keep your nose clean. Knuckle down, work hard. Concentrate on your goals. Keep going forward, never backwards."

"Will do Marcus."

"Oh, one more thing before I go."

"What's that?"

"Are you still hell-bent on suing the Cheshire police force?"

"What do you think I should do?"

"The decision is yours. But in my professional opinion. There's no better time to strike than the present. Considering you won your case."

"Well, when you put it like that. Let's do it. Let's crush those bureaucrat's and make them weep."

"Right guys, I've got to vacate my presence out of here. Good luck with the viewings and I'll be in touch in due course."

"Thanks again, Marcus."

"Take care, guys." As he got into his car, men like Marcus are not the best with handling compliments. Get to say I love you, that's easy like eating a bar of chocolate. But paying them one, forget it. They get very bashful and keep them emotions locked deep within from coming outside to the surface.

"Bye Marcus," I fondly said as he sped off down King's Road.

Everything about this area is affluent. The place is steeped in richness. From the way, the shops look on the outside, just by changing a shop sign. It's how it presented that makes all the difference. The way people act and dress. The only likeness to more impoverished areas is the colour of the roads. But the differences are noticeable. This is social engineering at its peak. But to be honest a girl like could get used to living in an area like this. So I was ready and looking forward to what Uncle had lined up for me.

"Erykah darling, I'll be two shakes of a cat's tail. I need to grab my coat."

"No problem, Uncle. Take you time."

As I waited for him, I leaned against his car, bust my shades on and folded my arms to take in the autumn sunshine. Even the goddamn air felt fresher. Inside I had to laugh. That in the same city, by crossing over a bridge, it's like stepping into another world.

"I'm back. Let's go, Erykah!"

"Let's Go, Uncle."

A Moment later, I was in the car, and Uncle was driving me to my first destination.

We ended up in a place called St. Mary Abbots Terrace, Kensington and on first impression Uncle did well. The flat he showed me was of a reasonable size for two. The area was beautiful and clean.

The second place was called Oakwood Lane in Kensington, another private road. This flat was an upgrade from the first one. It had a vibrant feel to it, and I liked this place much better than the first.

But the third place was the one for me. It was situated in Brunswick Gardens. It was steeped in richness, clean and vibrant, but I had enough money and a job, plus when I reach the age of 30 years, I'll have my fund monies from my compensation deals to pay for it all. So, I was set to go.

I told Uncle I wanted this one. After I signed the lease, Uncle handed over the tenancy and keys to the joint.

Uncle then kindly drove me back home. He came in and had a coffee and a catch up with me. Half an hour later, he left. The time now was 1:30 pm, and my hair and nail appointment was at 2:15 pm in Brixton.

My belly started to grumble. All that running around and I had forgotten to eat. On my way to the hairdressers, I stopped off at Subway. I ordered a 6-inch meatball sub and filled it with ranch sauce my favourite, and then I polished it off with a refreshing cup of Coca-Cola.

When I finished eating lunch, I had 10 minutes to get to my appointment. I walked there and reached in time. I was escorted to the nail chair straight away.

Forty-five minutes later and I was sitting in the hairdresser's chair. Justine became my regular only when I couldn't be bothered to go to Aunt Lola's Salon.

She knew exactly how I liked it done. But today I was going for a new, younger look—a bit on the rebellious side. I asked Justine to shave one side at the bottom of the back. The rest of my hair made curly into a Mohawk type of style. By the time Justine finished, I had left the Salon at precisely 5 pm.

I made my way home to get ready for this evening. Chantel's show was at 9 pm, but before all that, she had booked a table for us girls for 7:30 pm, and Nina was driving us up there.

On route, we would be picking up Syreena, and Kyndra. Danika and Kira were meeting us there. Syreena also informed me she was bringing along a friend of hers.

I asked why? She babbled on that the sister ran her own clothes shop and was very much into fashion. I said whatever as long as she was cool people, I didn't mind one bit.

Fifteen minutes later and I was turning the key into the front door of home for a little while longer. For a few seconds, I stood there marvelling in the realisation that in a few weeks from now I'll be moving into what I will be able to call a place of my own.

Inside I began to feel that warm and fuzzy feeling you get when your brain sends a signal to your heart telling it to feel content.

I had to try and catch my breath because all of a sudden, I became overwhelmed with joy. What got me was the fact of all the emotional trauma I had endured throughout my life.

So that coupled with my recent advancements, was beginning to bring on an anxiety attack.

I hadn't noticed that I must've been making a lot of noise. All I felt next was myself beginning to feel faint and ready to drop in the front doorway.

As I was about to fall, the door opened and out came two outstretched arms, ready to break my fall.

"Nina, get here quick?" Eric called out as I flopped sheepishly into his arms.

"What's up, bro?" I heard her. But to me, her voice sounded faint and far away as my eyes became heavy.

(A couple of minutes later…)

"Erykah, Erykah, can you hear me?" All I could hear was this robust voice and my face being slapped gently.

"Stop doing that, Eric?" I said as I put up my arm to wave his away. My head felt a little groggy as I began to sit up straight on the sofa.

"You okay?"

"What happened?" I said. My voice felt like it was beginning to get back to its normal state.

"You proper passed out," Eric replied astonishingly. Nina stood the other side of him with a bottle of mineral water in her hand.

"No, shit!" I replied as she handed me the bottle. I opened it and took a few swigs after I finished I gave it back to her.

"Are you feeling any better and what happened?" Nina asked, looking very concerned for my welfare.

"Yeah, kinda. I'm going to be alright. To be honest, I think I became overwhelmed with how fast things have turned around since I've been in London, that I've not had time to process it properly."

"I can second that notion."

"I'm going to be alright," I said as I got up from the sofa.

"Listen, you got one hour to get ready before we have to leave. So get a move on please."

"Take it, easy girl. My outfit has been ready since yesterday. My hair and nails are complete. All I need to do now is hold a fresh."

"Okay, well hurry up! I still got to use it myself."

"Well, why don't you go before me? I don't take long."

"Thank you. I think I will." Nina went ahead. So I took this opportunity to give Donte a video call.

A few moments later, my phone was answered.

"Hey baby, hold up a sec?" Donte instructed.

"Take your time."

"Where would you like us to take this Mr Williams?"

"Can you take that through to my office, thank you."

"No problem, Mr Williams."

"I'm all yours now, baby. So how's t'ings?"

"I'm good. Just waiting for Nina to get out of the shower."

"Ah yeah, you got Chantel's show tonight. I almost forgot."

"That's right baby."

"You looking forward to it?"

"What do you think?"

"Say no more. So what else is going on?"

"I got some great news."

"Well, don't leave me in suspense."

"I got my new flat."

"No shit, when?"

"Today, baby."

"Ah, that's what's up."

"Baby."

"Yes, my darling."

"I want to ask you something. But now I think I should wait until I see you in person."

"Nah, you dun know you can't do me like that, Erykah?"

"Okay, okay."

"Ite, so what's up?"

"Well basically, you know recently we've been talking, and in those talks, we discussed if the potential situation should it arise and if we were still madly in love, still very happy and sure it was the right move for both parties."

"Erykah, stop waffling and get to the damn point."

"Mr Williams, would you do me the honour and make me an even happier girl than I am already. Would you like to move in with me?"

"Hmm, let me see," Donte mockingly looked up towards the sky and rub his chin at the same time.

"See what?" I reiterated protesting in frustration.

"I'm just fucking wit ya. Of course, I'll move in with you. I got no doubt it's the best move for us on the next step in the evolution of our relationship. Even though it's come prematurely to our preferred arrangement, I couldn't be happier that it's happening now and with the number one girl in my life."

"Donte, I love you. You're the finest boyfriend a girl like me can ask for, you never cease to amaze me."

"Baby it's just you and me. We're a team, no doubt."

"That we are."

"By the way. Your hair looks amazing."

"You like it?"

"I love it. It proper suits your features."

"Ah, you're so sweet."

"For real."

"Cool, cool. Listen, babes, Nina is out the shower now."

"Ite, you gotta go get ready! Text me when you come out of the hotel no matter how late it gets."

"Will do babes."

"Oh, make sure you don't forget to pass on my love and wishes to Chantel and say wassup to Dominique as well, thanks babe."

"I will my love."

"Cool. See you soon. Love you."

"Love you too," I ended the call and headed upstairs. Half an hour later I had showered, got dressed and was out the front door. Nina was already waiting in the car and was pressing me to hurry up.

"Erykah come on, get a move on girl?"

"Alright, keep your weave on," I said back as I entered the vehicle and tried to get myself comfortable, but Nina was still winging."

"What took you so long?"

"I gave my bae a quick call."

"You know we're pressed for time already. You could've phoned Donte on the way."

"Well, maybe Miss, who's trying to control my life. Maybe what I wanted to say to him was meant to be said in private, teacher."

"Fine, what's done is done. Let's go already."

"Ditto to that sister."

After all the melee, Nina drove like some crazy-ass chick that was being chased by the cops. She was quite the driver, weaving in and out of traffic, taking over one or two other drivers that were driving below the speed limit.

After we picked up the girls, we finally arrived at the Savoy hotel at approximately 7:05 pm, which gave us 25 minutes to park up and make our way inside to our table.

As we entered a car park on the southeast side of Savoy place called the Adelphi garage, sitting in a toll booth, a security man greeted us upon entry.

"Afternoon ladies, are you all here for the wedding or the fashion show?"

"We are here for the fashion show," Nina stated.

"Okay, parking for that will be all the spaces on your right," he pointed out.

"Thank you very much, sir," I shouted out while Nina collected a ticket from him.

"You're welcome young lady and enjoy your evening."

"We intended too," Nina said back as she strutted about trying to put the car into gear. When Nina found a spot to park the car, she cut the engine dead. The four of us proceeded to make our way out of the vehicle, shortly afterwards.

As all the girls and I stepped out, we saw a couple of guys that looked like they were approaching us. There was three of them all neatly dressed the same in wedding suits. How I could tell was by the cravats they were all wearing.

Two of them were dark-skinned brothers, and the third was mixed race, who seemed to be focusing his gaze on me a lot. I found it quite flattering to my ego. But as handsome as he was, he hadn't a patch on my Donte.

By the time they had reached us, the first one that approached had this real cocky air about him, and I didn't like his attitude one bit from the off.

"Good evening, ladies, how y'all doing?"

Fucking great. Not only is he cocky as hell, but he is a yank as well.

"We are all fine, and who might you guys be?" Nina asked as inquisitively as I felt.

"I'm sorry, where are my manners? Let me introduce myself to you. My name is Clayton Rimmer; my two friends here are Raymond Francis and Teddy Haynes," the cocky dark skin brother said. But by the way, he spoke with his flatulent tone it gave him an air of authority that was powerful, yet calm from whence he first approached us.

"Nice to meet you guys," Nina pleasantly said.

"Pleasures all ours and your names are?" Clayton asked while rolling his right hand around in a circular motion in front of us.

"No disrespect Mr Rimmer, we are pressed for time. So if you don't mind, we all gotta go." I remonstrated harshly.

"Erykah, don't be so rude?" Nina said, trying to apologise for my outlandish behaviour.

"Yeah, girl?" Syreena said while she stared at me like a lioness who was about to tear into her unsuspecting prey.

"Erykah, Hun, you can see these brothers mean no harm?" Kyndra whispered in my ear and then she quickly went to take over the situation.

"Alright," I replied to my voice of reasoning.

"My brothers, my name is Sister Kyndra, you've acquainted yourselves with Miss Nina. The calm one now is Erykah, and the sweet, quiet one is Syreena, and her friend's name is Imani. Now guys before you say another word, let me break something down for you. We are all attached, and we are attending a good friend's fashion show, that's why we are here. I take it by the attire you are all wearing and your accents that you must be attending the wedding and are all from the States or Canada? So what's your business here if you don't mind saying please?"

"Well first of respect to you sister Kyndra and the rest of you lovely sisters. We all reside from the states in Atlanta, Georgia. Our business here is to attend the wedding of the UK director of operations at our company called BlackLivesMatter, which you may know off already?" Clayton said, answering Kyndra's questions.

"Yes Clayton, it's an organisation that has become world-renowned for upsetting one or two applecart's. Our organisation, The Black Resistance Movement, hosted an event last month which included a guest speaker a Mrs Olivia Stone who was expertly highlighting and spreading the message on companies like yours to our black community in South London."

"Well you have been misinformed Sister Kyndra, we don't upset we just advocate and highlight the ills that are happening internally and externally to our black culture and way of life. But if we do happen to upset a few along the journey, it's not meant in any malicious form. Also, we know Mrs. Stone very well. She is a great educator in the business of the history and the struggles of our people."

"Well thank you for the update Clayton, but we need to get going. We have a table booked."

"Hold up a sec, Kyndra?"

"Go ahead."

"Mr Rimmer, your statement it's weak at best. You seem apologetic before you even make a move? It's like you're coming across feeling very sorry for stepping on peoples toes and when I say people I know you ain't talking about black people."

"Miss Gaines, is that right?"

"I just said so, didn't I?"

"Miss Gaines, what do you think you know about my organisation?"

"What I think? I think your organisation are a bunch of self-gratifying, victim playing, self-seeking individuals who are looking to push LBGTQ agendas instead of black lives."

"Erykah, What's got into you?"

"Watch and see, Nina? Mr Rimmer, what's your answer to what I just said?"

"Miss Gaines, sexuality isn't the case here. It's about people that look like you and me."

"What in the Kentucky Fried Chicken is this Uncle Tom on? You one of them stupid-ass house negro's ain't ya?"

"No disrespect Miss Gaines; but you don't know me to call me that."

"Mr Rimmer do you think All Lives Matter?"

"Yes, I do! Why do you ask?"

"Because unlike your fraudulent organisation; all lives can only matter when black lives do."

"That's a ludicrous statement to make and I for one think it's unwarranted in this scenario."

"Ludicrous Mr Rimmer; how so? I'm calling it like I've been seeing it."

"A life is a life and it's as simple as that."

"I know All Lives Matter. But who is helping us?"

"Miss Gaines our organisation is all about the liberation of our people."

"How so? From where I'm standing your agendas are far removed from liberation and more about a specific group within our community."

"Where are you getting your information from Miss Gaines? Because like I said to Kyndra we are about black lives but all other life forms matter to. Don't you agree?"

"Do all lives matter? Of course they do! But in that statement when it's shouted out at your protests. Do you really believe it includes ours?"

"Yes, I do believe so."

"Look Mr Rimmer, I know we are under real pressures with what is happening to young black men and women in your country and in ours too. But surely it's naive of your organisation to be championing such notions?"

"Let me reiterate for you again Miss Gaines, Black Lives Matter and so does everyone else's."

"Well if you know that why does an organisation like yours exist?"

"Like you said, Miss Gaines, who is helping us?"

"So you think your organisation is?"

"I do if I say so myself."

"Cha dis bwoy yuh know! Mr Rimmer let me say this to you! A statement. Why do we need or have to beg other races to like us that's some lame-ass moves right there? Begging folks to be our friends. It would serve black people in better stead if we went around championing Black Power. Have you forgotten when people like the Black Panthers did such things? In Jamaica, we have a saying; 'Wi nuh beg nuh friend'."

"You're entitled to your opinion Miss Gaines, but it would be foolhardy to go around protesting or marching to a beat and making noise about Black Power!

We can't afford to loose any more lives, and that's why black lives matter."

"Ah beg yuh ah beg, da fuck is wrong with you Mr Rimmer. Are you mentally, alright?"

"My faculties are in perfect harmony, Miss Gaines. Are you sure yours are?"

"Mr Rimmer, before I depart from your heinous presence. I've got a question and a statement. Which would you prefer to hear first?"

"Oh, I have a choice! How delightful?"

"Hello! Get on with it please."

"The question first?"

"By your organisations standards of conjuncture. Why is the loss of black life more important when you protest when it's done by a White person compared to when a black person does?"

"That is not so? The perpetrator doesn't determine the outcome of how we protest."

"Oh really, okay, Mr Rimmer. Then why don't you explain to me when a fraction of your movement was protesting in Waller County in Texas against the unlawful killing of Sandra Bland when they were confronted by an outraged African lady who stated that your organisation is racist and also challenged them on what I said about you only protest when a White person kills a black person. Then she went on to say and I agree with her. She said why hasn't BLM ever protested in Chicago were more black on black crime is prevalent? And what were their answers?"

"Miss Gaines, I remember said video and that lady has been nothing more than a public nuisance at our protests."

"So, you do not deny that the BLM has ever stepped foot in Chicago, especially the South Side?"

"Classic Miss Gaines and you're entitled to your opinions. But what I won't stand for is you ridiculing BLM based on what one lady said and by way of definition that you probably have never stepped foot in the USA and know the work we do first hand?"

"That's bullshit, Mr Rimmer. Why are you deflecting from the question I asked of you?"

"I haven't deflected. I made a choice to not answer it."

"Alright, if that's how you want to go?"

"I believe you said you had a statement as well?"

"Yes, I did. Okay it's like this. George Soros and the other one-percenters fund BLM whose other agendas are to empty prisons. The reason for that is to let out the most violent of Racist criminals. The one-percent are funding BLM to cause a war and upheaval with white privilege. The war that we are in right now its a class and economic war and it's not a race war. It has always been a war between the one-per cent and the ninety-nine per cent - Divide and rule. The one-per cent don't care about Black lives matter, they only care about their agendas. They fund the open society companies who turn to challenge the one-per cent if the only option is the one-per cent funding BLM. Then Mr Rimmer, who benefits?"

"Miss Gaines, you're something else?" he said laughing out some nasty ass laughter.

"Erykah let the man be now?" Kyndra said. "We are going to be late for our booking?"

"You're lucky, Mr Rimmer, my friends, are here to protect you?" I said as I walked off in disdain for these fake ass people.

"Good to meet y'all. Please take my business card. Interesting chat there Miss Gaines?"

"Fuck you man." I said back at Rimmer as I walked away from him in abhorrence.

"Miss Kyndra, I would love to learn more about your organisation. If your people are ever interested, we run a competition where the winning company gets a chance to tour the states with us at BlackLivesMatter in the New Year."

"That's good to know Clayton, my people will get in touch with your people if they're interested," Kyndra wrapped up saying.

"I'll look forward to it. Have yourselves a great evening, take care now black people."

"It was cool to meet you all, have a great evening too," Nina concluded.

"Grade one dick head," I said to the rest of the girls as we made our way inside the Savoy.

We only had a few minutes to get to our table, but on the way, I wanted to question Kyndra quickly. Her response it wasn't the right time at the moment, maybe later she said.

When the three of us reached the room where our table was, at the far end it was adorned by the most beautiful stage I've had the fortune to lay my eyes on. It was draped in the most exotic of colours, yet it was simplified and kept to a minimal which gave it that class where hotels like the Savoy are world-renowned for.

As we all shifted a few feet forward together in unison, we came to a reception booth pretty much like the ones you see in American movies. A well-dressed, well-mannered middle-aged white man greeted us.

"Good evening, ladies," oh, it was refreshing to be called a lady by them for a change instead of other profanities. "Do you have a reservation?" He asked cordially.

"Yes we do," Nina replied softly. "You'll find it under Miss Lawrence," she concluded saying.

As he quickly typed in her details, I couldn't help but notice that he was staring through the whole exchanges at

Imani and why wouldn't he? It was the first time tonight that I looked at her properly. I mean for an older lady than us, she carried herself like she was twenty years of age. It's true what they say black doesn't crack.

"Oh, here we are, table for seven. I can see here you have two of your guests that's check-in already."

"Yes," I replied excitingly by literally jumping up and down and clapping my hands together in unison. I was glad Danika and Kira could make it, but the hall was so huge, and I couldn't for the life of me see where they were seated. All of a sudden, seeing this amount of people crammed into one space became overwhelming. I felt a rush of emotions come over me as my hands began to tremble, and my throat felt like it was filling up with salvia, trying to block my airway. I was having a panic attack, and my second one of the day so far.

I took a few steps backwards, trying to move into a space of my own. My breathing started to become more rapid. Sweat was beginning to perspire more profusely from my chest area, and my hands as well were trembling like I was riding a rollercoaster feeling very hot and clammy. As I tried to steady myself, I felt a warm hand in mine.

"Keep calm and breathe slowly." As I looked up, it was Nina. She grabbed my hand and led me out of the hall. "Erykah; take your time, slow your breaths down and think of calming thoughts."

But that wasn't helping, this was an immense one, and I didn't know what to do. To me, it felt like I was underwater, and no matter how hard I tried, I couldn't get the image out of my head.

Suddenly, through my episode, I could distinctively hear the voices of the other girls. I first saw Danika coming towards me, followed by Kyndra. With each step they took nearer to me, that was the point I felt my eyelids getting heavy, and the atmosphere around me was getting darker by the second. As I heard one or two of them call out my name, shortly after I fainted and passed out cold.

A few minutes had passed as I slowly came round to my name being frantically shouted. Once I was awake properly, I sighted Nina and Kyndra on either side of me. The worrying looks on their faces at first turned too sheer relief when I managed to utter my first words.

"What happened to me?" I said sounding all groggy.

"You fainted Erykah," Nina replied, sounding very concerned for my welfare.

"More importantly. How are you feeling sister?" Kyndra asked.

"I'm alright. Just very hungry and thirsty."

"Why do you think you fainted cuz?" Danika added.

"I'm feeling a bit overwhelmed, and it's been one heck of a long day so far."

"Come, let's get you up," Syreena said, offering me her hand as I was about to grab onto it Imani stepped in front of her and swiftly took over the situation.

"Wait?" She said elongating the word. "I'm a Doctor. Let me take a quick look at you first."

"It's fine; I'm good, Imani," I replied, pleading against her assertion.

"Nonsense Erykah! If it's all the same with you. At least for everyone else's peace of mind."

"Fine, but please hurry up because I'm thirsty."

Imani quickly gave me the once over. Once done, we all made our way back into the room, then we were duly escorted to our table.

We all made our orders. After our food came and we all finished it was almost nine o clock.

STAND IN YOUR POWER

It was nearly time for Chantel to perform. As we all began to set ourselves ready for the show, I quickly texted Chantel to wish her good luck. Then all of a sudden, the lights went out. So for a few moments, we were in complete darkness.

A minute or so later, it all started. The music came first. It was one of those instrumental tunes that most events used. Chantel's company chose the world-famous Star Wars one. In time with the music, white spotlights manoeuvred around the room, and then the smoke machines began to let off. As the smoke dispersed down the runway, the white lights weakened. A minute later lasers of different colours crisscrossed against each other, making the whole room light up like the most decorated of Christmas trees.

Then from the back of the stage out came the first of the models and weren't they something else. One by one, they sauntered down the catwalk with grace and elegance, each, in turn, adorning an outrageous but fabulous outfit.

I was beginning to get way too excited, waiting for my girl to come out. The anticipation was getting more and more intense by the minute, and the atmosphere was electrifying in itself.

After a few minutes went by, there she was my girl Chantel, and she was looking out of this world.

Then her moment came. Suddenly, the music changed, and with that, she took to the catwalk like the seasoned pro she was. She strutted her stuff and was by far the most sexiest and glamorous Supermodel on show. As she got to the end of the runway, I spotted her looking down and then she winked and blew a theatrical kiss towards the table directly in front of the stage.

I inched my head up, but I couldn't for the life of me see who she did that too through the melee of tables and people in attendance. I made a mental note in my head that I would investigate after. But not before I bought a round of drinks.

The first session went very quickly. Forty-five minutes had passed when the MC announced there was going to be a half-hour interval.

"Girls, this round is on me. What would you all like to drink?"

"You need any money?" Nina asked.

"I gotcha no worries."

"Alright then," she replied.

"So what's it going to be ladies?" I asked again as I stood there phone in hand, ready to take their orders.

One by one, they told me what they wanted.

As I about to vacate away from their presence. Danika called out to me.

"You want me to come with you?"

"Sure, let's go, girl", as she caught up with me. I put my arm in hers as we talked and strolled to the American bar.

A few minutes later, we reached the bar together. A young man whom I'd say was of Arabic descendant greeted us.

"May I take your orders please?" He asked in that sultry accent they possess.

"Yes, can I get a single shot of Remy Martin and a dash of coke for myself and what are you having Nik's?"

"Get me an erm, erm," she said as she scoured extensively through the drinks menu.

"I would like a glass of La Loupe Grenache Blanc, please."

"Right, so those two drinks please Mr Barman and a freshly squeezed Pink Grapefruit juice and an Apple juice. Also a single Snow Queen Vodka and lemonade, a single

Hendricks Gin and tonic and a single shot of Wray &
Nephews Rum and coke."

"That's seven drinks altogether. Is that correct man?"

"Yes, that is," I answered as he began making our
drinks.

"So cuz, how're things with you and Trae going?"

"Erykah, girllll, I can't thank you enough for bringing
that man into my life."

"It's going that good, yeah? So am I going to have to buy
myself a new outfit for y'alls wedding is the question?"

"Hold onto them thoughts for a little while longer cuz."

"Okay, Okay."

"Mam, your order is ready?"

"How much will that be?"

"That is a total of £66 please."

"Wow, that is not cheap," I said astounded by the prices.
I touched my credit card on the pdf reader, and the
barman put the drinks on a tray. As I was about to pick up
the tray, a waiter came over and carried it for us.

"Now this is something I don't see happening enough
on a regular!"

"Well, the next time you're up my ends. I'll take you to
some places where you'll see that all the time."

"Well, that maybe sooner than you think."

"Oh, why! What's changed?"

"Haven't you seen or spoken to your father today?"

"No, why! I came straight home from work, had a
shower and got changed. Kira came, and we both came
here together?"

"He found me a place today."

"Oh wow, Erykah; that's great news."

"Ain't it just?"

"So when are you moving in?"

"Within the next few weeks."

"Ah, you should let me throw a house warming for you?"

"I'm not sure about that Nik's!"

"Oh come on cuz it'll be great!"

"I don't know. I'm not comfortable with everybody knowing where I live!"

"Erykah; everybody you know is here today."

"That ain't so Danika? You know there's far more."

"A few here and there. Look at the end of the day everyone would be very responsible and respectable of your place. That you do know."

"True! But I'll need help with the list."

"Cuz I told you already I will organise it, and I'll help you with the list too."

"Deal."

"Good, now let's get back to our table."

As we both took a few steps, engaging in small talk too. I wasn't looking where I was going. Next thing I knew, I felt two strong hands rest on either side of my shoulders. As soon as I felt them, I instantly felt the urge to knock them off. Immediately I remembered the four stages of anger Aunt Lola taught me as I backed off from creating a scene. Instead, I decided to look up, and whoever it was I was going to smile my best smile and see who it might be.

"Erykah Gaines; you look cold, steady ready to hit me in the face."

"Dominique Sheridan; you're so lucky it's you. But thank you for stopping me making a calamity of myself."

"So are you enjoying the show?"

"Ah, it's magnificent! I can't wait for the second half."

"For sure! But did you see my girl up there?"

"Did I see her? Dominique; your girl is a superstar, the whole world has seen her. She smashed her walks to pieces. I mean, what's next?"

"Well, she wanted to tell you this herself. But you're her best friend and to be honest, I can't keep it a secret no longer."

"Maybe if it's a secret! Then you should keep it like that. But to be honest, I want to know now?"

"Hm, now I've got to tell you."

"Just tell me already, Dominique? You're always on some mysterious shit."

"Well, her agency informed her before she went on. Chantel has been offered a year's contract to work on the catwalks of London, Paris, New York and Milan fashion weeks. It's an exclusive contract which only four other Supermodels in the world have."

"Get out of here! Are you fucking serious right now?"

"Totally."

"I need to sit down," with that Dominique pulled out a chair for me from a table that had been vacated.

After I introduced him to Danika, she left our side and said she was going back to the others.

"You good?"

"Yeah, yeah I'm fine. I mean that must be a serious payday Chantel's getting?"

"She has a contract outlining that if she fulfils all her duties unless Chan is unable under extenuating circumstances, then she will be paid a million pounds per show and if she completes all four successfully including; celebrity appearances, media, and charity events and openings of stores and clubs then she will receive another million-pound bonus."

"Oh Mm Gee, This is unbelievable, I mean believable because she has beauty in abundance. But never did I think something this amazing would happen to her."

"I know it's crazy. I'm still trying to get my head around it."

"Wow, I can't believe how fast y'alls life has changed since the last meal the three of us had back in Manchester."

"I know, right? But to be honest it all feel's a little surreal to me right now?"

"I understand. I'm beginning to feel the same way myself."

"Listen whereabouts is your table?"

"Over there," I said as I pointed out towards the middle of the room. "Can you spot my cousin Danika?"

"Yeah, I see her. But I got an idea?"

"What kind of idea?"

"I've gotten to know the management here over the last few days, and if it's cool with you and your girls, I can arrange for a table to be set up by ours nearer to the stage."

"If it means I get to be nearer to my girl then I'm up for that. I'll ask the others and see what they have to say?"

"Sweet, give us a call in a few?"

"Will do," I replied, hugging him. After a few minutes or so, I was back at my table.

"Danika said you bumped into Dominique?" Nina inquisitively asked.

"Yes I did, and I got some good news as well. I'll tell you in a bit. But first Dominque wants us to join his table with his bredrin's, and I said I'd ask you lot first."

"Who's Dominque?" Kira asked.

"He's Chantel's Fiancé," Nina answered her before I could.

"Why does he want us to join him?" Syreena asked with a scrutinising nature, but it was understandable why she was being so pedantic.

"So we are nearer to the stage, and there are a few heads I haven't seen in a while, and I want to say hello."

"Well, I like the idea. Besides, I'm straining to see that far, and this pregnancy is messing with my hormones too." Kyndra stated.

"I'm good with it, Erykah." Imani relayed.

"Alright ladies, that's great. Dominique has just texted saying the table is ready."

"Come on then sisters, let's go?" Nina instructed.

As we all got up from where we were the seven of us headed towards the guy's table.

As we passed the other tables, we were getting as many stares as some of the models on the stage.

A few moments later and we had arrived.

Coincidentally all four of Dominique's friends and himself stood up one by one and waited for us to take our seats. My first thoughts were to tell Aunt Lola when I saw her next that Simeon alone wasn't the only one holding up chivalry amongst the young, 21st-century man.

"Pooki; ain't you a sight for sore eyes girl?" The man in question calling me by my rarely used nickname is none other than Quentin Starks; best friend of Dominique. "Come on over and give a brother some sugar?" From as far back as I could remember, he has been chasing the ass of me, begging and pleading for his emotional sanity at one point to go out on a date with him. But for the many occasion, I said no, never, in your dreams. This flamboyant brother never knew when to quit. I did admire his persistence. But I figured it must have been emotional torture for him to get rejected time after time. He would often afterwards tell me that he has girls queuing around the block for a piece of him. But I guess he wanted more than I could give him.

"Quit with the mellow dramatics Starkey; I'm a taken woman these days?"

"You married now?"

"No."

"Then I don't see a problem then."

"Same old Quentin, nothing's changed."

"Bro, stop harassing her and sit your ass down?" Dominique said as he put his arm across Quentin's mid-drift to stop him making more of a fool of himself.

"Thanks, Dom;" I thanked him by giving a knowing wink of approval.

"Anyway before you get settled. The guy sitting and observing to my left is Jeff Bloomberg and to Quentin's right is Cameron Johnson."

"Hey ladies," Jeff said first.

"Hey Jeff," we all said back in unison.

Cameron was a lot quieter. He mumbled a quickfire, hello and we all returned his greeting.

"Well, the three to my right and from right to left is my other best friend in the whole world, Nina Lawrence. Next to her is my new work colleague and mentor Kyndra Harris. This sweet little thing next to me is Syreena Williams," as soon as I said that everyone laughed. At first, I didn't grasp why they were laughing. But when I clocked Syreena giggling too, it was then that I comprehended what everyone was finding funny. When everyone finished, I continued.

"Wrapping up! To my left is Danika Briscoe, my cousin. Next to her is her twin brother's soon to be fiancé Kira Porter and last but not least is Imani. I've just met her tonight, so I don't know your surname Hun?" I asked her.

"It's Amune."

"Thanks, sweetheart, and there you have it guys?"

"Alright great, well...," but before Dominique could finish his sentence, he was interrupted in mid-flow when the room was plunged into darkness again.

Forty-five minutes later after the comedian who practically almost had me peeing myself and the rest of the fashion show, which my girl smashed it again. We were taken towards the VIP room.

Once we reached, we were escorted to our table. After we all settled into our seats, a few minutes later, a waiter came by and asked if we wanted any beverages. When he finished taking our orders, he went on his way. By now, everyone looked upbeat and happy. It was a rare sight to see a group of brothers and sisters sharing the same vicinity and showing each other the mutual respect they deserved.

"Chantel just texted. She says she'll be down in fifteen," Dominique relayed.

"Cool!" I replied.

"Hey, guys! Does anyone here watch 'Let's talk about black culture'?" Imani asked.

"I do," Syreena replied.

"I've seen a few episodes so far. But I missed last week's show."

"You missed quite the show Erykah," Imani stated.

"What was it about?" I was curious now.

"Syreena, you tell her?"

"Will do Imani. Well, they were debating about Black love?"

"What did they say about it?" Danika asked tortuously.

"Well, it's not about entirely what they said. It's more to the fact that they challenged the black community to put a group of three or more people together and each person to make at least one statement on the subject. The winners will be invited at a further date to debate the subject against another group. They also said for participants to film your talk, send it in, and it will be entered into a draw. The winning debate can win £100,000 for an organisation or charity that is black-owned, plus £10,000 per team member and an all-expenses-paid dinner and complimentary VIP tickets for their annual cultural event right here in London at the Dorchester hotel."

"Oh damn," Quentin replied.

"Did they say how many tickets?" Dominque pondered.

"As many as there are taking part in the debate. Each participant must at least contribute one answer however short or long for the debate to be valid." Imani stated.

"So who's going to film it?" Syreena asked.

"I'll do it?" Said a voice coming from behind me. Immediately I recognised who had said that. I turned around, and Chantel was standing behind my chair with a suitcase on wheels and her bright red Gucci handbag hanging from her forearm.

Immediately everyone gave her an enormous round off applause.

"Chan, Chan;" I said, screaming at the top of my lungs while deafening everyone in the process.

"Erykah; Ah," she said, screaming back in response. I immediately jumped up and threw myself onto her.

"I loved the show," I said out loud.

"Ah thank you, Hun."

"Yes Chantel, respect due. You did yourself justice up there. The show was incredible, and so was you."

"Thanks, Nina; so how are you doing these days?"

"I'm good. My career is going well! Things with the movement are taking shape. Plus Erykah is joining us on tomorrow's show for observation purposes only."

"Oh wow, that's great news Erykah."

"Thanks, babe."

"Hey baby, so where's my welcome?"

"Ah, honey, come on over here and let me give you some sugar darling?"

342

Dominique moved towards Chantel as she opened out her arms to take him in an embrace. As he rested his head on her shoulders, Chantel looked over at us and gave off a smile that was telling me; men are like babies. They got to be nurtured and never compromised.

"That's what I'm chatting about?" Dominique concurred as he moved away from Chantel's embrace with a big broad grin swept across his face.

Everyone one else saw the joke and laughed back collectively.

"How's everyone else doing?" Chantel asked, looking around the table.

"We are all good. Just waiting on you ma."

Quentin sarcastically replied first.

"Well, I respect that you alone Q was waiting?"

"I'm peeked that you've recognised."

"Duly noted Quentin," she replied in acknowledgement of his statement.

"So are you going to film this debate then Chan?" I urgently asked, trying to get everyone back to the matter in hand.

"Yeah, of course, and I've got the perfect thing too," she stressed as she started unzipping her suitcase. "Now where did I put you?" I could hear her mumbling to herself as everyone watched on in bemusement.

I was getting a little agitated on the amount of our time she was consuming.

"Chantel; what are you looking for?"

"Here it is," as she pulled out of what looked like a mini camcorder. I remembered she takes one to every show and event she does. So I quickly humbled myself because it was a brilliant idea.

"Finally," Quentin being his cynical self said as he began clapping in unison with his sadistic and annoying laugh.

"Yey, let's give her another round of applause." He continued in his drunken state. I got a distinct impression that something was troubling him. But you could never tell with Q because he is extremely good at hiding his true feelings.

"Come on man let me take you out of here?" Dominique lifted him from his chair with two strong arms. I mean Quentin was no lightweight. I reckoned he weighed around 185 pounds.

"Where we going?"

"I'm taking you upstairs to your room," Dom replied.

"Nah man, I'm good right here."

I was getting very agitated by his behaviour. I could see where this was going. I quickly decided to take over the situation, so I moved to where the guys were. I shuffled Dom aside, leaned down and then I whispered some words of encouragement in his ear.

Within moments, he lifted his head and looked at me, precariously through drunken eyes. He mumbled a few solemn words and began to lift himself. Dom stepped back in and helped his best friend in his time of need.

Being quiet most of the time, Cameron got up to help Dom carry Quentin to his hotel room. All the other boys, along with Chantel, were staying overnight.

"Hurry back soon, babe," Chantel said as she gave Dom a kiss on the lips.

As the boys carried him off, Chantel didn't take her eyes of Dom until he left the room. It was so endearing to see she was so loved up, and she was becoming my new source of inspiration. If she can make it as many have said. Then why couldn't I?

As soon as they were out of sight, Chantel began to turn on her camera. When she was ready to go, she gave me the thumbs up. I galvanised everyone together, and I was prepared to get this money and tickets for the cultural event.

The first part of the process, we all had too watch a five minute video about the title of the debate.

(Five Minutes and ten seconds later)

"Okay, guys. Who's going to kick things off?" I asked.

"I'll go," Nina replied.

"Cool, the floor is yours?" I replied in response.

"What's the topic of conversation again?" Danika said cutting in.

"Black love, Is it racist or preference," I answered back.

"Oh yeah! Thank you, Cuz."

"You're welcome. Nina go ahead?"

"Yes, ha hmm," she said while clearing her throat. "In my mind, it is a preference, and when a black person says it, it is coming from a place of pride and acknowledgement that black love is generally not celebrated in the media and by a lot of black people themselves. It's a kind of statement of self-love in a world that doesn't love you. However, I can see how some people particularly white people could take it as racist because if a white woman/human-made such a statement it would be taken as them saying black is inferior in some way."

"A'right, a'right. That's good Nina. Who's wants to go next?" As soon as I finished relaying my sentence, Kyndra anxiously put her hand up.

"I'll go?" She stated.

"Go ahead." I was so looking forward to what gem was going to come out of her mouth.

"Because we as a people have labelled our love with the same colour there is no problem! However, other cultures see a problem as they didn't think of a label for their love.

We have a right to call our love with each other within our own culture anything we like, and ours happens to be "black love". These other cultures seem to have a problem with everything we say and do. So now in my thought process, I don't see this terminology as racist or prejudice. I see it as a choice."

"It's neither racist nor preference, its self-preservation." Syreena's comment was short and sweet. But valid all the same.

"Well if I said I'm only attracted to black men, who are conscious, have an understanding of the issues black people have faced, is wanting to commit to me and raise our children with pride in themselves and their heritage...would that be considered racist? Because unless I'm missing something, that's what black love encapsulates." Danika argued.

"Black love is the key to our survival. It creates opportunities to illustrate our difference. Anything else will dilute and sow the seeds of our destruction." Jeff added.

"Why would loving yourself ourselves our own be racist kiss my teeth. Do people know what the word means? If white people get upset, that's on them as those same ones will say we are all human and originate from Africa but won't say Africans. So until they see us as parents, they will forever have issues." Cameron nicely put across his view.

"I fear your question may be malformed, the binary nature seems to want to shape possible answers, for example, my answer to the question would go like this, question: 'Black Love is it racist or preference?' The answer is No."

"Where did you come from Quentin? I thought Dom took you upstairs."

"He persuaded me not to. But instead, he had two coffees and some fresh air."

"And here I am."

"Okay, all good," I said, thanking him for his input.

"Do you have anything to add baby?" Chantel asked Dominique.

He looked over at her and smiled in a way that suggested he wasn't as keen on the idea of making a statement as she wanted. But all the same, he gave it a shot.

"It how he or she feels. Thinking they cannot be loved. Sometimes you need to ask this question, so you know the kind of person he or she is when it comes to loving someone."

"It isn't racist for a start, and if it's a preference it shouldn't be that either, it should be the NORM in my humble opinion," Jeff said in his second statement. He and Cameron have finally come alive.

"They could discuss how they each view themselves, as in what they feel they contribute to the upliftment of their culture, while also providing critiques at the same time. A sort of self-appraisal but in a public domain. Which would test the modesty in each character? A test to see who's bullshitting themselves." Cameron finished saying.

"A preference of Black love stated publicly to counteract all the preferences for Black hate is a long overdue response. And people get upset because it challenges the belief that black people are undesirable. A belief based on their very way of life, a way of life which means death to us, they hate us more than they love themselves? That's why they work so hard to get us to hate ourselves; it's called projection. They fight harder for the rights of two men being together than they do to protect male/female relationships. Black love is a revolutionary act," Jeff was making a valid but risky statement. But at the end of the day, it's a brilliant point of the truth, and it's his opinion." Jeff explained.

"Thinking hm no, I don't suppose that it is you have a right to love who you love." Short and sweet from Kira.

"Well said, girl?" I stated.

"The question should be is black love different from white love? If so, then the statement can seem racist, i.e. better or superior, but if it's just, I want a black man, she should've said that, and leave it like that." Quentin came again.

"It's racist by their standards because they are projecting their characteristics of 'white love' onto us. It is not racist for a black woman to acknowledge that she fits better with a black man - they're only calling it racist now because of all the race discussions going on now. They always knew black women preferred black men; they're just awkward. I've told a white man straight (when asked) that I wasn't into white men and he mockingly said 'that's racist', but as a joke, he knew it wasn't true racism." Imani's point was as bold and brash as her personality. Harsh and unapologetic.

"It is natural and preferable. The sad part is we have become alienated from each other because of white interference. Ghastly that there is even a question about this topic. Shows like Nicki Ring and I Am Me are belly warmer fantasy. They do not represent the majority of black women, at least here in the UK." I concurred with Nina on some points.

"It's a preference, no one questions when a white person only wants to be with or marry someone white, or for that matter if an Asian person only wants to marry another Asian. So why should someone's preference to only want to marry black be questioned or considered racist." Danika furthered.

"Saying that you're looking for black love to a white person, for me would just be about a mutual understanding without all the explanations," Syreena replied.

"And finally one more statement and were done. Because I'm doggone tired for real?"

"Me too, Erykah," Syreena pitched.

"Erykah take this?" Chantel passed me her camcorder. "I want to input. Can I make the last statement?"

"Are you sure babe that's wise?" Dom said, concerningly.

"I'm not going to say anything that impacts my career or jeopardises my future." In her mind, Chantel was adamant about it. We all looked at each other and shook our heads in disapproval of her statement.

"Chan, you're a Celebrity now. You can't say and do things like we're hanging around Moss Side's streets. Plus you know your publicist wouldn't approve. Filming and being behind the camera in this instance is one thing. In front of it for this is a big no, no!"

"Why are you always right, Miss Gaines?"

"Because I know better from experience Hun." Chan knew precisely what I meant and humbled herself into submission.

"I'm not going to disagree with you there, Erykah," Chantel concluded. She took the camcorder back from my clasp. She gave me the signal to proceed, so I did.

"There is no such thing as a preference when you are black and dating black. If as a black person you say you are not attracted to those that look like you, there is something wrong with you. I for one would not be offended if a White/Asian etc. person says they don't black women, I would, however, question a black man that makes such statements."

And that was a wrap. Everyone looked mighty pleased with themselves and so they should be. We all left the room and the hotel together after we left Chantel, Dominique and Quentin's side after Chan's media press conference.

She promised me dinner tomorrow after my show. I said I couldn't wait.

A few hours later, and I was back in the arms of the love of my life. As I laid there next to him, I was going through my day in my mind, and what a day it was? It was truly a memorable one for Chantel and myself. Everyone else left happy and upbeat.

I was also extra excited and nervous about my first assistant role at Resistance. But I couldn't wait to get started on there.

As I turned to face Donte; I stared and smiled at him for what seemed like ages. The next thing I knew it was the light of morning. The sun was blaring through the curtains, and his room felt fresh and warm for an Autumn's day.

The weather seemed it was going to hold up as I sat up and contemplated the events of last night in my mind. Donte was fast asleep next to me.

I was so content at the minute. Everything in Erykah's world was going swimmingly on all fronts.

I love my boo to death. But I'm glad I'm a chick that makes time for friends.

Chapter 21 - The Movement

I'm content with myself at the discipline and respect I've shown my body throughout the entirety of Chantel's modelling show.

I'm relieved I stuck to my limit because today marks my first shift at the Resistance radio station of which I'm optimistic of many more to come in the future.

I was motivated and also a tad nervous. I wasn't sure yet of what is envisaged of me. All I knew was that I was on trial today. I was foretold last week at the interview by the station manager that If I pass, I'd be offered the role as a training assistant to eventually take over Kyndra's position when she goes on maternity leave.

After I finished reading through my itinerary notes for the show. I couldn't help thinking about the discussion between Dominique's friends and my friends last night.

It became quite a heated topic of debate after we made the initial statements for the competition as people had different perceptions and feelings about it. I understood everyone's opinions, but I couldn't agree with everybody's point of view.

Being a politically minded soul, I concluded that I agreed with neither. I had two answers of my own. Firstly, it was about choice, a personal preference at that. The freedom to pick someone based on your principles of what you want and need from them, secondly, it was about self-preservation. Preservation in the sense of protecting our race from going extinct, I know that may sound a little far-fetched. But in all honesty, I'm sober right now. I'm not saying that I'm against us dating outside our race. Like I said before that's about choice and I suppose to a degree, preference. What I'm trying to say is that for black people to carry on procreating, a certain amount of us need to stick together. With the rates of us dying in many different formats, it's hard to argue against the point. If after you want to change your circumstances, then that's your call.

But what this is all about. It's about aiming to keep a certain amount of black families together.

I decided it was time to get my carcass out of bed. Donte was still fast asleep. He was such a quiet sleeper. Hardly a sound coming out of him.

I hopped off the bed and landed straight into my slippers. I then reached for my robe and flung it around my back.

Once I moved towards the door. As I was about to reach for the handle, I heard some stirrings coming from the opposite side of the room.

As I turned around, Donte had awakened. When he sighted me, he perched up his head and greeted me with the most amiable of smiles.

"Morning baby." All of a sudden, at first sight of him, to some extent I began to feel naughty.

"Morning gorgeous," he said back with a slight crackle in his voice.

I smiled again and winked back at him, and then I began to walk away and into the en-suite bathroom.

As I stepped inside the huge en-suite, I immediately walked over to the Jacuzzi. I pressed the button that turned on the water as it began to fill up the tub.

The Jacuzzi Donte had bought and fitted cost him nearly five thousand pounds. So because it was an express one, it would only take around ten minutes maximum to fill up.

In that time, I managed to shave my legs, underarms and private areas of my body and take a shower that was so refreshing that it almost relaxed me to the point of weightlessness.

I turned the shower off and reached for my robe. I stepped onto a plastic mat that was also housing my sliders.

I got to the Jacuzzi in time, and It had filled nicely, so I checked the temperature on the Gaige, and it read 100 degrees Fahrenheit out off a maximum of 104.

I was satisfied, so I stepped into the Jacuzzi. That's when I heard Donte walk in. He wasted no time and came up right behind me with nothing on but a small white towel barely covering his never regions.

She pressed her lips together, which made a buzzing sound.

I was getting turned on neatly as Donte's six-pack glistened, reflecting the light.

She took off her robe and let it fall by the side of the tub. For a few brief moments, she stood there in all her nakedness like she was anticipating I would come up behind her, and so I did.

As he pressed his body against mine, our skins touched, and I felt that warm fuzzy feeling you get from it. Instantly my dopamine level rose in time with the sensual vibes that were coursing through my veins.

I took her silky-smooth hand in mine and summoned an emotional force-field, locking tight the feelings I had for her in one big, huge embrace.

He could sense my breathing becoming harsher.

As she tilted her ass out and began grinding against my dick, my nature began stirring, and I could feel the tingling sensations of my pre-come coming to the fore. Within a minute, I was fully charged.

I felt him poke me, so I turned around to meet the meat that had given me so much ecstasy on many an occasion.

As he stood there with a grin planted on his face, I read his mind and knew exactly what he wanted first.

When I anticipated her knowing what I wanted, I sat down on the edge of the Jacuzzi. At the same time, she went down on her knees.

When I adjusted myself and was comfortable, I took his dick in my hand, and I began to stroke it slowly back and forth several times. He instantly tilted his head back and let out a shallow moan of delight.

I was beginning to drift away from my everyday stresses as Erykah was taking me to the point of no return.

I was sensing he was getting into this, so I initiated to up the tempo. I lowered my head forward and took his manhood into my mouth.

She began to go up and down on my shaft, expertly like a seasoned pro. Sucking and licking like her life depended on it.

As I sped up my speed on his nine and a half inches, after several minutes, I was sensing he was about to come.

As she continued to galvanise me, she looked me dead in the eyes, and without warning, Erykah jerked the base of my dick upwards, and at the same time she sucked down hard on it. I've never felt such sensations as I was feeling at this moment.

I caught him out with that move. He had no idea as it was the first time I tried it out on him. I continued in the same fashion, and after several more times, I could feel his spunk rising through the chambers of his manhood. It was like everything had slowed down for a few moan-ments, and time was of the essence.

I could feel I was about to bust a nut as Erykah jerked and yanked for the final time.

"Ah yeah, that's right, just there baby! O damn, you got it, you got it."

"Baby, right there? Like that?"

"Yes girl yes, talk dirty to me, baby."

"You gon cum for me boo, cum all over my breasts baby, you nasty boy you?"

"Yes baby daddy gon cum for you, here it is, here I cum, ah, ah."

"Mm daddy yes! Fuck that shit up all over me."

"Ah, ah, Oh, Oh shit, yes, yes you sexy mother, God damn, Erykah, fuck, fuck, fuck, yes, yes, ohhhhhhhhhhhh, O, O, O, O, damnnnn."

"Oh, Daddy, that's it! Fucking yes."

She stopped talking and looked at me for a long moment quizzically then tilted her head slightly to the side as her eyes took on a hungry predatory gleam. Her lips curled into a playful and seductive smile; then she slowly began to circle me with her eyes, flirtatiously looking me up and down and lightly tracing with her fingernails my chest, my arm and my back in her wake. Her voice lowering into a soft, husky feline purr.

"Are you satisfied, Mr Williams?"

"Miss Gaines; I'm all good. But is there anything I can do for you?"

"Well, for the matter of fact there is one little thing."

"Name it?"

"I want you to do something physical for me. Not sexual, because I'm still recovering from last night's session. But physical in the sense of making me a hearty breakfast."

"You want all the trimmings baby?"

"Miss nothing out. I want everything."

"You got it."

Half an hour later, I finished from the Jacuzzi feeling rejuvenated and fresh, dressed and sitting at the table waiting for my breakfast.

"Mm, that smells perfect baby."

"You wait until you've tasted it. I've added something a lil extra as a treat."

"Oh, you know how I hate surprises, Donte. It's better if you tell me."

"I know that boo-boo! But trust me when I say you gon' love this."

After Donte finished cooking, he served up a scrumptious looking feast.

Not only was Donte an attentive and skilful lover, but he was also equally as good in the kitchen as he was in the bedroom. Which always puts a smile of gratification on my face.

"How's the food?" He asked joyfully.

"Mm, hm, mm." I murmured back through a mouthful of food.

"I take it you like it?" He reiterated with laughter.

"Baby, you remembered. You know how much I love black pudding."

"Indeed, I do."

I grinned at him as we continued to eat and converse about work and my impending appointment.

Donte was coming along as he had a meeting with Calvin and the station manager about how he set up First Approach gyms and also to do a radio advert for the relaunch.

"Babe, you ready?"

"Give me five minutes to freshen up."

"Ite! I'll go warm up the car then."

"Don't forget to lock the back door first."

"Already done!"

"Cool, see you in a bit."

"Ite."

Five minutes later, and I was sitting in the front seat of his car buckling myself up.

"You good?"

"Yes, baby. Let's go."

Another five minutes later, and we were inside Costa grabbing ourselves a morning latte.

After we finished our beverages, Donte drove us straight to the radio station. Within a few minutes, we were parking up outside. We both got out of the car and walked the short journey across the ground to the building that housed the whole empire that is The Resistance Movement.

"How many floors up?"

"Fourth-floor babe," I whispered.

"Let's get the lift?"

"Obviously."

As we began to make our way towards the entrance, another guy from the other side was exiting out.

"Erykah; wah gwaan?" The guy said all cool and calm heading towards us.

At first, I didn't recognise the voice or the face who was hollering at me, because the reflection of the sun against the glass door was obscuring my vision. But as the body came through, I instantly could see who it was.

"Hey Keionte, you good?"

"Mans calm."

"Cool!"

"Suh dis mussi Donte?" Keionte held out his right hand for Donte to greet. He was old school like that.

"Bless up, sir."

"Respect, junior."

"Nice, nice."

"Suh Erykah a yuh a luk faawud tuh a bi involved eena yuh fos show?"

"Involved! I thought I was only observing?"

"Unfortunately yuh covering ah situation dat arose."

"What do you mean by, unfortunately? What kind of situation?" I was hating the tone of voice that was coming out of his mouth. I didn't like his actions one bit.

"Eh Kyndra."

"Oh my days, is she alright?"

"Eh nutten. Shi jus a call an seh ih did di Braxton Hicks."

"Oh, okay. Is she going to be alright tho?"

"Yeh Yeh. Mi pan fi mi way tuh pick har up fram di hospital."

"Oh, is it? Which hospital?"

"Kings."

"You're bringing her back here, right?"

"Eff shi a up fah ih den kool. Buh mi nuh gwine pressure har. Dat a wah mek mi hav seh git ready tuh bi involved jus eena case. Anyway Nuh worry Kaniah will bring yuh up tuh di time? Fram wah Calvin an Kyndra ave did tell mi bout yuh. Mi tink yuh a guh bi kool eff Kyndra decides tuh guh yaad."

"Well if you're sure, then I'll do it."

"Mi sure. Cah Ih did Calvin's idea yuh know."

"Really? Then I feel privileged. Thanks."

"Nuh Eh fi wi privilege. Suh nuff respeck si."

"Seen."

"Rite Mi ah run. Mi wi ketch yuh wen mi a cum bac."

"See you later?"

"Donte bless up. One luv."

"Yah mi bredda Waak gud."

"Criss."

As soon as Keionte left our side, Donte and I made our way inside the complex.

Once we were safely in. I couldn't get over how intricately designed the place was.

The walls were decked out with picture frames of what I could only see were our ancestors. I spotted one of Queen

STAND IN YOUR POWER

Nanny of the Marrons and another of Marcus Garvey wearing some military uniform and inscribed underneath him were the letters (UNIA).

On either side of the reception desk, the place adorned two identical, tall, black African statues resembling the Abyssinian people and written on the inscription it said; 'They are politically and culturally a dominated group in Ethiopia and Eritrea. Their military history dates back to the Axum period where they conquered and colonized the southern Arabians. They are a powerful mountainous people and with their perfect terrain, they were able to resist most invasions successfully and have a long history of their successful warfare skills'.

After I finished surveying the reception area, we continued our walk until we reached the reception desk. Both of us had to sign in. The security gave me my pass and Donte was given a visitors pass.

When we got through the electronic barriers, we made our way towards the lift area.

I pressed for the lift to descend. Around thirty seconds later, we stepped inside and made our way to the fourth floor, which is where the studio is situated.

When we finally arrived, we strolled out of the lift and began walking until the far end of the corridor. As we were about to enter the studios, Calvin strode out.

"Erykah Gaines, what's happening ma?"

"Calvin Felix, it's good to see you again. How's t'ings?"

"I'm good young lady. How's you?"

"I'm a bit nervous, to be honest."

"Oh yeah, Keionte informed me of the changes and its all good with me."

"Alright, alright, that's good to know," I replied.

"Don't tell me this handsome young man is your better half?"

"Oh Calvin, that's so cheeky of you."

"Mi rampin."

"Calvin, it's been a minute. Wah gwaan?"

"Same here, brother. It's been how long?"

"Three maybe four years."

"Too long!"

"Wait! You two know each other? How come?"

"His oldest sister is my ex-girlfriend."

"Wow, what a small world we live in," I sarcastically said.

"Indeed."

"So what you want me to do first?" I asked precariously.

"First, relax. The show doesn't start until another hour from now. Secondly, let me show you where the staff room is. Have yourselves a drink. Then in about fifteen to twenty minutes, we will be having a staff briefing. If there's any time leftover, otherwise I'll make time. I'll show you around the headquarters."

"Why don't you show us right now?"

"I'll tell you what. Come and find me in five. I gotta make a quick call first."

"Okie Dokie Calvin," with that, he walked away from our presence.

"Come, babe. Let's go to the staffroom?"

"Ite, let's go!"

Moments later, Donte and I were seated in the staffroom going over the script for his segment of the show.

Donte a man of many words, pun intended, asked me if I was nervous. I told him to stop asking me obvious questions he already knew the answer too. At that moment he looked at me baffled, and that's when I realised there were details about each other we still didn't know yet. Well, what do you expect we've only been together a few months?

Ten minutes later Calvin was ushering us out. We followed him as he gave us a tour of the studios. He also suggested he'd provide us with the grand tour of all the other three floors if we wanted. I immediately gave him the thumbs up, and Donte nodded his head in agreement too.

"Well, this room here is the main studio for where the talks take place. The adjacent room is where the studio engineer is. Any questions?"

"No," I said in response.

"Let me show you the rest."

As Calvin showed us around the other three floors, he introduced us to everyone. Even down to the tea lady. Call it thorough or call it extra. One thing I noticed more than anything about him that he was always on point.

Time was up, and we had to get ourselves to the briefing. In attendance was Calvin, Keionte, Leon, Kaniah, Donte and myself.

The briefing was about today's topic 'The War on Blacks' and the shows breakdown order. The subject in question is something that continues daily to affect the black community in a big way at this moment in time.

After the briefing had concluded, Calvin and I headed back towards the studio. On the way, he gave me some last-minute words of encouragement.

It made me feel a lot less nervous that I had his immediate support. But to be honest, I could only feel myself fucking up.

No matter what positive spin was being fed to me, in situations outside my comfort zone, I always felt helpless. Just like I did the day I was told my mother had gone to heaven.

It wasn't the apparent disaster that threw my world into a tailspin of intractable pain and suffering. It was the settling period as I got older and the coming to terms with that I'll never have her by my side with me on this earth anymore.

I tried as hard as I could to get my feelings in check and in time for the beginning of the show.

I needed to make a good impression. Considering the talk up and credence Keionte and Calvin had in me.

So here goes my reputation.

"Erykah, are you ready to go?" Leon asked.

I gave him the thumbs up as I slotted my headphones onto my head.

"Calvin?"

"Mi Kool bredda."

"Right, good. Calvin do your usual introductions and introduce Erykah as your temporary assistant for today and give a brief explanation on why Kyndra isn't here. Tell the public the topic of discussion today and its breakdowns and then let's get the live link up and running after?"

"Gotcha Leon."

"Alright everyone, stand by and in five, four," Leon relayed by doing the five-fingered countdown. "Three, two, one and we are live."

"Good afternoon England and welcome to the 'Culture Show' on Resistance 89.6 FM. We have a packed show in store for you lovely people today and another weekly dose of knowledge, empowerment and the truth according to me. I'm Calvin Felix, your irrepressible host and with me for today is a young lady who is a virgin to this show, and she has kindly accepted the invitation of being my co-host in place of Kyndra. Don't worry, folks Miss Harris is okay last time I know. As most of you know, she's heavily pregnant but had a false alarm. As a precaution, she's been told to rest. I'm sure she'll be back larger than life next week. No pun intended if you're listening Kyndra. So in her place is Erykah Gaines. Please England be gentle, to begin with. You know how t'ings run suh." Calvin said as he gave me a reassuring wink.

"Right before we get started, I wanna make sure the live link is working. The number to call is 07891 412 268. I want a call please from up North as far as Manchester or Leed's to east in places like Bristol or Reading. West and south too. If I get one call from all four corners, then we will proceed with the show."

The first call came within seconds of Calvin's announcement.

"Caller you're through to Resistance 89.6 FM. This is Calvin Felix. What's your name and where are you calling from?"

"Afternoon Mr Felix, this is Krystal from Manchester."

Straight away, I recognised the voice. I whispered to Calvin that I knew who it was, and if I could take the call. He obliged, so I took to the mic.

"Krystal," I expressed excitingly.

"Erykah Gaines is that you, girl?"

"Yes, it's me, Hun," I replied, laughing at her surprise.

"I knew I heard, right. I was just saying to my mother I listen to this show religiously, but this is the first time I've ever called. Hello Mr Felix."

"How's it going, Krystal?" Calvin asked.

"I'm good. By the way, I loved last weeks show. It was very insightful and informative. A real eye opener."

"Thank you. Hang on a minute. You wouldn't happen to be the same Krystal that texted in last week about black on black crime?"

"Yes, that's me. You have a great memory."

"I never forget such deep and perceptive material. You're a Youth worker if my memory serves me correct?"

"Yes, that's right."

"A'right good. You can hear us loud and clear, I presume?"

"Yes."

"Nice. I'll hand you back over to Erykah, take care."

"You too, Mr Felix."

"Please, in future. Calvin will suffice nicely, a'right."

"Okay."

"Kris, so nice to hear your voice."

"Oh my day's Erykah, how and how did you get on this show?"

"It's a bit of a long story."

"Oh, I see. I'm still in shock, you know."

"I know."

"Can't believe it. Wait until I tell mother."

"Kris, can I give you a call after the show?"

"Yeah sure, you can."

"Nice one, I'll speak to you later."

"Speak to you then, bye."

"Bye, Krystal."

With that, the line cut dead.

"A'right, the number to get through to us here in the studio is 07891 412 268. I repeat 07891 412 268. Thank you, Krystal, from Manchester for the confirmation. Also, the links to the social media accounts are www.fackbook.com/resistancemovement and www.twitter.com/resistancemovement."

The phone rang out again four times. Calvin pointed to me to answer it.

I looked at him hesitantly. But he kept on pointing towards the phone.

On the seventh ring, I took the call.

"Hello, Caller. What's your name and where you are calling from?"

"Hi, Miss Gaines."

"Hello there. What's your name?"

"Oh, sorry, my bad! I'm Eddie, and I'm calling from London."

"Nice to meet you, Eddie. How do we sound out there where you are?"

"Perfect."

"Alright, Eddie thank you! Is there anything you'll like to say to the UK?"

"Yes! What's the first subject of the day?"

"We are going to discuss the war on black people first."

Calvin looked over at me and gave a thumbs-up of approval.

"Wow, such a huge subject and spot-on at the moment. It's a war, indeed."

"So, Eddie! Do you have anything you want to say to the UK?"

"I have a question for Mr Felix."

"Cool, go ahead and ask?"

"Mr Felix! With all the profound things that are happening to us and the continued rise of black on black crime. I want to know, in your opinion. What is the role of the White Power world elite concerning the system of Institutional Racism and the responsibility of the regulators of the system of Institutional Racism in the demise of the black race?"

"Great question Eddie. So here goes; what is the role of the White Power world elite concerning the system of Institutional Racism? The White Power World Elite (WPWE) are the designers, promoters, financiers, maintainers and enforcers of the global network of Institutional Racism with their non-white allies and hostages. They, like the White banks of this White World, provide settlement of obligations between racist organisations against the security of certain people's lives or deaths to help racist organisations manage their public relations. White Power and domination, racist organisations, typically plan to hold power sufficient to meet expected disagreements. Still, if they need more power (violence) on a given project, they can contract the lives or deaths (Police, Military, Civil Services, etc.) of certain individuals to WPWE. This role of the WPWE (like International Banking) also enables them to influence interest on people's life and death value in the marketplace of political and religious ideas and thereby pursue their main objective of power and stability, or low inflation of life and death value and what is the responsibility of the regulators of the system of Institutional Racism and how do they supervise Racist Activity? Because of their essential role in the economy, White Power, racist organisations have to be regulated to ensure they are prudently managed. The responsibilities of the regulator include the licensing of covert racist activity, prescribing appropriate prudential requirements for racist organisations to comply with, and monitoring how racist organisations manage their risks. In countries under the influence of the political ideas invented by White Power the regulation of White Power and domination ideology and the system of Institutional Racism is governed by racist control of the legal system, which confers on the registrar, like the IMF (International Monetary Fund), of racist organisations the necessary powers. A department of the WPWE and their allies and hostages carries out this function, but the registrar mostly regulates life and death value independently from the WPWE."

"Mr Felix, you're one of the most intelligent minds of our time in my humble opinion. I got nothing more to add other than thank you."

"Respect, Eddie! It was your question that sparked off that."

"No problem! Big up yourself, Mr Felix."

"You too, Eddie."

With that, the line went dead.

"07891 412 268, that's 07891 412 268 for the live link number which gets you through right here in the studio?" I repeated over the mic.

Around a minute later, the phone rang and was answered by Calvin.

"Caller you're live on air. What's your name and where are you calling from?"

"Hi Mr Felix my name is Donna, and I'm calling from London. Also big up the new girl Miss Gaines as well."

"Big up yourself to Donna," I shouted from the other end of the studio.

"Ah bless you, Hun. You're doing a great job so far."

"Thank you," I shouted again.

"So Donna, is there anything you want to add to the discussion?"

"Well for the matter of fact there is."

"Go ahead, Donna; ask away."

"I got a son who turned fifteen last week. My son is a good lad. He helps around the house with chores. Keeps a clean and tidy room, is a grade-A student, is popular and teachers love him. Yet, when he is out and about without his school uniform, he is targeted by police almost every other week. For example, he was going shops for me one evening. It was latish around 9:30 pm. He was only going to get me some formula. I have a 4-month-old daughter. Their dad was at work. He works in security and runs his own firm. I gave up my job in a school to bring up my daughter. I plan to go back to work when my daughter reaches full-time schooling. We are a good family.

Pay our bills on time. We are good neighbours and I'm on the board of chairs for our local tenants association. The police have stopped my son on more than one occasion may I add. But on this occasion, he was stopped and searched, and the reason they gave was that he fitted the description of a recent burglary in the area. So, my question is. Why is a good kid like my son. Who isn't in a gang, who has never been arrested or in trouble with the police. Why is he been constantly targeted and harassed?"

"Donna; this goes back to my long statement I made earlier about how white racist power works. You see, the places where we live are known as ghettos. Ghettos are places where the majority of minorities dwell. So, no matter how affluent you become or how much money you're ploughing back into the community where you live. We are and have always been a targeted group more than other races. From time to time, they highlight another group to look efficient in their so-called fairness policies. That's some bullshit propaganda?"

"So what am I meant to do? Keep my son locked up?"

"No, Donna; that's unethical? But understand this as a people we are under pressure from so many parts of the world. Internally we lack self-control and the ability to make good and sincere relationships with other people. We are not in a great place, and we lack developmental energy."

"What about them? The Supremacists?"

"What the few are doing is enslaving us all over again. By dumbing us down and bringing forth the dumbest of people and we don't understand where to go!"

"Doesn't sound promising Mr Felix?"

"Donna, I'm not trying to be negative. But this is the truth right now and as bad as it sounds. It needs to be told?"

"No, it's okay Mr Felix! I was just relaying to what you were saying. I can't help but think what kind of future my son and maybe his children and their children are going to have when his father and I are not around anymore."

"Seems bleak. But until everyone realises they are enslaved. We can't come together as a collective and build a blueprint for purposeful plans that will find solutions. After this call Donna phone the offline number and Erykah will give you the details to the next Resistance event. Come along and see first-hand the work we do. They'll be someone there that I know that will be able to help you with your situation."

"I'll do that now. Thank you, Mr Felix, for the insight."

"You're welcome, Donna. Stay strong!"

"I'll try. Goodbye."

"Take care."

"Calvin where's the Information?"

"On the wall to your right."

"Thanks."

"UK I'm turning off the live link number for a bit. You can still text the offline number."

"Calvin; do you want me to erm?"

"Yeah."

"Cool."

"Now continuing. In America, the blacks are gone, and their leaders are shot, worn out. Music artists make no sense they talk business like retards. If you earn enough money, it's easy to hire lawyers. But that doesn't make those that hire them clever. People are still thinking about guns. Don't you see how enslaved we are? How powerless you are? We don't have anything! The J.A Government are weak at the knees. For example, people that are dumber and more illiterate want to effect progress because of the need to be safe. There's no attack on the attitude? As soon as some blacks get money or an edge, they want to live away from other black people and go live with white people. There's nothing wrong with that. It doesn't apply to those that don't forget where they come from! Other groups want to be super, triple black segregating themselves and want to be blacker and chat about Africa. When you go the USA, J.A there's no talk about post-slavery population or generations. They chat about like they were only slaves a few generations ago. It's like the white man has edited out the past 400 years. I don't know who is more savage? Black or white people. Whites use people like instruments, like animals. They created a culture from their governments and business people. So you see how easy it is to make black people kill each other? From songs and they realise this is the game they gon' play and how they've taken homosexuality of the schedule, but still, have songs about killing or girl's underneath etc. In the states, they never address the issues. But they always big up the egos of dumb ass rappers. Behaviour, there are elements of them putting videos like beating their kids to actual violence and fights. Black people have lost it and are on a spiral downwards floating in the air—all being posted on social media for the world to see. We put ourselves in situations of stress. You have men in their 50's having kids, and they have kids all over the place? They only know who has got more money. Who is badder than who? It's important to be tough in black culture. In black culture, they are quick to get too Gangster or screwface because they can't control their emotions. Youths only see beef and confrontation. Songs don't help! People are chatting murder you; I'm gonna murk mans to each other like that. No one cares what we do in the black community unless it spills into theirs. Some of you don't care because you're stupid. The way we live our lives is stupid, and we have suffered from post-slavery trauma in the last 100 years. We have done nothing exceptional to address the issues. Question! Do people think everything is safe? With all this brother and sister shit when all the madness is around. Black people have no respect for other blacks work because they are black. From copyright control, there's no communication, and all you get is more screwface and a badman attitude. Not to say everyone else is perfect and we are not. To allow our musicians to formulate violence and porn into our music that affects our children, and there's nothing anyone can do about it. That's a testament to the weakness of black people all over. No judge or president is saying jack because they are like jobsworths. Big ass celebrities can't do shit. They are the top slaves because they make money for the white man, and they are not free. If you wanna be like them, then you're just as dumb. All you do is continue your ego all your life. To come up against a politician with no power, you can't. They lock us up and give different sentences to whites. They're way smarter than man on ends. Bunning spliff and chatting about the Illuminati?"

"Can I add something, Mr Felix, in response to Donna's comment earlier?"

"Sure go ahead Erykah."

"Okay, so I get the frustration and fear due to the way the streets are set up and the way our youths are behaving. But I'm seeing a lot of arrogance, ignorance and blame going on. I'm seeing 'society' being blamed, schools being criticised, the government etc. and I can't help but see a theme of blame rather than responsibility. I'm continually seeing folks on social media sharing posts of fights, news articles etc. of negative happenings as though we're stuck on it. We know there's a problem, have a rant and be angry. Anger is the stem for action but don't be consumed by it. See that as much as the negatives are portrayed; it's not the norm of our young people. Do what you have to do for your child, take responsibility - if it's society, be sure that your home teachings outweigh their peer's influence. If it's a school, engage with them highlighting your concerns if not move your child. And most importantly be true to yourself, as much of the time the problem is internal, not external. Take responsibility for yours and stop blaming others."

"Well said Erykah. Let me add a short story of my own."

"Go ahead."

"I got a unique perspective on this. I'm from the rough streets of Brixton. I'm 37 years old. If I don't tell you my religion, you can't guess it. If I don't tell you my mother's name, you can't guess it. When I was young, I lived in a two-bed council flat in Brixton, and we were so poor I shared a single bed with my brother. Six siblings were sharing one small room. I'm doing a'right now. The one thing that I've always been, the very thing you can see is black. This is what you see. You don't see my religion. You don't see my orientation. You don't see my political affiliations. But you see this." Calvin finished speaking by making hand movements around his face.

"Calvin; you're so right. That's spot on!"

"Enuh ih goes suh."

"Let me add something else," I asked.

"By all means, Erykah. The mic is yours."

"I think what is interesting is how these things are being perceived based on individual experience. I've listened to people over last few months and what I got from that, to be pro-black (advocate the positive progression of black people) you do not have to be anti-white but rather anti-white power. You can be pro-black and still maintain successful relationships with individual white people who's privilege benefit from institutionalised racism and the system it functions in. How does institutionalised racism work? Institutionalised racism is designed to benefit the advancement of white people as a group, not as individuals. Poor white people are often used to keep the core of this system alive even though they receive little privilege in return. Sure they may have minor privileges in terms of better treatment based on the colour of skin in certain circumstances and are more likely to get off with particular crimes. Still, in terms of real social and economic advancement, their prospects aren't significantly better than non-white people. Their role in today's society is a little like the overseer. This section of society are least likely to recognise racism because they do not see the social and economic benefits of being white. What people have to understand is that speaking about racism is not going to separate people from each other it's going to encourage honest discussion about how to deal with what already exists. The system is there to suppress one group and advance another. The question that is asked is, are white people prepared to fight against systemic racism which is designed to benefit them as a group? I'm not saying all white people are racist. I'm genuinely interested in why this is the message some are getting. To me, it's the opposite."

"I'm not going to argue with that. I concur."

"07891 412 268, is the number for the live link," I said. "I got some text messages to readout. First one is from 407; it says Big up yourselves! Erykah you're the new queen of the mic. Your statement on being pro-black was spot on. Keep up the knowledge? Thank you 407 your comment is greatly received. I'm humbled," but before I could read the second text. The live link rang. Calvin answered it.

"This is Resistance 89.6 FM, you're speaking to Calvin Felix. Caller what's your name and where are you calling from?"

"Hi, Mr Felix," The young-sounding voice said excitingly.

Calvin asked her name again. When she regained her composure, she took on a serious tone.

"Sorry, my name is Cleo, and I'm calling from Fulham."

"Hi Cleo; do you have something to say for the UK?"

"I do."

"Go ahead."

"Calvin; I'm a 19-year-old black girl, and I'm in the second year of doing a communications degree. I've been told I have a vibrant and sunny personality, and I get on with most people. I went for a part-time job in a newly opened Caribbean and American Soul food restaurant. In a nutshell, I was told I don't fit the image of what they're looking for? I was mortified and offended. So another time I wanted to check out the place. So four of my friends and I went one evening. All that there was to greet us at the reception was some miserable old black lady. Which could've been his mum yeah? So anyway we all expected the food to be lit. It was far from it. All our meals tasted like it was cooked nearly two days before and heated up in a microwave. There wasn't one black worker in sight. All the servers were Eastern European and half of them they had no idea of certain foods we were asking for like Okra for example. The owner was a rude, arrogant forty-something black man. So Mr Felix; why is it that when any new black-owned restaurant comes into town. Why is it hard for someone like me, who knows all the foods as my parents are Caribbean and American and I was taught about them? Why is it that I'm told I don't fit the image they want to portray unless I relax my hair and look more street? At the end of the day, Calvin! I'm proud of my natural hair, and I maintain it in respectable order. Maybe it's the way I speak? Because my family are middle class. But I'm not ashamed of who and what I am. So why is he? I thought my image would fit more? I'm not against the other girls working there. Everyone is entitled to work."

"You're right Cleo; every one with valid papers is entitled to work. I'm assuming you were born here?"

"Yes, I was?" Cleo said in response to the question asked.

"I thought so. To be honest Cleo as sad as your situation is. It's ubiquitous, and I'll tell you why? Your image, as you described, has no bearing with employing you. That's his easy excuse to put you off. The real reason you have here is that he probably isn't the owner. He probably isn't even the manager. To me, the old lady is. Well her name is on the documents, and she signs everything. But she allows her son to take care of the staff. The real owners are rich middle-aged to old white men. Like you said the food is shot. He probably employs mediocre chefs, and he employs the Europeans for two reasons. One, because they are cheaper labour. Two, they won't give attitude or take the piss with breaks etc. if they try to slack! He's probably got one or two of them over a barrel. Meaning they work there as self-employed that way he doesn't have to pay any national insurance contributions or tax on any employee. He is a modern-day Castro in a small sense. But add up more of them they're like a little army who are making money for the white man by taking money out of black people's pockets and not giving value for money. But the downside is your better off not working there. But these so called black businesses are not helping their own or ploughing any money back into black commerce or re-investing in the black community as a whole?"

"Oh, my days Mr Felix; that's such barbaric behaviour. Is there anything that can be done?"

"Boycott their businesses until they are willing to shift the goalposts. I'm all for the black pound and supporting black businesses that serve the black community in more ways than one. But I'm not an avid supporter of the ones that sell us out."

"That makes perfect sense. I've got to start somewhere."

"Listen Cleo; give Erykah a call on the offline number, and she'll give you the details to our next event?"

"Okay Mr Felix; and thank you for the advice."

"No need for thanks. It's all part of the process! Have a blessed day. Bye."

"Goodbye, Mr Felix."

"07891 412 268, that's 07891 412 268, we have half an hour left for the show. We can take two more calls. Big up to those that rang and texted today. Eddie, Donna, Krystal, Cleo, Diamond, Lex, Mary, Trevor and Wayne. Big up all your message's on social media too."

The live link number rang twice before Calvin instructed for me to answer it.

"Resistance 89.6 FM, this is the culture show. What's your name and where are calling from?"

"Sup Miss Gaines; this is Raymond, and I'm calling from East London?"

"Welcome Raymond; what's your question?"

"Mr Felix; I want to know what your stance is on the dynamics of supporting black businesses?"

"Raymond this is a purely philosophical rant! While I'm an ardent supporter of Black business & believe, as Marcus Garvey so eloquently put it 'be Black, buy Black, think Black and all else will take care of itself' there are certain factors that need to be clarified when speaking on Black group economics! While I acknowledge it's our solemn duty (not to mention the key to our survival) to support our brothers & sisters businesses, we have to stop being dogmatic about things, just because something is labelled a "Black business" doesn't mean it's for our betterment. Quid pro quo, while co-operative group economics is our responsibility to practice, we need to be discerning & make sure that business is beneficial to the collective. That drug dealer in the trap house is technically a 'Black business' should I buy some smack & support him? That pimp is technically a 'Black business' should I go trick off my money with his bottom bitch to make sure he turns a profit? See where I'm going with this? Does that Black business (a) Support, deal with, & network with other Black businesses? (b) Invest in our communities or take their earnings and spend them/ bank with the white, Asian, Arab communities? (c) Employ brothers & sisters from our communities, or mentor young brothers & sisters who have that entrepreneurial spirit? (d) Project a positive image of our community to our community? And finally (e) Are they a benefit to our specific needs in the community (i.e., for example, a fresh produce market that has fresh produce). Now I know some people will say 'Hey Calvin', "Why are you so hard on us? We don't ask that much from the Asian & Arab businesses in our communities?" Yeah, you're right, we don't. Why should we? We're not their responsibility, their family, or their ward. They have their responsibilities to look after. In short, as I stated earlier, it's quid pro quo, in group economics, both the consumers & the producers have a duty to themselves & the collective as a whole. So does that answer your query?"

"Yes, bless man! I couldn't have put it better myself!"

"Okay Raymond; thank you for your brilliant question. Bless up and one love brother!"

I quickly jumped back on the mic.

"Raymond, wait before you go! Can I say something?"

"Go ahead, Miss Gaines?"

"Cool, I was listening to a video on YouTube last week and in it was a black woman that broke down a few parts about the current state of things in America?"

"I'm interested. Go ahead?"

"Raymond, let me give you the criterion of what she said about black economics?"

"Ite, I'm listening."

"When African slaves were taken there, they were used for two patronages, textiles in the north and agricultural work in the south. Is that correct?"

"Yes, Erykah," Calvin answered.

"Now imagine you, and I play a game of Monopoly, and in that game, for four-hundred rounds, I don't let you have any money or anything on the board. Then we play another fifty rounds, and everything that you gained or earned is taken away from you. That's places like Tulsa, Oklahoma, Rosewood. Those are towns where they built black economic wealth, where they were self-sufficient, where they owned their stores, where they owned their property, and they burned them to the ground. That's four-hundred and fifty years of playing. So for four-hundred of them you don't get to play at all, not only do you not get to play but you have to play on the behalf against the person you're playing against. So you have to play and make money and earn wealth for them, and then you have to turn it over. So for fifty years you get a limited morsel, and you're allowed to play, and every time they don't like the way you're playing or catching up or doing something that's self-efficient they scorch your game, they burn your car, they burn your monopoly money. Now on the release and the onset, they tell you to catch up?

The only way you're going to catch up is if the person shares the wealth? So what if every time they share the wealth, there is psychological warfare against you that you're an equal opportunity hire. So if I had to play four hundred rounds of monopoly with you and I had to give you every bit of money I made. Then for another fifty years every time, I played, and you didn't like it, you got to burn it down just like they did in Tulsa and Rosewood. How can you win? You can't win because the game is fixed."

"And that's why economically we are always at a disadvantage. We own nothing, so why should we care? Take the UK riots in 2011; we know how it started and why? What transpired are folks taking back what was stolen and never given to them when they earned it in the first place?"

"Exactly, Raymond."

"Don't get me wrong, Miss Gaines I'm not in any shape or form condoning or have I ever instigated violence or criminal damage?"

"You're not the one on trial here, Raymond. Talk your talk?"

"Cool, Mr Felix."

"All I'm saying is that although I don't flex like that. I understand the anger and frustrations of the people in all their actions but not in its entirety."

"Well said, my brother? Raymond stay bless."

"Peace Mr Felix."

"Take care, Raymond. Thanks for calling in?"

"One love, Miss Gaines."

"We got time for one more call," Calvin said.

The phone rang for last time today.

"Caller you're live on Resistance 89.6 FM. This is Erykah speaking. What's your name and where are you calling from?" I asked, still feeling rejuvenated; I didn't want the show to end. Four hours had passed quickly.

"Hi Erykah this is Deniqua, and I'm calling from Leicester."

"How you doing Deniqua? Do you have a question or anything to say to the UK?"

"I do. I have something to say."

"Go ahead?"

"I'm aware of the pressures of being a black girl and how I'm supposed to present myself in comparison to other people around me. Right here in the UK, people don't understand the journey of a black girl or black woman."

"What kind of pressures are you personally under?" I asked precariously.

"What you mean apart from socio-economic problems?"

"Yeah?"

"How I'm frowned upon in society when I'm walking around with my hair all out in it's natural-state. Or maybe another day my hair is in braids. I went for a job interview once for the position of a secretary. The interviewer told me I had the job, but only if I took out my braids and got it relaxed or something. The interviewer was a middle-class, middle-aged black woman with whom I told after feeling sad and angry that had she gone completely out of her mind and that she'd sold her soul to the devil."

"No, you didn't?"

"I did you know."

Calvin was in the background, shaking his head in disbelief.

"So, what happened next?"

"Well, you won't believe it. I couldn't at the time. She only went and offered me the job."

"No blooming way! For real?"

"No joke and three years on I'm still there."

"So why all the drama about your hair?"

"She said it was a test of my character. She went on to explain that if such a situation arose in the office would I be able to stand up against a male-dominated environment. I did ask why I would need to be like that. She answered that I possibly couldn't be that naive."

"So was she right?"

"Right on the money. But I gave back as good as I got. The day I earned their respect was the day they invited me to lunch. Nowadays I'm one of the lads, so to speak."

"Thank you. Getting back. As black people, we need to get back to basics and have each other's back both male and female. Because by tomorrow they will go back to calling us bitches and hoes. In relation to your skin tone, hair texture, length and overall appearance, this story is an eye-opener for me. I know that colourism can go hand in hand with racism, but my understanding has always been that dark-skinned people like myself with a certain hair type always got that pass as a coolie, therefore, better than a dark-skinned girl with tightly coiled hair. Most black people should know what I mean! Hair type also goes hand in hand with colourism. It's not just about skin colour! This is why I'm very conscious of the imagery I share of black women or occasionally children. I always try to bring balance when sharing images of 'beautiful black people'. I have also witnessed well-established pages of empowerment showing only black women and children with a particular hair type as beautiful. It's a little irritating because this only shows one version of beauty while suppressing another. What you're describing would fit the description of what would be acceptable blackness as a prized dark-skinned beautiful girl to many. I can assure you being prized to many mainly because of that kind of hair type. I can tell you now these people will make you feel ugly, and you will lose confidence. You probably even don't suffer or ever have from low self-esteem. You've probably been bought up in a way that you was told you're beautiful. But as soon as you rebelled, you stopped believing in yourself, and it was further coupled by what you have phoned about. I guarantee you will go through life being told this over and over again. To be blunt, your hair texture plays a big role in how you will be perceived in life. It is not the entire source of your beauty, but in terms of you being accepted, it will help. But yes, you're 100% a beautiful dark-skinned woman. But it is essential to highlight that you are not the only version of a beautiful dark-skinned woman. I have noticed that beautiful women like yourself with the accepted hairstyles are becoming the face of dark skin woman, and I simply say there must be a broader representation to reflect our vast diversity. In my terms even the hairstyle you're sporting in this photo you just sent in. The well-kept natural look. It's another version of us."

"So basically you're saying that for me to be accepted, I must represent myself to fit in with the norm?"

"No Deniqua, what I'm trying to say is when needs must just go with the flow until you're established where you are."

"Alright, I understand. Thank you so much, Erykah. Goodbye, Mr Felix."

"Take care Deniqua," I said

"One love," Calvin answered.

Well, folks, we have come to the end of our show. Next up, is a man like DJ Suss 2 on the wheels of steel. He'll be playing you the very best in old school sounds. Big up again to everyone that phoned in and another big up to all the other listeners too. Until next week this is Calvin Felix, and you've been listening to the culture show."

"Goodbye and take care every one," I finished up saying.

Moments after the show, we went into another room for a debrief.

Everything went well from my perspective, and Keionte expressed he was happy with the show. So much so he offered me the position permanently, and it had Calvin's approval and Kyndra's endorsement as she informed Keionte that she was quitting the party to become a full-time mother. He then asked her not too entirely, and that could she after the birth come back as an advisor. She said that was a great idea, and everyone left the headquarters happy and with the sense of empowerment, but also with a lot of work to do.

Chapter 22 – The Party

"Your rage is blinding; Dad; you have to let it go. Cut it loose, before it destroys your relationship with mother?"

"I'm trying babygirl; I really am. But nothing seems to work."

"Try harder Dad? Bernie loves you! I know it's not our belief. But she is your girlfriend, and sometimes you got to indulge and make sacrifices for the betterment of your relationship."

Father and Bernie were in town for Daniel and Kira's engagement party. They arrived two days ago, both looking expatriated and out of joint with each other. Neither has said a word to the other since.

"Look, Dad, I'm not trying to lecture you? But may I remind you of the sacrifices Bernie has made helping you finally get off your addictions after all these years. I know first-hand what she has experienced don't I dad?"

"Why are you brown beating me with that brush?"

"Because Dad, you have been getting away with all your self-indulgent behaviour for far too long?"

"That's an unfair statement to make in this timeframe. I'm not the same man I used to be."

"Why are you telling me this? Go and tell Bernie! Better still, prove to her and yourself you're this reformed character you like to converse about."

"Fine, okay."

"What are you fine about, dad?"

"Once again you're right. It's not much to give Bernie a little smidgen of support. Even if it's against my philosophies," he said that statement with intent in his voice and a smile, finally, on his face.

"I'm glad to hear it. What you gon' do now?"

"I will find Bernie and do one hell of a make-up session. I don't relish my chances, but I'll give it a go."

"Last time I saw her she was in the kitchen packing some food together."

"Thank you, baby girl, I don't know where I'll be without you."

"No problem dad. Just get down there and do your thing."

"A'right, here goes everything I have."

My father and his statements always crack me up. To be honest, they were always the perfect antidote for when I needed picking up. But on this occasion, fathers antics weren't required.

After I finished getting ready, I went to check to see if Nina and Eric were ready to go. Simultaneously, they both bellowed out another ten minutes. If you didn't know them, I swear down you'd think they were joint at the hip.

I then made my way gallantly downstairs and headed towards the kitchen at the back of the house.

The place was in sheer silence. All I could hear were the birds chirping outside. The different smells that came wafting past me prickled my nose. The sensations were overwhelming that I had to investigate.

As I moved closer to the kitchen, the smell got stronger. When I reached the door, I opened it only to find Bernie packing the food and singing songs to herself.

"Hey, mum," I shouted louder above her singing.

By the way, I had startled her; it looked like she jumped right out of her skin. I tried my best not to crack up.

"Erykah, why yuh ah creep up a mi like so?"

"Mother, stop over-exaggerating! I came in normally. You're the one in a world of your own."

"Never mind that. I've got to get to church for a bit. Make sure to put the food in the fridge when it cools down. Give it ten or so minutes. Then load into the car. Now I've got to go and say three prayers."

"Only three mother?"

"Yes, dear. One each for Daniel and Kira and one for their engagement."

"That's decent of you Mother! So which church are we picking you up from?"

"UCKG Help Centre on Brixton Road."

"So I take it you forgave Dad?"

"There was nothing to forgive. He's coming along, so that is that."

"Good, okay. You better get going! I'll finish up here, and by the time church is done, we'll be there to pick both of you up."

"Bless you chile, mi ah go now."

"In a bit, mother."

"See you later, babygirl," Dad said as he came rushing past me.

"Bye."

After dad shut the door behind him, Nina and Eric came down the stairs. When they both reached the bottom, I noticed Nina was looking a bit weary.

"Hey girl, are you feeling alright?"

"I'm a bit hungry. I've been running around doing a hundred and one things for your parents and myself that I didn't get a chance to have breakfast."

"Bernie made some food. Let me see what's there."

"If there's stew chicken and rice and peas, I'll have that?"

"What do we have here? Jerk Chicken, dumplings, patties, coco bread, curry goat and hang on Stew chicken."

"Any rice and peas in there?" Nina asked anxiously.

"Lemme see! We got white and in this one, rice and peas."

"Great, can you add a dumpling too please?"

"Sure thing! Eric, you want anything?"

"Gimme some Curry goat with white rice and a festival?"

"No worries. All this plating up has made me peckish. Think I'm gonna have myself a lamb Pattie in coco bread."

After I finished serving up the food, an hour later, I got a text from Dad to say they were ready. Five minutes after we all left the house.

"Eric, would you mind driving there and because I won't be drinking? I'll drive us back."

"No problem Sis. Come you two let's go?" As Nina handed him the keys.

When we all reached outside, Eric got to the car first as he got in and started it. Shortly after both Nina and I got in. She turned to me and asked.

"Where are your Aunt and Uncle staying Erykah?"

"They're staying with my Aunt Lola and Uncle Sebastian."

"Oh, I see. So how're things between them?"

"Well, apparently they're looking into marriage guidance."

"Wait for real! Since when did elder black folk go seek counsel for anything in this country?"

"I don't know. All I know is Mum and Dad have tried talking to them, and for sure you can guarantee Aunt Lola will say something."

"I see, that's good, isn't it?"

"I don't think it will matter. You see, my Aunt CeCe is a woman unto her own. She is one woman that defies every stereotype. The stereotype of what it is to be a good wife, a good mother, a good friend, a good businesswoman. She once told me that it's alright not to be perfect. If your workload becomes too much, It's okay to drop the ball and see if someone else will pick it up for a bit. When you try and delegate responsibility, and it's not reciprocated, that if it plays with your sanity, you need to know how to release the stress and move on,"

"I can't wait to see you Aunt again," Nina replied, looking a bit more upbeat and perky. The food did her good. In fact It did us all good.

Donte was making his way to the party with Trae, Syreena and Simeon.

The first stop for us was to pick up Mum and Dad. When we arrived, I spotted them outside on the pavement, both acting in a cheerful mood. They were laughing and chatting with other church-goers. It took us nearly ten minutes to prize them away.

I got out of the car and walked towards them. Dad saw me first and wasted no time in introducing me to the whole street.

"Everybody this is my one and only beautiful and intelligent daughter Erykah,"

"Hi, Erykah." The lady who welcomed me first was sporting a rather beautiful Crown hat on her head.

"Hey, Erykah." A gentleman around fathers age who was standing next to the lady with the lovely hat said that.

"Baby girl, this is Yvonne and her husband, Thomas?"

"Hello, hi," I said back.

"This two lovely people are Mitchell and Jannah?"

"Hey."

"Your father was just telling us that you run a gym and you're a Radio Presenter too?"

"Did he now?"

"Yes, indeed, and he was quite vocal about it."

"Well, father should know I'm a very private person."

"Oh chile, what's the big deal?" Bernie remonstrated.

"Nothing, yes I'm the deputy director of the Body Active gym group, and I am an assistant social-commentator on the Culture show on Resistance 89.6 FM. You people should check it out one time. It's on a Sunday afternoon between two and six pm?"

"Sound's intriguing!" Mitchell said all happy and excited.

Miraculously, these elder folk did have the sun shining from within.

"I'm sorry, everyone. I would love to stay and chat some more, but we have to get going."

"Yes, we do!" Dad replied as he looked at his watch, then back at me.

"But here, take my card," I said as I handed two cards out for both couples. "Just text me if you want a personal trainer or a workout at the gym. Please book twenty-four hours in advance so I can sort you one and that come's with discounts. Same with the radio show so I can send you the details if you forget today."

"Howard, your daughter is such a blessing?" Mitchell referred.

"Don't I know it," Father said, cracking up to himself while acting like he didn't know what to do with the comment.

"Anyway, Dad, we got to get going now," I said as I started making my way back towards the car.

"A'right, a'right we are right behind you. Let us say our goodbyes first, and we'll be there in a minute."

"Fine, make it quick, as we are pressed for time as it is." Father bowed his head back in compliance. I hope he doesn't take the piss.

When I got back to the car and got in, I didn't even get settled before the brother and sister combo launched in with twenty questions each.

"Your father is still the ardent character he's always been and I can see where you get your fiery nature from," Nina questioned first.

"And don't I know it?" I replied sarcastically as mother and father made their way to the car.

When they finally reached, father opened the front door so that he could let Bernie in. Regardless of what he has been through the years. He still kept his old school mannerisms about him.

On the rare occasions when I used to ask him what mother was like, he would fill my head with the most beautiful adventuress stories, each one more extravagant than the one told before.

Bernie slowly manoeuvred her large frame into the car as she huffed and puffed herself into her seat.

"Dear God, I'm getting old." She turned and said to Eric.

"You don't look a day older than twenty-one Miss Clark." He remarked back.

"Ain't you ever the charmer?" Bernie replied as she playfully hit him on the arm and giggled like a schoolgirl.

"It's true, Miss Clark. Yu know seh how Mr Gaines love im yung t'ings."

"Oh, stop it," she continued giggling like it was going out of fashion.

"Hey mother, you better watch him, you know?" I said.

"Watch what Erykah?" Eric remarked while giving me a knowing wink.

As soon as dad entered the car, I took one look at him and burst into fits of laughter, Nina followed suit, then Eric and finally Bernie.

"A wah yah laugh so?" Father asked, looking a bit perplexed.

"It's nothing father. Don't worry yourself."

"A'right, if yuh seh so!" He answered back as we continued to chuckle amongst ourselves, father stayed looking perplexed.

As mother and father hailed and waved goodbye to their newfound friends. Eric started up the car again, and when he'd done all his checks, we sped off in the direction towards Acre lane.

Before I knew it, we were passing through Clapham Junction. Even though it was Sunday, I noticed one difference between London and Manchester that life doesn't slow down in London, no matter what day of the week it was.

We kept on going, and within a few minutes, we were cruising along Battersea Bridge road.

The sun was out, even though it was an overcast day.

As we slowly went over the bridge, halfway through we had stopped because of traffic. For the few minutes we were waiting to move, we took in the marvel of the River Thames and the surrounding buildings. I took a few pictures, and so did everyone else. The Royal Borough of Kensington and Chelsea is a part of London that makes you feel it doesn't have the trouble it possesses.

"How far mi sista house from ear?" Father blurted out.

"Just a few more miles, dad."

"A'right, gud. Cah mi hungry bad?"

"I swear down you ate before you left for church?"

"Mi did! Buh mi a wuk up an appetite before mi led."

"Well, no worries. We will be there in about ten minutes."

And I was exactly right. Ten minutes later and we were pulling into Aunt Lola's mansion forecourt.

There were cars of every kind that boasted money. I spotted two Lamborghini's, a couple of Ferrari's, a Maybach, Rolls-Royce, A few Bentleys, to name a few.

Black people were everywhere. Some had arrived before we did, and others were walking into the Mansion. Outside I spotted some men in light red jackets, white shirts, sporting a black bow-tie, black trousers and shoes.

As we drove a little further, one of them approached our car. Eric came to a sudden halt and wound his window down.

"Is everything good?" Eric suspiciously asked.

"Yes, sir, everything is fine. Hi I'm Steven, and I'm a parking valet," he said, introducing himself.

"Wah gwaan Steven?" Eric sarcastically answered.

"I'm good. We have to ask are you family or friends of the couple?!"

"We are family!" All of us answered back in our sing-song voices.

Steven first laughed at our antics, and then he pulled a small book from the inside of his jacket, opened it out and then he ripped off what appeared to be a ticket.

"You're in bay A7, which is at the back of here and to your right." He instructed by pointing his fingers all over the place.

"Bless up, Steven," Eric said as he handed him a twenty-pound tip.

"Someone's a bit flush with their money?" Bernie shockingly stated to Eric.

"It's nothing, Miss Clark."

"Wah yuh mean nothing?" Bernie angrily sneered back. "In my day we didn't tip people for telling us where to park."

I felt one of Bernie's sermons coming on. I instructed Eric in a language that she would find hard to comprehend to stop.

"Fair enough, Miss Clark. Do you think I should ask for my money back?" He said as he looked at her with anticipation.

"Don't be so foolish young man!"

"Eric, don't indulge her?" I whispered to him.

He looked back at me and then to Bernie and continued to park up the car while saying nothing else.

"Respect young man," Father said as he patted Eric on the back.

The stone-cold look Bernie gave father even gave me chills. I didn't think she had that in her. But a woman scorned or unfairly treated is a woman to be wary of.

Shortly afterwards, Syreena texted me first and said they were five minutes away. I instructed the others to make their way in as I waited for Donte and his lot to arrive. Secondly, Chantel left a WhatsApp voice note saying Dominique, and she just landed at LAX airport in Los Angeles for a fashion shoot for Vogue Magazine and then onto Essence Magazine in New York for another. I was so thrilled for her. She also said these were the prelude shoots until the big fashion shows that start in February 2016.

As I watched my dad and the rest of the clan make their way into the mansion. I couldn't help but think about how much progress he has made since the last time I saw him.

It was never easy dealing with someone who was going through the same pain for years as you have. But the only difference was that I was a child.

Not that I'm saying it's any easier.

When they all reached inside, something quickly took my gaze away from them. As I looked across the forecourt, I spotted Marcus and his wife, Nicci.

Within seconds of me staring, Nicci saw me first walking towards them. She lightly tapped Marcus on his arm and then pointed towards me, coming in their direction.

It didn't take long for me to reach where they were. But as soon as I did Nicci stepped to me first, held my gaze for a few moments and then she threw her arms around me and gave me an almighty, yet emotional hug that seemed to last forever.

When she finally took herself away from the embrace. She stared at me again. Then all of a sudden out of nowhere, she burst into tears.

"What's the matter, Nicci?" I asked concerningly.

"Ah Erykah, I'm alright. It's overwhelming seeing you in the flesh again."

"Overwhelming, but why?"

"Everything, everything that has happened to you recently. Marcus has been filling me in."

"Oh, Nicci, it's okay. Everything is good now."

"Are you sure? You have been through a hell of a lot recently."

"When is anyone ever sure and yes, I've been through a lot. But some people are going through a lot worse. Besides, I got a lot of support. Your husband has been tremendous throughout the court case. He's gotta be one-off if not, the best defence lawyer in the country and today is my cousin's engagement, and I intend to enjoy it to the maximum."

"Don't say that about him? You're going to give him a bigger ego than he has already."

"Nicci, I am standing right next to you." Marcus reiterated.

"And so you are," Nicci sarcastically replied as she dismissed Marcus's comment in a friendly manner. But you could tell she wasn't a woman to mess with.

Nicci," I said, raising my voice a little louder, enough that she could hear me.

"Yes, Erykah?" She replied.

"Where's Tiffany?"

"Oh, she went inside with two of her friends to get changed for the pool."

"I must catch up with her later?"

"Definitely! I'll let her know. You know she's very fond of you?"

"I do indeed. I love that girl. Your Tiff is a very astute and clued up fifteen-year-old. There's no doubt with you two for parents. She'll go far."

"Ah, that's such a nice sentiment, Erykah. Bless you, girl."

"So how's the bump?" I asked.

"Keeping me up half the night. You wait until you have your first, you'll see what I'm on about."

"And that won't be for a long time yet? And on that note, I better catch up with the others. I'll see you lot inside. Take care, guys." As I gave each of them a hug, and then I made my way inside.

Moments later and I was inside the mansion. On my arrival, I was greeted by another red coat who offered me a glass of Champagne.

I took a glass, smiled and said thank you. Then I proceeded to look for Daniel and Kira. But as I searched through the melee of people, I ended up in the back garden near the swimming pool.

"Erykah, over here?" Came a voice shouting over the music and there was only one voice capable of doing that.

"Godfather," I shouted back to my surprise, as I galloped towards him. As soon as I reached him, I didn't care in the slightest who saw. I jumped on him and hugged him for dear life.

"Hey Goddaughter, how's t'ings?"

"I'm good Winston. For once in a while, I can't complain."

"That's good. So where's this boyfriend your father has been telling me about?"

"He'll soon be here. He just texted me."

"A war! Yah know seh im ave fi pass mi test."

"What are you on about Godfather?"

"My test to see if he is man enough for you."

"You're joking, right?"

Godfather gave me one of his formidable tilt your head to the side kind of looks that looked very menacing even when he was joking. Then he turned his attention to Bernie, father and his wife, Rachael. Then after a few moments, he focused his attention back to me.

"You're not joking, are you?"

"Babygirl, yah know seh yuh Godfather neva joke bout dis kinda things."

"Okie Dokie dad?" I answered back while I chuckled to myself inside.

After I briefly had a catch up with Rachael, I left the elders to chat amongst themselves as I proceeded to try and locate Daniel and Kira.

I walked a little further on, my phone rang. I took it out of my handbag. Donte was calling me, so I answered it straight away.

"Hey, babe, where you at?"

"Erykah, I've just pulled up in the car park. What's with all these redcoats everywhere"

"They're working here. Do you want me to come and meet you?"

"Yeah, sure."

I made my way to the front door; I noticed these two big burly looking guys approaching from the opposite direction. As they went past me, I look at them both square in the eyes. They seemed familiar, but I couldn't for the life of me, remember where I've seen them before. They, on the other hand, looked at me in a cold-hearted manner. The vibes I was getting from them was chilling me to the core, and they were two of the darkest complexions I've seen in time.

As I exited out of the mansion, I continued my march towards Donte's car, the sight of those two guys had my brain bugging out. With each step further I took, bit by bit, I began to remember as I pieced together my memory of them.

"I got it?" I shouted out in jubilation because I recollected where I saw them last.

"Baby, are you feeling alright?" As soon as Donte said those words, my joy turned into fear. I look at him as my body began to tremble. Donte stepped towards me and behind him was Syreena. I felt my breaths getting shorter and shorter as my body began to shudder as a result of my instantaneous revulsion.

"Erykah what's the matter? Why are you shaking like that?"

"Donte, I, I, I, saw, s, s, s, saw," I couldn't give him a proper answer because I was stuttering my words. As my abrupt memory of the burly fuckers became more transparent, the velocity of my anxiety attack became more violent.

"Erykah, what are you trying to say?" Donte asked.

I looked at Syreena and then beyond her. I noticed quite a few onlookers were standing there and staring. Trae, Simeon and Eric identified the same folk and began to proceed in the direction of the people taking the liberty of filming me like I was some kind of freak. Fucking bastards instead of trying to help they stand there like I'm some form of entertainment, arseholes.

"Erykah, what are you on about? What did you see that's got you wound up like this?"

I couldn't answer Donte. I tried to speak, but no sound was coming out. Everything around me went silent as my head began to spin into a frenzy, and my body was doing a dance of its own.

Donte and the others were talking to me. But everyone looked like goldfish with their mouths bobbing open and shut.

Syreena tried to take my inhaler out of my bag, but it was proving a difficult task for her. It took Donte and a redcoat to try and slow me down and bring me back to normality. But it was clear. The attackers from the hospital were here as I recounted the recollections of that night, I began to pee myself when I noticed Nina and Kira coming towards me first then the others were following suit.

As soon as Danika jumped in the way and took over my situation, she put her hands on my shoulders, trying to steady my out of control body. I smiled a happy to see her smile, but all the same, I couldn't control my fear. Syreena tried to give me my inhaler. The last thing I noticed was her hand coming up to my mouth as the light of day around me was getting darker and darker.

What seemed like ages later? Only five minutes had passed. When I woke up, my head felt groggy, and the inside of my throat felt like it had been slashed with a razor.

As I held my hand gently around my throat, Aunt Lola and Danika were sitting nearest to me. Donte and Nina were situated behind them.

"Water, I need some water please?" I said as my voice kept cutting up.

Aunt Lola poured me some water and handed it to me. As I took the glass, my hand shook a little; so I couldn't hold the glass for myself.

Danika kindly took it from me and fed me a couple of sips before she laid it to rest on the side table.

As the fogginess in my head began to disperse, I noticed I was in Aunt Lola's and Uncle Sebastian's bedroom. I wasn't alone, either. Mother, Father, Winston, Rachael, Daniel, Kira, Trae, Danika, Syreena, Simeon, Aunt Lola, Uncle Sebastian, Aunt CeCe, Uncle Jeb, Darius, J'nay and their toddler son Terrell, Nina, Xavi, Eric, Marcus, Nicci and Donte were all present in the room too. That's how big it was.

Everyone focused their energy on me, waiting in anticipation for what I had to reveal.

I half managed to sit up with the help of Danika I was tucked in and felt slightly less fearful.

"Donte, Godfather come over here please?" I ordered.

The two of them came over and sat on either side of the bed. They looked at each other and then back at me with perplexed looks on their faces.

"Relax guys; I want to introduce you two properly to each other. That's all."

"Erykah, you're funny. Don't you think we have already?" Godfather stated.

"Yeah, babe, who do you think carried you upstairs?" Donte said.

"It was your Godfather baby girl!" Father yelled out above everyone else.

"Thank you, Dad and thanks, Godfather."

"No sweat," Winston replied.

"So are you going to tell us what your shakes were about?" Kira impatiently asked.

"Yes," I said as I held onto Donte's hand.

"It's alright baby I gotcha." Donte looked at me with a reassuring smile. I began to hold my breathing down as I took two squirts of my brown inhaler. When I was ready, I signalled for everyone to come closer.

"Fam, don't be alarmed until I've finished?" I authoritatively said.

"It's cool babe. Take your time?"

"The reason I had an episode."

"Yes, Yes," a few of them shouted out.

"Remember, baby, don't be alarmed."

"Erykah, you're freaking me out. Just tell us?"

I gripped Donte's hand a little tighter. By his non-reaction, I gathered he didn't feel it.

"I saw the guy that attack me in the hospital."

Straight away, there were gasps and groans. Uncle Sebastian, Father and Uncle Jeb began walking towards the door. Donte tried to free himself from my grasp. But I held on tighter and shook my head in disapproval.

"What the fuck?" I watched Donte's pupils enlarge, and his face began to contort with rage.

The rest were whispering amongst themselves. Father and my Uncles were about to open the door. That's when I bawled out towards their direction.

"Stop!" I yelled for dear life. "Please wait?"

"Erykah a wah di rass?" Uncle Jeb was angry and out of joint and ready for war. That was good, but I had a plan.

"Hold your horse's everyone? First off sekkle yourselves if you go steaming down there like raging bulls, you're going to alert them of your presence and expose yourselves maybe into a trap. Who knows how many of them are here?"

"So what do you suggest we do Cuz?" Daniel concerningly asked.

"First off we need a plan."

"Good Idea Erykah. Do you have one?" Marcus asked.

"Yes, I do. If Nina agrees."

"Agree with what?" She reiterated.

"We all go down and spread ourselves about but near enough to get to myself and Nina quickly."

"Da fuck you talking about baby?"

"We go down all of us, exactly twenty secs apart. The couples that are left stay together and act normal. Pretend nothing has happened and appear to enjoy the party. So we don't arouse suspicion that we are onto them. Uncle Sebastian, Father, Uncle Jeb and Godfather get tooled up and wait in the background ready to pounce."

"Pounce for what Erykah?" Aunt CeCe asked with grave concern in her voice.

"Nina and I will be bait."

There were more gasps and groans.

"I don't like the sound of this; I don't like it one bit?" Syreena said with her fragile self. I instructed her to come over. As she sat down next to me, I cradled her in my arms. I could feel how scared she was. She was trembling with fear. This was defiantly bringing back her childhood attack. The expressions and emotions were plastered all over her face.

"Simeon take Syreena and yourselves to one of the guest rooms. Danika will show you where to go. Kira, you go as well. Nicci too. You're pregnant. Cousin Darius and J'nay you go too. We need some men in there to protect the women. Uncle Sebastian will come and give you a piece in a bit."

After they all left, I continued.

"Right listen up y'all. We are going to do this the Gaines and Briscoe way. That means no police and not alerting any of the guests. I got the perfect plan. Nina and I will lure them simply into the library. For a few moments, we play the part. Marcus, you're hiding in plain sight opposite the library. After you have seen, all of their men follow Nina and me into the library. Give it approximately 120 seconds then you make some excuse you're looking for the master of the house. They will be suspicious, so they'll probably send you on your way or take you captive as well. Are you cool with that?"

"You know me, Erykah? I'm down for whatever."

"Good that's great to hear. Then after another five minutes from the front door, Trae, Xavi, Daniel, Eric and Donte come into the room locked and loaded just to startle them. Not shoot, unless they fire first if they have guns. But I presume they will. That will render them all to face in that direction. One of them will have a gun on us. That's when Uncle Sebastian, Father, Uncle Jeb and Winston come in from the adjoining study and get them from the back. Not if, but when they surrender. That's when Donte's Uncle Mike turns up, and the rest is history."

"Donte's Uncle Mike, and what does he exactly do?" Aunt Lola curiously asked.

"My Uncle is a specialist in getting rid of things that can't be found." Donte remonstrated by answering Aunt Lola's question.

"Oh, is he now. I think I like the sound of your Uncle Mike," Aunt Lola said with a big smile on her face. In turn, Donte shook his head at her in recognition.

"Okay, how we gon' execute this first?" Daniel questioned.

"First off, Mother, Aunt Lola, Aunt CeCe and Rachael make your way towards the back garden and keep those guests occupied by getting the DJ to ramp up the party vibes and get people raving. Then Nina and I will go downstairs and casually make our way towards the library. Afterwards, Marcus, you get yourself into position. Donte and the rest you follow suit. Allow exactly three minutes to pass after Marcus has entered the library, and that'll be your cue to go in."

"Howard, Jeboniah and Winston follow me. I got a back staircase that leads into the study." Uncle Sebastian instructed.

Everyone began to get themselves into position. I looked at Nina and signalled for her to make moves.

As I began to make my way out of the bedroom, Bernie came and stood right in front of me, which forced me to stop abruptly.

"Mother, is everything good?"

"Yes mi dear, hol' mi hand real quick? Mi wan fi seh a likkle prayer fa yuh."

Bernie took my hand and Nina's in hers and began to say a prayer for us.

"Dear Lord, please bless an protect mi daughter in the bravery she is about to perform. Even tho mi nah agree wit it. May yuh also bless an protect her friend Nina. What they are about to do is for the good of all the family. Those bad guys, may they be weakened in their efforts to try and hurt anyone. Praise the Lord, Amen?"

"Thank you, mother, much appreciated."

"Please, be careful?"

"It's alright. I know what I'm doing."

"I hope so chile, mi hope so."

I took another look at Nina, as we both made our way downstairs.

I could hear people raving already, and the music was thumping out some intense bass and treble.

That was the final signal to get our asses downstairs.

As we reached the foot of the stairs, people we haven't seen in years were coming up to us. As I returned their greetings, I spotted two more guys that didn't seem to fit in with the atmosphere.

I gently nudged Nina in her arm while she was hugging and chatting to the guests we knew.

"What's up, girl?" She said in response.

"Don't look too fast. But over my shoulder to my left. You see those guys over there dressed in black?"

"Oh, my gosh Erykah, they're part of the same crew aren't they?"

"Well, they don't look like anyone the family would know?"

"I concur. They look well shifty for my liking. So what do we do now?"

"We stick to the plan and carry on as normal."

"Okay, let's lead them to the library."

"Cool, let's go!"

We said our goodbyes to the guests and continued heading towards the direction of the library.

"Erykah!"

"Yes, Nina?"

"Ain't you scared in the slightest?"

"Inside, I'm petrified. But it's vitally imperative we keep our cool. Otherwise, the plan will be preposterous."

"I know. But we are playing a dangerous game."

"Don't worry! My family are very professional when it comes to matters that affect the livelihood and lives of all of us."

"There is some comfort in knowing that."

"Good, let's focus on what needs to be done and get this over and done with."

"Alright, let's do this?"

We continued to make our way towards the library and just like that the burly fuckers started to follow suit.

"They are coming, so be ready to count two minutes from when we are inside?"

"I gotcha, girl."

As we gathered pace, so did our followers. Where he was meant to be, Marcus was in position. I gave him a knowing wink as we passed him. When we reached the entrance of the library, Nina opened up the door as I had a glance back. They were still coming. Good, I thought to myself.

When we finally got inside, straight away, we acted like we were lost.

"Where are you on the countdown?" I precariously asked Nina.

"Another fifty seconds to go?" She said with anxiety in her voice.

If I wasn't feeling scared before, then it suddenly dawned on me that this shit in a matter of seconds was about to happen and I didn't feel prepared or ready in the slenderest.

We started to pace around in circles, pretending to scrummage through the books.

"What did you say the name of that book was?" I said as I heard the door handle turning.

"Figures Of The Fallen by Reese Brown?" Nina answered.

"That's the one?" As I gave Nina the signal, the door began to slowly open. My heart started beating ten to the dozen. I kept on telling myself, don't panic. Things must go according to plan.

When the door finally opened, the burly fuckers came in with some mean-mugging looks on their faces. My heart rate sped up some more as I spotted a few beads of sweat falling from Nina's forehead.

"Hello, can I help you?" I first said to the bigger one of the two.

"Yeah, you can help us?" He said in response as he slowly moved his already unzipped jacket to one side, brandishing a gun that was neatly tucked into his trousers.

Behind myself, I heard Nina gasp. I, on the other hand, wasn't at all surprised in the least.

As I was about to respond, the door opened again and in walked Marcus looking all startled and confused. The smaller fucker grabbed Marcus by his upper arm and shuffled him over towards us.

"Are you girls, good?" He asked, whispering.

"Kinda, did you see the boys outside?"

"Yes, they are waiting for their time."

"Oh, good. Let's hope these sons of bitches don't kill us first."

"Quiet you lot over there?" The bigger one said.

The smaller one was pointing his gun at us. My nerves started to play havoc with my mind. I was getting that feeling my life for all it had succumbed too was coming to an end right here and now.

"All of you move over by the bookshelf behind you." The smaller fucker angrily said while maintaining his gun pointed at us.

We didn't take a second longer than we had too. As he instructed, we all sheepishly shuffled ourselves towards the bookshelf that was behind us.

"Tie them up, Gee?"

The other one did as he was told and began to tie us up.

"What do you want from us?" Nina nervously blurted out. But she was ignored.

"Take it, easy girl," I said as I tugged at her forearm.

"When are the guys coming?" She continued in her nervous state.

"In about," I said as I looked down at my watch. "Five, four, three, two and one!"

Right on cue, Donte, Eric, Trae, Daniel and Xavi entered the room; they spotted that the burly fuckers were packing, immediately they all drew for their pieces as soon as the fuckers aimed their guns at them.

"Drop your fucking weapons right now and put your hands up?" Donte instructed in a take-charge kind of manner. "Erykah, Nina, Marcus, are you all alright?"

"I am now," I replied.

"Yes, Donte," Nina answered back.

Marcus gave him a knowing nod of the head.

"Who the fuck are you lot?" The big one asked first with his hands up.

"More to the question is. Who the fuck are you, and why are you holding my girlfriend and her friend's captive?" Donte said as he held his gun up, pointing towards his head.

"I ain't telling you shit?" He replied. As he did, I noticed the smaller one was beginning to sweat more. I somehow managed to signal Trae without the fuckers seeing that the smaller one was the one to get too.

While Trae was whispering to Donte, Daniel and Eric came over and untied us.

"You lot good?" Eric asked.

"We are fine, Eric," I replied.

All of us stayed put where we were seated. Donte, Trae and Xavi were still holding the fuckers captive.

Moments later, both my Uncles, father and godfather ambled in through the adjoining door.

"Is everything under control over there?" Uncle Sebastian quizzed.

"It most certainly is, sir," Donte replied.

All the men looked cool, calm and collected as they handcuffed the criminals. Nina began to form a smile on her face as she watched the love of her life become one of us right in front of our eyes.

For once, one of Uncle Sebastian's toys came in handy.

All this time and I didn't feel I could let these guys go without at least questioning them first.

I walked over to where the boys were holding them. I turned my attention to the giant guy first.

I took one look at Donte and gave him the nod. He knew what it meant.

"Listen fucker," I said first as I slapped him hard across his face. He didn't even flinch, but instead, he bought up the biggest screwface and didn't take his weed-induced eyes off me.

I took it upon myself and placed myself on his lap. Both my legs were either side of him in the straddle position. Donte handed me a gun as I began to get information from the firm that has been making our lives a misery.

"So, motherfucker, this is how things are going to go down?" A bead of sweat began to break out from his forehead. "I'm going to ask you some questions. If I like what I hear, we may consider letting you go so you get to live another day. If you don't comply, then there will be consequences."

"Well, you're wasting your time. Coz I ain't saying shit, bitch."

Now he was getting me vex. I took the gun and turned it the other way around and butted the back of his head. It instantly knocked him out.

I took myself over to where Uncle was holding the other guy.

I did the same manoeuvre to him as I did the other guy.

As I set myself upon his lap, as I did, I could feel him beginning to shake. This dude couldn't be more than twenty years old.

"Please, please, I beg you. Don't kill me?" He pleaded so desperately. Something about him wasn't sitting right with me. This dude didn't feel gangster at all.

"Uncle Jeb, untie him please?"

"You say what?"

"Uncle, I know you heard me the first time."

"But why, Erykah?"

"Trust me. I know what I'm doing, Uncle."

"Cha Jeb, a dat what she seh," Father reiterated.

Uncle gave father a look of discontent. Father held his gaze equal to Uncle Jeb's dissatisfaction. In the end, Uncle gave in and untied the man.

"Move other there?" I instructed him by pointing my gun in the direction of the sofa.

He slowly shifted his body to where I told him to go without even taking his eyes off me. When he finally settled down, he was trembling far worse than before.

"Alright young man, start talking?"

"What do you want to know?"

"Everything? First off, let's start with your name."

"Ma, ma, my name is Jamal miss."

"Good! Now that wasn't so bad, was it?"

"No mam."

I gave everyone else a cheeky wink. Donte was shaking his head at the way I was toying with the boy.

Father knew what I was up too. He began to chuckle to himself. But I could see, the more he thought about it, the more it made him laugh harder.

"Well, Jamal, what you got to say for yourself young man?"

"To be honest. I didn't want any part of this."

"So if that's the case. Why in the hell are you on this mission?"

"I was forced, Mam."

"Forced, how?"

"They have something over my family."

"Like what?"

"These people ain't no joke. They will kill me and everyone in my family if I say anymore."

"What and you think we are?"

"No mam, I don't underestimate any of you one bit. But I can't afford to be as expansive as you think I should be."

"Look, Jamal, let me put this another way. I could tell from the moment I first saw you that you ain't a bad person. Whatever you may think your ex-bosses will do to you. I know you have a good heart, only by the way you speak and express yourself. I was in your position around thirteen years ago. So I know what you're going through! But deep down, you know you got to do the right thing and don't worry about them. If you tell us what we need to know, I'll personally make sure we protect you! Ain't that the truth guys?"

"Yes." I got a resounding response from everyone.

"Okay. I'll talk."

"That's good. Go ahead."

"Well, the name of the organisation is run by some Jamaicans from yard. The head manz in charge is a guy known as Trevor Foster. He's a nasty piece of work."

"Bloody hell, that motherfucker," Donte blurted out.

"I take it you have heard of him, babe?"

"I've more than heard of him."

"Who is this son of a bitch?" Father chipped in anguish.

"The man Jamal is saying who his boss, is none other than Trevor Foster. He used to work for my father's firm back in the day."

"So, something dread must've gone down for his firm wanting your family and anyone associated with them, dead, babe."

"Trevor was head security at my father's nightclub, Little Jamdown."

"The one we were at last week?"

"Yes, baby. I'm surprised you remembered. After the way."

"Shush," I whispered in his ear. "I don't want my father or Uncles hearing about my shenanigans."

"Duly noted, sorry."

"It's alright babe. Finish up."

"Well, my father found out through a valuable source that Trevor and his henchmen were planning a coo to take over all our families businesses. Father confronted him one night while he was at work. Foster didn't even deny it, and he went on to say that he was relishing the opportunity to take the William's family down."

"I take it he hasn't succeeded yet? Hence me stating the obvious."

"Now I know what all this coming after us is about. It's time for me to go phone Uncle Mike and tell them wah gwaan."

"Wait before you go! Are you saying that they are the same person's that came at us at Rich Mix and the hospital?"

"I have no fun in saying this. Yes, they are the same firm."

Based on what Donte just relayed to me. I took the opportunity to give the unconscious fucker a few more kicks to the back of his head.

But it still didn't feel enough.

"So, what now?"

"Like I said. I need to know what my mother feels to do first."

"Alright, you go ring her and your Uncle, and we will wait upon you until you get back?"

"Alright baby, in a bit."

"In a bit babe," I replied.

While Donte was gone, I delegated Xavi and Nina to tell the rest of the family everything was under control.

Father, both Uncles and Godfather, lifted the big fucker off the floor and tied him to a chair.

While they kept a close eye on him, I took the opportunity to ask Jamal a few more questions.

"Jamal."

"Yes, Mam."

"Enough with the mam business, I'm not old yet. Just Erykah will be fine."

"Yes, Erykah."

"I want to ask you a few things about yourself?"

"Anything, you name it?"

"First off. Is there any more of your crew here at the party?"

"No, Erykah."

"Alright, good. Daniel, Trae and Eric make sure the party is still running smoothly. Make sure to act like nothing is happening. By then the others will be down to mingle after Xavi and Nina informs them."

"Cool Cuz, see you in a bit," Daniel said.

"Secondly, Jamal, is there any more coming as a backup?"

"No, but we have to check-in at around 18:00 hours."

"Which is about half an hour from now."

"Yes, but Vincent has the burner on him."

As soon as he said that Uncle Jeb searched Vincent, moments later, he emerged with it.

Afterwards, Donte appeared. I quickly filled him in on what happened between Jamal and myself. I didn't hesitate in asking him if it was cool to take Jamal under our wing and give him a job at Body Active. Donte concurred it was a great idea because we could pick Jamal's brains on the whereabouts of Foster's base while protecting him at the same time. So now I had a proposal to put to him.

"Jamal, do you live with anyone?"

"Yes, my babymother Shanice and our one-year-old son Jesse."

I had a quick word with Uncle Sebastian and Marcus, and they both agreed with what I'd asked of them.

"Good, listen up Jamal. From the moment you don't deliver our dead bodies to Foster then it's game over for you. So what we are proposing may seem a bit radical to you at first, but if you want to live, we can set up a whole new life for you, your girl and your son. First off this is Marcus, our family lawyer."

"Hey Jamal," Marcus extended out his arm to greet him.

"Nice to meet you Marcus, sorry about before."

"It's okay kid. You didn't do anything."

"Thank you."

"You're welcome."

"Marcus here knows a man that can give you a whole new identity."

"I'd rather take my chances than having plastic surgery."

"No one said anything about plastic surgery? I'm talking about a change of name, social security number, a new passport and a new location to live where Foster can't find you. You get my drift now?"

"Oh, my days. You must think I'm a fool?"

"On the contrary. It doesn't matter."

"Oh, okay. Man, I thought I had to, you know? Damn, phew. Thank fuck for that."

"Jamal, how old are you?"

"I'm nineteen."

"Alright cool. Also what else we're proposing is that you come and work for Donte and me at our new North London gym. Thirdly, my Uncle Sebastian has agreed and if you want it. He will find you a house for your family. He's agreed to pay for the 1st years rent and home insurance in advance. After that, you're on your own with all that. Plus I suggest in the inevitability that things go belly up you take out some life insurance on yourself, so you have something to leave Shanice and Jesse, Okay?"

"I got it and thank you all so much. I'm stoked. I've wanted for the longest time to get away from Foster and his goons. But he has had my family over a barrel for the longest time, and my people haven't been able to live normal lives."

"Don't worry about all that. That will be taken care off. Let's just say for now that Foster won't know what hit him."

Half an hour later, we instructed Jamal to contact Foster. He told him that Vincent got caught up in the crossfire and was dead and that all of us got away. Immediately Foster was enraged and ordered his crew to come after Jamal and us.

Straight away, we collectively put a plan in motion real fast.

First things first, we shut the party down and got the redcoats to clear everyone out safely.

Donte called upon his best friend Elijah who ran his own security company. We got him to pick up Shanice and Jesse and pack some belongings too. With an hour of him doing that a neighbour across the road who was good friends with Jamal, informed him Jamal's house was on fire. Elijah bought Shanice and Jesse to where we were. When they reached, we informed him and Shanice of everything.

Secondly, Uncle Mike came and did his thing.

Third off, Uncle Sebastian and Aunt Lola's mansion was compromised. Over the coming days, they organised the sale of it and moved into a mansion in the heart of Hampstead Heath.

Everyone else was fine because Foster had no idea where anyone else lived, and it proved to be the fact.

For about a week everyone else stayed at one of Uncle Sebastian's safe houses, in that time Donte's Uncle Mike and a whole bag of his crew went to war with Foster.

On the eighth morning at our safe house, Donte got a call from him saying that Foster and his firm were no more. It became widespread news all over the world. The media and the government labelled it as terrorism at first. But when they realised it was Jamaicans involved they quickly blamed it on drugs.

Those stereotypical notions kept the heat off our families and friends.

For the rest of us, we went back to our lives. Jamal and his family were settling in well into their new home and had no trouble yet? He was now known as Ethan and Shanice become Sara, and baby Jesse was called Anthony. He was also thriving in his new role as a personal trainer too.

Aunt Lola, Uncle Sebastian, Daniel and Danika were doing fine in their new surroundings. Once everything had calmed down, they organised another engagement party, and this one went without a hoot.

Everyone made an oath as not to talk about this to anyone else.

As I reflected over the last few weeks, I couldn't help but feel that this wasn't over. All any us could do for now was to keep extra vigilant and to make sure we were looking over our shoulders when exposed out in public places.

Chapter 23 The Pain We Feel

Nothing is as painful to the human mind like a prodigious and sudden change. We have to distrust each other as it's our only defence against betrayal.

Great Britain and America I don't even know what to say anymore. I wonder if we have the most malicious people in the world.

It's not what's going on in the world that flummoxes me; it is people's mean reactions. The nasty, spiteful, hateful comments, the entitled silence on things that don't affect them and the lack of humane perspective on anything. The judgemental non-empathy and venomous ideologies. I don't know what's happened to people.

And what about this so-called democratic system which is failing us time and time again? It's a well-calculated system, so much so that many people dismiss the depth and breadth of it. I was born and raised in the "hood" nothing to be proud of, merely the facts, so this thinking is saying. At the same time, I lived in the "hood" I am the victim of racial prejudice but once I'm no longer living in the "hood" and have overcome the hurdles placed before me I can no longer experience prejudice? That, unfortunately, is a masterful stroke that not even the practitioners of racism could hope for.

Also, If slavery persists as an issue in the political life of a minority black continent? It is not because of an antiquarian obsession with bygone days or the burden of a too-long memory, but because black lives are still imperilled and devalued by a racial calculus and a political arithmetic that were entrenched centuries ago. This is the afterlife of slavery-skewed life chances, limited access to health and education, premature death, incarceration, and impoverishment.

But like always, on point, sadly many don't get the politics of divide and conquer. Anyone who thinks that any of us who are targeted are somehow not qualified to be considered a target is simply a fool!

Racism is a system. Unless you understand that system & how it works, everything you think you know will only confuse you.

Divide and rule is another tactic our enemy executed to perfection until today you have complexion based light skin vs dark skin internal warfare, class warfare, etc. And of course the 'I made it, emphasis on I made it. Mentality is a good isolator; it creates vulnerability & breeds jealousy.

I have often wondered if the reason why our people can't seem to come together in solidarity and support Black-owned and operated businesses; promote and implement home-school programs for our children; form community protection groups, etc. is because of our unconscious fear of immediate annihilation based on our achieving self-sufficiency and independence as opposed to the slow genocide of being fodder for conspicuous consumption and Fake Power entertainment.

The struggle is real. For some of us, it's merely a blip of interference in our daily grinds. For others, it is a prevalent occurrence, which is no different from the nightmare's that play out in their sleep.

At the end of the day, do you understand what debt is? Do you know what inflation means and how it works? Do you know why the poorly paid keep costs down for everybody else? Do you know-how stocks and shares work? Do you know why being black and poor is different from being white and poor? Do you know why being a woman and poor is different from being a man and poor?

STAND IN YOUR POWER

Do you know why there are pubs and betting shops in every poor area? Do you know why the young and the elderly are not taken care of?

It is so in your face obvious now. It is not mysterious anymore. It is right there. Just how crazy it is. There have been people along with each wave of idiocy that deny ignore and glamorise the insanity that justifies it and or pretend it doesn't matter. Hoping things will get better and saying it's not their fault when instead by way of mass apathy it got worse. You are the history of the future you are the people history will look back on as the people who did felt and observed nothing.

Let me say something to you. At the end of the day, what it comes down to is defining Black Power and being powerless. The business you're doing is white business and that only profits the constitution of the wealthiest people on the earth.

We as a people are powerless all over the globe and have mistaken money for power. Ghetto people are wasting money on expensive things instead of investing in wealth management.

In the last 2,000 years, we have been losing on all continents. What they're trying to do is to eliminate the original man of this planet 'The Solar Man'.

There is a particular continent that is racist. It's always been racist and was founded and built by racists.

Some of us may know that certain Fake Power entities financed the slave trade, owned slaves and got rich on the back of slaves. The poverty, violence and dysfunction in the black community is a product of the slave trade and centuries of ongoing racism, perpetrated by amongst others, the FPE. We don't need advice from the FPE. The FPE who helped create the society in which blacks struggle to get a fair shake and have no standing to give any advice.

They run the media that minute by minute demonises, vilifies and creates murderers, rapists and violent thugs out of us.

The narrative that you are circulating perpetuates that perception and is part of the system they help sustain that perception. I know plenty of black People, wealthy and not so wealthy, who care about their community and actively engage in bringing others up. Who watch black, buy black, hire black and support brothers and sisters. We're not all killing each other, and the killing that occurs is, without doubt, a direct product of poor housing, poor education, poor nutrition, poor work opportunities, broken communities, a broken criminal justice system and a destructive, ongoing media narrative that the FPE play a disproportionately significant role in maintaining. Don't always believe the hype?

So to my final declaration of truth for you to all remember. So take heed. 'Slavery hasn't been abolished it's been redesigned?'

As I sat at the edge of my bed pondering on all those statements in my mind. It also reflected some of the negatives I've endured since I moved to London.

The last few weeks had been a torrid affair. But for the meantime things were more settled.

As I finished packing the last of my belongings, Eric popped his head around my door.

"Hey, have you finished yet?"

The day had finally come. I was moving into a place of my own. I didn't have much to take, as all the big gear I had ordered online, and everything was due to be delivered tomorrow.

All I was waiting on now, was the arrival of Donte. Finally, we were taking the next step in our relationship and moving in together.

But don't get me wrong, I tried and tested first by doing a few trial runs.

Over the time we have been together we have had periods of staying at each other's houses for a period of a week at a time. Some days maybe more.

Each time everything went swimmingly, as it should be for us and I'm not boasting either—it's just how it is.

"I'm done now, Eric. Just gotta take these last few boxes downstairs."

"Let me help you with them?" As he grabbed two of the boxes and piled them on top of each other.

"Thank you."

"No problem. So when is D arriving?"

"Anytime now."

"Do you want me to load them by the front door?"

"Yes, please. If you don't mind?"

As he took the last of my boxes downstairs, I took one more look around the bedroom I've been occupying for the previous few months. Already in that phase, many good and some bad memories had been created.

As I shut the door, Nina lethargically came shuffling out of her room.

"Hey, girl." She said in the most croakiest voice I've ever heard her display.

"Hey, how are you feeling?"

"Like a bear with a sore head."

"Oh, dear. Why don't you go back to sleep?"

"No! I've slept enough."

"Girl, you look like death warmed up."

"No thanks to you."

"And how have you come to that conclusion?"

"You know I have a limit and when I reached it, I forgot to stop because I was engrossed in deep conversation."

"I still don't see how your sore head has anything to do with me?"

Because I told you to stop me when I reached my fourth glass of Prosecco."

"But I was engrossed in deep convo too."

"Erykah, please, take some responsibility!"

"Nina, you're one of my besties. But right now you're beginning to piss me off!"

"Fine, Erykah, have it your way as per usual."

"Hey! What's that supposed to mean?"

"Since you're so clever and you think you know it all. Why don't you figure it out?"

"I won't even fathom an answer to that. Instead, I'm going downstairs to wait for Donte to come. So I hope to see you at the house warming tonight?"

"If I can be bothered. I'll let you know."

"You do that."

"I will."

"Fine!"

"Fine!"

I made my way downstairs, still feeling the heat that had me seething with so much anger from within. When I got to the bottom, Eric was taking the boxes outside. As I walked a little further, I sighted Donte making his way back towards me. He bypassed Eric and came straight over to where I remained glued to my spot.

I dropped my rucksack onto the dining table and first placed my arms over his shoulders. When our eyes met, my anger quickly subsided as I smiled so hard I felt my face muscles working individually to pull off the pose.

"Hey, baby," he first said in that deep-husky tone he possessed.

"Hey you," I answered in a dream-like state. This man's sexiness never ceased to amaze me, even after all this time.

"How are you feeling?"

"Good, apprehensive, scared, good."

"Ah, baby! Aren't you looking forward to the next chapter in your life?"

"I am, I am. It's just I feel so settled here, and to the fact, I've only been here a few months,"

"I know. But times must and do change."

"Well then, let's keep it rolling."

"For real. We out."

When Eric came back inside, Donte and I said our goodbyes and began heading out the door.

I decided to take one more look behind me, and as I did so, I could hear Nina calling out to me as she came running at full speed towards us.

"Erykah, Erykah, wait?"

"Can you believe this? This is the same way you greeted me when I reached here for the first time."

"I know. I remember," she said through the tears of laughter and regret.

"Look, I'm sorry about what I said."

"Why're you sorry? I'm the one that came at you."

"For saying you look like death warmed up."

"Forget about it. I was the one being grouchy and blaming you for my shortcomings last night."

"Well, ain't that the truth?"

"Forgive me, please?"

"You're forgiven," I said, smiling.

"Thank you."

"Eric?"

"Yes, Erykah?" He replied.

"Is Regina coming tonight?"

"Yeah, she is. She's finishing work around 7 pm, so Sis and I will be picking her up at 9 pm, and then we will make our way to yours."

"Alright, good. Well, things are kicking off around eight-thirty."

"Erykah, did you inform your neighbours?" Nina asked.

"I've informed and invited everyone in my block."

"Smart. Is any of your family from Manchester coming?"

"No! Not this time. Only the London lot."

"Well, at least some of your family will be there representing you."

"I'm happy for those who are coming. It's too much to ask them to come again after they went back from Daniel and Kira's engagement party. Besides I'm going to do a Skype link around 10 pm."

"Ah can't wait to see them all."

"Yeah, I know. Besides with all the recent dramas everyone has been through. That's another reason for them to stay put and get back to some kind of normality again."

"I guess so. I saw it took its toll on your father and Bernadette."

"But weren't my father brave or what?"

"Oh gosh yes, Erykah. That's a side to him I've never seen."

"I know, right. I couldn't quite believe my eyes on how composed and calm he was. Usually, he is all erratic and emotionally unstable."

"I'm happy for you Erykah. Because, finally, after all these years, your father has evolved into the person you've always hoped and dreamed for."

"I'm elated about it, Nina! All I ever wanted was for him to bring stability into his own life and be a person I can call and rely on."

"Baby, I'm sorry to break-up your little make-up session. But may I remind you we got bare t'ings to do before the party tonight."

"Okay, Donte, I'm coming right now."

"Good, I'll go start the car. See you later, Nina! Eric, bless up."

"Take care, Donte."

"One love mi Breda."

"So, see you tonight?"

"Yes, the four of us will be there."

"I'm so glad."

"Do you want me to come a bit early so I can help you out?"

"No need! Uncle Sebastian has organised and paid for caterers, a barman, two waitresses and his very own butler Jameson to help out. Also, Danika is coming to oversee the staff."

"Oh, wow, your Uncle is amazing."

"Ain't he just. It's a house warming gift from him and Aunt Lola?

"Ah, that's so sweet of them."

"That reminds me. Aunt Lola is coming to mine in an hour to do my hair."

"Right, you two better get going."

"I'm out. See you tonight." As I gave her a significant hug.

"See you later."

"Bye, Eric."

"Laters, Pooki."

I said my goodbyes, and then I headed straight to the car. I couldn't wait for tonight. I hope it was going to be as epic as I had endured in my mind.

"Finally! Are you ready now, Miss Gaines?" I bobbed my head in acknowledgement, laid my head back on the seat rest, closed my eyes and drifted off to sleep.

Half an hour later and I was awoken by the sound of Donte honking his horn repeatedly and the cars sound system.

"Erykah, wake up?"

"I'm awake, I awake," I repeated as I outstretched my arms up above me.

"We're here."

"Wow! It looks even better than the time I came to see it with Uncle Sebastian.

"Really?"

"Yeah, it is pretty amazing. Wait until you see the inside."

"You go open the door, and I'll make a start with the boxes?"

"Right ahead of you."

I made my way to the main doors. As I stopped, I began to fumble around in my bag for my keys. I started searching everywhere, but I couldn't find them. In my panic, I tried to think where I had or saw them last. A minute later, it came to me as Donte approached with the first of the boxes.

"What's up babe?"

"I forget my keys."

"Oh, damn! Where did you have them last?"

"You got yours, right?"

"Yeah, right here." As he took them out of his pocket and dangled them in front of me.

"Oh, good! I remember putting them on the table when you came inside the first time."

"Ring Nina, to bring them with her tonight."

"I'll call her right now."

I took out my iPhone and dialled her number straight away. She answered on the first ring.

"Erykah, is everything alright?"

"Nina, check the table in the front room and see if I left my keys there?"

"Let me go check."

"Cool."

Moments later.

"Yes, they are here."

"Thank goodness for that."

"I'll bring it with me tonight."

"Thanks, girl."

As I checked off the phone, Donte had already taken all the boxes inside the foyer.

"What's our flat number?"

"Number three, sugar."

I grabbed a few boxes myself while Donte pressed for the lift. Moments later, the lift came. I first took my boxes and put them inside. Then I held the doors open while Donte loaded the other eight boxes.

When we reached our destination, we repeated the same process.

Donte gave me his key as I opened up our front door as a couple for the first time.

I began to feel that warm fuzzy feeling as I grabbed a few boxes and instructed Donte to follow me.

After another ten minutes had passed, we had bought in all ten boxes, found the kettle, two cups and the condiments and sat down in the two chairs I had bought the other day.

It was so refreshing not to have to worry about electric or gas meters. Plus Uncle had paid my mortgage and council tax upfront for a whole year as another house warming gift.

Besides I had already paid £50,000 of the mortgage from the money he and Aunt Lola had given me a few weeks ago.

Donte's mother had also given us another £5,000 and Donte himself matched that. So £60,000 went towards mortgage, and I used as promised the other £10,000 to kit out the already decorated flat which was another gift from Aunt Lola and Uncle Sebastian. My thanks were beyond wow. We were delighted and overwhelmed.

After we finished our refreshments, I gave Donte the grand tour. The flat boasted two bedrooms with our room having an en-suite shower. We also had another separate bathroom which also housed a Jacuzzi. The rest of the flat we had a kitchen and decent size front room with a great outdoor balcony.

"Yes, that's what I'm chatting about."

"I take it you love it then?"

"For real doe, your Uncle did well."

"Come we better tidy up this mess before my Aunt gets here?"

"I'm on it."

Precisely ten minutes later, Aunt Lola arrived. As I buzzed her in, I could hear her cussing out somebody. At first, I thought it could've been Danika. But when I overheard a radio in the background, I immediately grabbed my keys and ran out the door, heading downstairs.

"Erykah, where are you going in such a hurry?"

"My Aunt! It sounds like she's caught up in some kinda commotion."

"Wait, it could be dangerous?"

"Then come with."

When I reached the ground floor, I continued my run towards the double doors. Through the glass, I could see five O outside.

When I got out, I spotted two patrol cars and four police officers. Donte was right behind me.

"What's going on Auntie?"

"These officers seem to think I was speeding, and now they want to breathalyse me."

"Excuse me, officers. But is this some kind of sick joke?"

"Young lady, I don't know who you are. But may I suggest you keep your nose out of this."

"Or what?" I said sneering at him.

"Or I'll arrest you for obstruction."

"Erykah, baby, fall back?" Donte instructed as he pulled me back by both my arms.

"For fuck sake Donte," I said muttering quietly under my breath.

"Can I see your driver's license and registration please?" The officer asked my Auntie in a patronising manner.

I could tell by the expression coming from her fed up persona that this was so embarrassing for her. I sighted one or two neighbours watching from their windows, and some even came out of their houses to be nosey. At least the neighbourhood watch around here was on point.

But no matter how affluent you become or where you live, being black makes no difference to this institutionally racist organisation or gang as I see them.

"Officer, I want to know why you have stopped me?"

"Mam, you were driving below the speed limit."

"Was I? I didn't realise." Auntie protested in vain.

"Look, mam, for your sake, let us breathalyse you. If you pass, then you can be on your way."

"As easy as that?"

The officer went back to his patrol car, and from what I could make out he was reaching inside the glove compartment.

Moments later, he emerged and came back to where we were situated. By this time more neighbours came out of their cribs to see what all the commotion was.

I guess you can say an area like this probably never sees action like this. For myself, this is a regular daily occurrence.

"Mam, blow into the mouthpiece when the green light goes off."

With a cautious eye on the officer that was trying to breathalyse Auntie, she reluctantly against her will complied with a foot soldier of the DEMON-CRATIC state.

"Thank you, mam," he concluded as he pulled the breathalyser away from Auntie's mouth and analysed it.

After a few moments, he gave her the result.

"Well, it looks like you're luckily under the limit."

"So am I free to go now?"

"Yes, you're. But in future Mrs Briscoe keep an eye on your speed limit."

"What for?"

"Because you were driving way to slow."

"Oh, was I?" Auntie reciprocated as she began to chuckle to herself. Deep down, Auntie knew she was. Only because she got off lightly it was in that moment that she was toying with them, but not in a civil manner but a manner of disgust and disappointment.

As soon as the officers drove away, Auntie began her orderly round of how unfair the system is and how it victimises even the richest of us.

"Auntie are you alright?"

"I'm fine. I'm used to things like this. But it's been a long time since it's happened to me."

"What gives?"

"I think I have an idea."

"Tell me?"

"First, the thing I need to establish here is all I had was my usual one glass of red wine before I set out."

"Oh, I see."

"Although it's got nothing to do with how fast or slow I was going. I was driving appropriately like I always do."

"So what is this all about, Auntie?"

"Erykah, at least let your Aunt get upstairs first."

"I'm so sorry, Auntie."

"It's fine. Let's go, and I can tell you both over a nice cup of coffee."

"Amen to that," Donte added.

Ten minutes later, and the three of us were sitting in my new front room. Auntie had laid her styling kit by the window, as we all settled, Auntie continued.

"What you young folks got to understand is that this is a political issue. Back in 2011 your Uncle, if you remember, ran for office to become London's next mayor. In 2012 he lost by eight votes. But on the campaign trail, his strategy focused mainly on the metropolitan police force and particularly the killings of young black men in incarceration. The then Police commissioner made it his career to define your Uncle's campaign as the most vilifying and slandering ever. This battle further fuelled the way black and ethnic minority Londoners incessantly thought about the Police. This goes hand in hand with the way the 44th President-Elect was shut down on many an occasion to get bills passed. So, this is why your Uncle and I are subjected to this way of treatment."

"This was the exact subject we were discussing on Resistance a few weeks ago."

"You mean the show about the War on Blacks?"

"How did you know?"

"Your father."

"I'm shocked. I didn't think any of the family would be listening."

"Locked and tuned in. You know your Uncle, and I have a vested interest in your career."

"I guess you do."

"Anyway ladies. Are any of you hungry?"

"I'm glad you asked. I'm bang in the mood for some Oxtail with rice and peas and get me two dumpling with some hard dough bread as well. Thanks, sweetie."

"That's quite an appetite you have there Auntie?"

"Well, with my run-in with the police. Doing your hair and helping with the preparations for the party. I guess it's very much needed Erykah."

"Babe, can you get my some jerk chicken with white rice and a juice?"

"What kind?"

"Sorrel and ginger, please."

"Alright, see you in a bit."

"Which takeaway are you going too?"

"There's only once place I go, baby."

"Refill's in Brixton."

"That's right."

"See you in about an hour then."

"When Donte left the flat, I made Auntie a cup of coffee and then she got straight down to doing my hair.

Today I was changing my Mohawk style back into a short, relaxed hairstyle cut to shoulder length with one side at the front swept over my forehead. I saw the haircut in a film I watched last week, and if I do say so myself, I think it will look the bomb on me after Aunt Lola is finished.

"Auntie, what time is Nik's coming over? After all, this was her idea."

"She should be pulling up right now. One thing with your cousin is that she is always on time."

Within a few minutes of Auntie's prediction, the intercom buzzed. I had one of those where you could see the person who was trying to enter.

"Danika, come on up it's the top floor."

Moments later, Danika reached.

"Damn cuz, you ain't even out of breath."

"Hey girl," she said as she came towards me with her arms outstretched. "How are you?"

"I'm fine. How's you?"

"I'm good girl. I just came from the gym."

"That's why you look so fit."

"I'm getting in shape for tonight. I want to look my best for Trae."

"I saw him earlier. Man is looking all fresh with his new cut and the outfit he is wearing, damn, you two are gonna look the business together."

"I think we should add Swag to the Williams brothers name?"

"Good idea. They certainly will live up to it."

"Where is Donte anyway?" She asked as she stepped inside.

"He's gone south to get some food for your mother and me."

"Ooh, where has he gone too?"

"He went to Refills in Bricky."

"Tell him to get me something? I'll give him the money when he comes back."

"Don't worry about paying him. I'll ring him for you."

I took out my phone and called him. On two rings, he answered.

"What's Up?"

"Baby, can you get Danika something too eat?"

"What would she like?"

"Nik's what do you want?"

"Let me speak to him?" As she grabbed the phone out of my grasp.

"Hey Donte, how are you?"

"Sup Danika, I'm all good. How's you, Hun?"

"I'm great. I came this second, and I'm all ready to do the preparations for your party."

"I know. Erykah told me yesterday. Thank you so much for all your help."

"No sweat. Anything for you two."

"Cheers. So what do you want?"

"Can you get me some Stew Chicken with rice n peas and a sour sap juice."

"No worries. I got you."

"Thank you."

"In a bit."

Donte cut the lines of communication dead.

"So, how's work Niks?" I asked.

"Works fine. We're are getting some interesting cases at the moment. Hey, mother."

"Hey, Danika."

"Is Marcus, putting you to the sword?"

"Nah, he's a good boss. Can't complain."

"Yeah, no doubting he's a wonderful person."

"He's cool for a solicitor."

"Danika, I'm going to make a start on Erykah's hair. You can get going with the decorations. When I'm finished, I'll give you a hand."

"That's okay mother; you'll be exhausted by then. Besides, you'll have to get ready before us."

"Danika, that's why I love you, darling?"

STAND IN YOUR POWER

"Love you too, mother."

"Ah, I love y'alls relationship. It so real and authentic yet uncomplicated at the same time."

"Thanks, cuz. But we do have our share of disagreements."

"I see that as keeping you on your toes. It's not always healthy to agree on situations where there are no solutions on offer."

"Touché, dear niece. Debate and formal debate is one factor that makes the world go around. If we all agreed on the same subjects wholeheartedly, one, there be no point in democracy. Come to think of it; regardless there is still no point unless it serves the masses. Two, you would never see flaws if your head is in a cocoon of sublime bliss?"

"Wypipo then, Auntie?"

"Spot on, Erykah."

"Privileged arseholes."

"Somethings never change."

"Aunt Lola, I should get you on the show?"

"That's a sweet offer. But I'll have to decline and leave all that to you, youngsters."

"Well, as long as I'm on there, the offer is open."

"Thank you, Erykah. I'll keep it in mind."

"What time are the staff coming mother?"

"Around four hours from now."

"Great. That gives me plenty of time."

Forty-five minutes later, Donte came crashing through the doors all huffing and puffing and out of sorts.

I went towards him and took the bags of food off him.

"Is everything alright, babe?"

"Not really, but let me catch my breath first."

"Sit him down on the couch, Erykah," Auntie instructed.

"I'll get him some water," Danika offered.

I went and sat down next to him. He stared at me with a look of disparity in his eyes. It was like he'd seen a ghost.

Danika came back with the glass of water and handed it to me. In turn, I feed Donte a few sips as he was unable to hold the glass. He was shaken up and sweating like a pig on a hot roast spitfire.

I gently removed his jacket. He managed to hold the glass on his own. His breathing was slowing down, and life started to come back into him. After a few minutes when he managed to compose himself, he spoke.

"Sorry if I've frightened you all."

"Don't be silly, Donte, take your time," Danika shouted out to him.

"I'll heat the food." Aunt Lola offered to do.

"Thank you, Auntie."

"So Mr Brixton, what's going on with you?" Danika asked.

"Dread Man, dread!" He said, shaking his head as a few tears began to fall from his solemn looking face. Seeing Donte like this, It was starting to make me feel uneasy. I hated the vibe he was projecting right now. I took my hand in his and rubbed it a few times and gave him a look of solidarity. Then he continued. What he said next blew all our minds simultaneously.

"Go ahead baby it's alright."

"Boy, I just found out that a good, good bredrin's teenage son got stabbed, while I was driving back here." He relayed as more tears flowed. I've never seen him like this until this present moment. I was feeling for him so much.

"Oh my gosh, Donte. Is he okay?"

"No Danika, he died ten minutes ago."

"Oh shit?" I said as I hugged him for dear life.

"I'm so sorry to hear that Donte? Tell your friend when he has processed today. If he wants, Sebastian and I will take care of any funeral expenses."

"I can't ask you to do that Mrs Briscoe?"

"Nonsense. It's nothing. Your friend right now has just lost a child. He and his family will be in no fit state to think about anything. After dinner, please ring him and tell him of my offer. If he excepts, get his bank details, and I will transfer ten thousand pounds into his account."

"Thank you, Mrs Briscoe."

"Donte, it's my pleasure. We have to stick together and help our own, especially in times like this."

"Does your friend know how it happened?" Danika anxiously asked.

"No, not yet. He didn't say anything other than ball down the phone after he told me."

"Fucking shit babe. This is so, so wrong. Something needs to be done about this?"

"That's the second black teenager to be stabbed to death this week. That total's 16 youths shot and killed in the Capital this year, and it isn't going to be the end. Between this and the acid attacks. Question is as a community what can we do in our cliques to change and re-educate the mindsets of these youths that kill. We have a collective responsibility! Those in power won't do shit. It's time we rally together and start something purposeful and full proof. Just saying."

"I agree with you, Danika, something needs to be done. But those statistics are so wrong! Someone's trying to cover up the severity of knife crime or black youth deaths. There have been far more than 16 deaths of black youths by stabbing or gun crime in London. The media only report a small fraction, Donte can clarify this. I know of two stabbings around Nina's neighbourhood that never made it to the news, nor were they counted among the sixteen. Yet, they're well and truly dead."

"We all know what's going on. The UK is not the USA. The numbers are small by comparison. What's happened here is not the fault of these children, alone. It's the adults, us! Some of us have become so scared of our kids. We are not like our parents in terms of being strict. Many of us rebelled against the strictness, despite the beatings, and today, we have children, that are a consequence of parenting styles, that are based on friendship as opposed to being a parent that run things. Factors like legislation, and the outlawing of corporal punishment, and chastisement in the home, we are not paying the price on a whole new level, that is instead of paying college fees, many parents are going to end up spending more and more on funeral costs. Sorry to be so real, Donte!" Auntie said.

"Don't worry; It needs to be said. Modern life feels like the end of time. One generation builds, and the other break's it down. Our fore Father's struggled, we decided our children should not. So we paved a solid pathway for them, leaving them nothing to fight for. All fucking fed with golden spoons, with all the time in the world. The enemy fine works for idle hands." Donte relayed back to Auntie.

"Our forefathers were around to struggle. These kids have no fathers around!" Danika said.

"Parents of today are too damn soft and scared of their kids and the laws that give the kids the audacity to do what they're doing with impunity."

"Not all Auntie. There are many with great upbringings and still end up losing their lives innocently. It's bigger than simply being a good parent. If things don't change in the future, I would fear for my children always because of other children." I said in response to Auntie's point.

"Erykah, you do have a valid point here. Sometimes peer pressure and a bit of bulling compel some of them to partake in delinquencies they wouldn't normally get involved in." Auntie stated.

"True and also those simply going about their business are attacked too. There are too many scenarios for me to put it down to parenting although this too is a big aspect,"

"Good point Danika. But your brother and yourself didn't do martial arts for anything. That aside, it's not as black and white as most of us are led to believe. As a parent, it's safer to give them the most protection we can offer, than folding our arms hopelessly and doing nothing about it." Donte said.

"What did you have in mind, babe?" I asked.

"For starters, let's lobby our local counsellors and MP to increase the budget in youth provision, clubs and workers. We could get Resistance involved?"

"I'll talk to Calvin before we go on our holiday."

"You could also bring successful people into the schools and communities to show kids that they can create a future worth living for, rather than the scraps of being some kind of 'bad man on-road'," Danika said.

"We could also send our kids to self-defence classes, so there's an alternative to carrying a weapon for supposed protection?" Aunt Lola added.

"It is not nice knowing that the sixteen or more youths that got stabbed and hugging a child not realising that last hug you gave them before they died always will have an impact in my life. I am so scared now for our children's future. It's not nice seeing people returning from their children's grave its so sad." I said.

"So true these days youngsters are attending more funerals and the effect this has on them also."

"Donte in relation to your statement. If they're under sixteen, charge both parents. I don't care if the father is not in his life. Find him and charge him for his delinquency too for not being in his teenage son life."

"Danika, what can be done as a community is for older men to mentor young boys. Like I noticed already in the college of boys who had lost their lives, I doubt any or more than twenty per cent of them had their fathers as positive role models in their lives. Youth offending institutions are full of young men without good fathers. That's the key tool to stem the flow. Mentoring is important. Stop claiming that whooping kids works. You're complaining about youth violence but want to explain that an adult inflicting violence on a child is discipline."

"Hello, it worked well on me and the generation before me. Granny and the villagers were the judge and juries. Don't spear the rod and spoil the child. Bend the tree while it's young. Have you ever heard the saying? Who don't hear will feel."

"Aunt Lola, I differ to say for the older generation it didn't work. The mistakes imparted on adults by their parents don't need to be passed down to other generations. You can't model violence in a violent world as a means of teaching kids not to be violent with each other. All that happened in the older generation is there was a better sense of family, better food, and fewer distractions that's what held damaged kids of yesteryears together. As a result, these parents that were 'whooped' suddenly didn't know how to hold down a family as their parents did. They all seem to scream about, whooping working, but few of them copied their mothers or fathers examples and kept the family together."

"Whooping by the parents or the police? I have seen it." Aunt Lola added.

"As I said, we pave the pathway solid. For example, fathers plant their seeds and run like crazy. Mother's are playing the role of mom and dad, with little chores around the house to do. Give the idler more time to find work to do."

"Erykah, you forgot to tell about the place of money. Money is the absolute benchmark of this society. Let's teach our children that it is less the case and that there are other things."

"Danika, we need to take a long hard look at the culture we are passing on to our children because it takes a village to raise a child," Donte said in response to Danika's statement aimed at me.

"I do agree with you and love the sentiment. But how can you do it because you can't get children by the clip of their ear when they are misbehaving in the street and bring them to their parents because it is forbidden to get a child by the clip of his ear and because that would turn against the person doing and asking him. 'What are you doing to my child leave him alone?" Aunt Lola made a valid point.

"It shouldn't have got to that stage in the first place," Danika said in response to her mother's point.

"The problem with our children is a reflection of bad choices we make as adults. We are the only community on earth, where the males that make the best providers are rejected solely based on the fact that he doesn't fit the criteria of dysfunctionality set out by the entertainment industry. It's about supply and demand, the dude with the very low IQ that shouts coon at any black dude in a suit that can read. It wouldn't exist if black women had the same permanent husband selection process as other women from other cultures. Relationships and the way black men and black women treat each other is the cause off most of our problems." I added.

"Hello. My first idea would be a bit tough but what about starting a curfew to take our children out of the street and create solidarity between parents where an adult will take them to activities and escort them back home. Or a group of benevolent parents. No children in the street on their own after school. This curfew doesn't need to be forever but for the time to break the habits for these young people to hang out together and do stupidities. Social media can help to make it possible. Maybe asking clubs to take children who can't afford it on board. Organise safe spaces in libraries or other places for them to work. So they can listen to music, no bloody rap though. But classic or traditional. Having storytellers coming from Africa or the west indies to hear stories about where they are coming from. No more black children in the streets of London around unsociable hours. My second idea would be to create a task force, mainly men going into the streets and urging children to go back home and not staying on road." I felt what Donte relayed.

"Families must take control of there young people," Auntie said.

"It's unfair to say it's all on mothers and fathers. I'm saying all extended family members too. Rope their young people into business or get them into something constructive. Teach them about wealth and Money Management. It's everyone's responsibility in a family setting to take care of each other. This would reduce some of the fatalities." I said.

STAND IN YOUR POWER

"I remember reading an account from a young murderers mother after he was sentenced to life at the Old Bailey aged sixteen years. She said his anger and bad behaviour drove her insane, and when she knew she couldn't manage him, she went to social services; however, she says they did nothing to help her. He was kicked out of school, smoking cannabis and carried knives. He committed the stabbing in West London after going to look for the victim. I'm thinking if there was like a community task force that a case like this that could be referred to then they could work with the kid to tackle his issues he's having with another kid and squash the problems which make him arm himself with a knife," Danika said.

"I recently heard of another three boys, all with knives looking to stab up another boy. The mother found out and went to meet them. She cussed them out and also managed to talk to them, and through it all, it squashed the argument. So they will not be stabbing her son. The power to save our children has got to come from some of us." Donte passionately relayed.

"Donte, I hear you, but all you are suggesting is placing a plaster and kissing it better when what you should be suggesting is ways the set broken bones and nursing the patient back to full health. The problem is with Western black culture and the demise of two-parent black families." Danika countered what Donte said and called him out on his statement.

"To get to the bottom of fixing our problems, some of us will be very offended."

"Auntie, you are suggesting a ground treatment which is going to take years. How do we act in the meantime to what is an absolute emergency? The death of black children killed by other black children in a deafening silence."

"What about a straight name and shame of the kids convicted of knife crime. Put then in the public eye & their parents."

"Danika, those boys are like that because they don't have a real man in their lives to look up to. There is no solution if the boys goes home from school to a messed up family life. The best thing we can do is separate them from those that have a chance."

"Donte, the only way your suggestion will work is if we have an all-out war on all forms of black counter culture. Black people with those traits have to be shamed and know where they stand in the food chain, which should be at a level as white, red necks and white trailer trash. A dumb white underachiever wouldn't dare discredit anyone above him. So are we seeing it in all black groups? It's as if to be accepted as black you have to be thick as pig shit."

"To fix knife crime, you have to look into the cause of the problem, not the symptoms."

"Auntie, I believe women are the key to solving our problems. If they were to rise to the level men did when they had their million man march. I am confident that most of the problems we see today would be sorted overnight."

"If they for example overnight saw counter-culture as very unattractive. Your thug with his gold teeth would start wearing a suit and learn to read."

"Donte, that's where our analysis differs slightly. Today money is the absolute benchmark and if you have money no matter how you get it your place in the society is better than the place of being knowledgeable. It's okay not to work hard and to sell poison to others to make money because society allows it. Wearing a suit is not the alpha and omega of life. What would be the alpha and omega of life is a bit more solidarity between people from the same neighbourhood would help."

"The suit is a metaphor of being able to adapt and succeed in this society we live in. Some misguided black people adopt a street culture that is incompatible with the modern age in any society even authentic black African and Caribbean societies. Not being able to adapt to the society you live in is unnatural." I said.

"I agree with you on that one, two-hundred per cent." Danika finished of saying.

"Come on, you guys. Let's wrap this up and eat some food?" Aunt Lola belted out.

"I second that notion," I answered.

As we all sat and ate together, we continued discussing and debating the same subject.

Six hours later, and the first guests started to arrive. When Calvin entered, I ran by the idea of doing a show about what was discussed earlier in the day. He agreed that it was an immediate subject to discuss and we could do it as early as next week before I fly out to Brazil.

The party went well. Mostly, everyone, we'd invited turned up. It carried right on into the early hours. Uncle Sebastian, Danika and Aunt Lola did Donte and me very proud. From the catering to the music and the decorations, they smashed it.

I managed to Skype Bernie and Father. They were ever so pleased for Donte and me. Dad was telling me he passed another year of remaining drug and alcohol-free. That put the smile of all smiles on my face.

I also found out that cousin Darius was on the verge of signing a new and improved football contract with City. I was so pleased for him and his family. He was going to be set for life.

As for myself, I cuddled up next to the of love my life on our first night in our new digs. I began to reflect on the whole day gently. On a positive aspect, everyone's life at the party was going well as could be expected at these moments in time. On a negative, there was so much work to do in regards to tackling the issues that affect us as a race at large.

As my eyelids began to sag, I turned to Donte and stared tentatively into his eyes as I did so, I told him how much he meant to me.

In return, he said he loved me with so much passion, that he was making me feel it on whole new level.

For the next few hours, we made love to each other like never before. Afterwards, we cradled up in each other's arms until we both fell asleep.

Chapter 24 - Different Shores

"Erykah, what if when we die that light at the end of the tunnel is the light to another hospital room. There, we are reborn, and the only reason why you come out crying is the fact that you died and lost everything. As you grow, you start to forget your past life and focus on the life you have now. But patches of memory stay behind, and that memory causes Deja vu. Think about that for a second."

"That's some bold insight right there Xavi. Clever, but it's out there still."

"Unfortunately it's not mine to claim."

"Oh I see."

"But, Erykah, you more than anyone I thought would appreciate this analogy."

"Xavi, I'm going to tell you one valuable thing about a black girl. Never touch our hair, never touch our hair, never touch our hair."

"Ah Erykah, go easy on him. He is still learning."

"Well, teacher. You better start putting in overtime, so you can get him up to speed for real."

"She puts in more than overtime. If you know what I mean?" Xavi said with the most prevalent grin I've ever seen on a person.

"Ewe, too much detail thank you very much."

As Donte, Xavi, Nina and myself were catching bare joke. We were perambulating through terminal two at Heathrow airport.

As we all carted along with our luggage on the trolleys towards the waiting area, Xavi was trying to tell me something that I had no interest in at this point in my life.

"But Erykah, if a non-believer like you can't grasp it, then who can?"

"Xavi, dear, patience has to be ascertained here. It's an area of study that needs time to master it. But right now it's not a priority in my life."

"Why does it have to be a priority? It's a simple process of elimination."

"Don't you think I already know that?"

"Xavi, baby! Leave it alone know."

"Fine, only because you say so my sexy señorita."

As soon as he said that, they began snogging each other's face off. Donte and I gave them a bemusing look each and carried on towards our check-in like we didn't know them.

"Damn! The more I see off Nina lately, the more cheesy she gets. Don't get me wrong; I like Xavi. But he has changed her. Not sure if it's a good thing in its entirety." Donte explained about Nina's changing of character like it bothered him in a bad way.

I decided to address him from a different perspective as I was about to do so. A brother who looks in his late twenties strolled right past us holding a sisters hand, but with one thing that put Donte's and mines nose out of joint.

As we continued to stare, Xavi and Nina finally caught up with us. The four us just stood there staring at these brothers jeans which were halfway down his legs. Well, they might as well be.

But that wasn't the worst thing. His brief looked all out of door like he'd been wearing them for a few days. Plus his crack was showing as well.

"What the fuck?" Donte said as he shook his head from side to side several times.

"Oh, dear." Nina remonstrated by covering one hand over her mouth.

Xavi gave that judgmental look all white men do.

"I got an insight into this," Nina said.

"Go ahead, girl. Enlighten us," I said, answering back.

"You see, many think 'Sagging Pants' started in prison. But it comes from a place much worse than that."

"So where does it originate from?" Xavi asked expectantly.

"Well, with the evolution of hip-hop and urban culture over the past 30 years, there have been so many arguments about the origin of sagging pants.

Of course, most people have probably heard that 'the word "saggin" spelt backwards spells niggas and all types of other things. But most people think of rap music when they see sagging pants.

Many people believe the trend is the result of people glorifying rap culture and fashion trends seen in music videos.

Back in the late 80s and early 90s, the sagging trend was introduced by rappers like Ice-T and Too Short. Then, Kris Kross took things to a whole new level.

Although the trend started in prison systems and correctional institutions around the country, soon, black youth on the outside began adopting the fashion trend. However, it's much deeper than something you see on television in this day and age.

Then there's the Prison Systems. Of course, you've probably heard a number of different theories, including the one about sagging pants in prison. If you haven't heard about the prison theory, there are claims that incarcerated men who wear their pants below their waist do so to let other inmates know they're okay with homosexual encounters.

I read an online article one time according to it 'A prisoner would claim another inmate by having him wear his pants down low for easy access and to show that the inmate belonged to him as his property, although some disagree with that theory.

But there's a dark truth about the origin of sagging, and it goes all the way back to the days of slavery. Back then, there was a practice known as "breaking the buck", and it's probably the most horrible thing you'll hear today.

If you haven't heard of the process of "breaking the buck," you'll never look at a man wearing sagging pants the same. According to another article, I once read online the process was a heinous act used during times of slavery to break down defiant male slaves.

During this laborious process, the slave owners and overseer would make an example of the slave in front of the entire slave congregation by beating him relentlessly. But unfortunately, that's not the worst of the punishment. Then, they would cut down a tree and force the battered male slave over the tree stump with his britches removed so he'd be exposed for the entire slave congregation to see.

The slave master would then make an example out of the slave and promise others the act would be their fate for defiant behaviour.

The slave owner would then remove his clothing and savagely sodomise the slave in front of his family, wife and children and his friends. But sadly things didn't stop there. Slave masters were also known to invite their associates from other plantations to participate.

Then the owner would make the slave wear his pants below his bottom, letting others know that he was broken.

The defiant slave's male children were required to be front and centre while the horrific acts were taking place in an effort to break them down mentally at an early age as they witnessed their father's humiliation.

Sadly, the process was successful. The disturbing process evolved into a "Sex Farm" practice where slaves were put on display for the twisted sexual desires of homosexual slave owners.

According to another article, I read online, the 'breaking the buck' process evolved into what was known as "sex farms." With disturbing sex farms, slave owners would put enslaved Blacks on display for their friends to see. Slaves were forced to have orgies while being watched by white men who'd come from other plantations. In many cases, white men would often participate in sexual acts.

So for the guys who wear their pants below their waist to make a fashion statement, it would probably be wise to think about what it means because it's more than just a look. It's a reflection of a harrowing past and a warped mentality."

"Wow, Nina, that's some heavy shit right there? Who would've thought it that it traces back to our forefathers?"

"Donte, growing up in the streets. You did often hear it had something to do with when po-po arrested you, and you were forced onto your knees and made to put your hands behind your head."

"Erykah, the streets adopted that method. Most people nowadays don't have any idea how far it traces back. Hence why you see young boys and young men carrying on a horrific tradition without them having the education on why they consciously do it."

"It's sad because what a lot of young men think is cool and up to the time. Shake my head, Nina! Resistance has to do a show on this and other trends that are not good for us."

"I agree, Erykah! With such a platform Resistance has. We can reach out online now."

"Meaning we can tap into other black communities around the world," I said quite excited at the idea of speaking to thousands if not millions of black folk around the globe. This subject with the online set-up now could catapult my career onto a whole new level.

After Brazil, pitching the idea of Gun and knife crime will be a foregone conclusion. That's happening, standard. Sagging pants will tie in neatly with it.

Two hours later, and we all together reached the check-in desk. First up was me.

"Passport please?" The kind young lady asked from behind her desk.

"Here you go," I said as I handed it to her.

She took one look at the passport then at me and back to the passport again.

"Is this your first time abroad?" She asked in a softly spoken manner.

"Yes, it is," I answered back.

When she was satisfied that the girl in the picture was me, she duly stamped it.

"Have a safe flight Miss Gaines."

"Thank you very much."

I walked through and waited for the others. Five minutes later and we all headed towards the plane.

We continued our walk through the tunnel and had a bit more conversation about other things that affect our people daily. It's quite incredible when you bring it to life on how many attacks we suffer.

We can't even rely on any authoritative establishment on mass to help us. Throughout history and time, our existence has been about them against us.

You see as a people it's not something we would wish on our enemies if the tables were turned.

We didn't asked to be pillaged, raped, chained up in ships and taken from our motherland on the back of our people trading us out to the white man to work on plantations in a foreign land for a slave master.

STAND IN YOUR POWER

Then on top of that, we were beaten, hanged, quartered, raped again, the list is endless.

So when I see how slavery hasn't died yet. Dealing with 21st-century politics does not have a patch on what our forefathers went through. But they thought as hard as they could for our freedoms.

Yet after the civil rights movement. We made a lot of progress for a short period. But by the 1970s, when crack cocaine was introduced into the black communities in America at first. That's when they began enslaving us all over again, and the struggle continues.

At the end of the day, slavery has never ended. It just got altered.

Fifteen minutes later, after more checks, we finally boarded the British Airways jet. This is obviously due to the country being on a severe level of threat against terrorism.

Once we were all settled, the captain welcomed everyone onto the plane. He mentioned that the flight was non-stop and would take around 12 hours and 15 minutes to land at the São Paulo international airport. Xavi mentioned locals called it Cumbica airport.

On the flight over we drank and ate several times each, and we all watch a movie in our own spaces. I decided to watch an old classic, and it seemed befitting to my current situation. 'How Stella Got Her Groove Back.'

After a couple of hours, Xavi and Nina fell asleep.

Donte and I decided to tick off something on our bucket list. Half an hour later and we officially became members of the 'Mile High Club' I couldn't stop grinning.

When Xavi and Nina finally awakened. Xavi gave us the lowdown on how to survive in Brazil. He also went on to tell us that his family lived in the wealthiest neighbourhood in São Paulo.

His father worked as a Science Director for the Brazilian Government. He said his dad earns up to $135,000 per annum.

My head exploded with all the information. I couldn't believe where we were going to stay. And there was me thinking he lived on a farm with two goats and a pig. I feel so bad for stereotyping him in my mind. As a people, we don't like it. But I guess it's a preconditioned human trait in some of us.

When we finally landed, feeling all jet-lagged and a bit noxious. I was so glad I took one of those pills to cope with the long-distance.

At the airport, we were greeted by Xavi's older brother Luís. He drove us to their parent's mansion, which was in Ibirapuera / Vila Nova Conceição, which is the most expensive neighbourhood in São Paulo city.

Fifty minutes later and we arrived at the Mansion. The whole neighbourhood made Kensington and Chelsea look like a run down nightclub.

Straight away Xavi and Luís parents took to Nina like a duck to water. Well, after a few Skype sessions, it made that initial first meeting less awkward.

After we got settled and was shown to our rooms, there were five bedrooms in all, and each one was equipped with its walk-in wardrobe area and an en-suite bathroom.

After Donte and I had our showers and got dressed. We met up with Xavi and Nina at the top of the landing and made our way downstairs.

I felt already at ease in this new and first country I have ever visited.

The weather for this time of year was a cool 21c—such a contrast to London at the same time.

Xavi escorted us into the dining room where Luís introduced us to his wife Camila and their five-year-old daughter Gabriella. She was ever so adorable and funny. She took a shining to Donte. I whispered silently into his ear. 'Seems like I got competition then?' In return, he laughed and then said. 'Even with all the millions of beautiful women in Brazil. No one in my eyes captures beauty the way you do'.

Damn, he was making me feel as mushy as soggy peas and just when I thought I couldn't love him any more than I already did. Bang, he surprises a sister again. I now know that it's him that I want to spend the rest of my life with.

For dinner, we ate a traditional Brazilian dish called Moqueca Baiana, which is a fish stew. Then for dessert, we had some Pudim de leite, which is a flan. To wash it all down, we drank some Red currant Caipirinha. Delicious.

After dinner, Xavi's father, Felipe. Filled us with stories about his career and how he met his wife, Viviane.

In return, Viviane asked how long Donte and I had been together and if we were planning on getting married and starting a family of our own someday. We both said in unison maybe in the next year or two.

Nina first, then Xavi and then the rest congratulated us even if it weren't official yet.

His father was particularly interested in our livelihoods and asked me about my role at Resistance and how I got into it.

They already knew about Nina, so they concentrated on getting to know us.

Donte filled them in about his businesses. But none of us revealed about what happened at Daniel and Kira's first engagement party. We agreed back then It was too risky to tell anyone who wasn't there.

After I finished telling them about my family and my harrowing past, it brought Viviane and Camila to tears.

Felipe, Xavi and Luís had similar looks of astonishment on their faces.

Him being a very religious and spiritual man, that was the moment when Felipe made a bold prediction of what I was going to become in the near future.

I stood up and went up to him. With the permission of his wife out of respect, I kissed him on both cheeks and turned around and said; 'If you're right I will buy you all another mansion each'.

He didn't laugh. All he did was give me this intense stare. It made me feel like I was the most crucial person in the world, and I said that statement out loud for everyone to hear.

That's when he grabbed both my arms lightly and said. 'Erykah,' his English was perfect. 'If you become the most powerful female politician in the world. You could buy a damn country, and that is a fact.

After the power trip, we all laughed and joked about a bit.

In the end, I gave them all some strong subjects to debate. Which evermore cemented Felipe's prediction.

Over the month we were there we saw the whole of São Paulo and even visited Rio de Janeiro. We took in a Brazilian league football match between Santos from São Paulo the team Xavi's family support and Corinthians from São Paulo too. It happened to be a local derby match.

We also visited historical places such as the world-famous Christ de redeemer in Rio de Janeiro. We hanged out at beaches in Rio and I did some much needed retail therapy with Nina, Viviane and Camila while the men looked after Gabriella.

We went to some cool nightclubs in Rio and São Paulo. Xavi and Luís taught us how to do the latest dance craze called Passinho.

STAND IN YOUR POWER

Felipe treated all of us to some of the best restaurants in São Paulo. Donte, and I even took part in a Samba competition. Surprise, surprise we even won it.

After we step off the stage, trophy in hand, Donte walked back to our table, and I headed towards the ladies toilets.

When I was finished with my lady business, I washed my hands thoroughly and then I exited out. First thing I sighted was Felipe who was coming towards me from the opposite direction, which I presumed he was heading for the gent's toilet.

Instead, he approached my personal space and stopped me in my tracks, smiled and then looked at me with an energy that was unreal. It felt very regal in a sense.

He opened up his mouth, his breath smelling of alcohol and said.

"O que eu disse-lhe. Você é um vencedor nascido. Você nunca esquece jovem senhora. Se você se tornar o que eu sinto que você será. Eu pessoalmente prometo uma doação para sua campanha."

Which translates as; "What did I tell you. You're a born winner. Don't you ever forget young lady? If you become what I feel you'll be. I will personally pledge a donation to your campaign."

This was all too much. Another millionaire in my life wanting to endorse my career. I didn't feel I was that special. Well, not yet.

Right there and then I fainted into Felipe's arms.

Five minutes had passed when I came around. I was still in the restaurant. Everyone was still there attending to my need. The only thing that was feeling different was me.

I couldn't quite put my finger on how I felt. All I knew for the first time in my life and what a moment this was and what a revelation I was having at this stage of my life thus far.

All this month, being in Brazil. The land of the spiritual. I Erykah Gaines, born and breed in Moss Side Manchester. Who resides now in Kensington, London. Has evolved onto a whole new level.

I felt, no, I knew what I wanted to be now, and it was a frightening prospect for myself. But even more, now I so felt Felipe's prediction in the core of my soul, and that was even more of a fear-provoking prospect towards anyone that would cross my path from here on in.

STAND IN YOUR POWER

Chapter 25 - Results Are In

I live in a world where hashtag this and trending that is cooler than picking up the phone and liberating yourself.

A world filled with a bunch of self-obsessed, attention-seeking, narcissistic individuals who are probably deep down insecure, lonely and seeking approval and love, in the wrong way.

A world gone mad. Where someone would rather film a fight taking place to post on social media for the world to see than get involved and help or get help for the person being pummelled into tomorrow.

A world where some of us deem it necessary to document our every movement, I mean come on now! Do I have to know what you're having for dinner? Yes, it's harmless and a bit fun I concur with that to a point. But if you're going to do that, the least you can do is provide a recipe so I can go and attempt to make it my damn self. Instead I'm left lusting for some food like it's porn and no means of knowing where to start.

But where it gets idiotic and dumb is where some of y'all tell the world you're going out for the day. This is the point the alarm bells should be ringing in your head. Not only are you out, but you also leave your location on. Do I have to spell it out?

Word to the wise ladies and gentlemen, if you're going out for the day and leave your house empty, to tell people all over social media where you're exactly going. My advice, do that shit after you've got back home safe and sound, okay? Or better still. Don't say anything at all!

"Xavi, I don't quite get it? Your family are wealthy people. Yet you work as a head waiter no pun intended, and there's nothing wrong with that. It's an honest living for an honourable man, yet you're earning just above the national minimum wage. When you could own and run a restaurant at the drop of a hat."

"It's simple Erykah; I want to stand on my own two feet without my fathers help."

"Yeah, Yeah, Yeah, I know all that. But many people in less than fortunate positions would grab an opportunity like what your family has got and run to the highest mountain with it."

"But I'm not everyone else. I'm me. This is how I am."

"I've heard it all before Xavi. But at the same time, I do admire your tenacity to live a life of solitude from your parent's money. Even if it's foolish for someone like you."

"Why foolish? Are you saying that you're these so-called less fortunate?"

"Xavi, please! In three years from now, my compensation money all two hundred and fifty thousand of it will be in my bank account. But if your father is right. I will become one of the most powerful and richest black women on this earth."

"If, is the operative word here."

"You two, give it a rest now?" Donte ordered.

"Yes please, I still feel like I'm jet-lagged and I'm doggone tired. All I want is a nice cup of Horlicks and my bed." Nina remonstrated.

"Ah, the black female form."

"What about the black female form, baby?"

"Nina, darling! It's what I love about you."

"Isn't the tough ones always a little extra softer on the inside. The black female form, I've grown protective of it. My foolish attempt to control the gaze of the gophers, who think the black female form is simply here for their consumption, their scrutiny, their enjoyment, their grabbing hands. When all the black female form wants to be is free."

The four of us have been back in London for exactly a week now and today was the day of the impending result from the 'Let's talk about black culture debate. If our entry was a winner out of the two finalists, then we get to go on the show to debate another topic and see if we could win the £100,000 Grand Prize.

But in the present tense. I was getting into another heavy conversation with Xavi.

I mean, here was one man that knew how to press the destructive buttons within me and I hated him for it.

"Listen. I hear you. But all I need to know about the black female form is that I've explored it in its entirety. The many parts and places. The grooves and most sensual of erogenous zones on that body. Você sente um irmão brasileiro."

"What does the last bit mean?"

"It means Miss Erykah, you feeling a Brazilian brother."

"Blooming cheek. You got some nerve, Xavi Oliveira."

"Girl, you know how he is, and you always play into his hands."

"Well if that's the case, then tame the beast for real."

"Babe, you're hilarious. Your one-liners always crack manz up."

"You know it?" I answered back as I grabbed him by the waist and pulled him in.

"Miss Gaines."

"Yes, Mr Williams."

"Nothing."

"What is it?"

"Just wanted to say. How much I love you." As soon as he said that he did something that made me run from him immediately.

"Ewe, Donte, Why did you kill a perfectly good moment?"

"Ha, ha, ha," he continued unapologetic, crying his eyes out like I told him the joke of the century.

"What did he do?" Nina asked. Within a few moments, it hit her. "Oh my gosh, Donte Williams, you're a fowl brother sometimes."

Donte was on the floor in stitches. He thought to pass the most excruciating smelling wind was as funny as he was laughing at himself.

Nina and I looked at each other, and she knew what I was thinking. Within seconds we got our revenge.

While Donte continued in his self-appreciation state, I headed over to the fridge. When I got there, I was looking for the ice tray. Nina marched towards the sink cupboard to grab the bucket that was housed in there.

After we both collected our retrospect weapon of choice, Nina put the bucket on the table as I filled it up with ice.

Nina took the bucket over to the sink and filled it up with water.

I grabbed the other end of the bucket, and then we both proceeded towards Donte, who was still crying his eyes out.

As we both lifted the heavy bucket, It seemed like Donte sensed something terrible was going to happen to him.

But it was too late. As we titled the bucket over, the fear on Donte's face on what was about too happen suddenly dawned on him.

He threw his arm up in protest, but for him, it came to no avail.

STAND IN YOUR POWER

As the ice fell upon him and the water drenched his clothes, I had to hand it to him. He hardly made a sound when we did.

"Babe are you alright?" I asked anxiously waiting to see how he'll respond.

He got up from the floor, and at first, he stood glued to the spot. After a few moments, he began to work his way slowly towards me with a predatory glare that penetrated right through my body.

I knew exactly how I was going to be punished.

Nina and Xavi sensed it was their time to go and swiftly they made their exit out.

"Donte, I'm sorry about all that."

"It's okay, Nina; it's just jokes."

"Alright well, I'll see you soon."

"Take care, Nina."

"Nina, Nina, wait!" I said, rushing to catch her.

"What is It Erykah?"

"I just got a text, and the results are in."

"Hang on! I got one too."

"Oh my gosh, I can't believe it. We've made it to the final."

"Ahh, Erykah, this is so amazing!"

"What does it say, babe?"

"Donte, it says; 'Dear Group Member, we're pleased to announce here at the studios of Let's talks about love that your team has won all the preliminary rounds in this year's debates and as a result of that you and your fellow members have won a place in this year's grand final where your team will get the chance to battle it out for the £100,000 grand prize. The subject for this debate will be about Black Men that hate Black Women. Also, we have sifted through many videos and a diverse amount of debates from different rounds. We have chosen your crews entry on 'Black Love - Is it Racist or Preference' as this year's winner of the £10,000 and all expenses paid dinner at our annual cultural event in London's Dorchester hotel. We hope to see you and your team on the evening of the 25th of November 2015. In the case of your team is less than three people. We will deem it as a forfeit. It ends with from The Adecco Studios Team."

"Ah, you dun know man. That's peak."

"I'm going to go now. I'll phone the others on our way."

"Yeah, trust me. It won't be long before Danika's blowing up my phone."

"Cool, I'll speak to you tomorrow Erykah."

"Alright, see you later. Bye, Xavi."

"Bye Miss Erykah, bye, Donte."

"Take it easy Xavi and thanks again for taking me to meet your folks in Brazil. It was a blast."

"It was my pleasure. Maybe we go again next year?"

"I'm up for that. Stay safe man."

"You too."

With that, they both left.

Together we walked over to the front room window and watched as they both got into Nina's car. Within a minute they were speeding down my road until they were out of distance.

I was starting to feel tired, and it was beginning to take its toll on my mind. Donte looked bright as the day. Like he didn't travel at all.

So, I look up at him with a sultry look in my eyes and then gazed towards the bedroom door.

In one move, he lifted and cradled me into his arms like a baby and carried me across our flat.

I smiled inwardly as we both entered the room excitingly and me knowing what was about to go down.

STAND IN YOUR POWER

I've been waiting for his manhood all day. At one point, I thought Nina and Xavi were never going to go.

But go they did and as the tiredness began to disintegrate slowly. The adrenaline that was coursing through my body was taking over my senses.

Donte just stepped us his game and started by taking off my garments in a sequence methodically, one by one and began the night lovemaking that will probably have me sleeping for half the day tomorrow.

Chapter 26 - Show Your Worth

The evening sun was settling into night. Nina, Syreena, Kyndra, Imani and myself were making our way to the Adecco studios in central London. We were riding in a twelve-seater limousine that was hired by the company that produced the show.

On the journey up here, I noticed bare people mainly twenty-something Wypipo that were dressed in the minimal amount of clothing.

They were out in force on this cold November evening mixing with the night air, looking like they didn't have a care in the world.

But I guess they don't have to carry around half of the problems we as a people have to on our shoulders.

As I sat there quietly reflecting on my personal journey so far. Between themselves, all the girls were having a heated discussion on why some black men hate black women.

For myself, I was feeling a lot more appreciative of my race as I remarked on the black scholars that were going through my mind that shaped the course of history and time, which also paved the way for the kind of platform on which we were combating to win a prize for.

But vitally, it was about our pride, and as black females, it was also about showing to our black brothers that black girls rock.

Not that it's in the effort of improving to be excepted entirely for who we are. But more to the contrary in the context of saying you don't need to dislike us as much as some of you do.

For it is we are the most underrated and unappreciative of peoples. We are the indigenous race of this earth and when we were taken from our lands and thrown into a cluster of cultures which we had no business being in for the sake of our humility.

The African diaspora is our black communities throughout the world that have resulted by descent from the movement in historic times of peoples from Africa, predominantly to the Americas and among other areas around the globe.

But over the generations, we adapted, but we were and still are in a lot of ways a lost people. We are also indeed racially naive, juvenile and viscerally unaware and insane race of people. We scream for loving others while these others don't love us as we do.

Just look at how they treat us in our lands and theirs. We don't even question it. Then another African comes into our country, and we are quick to attack them and want to run them out like it's done in South Africa.

But in hindsight, we were all equal humans until race disconnected us, religion separated us; politics divided us and wealth classified us!

Nevermore a true word said as the limo pulled up to our destination.

The driver also instructed us he would come inside the studios to collect us and drive us to the After Party.

This was getting a bit too much. For the first time in a long time, I was feeling overwhelmed with joy about something real and authentic.

"Erykah, you seem very calm and relaxed. Are you not in the slightest a little nervous?"

"Syreena, of course, I'm nervous. I'm trying to keep my cool in case I get one of my panic attacks happening."

"Oh okay, we wouldn't want that to be happening to you. You're our best asset after all."

"Syreena, Erykah is just getting into her zone right now. This is how she do when she is getting ready for battle."

"Damn straight Nina! You know how we roll from way back."

"Hey, do you remember that time at college when we had that debate with those dudes. What were their names?"

"Ah damn, for the life of me their names have evaded my mind."

"I've remembered one of them. His surname was McKenzie."

"I got it! Anthony McKenzie and Travis Alexander.

"That's them! Those dudes were so wild. They proper got heated like they were going to pass out or something."

"Do you remember what we were debating about?"

"If my memory serves me correct, I think it was something similar to tonight's topic! Let me think for a second." A few moments later, and she had it. "The question was; if your partner is talking to another female for five minutes and three of those minutes, he is staring at her breasts. Is that considered cheating?"

"Yeah, that was it!"

"In ten years look how that discussion has evolved into what's current now," Kyndra added.

"Well, in ten years, I don't think much has changed."

"That's one thing I agree with Erykah."

"Well it's a sad case of ignorance isn't bliss."

"Nina, sad case or not. It is still relevant in today's society."

"I know Sister Kyndra, I'm reflecting on how gloomy it all is."

"Ain't that the truth?"

"Amen to that."

STAND IN YOUR POWER

"Ladies, no matter how much we sit here and debate this. Most men's behaviour towards women is hereditary. Throughout history and time, this has been the case. So if anything new is going to come from this debate tonight, then we better be on our A-game for real!" Imani added.

"Oh we gon' be on our A star game and that's the deal."

In unison, all of us stretched out an arm each, and then we put one of our hands out in front of ourselves. We laid it on top of each other and made one of those solidarity packs and a promise to have each other's backs tonight.

The driver went over the instructions again.

When we all said, we understood, one by one, we all got out of the limousine.

Moments soon after, another limo pulled up next to ours. When the people got out, I knew it was the other team. Funny thing was the black women gave us all a pretentious smile. What got me was the way this two hardcore looking white women screwed us.

Without delay I wanted to go over there and punch them right in their faces for being rude and showing a lack of respect. But Nina sensed my desire to reap destruction and held me back by my arms. Kyndra defiantly whispered a few words of empowerment in my ear.

"Sister Erykah, whatever negative occurrence you're about to do don't. Please don't spoil it for all of us. Instead, use that negativity and fuel it into the positivity you're going to need and leave your annihilation all out in the debate."

Even though my nostrils were still flaring through her mini-speech, my heart was beating ten to the dozen also.

But as always. Moments later, Kyndra's words of astuteness had calmed me down.

The white girls sensed I was a bit rattled. So they carried on trying to taunt me. But I was covered by the best group of friends a girl like me could have, and that goes a long way in this life.

After my little melee, in my mind, they were simply a bunch of buffoons that I was going to murder on that stage floor.

When they left, a short while later, another limousine pulled up on the other side of ours.

From it, two people emerged. It was my cousin, Danika and Kira. I immediately went crazy as I always do and was so delighted they made it.

"Danika," I shrieked so loudly that probably the whole studio heard me.

"Erykah, cuz," she said as she ran towards me. We embraced and exchanged a few more words between us.

After I greeted Kira as well, the two of them got aquatinted again with the others. No one had seen the two of them since my house warming.

As we were about to walk away, another limo pulled up. From this one four bodies emerged and it was the guys. Dominique, Quentin, Jeff and Cameron.

"Hey, ladies," Dominique said, first. The rest followed suit. But Quentin gave me one of those stares like he wanted to rip my clothes off and have wild passionate sex with me right there and then. Trust me Quentin Starks would if I let him.

"Hey, Dom."

"What's good, Erykah."

"Quentin."

"Erykah Gaines, you're looking sweeter every time I see you."

"Is that so Mr Starks?" I replied by nearly kissing him on the lips. But instead, I turned his head and planted one on his cheek. He tried to grab at my waist. But I quickly ushered his arms away from me. In return, he kissed his teeth and sniggered at the same time. Crafty bastard, I thought to myself.

"Hello, Jeff, Hi Cameron."

"Hey Erykah," they both said at the same time in return.

After the guys and girls got aquatinted and all the formalities were over, we all made our way through the car park.

Foremost we had to get pass the main gates. I rolled up first, and the security guard asked who we were.

After giving him our names, all the girls got searched by a female guard and the guys by a male one. When they were finished searching us another one of his colleagues escorted us to the main reception area.

Once inside we signed in and was given access passes to the studio, except for areas that were restricted.

"Good afternoon, Team Black Resistance! I hope you all had a pleasant journey up here?" Said the brunette with the secretarial looking glasses.

"Yes, we all did Miss," Kyndra said, speaking for all of us as we all nodded our heads back in agreement.

"Sorry, my name is Sarah Cummings, and I'm your studio rep for the entirety of your stay. Anything you need during your whole experience I'm here for all that. But first things first I'm going to give you a quick rundown of the studio rules. Afterwards, I'm going to give you a quick tour of the important places you need to know, then it's off to make-up and wardrobe if necessary. Then of to the canteen if anyone is hungry. After that, you get an hour to chill and go over any material for the debate. During your relax time the floor manager will give you a rundown of what is excepted of you and the order of the show's content, is that alright with you ladies?"

"Yes, that's fine with us," I answered for all of us.

"Okay, then! Let's get going. First off, just a few of the basic rules that apply to contestants as to keep yourselves safe. So, no food or drinks allowed in the control room or on the studio floor. Do not hang or tape material to the studio walls. Do not attempt to move lights in the grid without the assistance of the Media Centre. Do not download any software to control room computers. Control room computers are for TV production use only. Okay, does everyone understand the rules?"

In Unison, we all said yes.

The next stage, Sarah gave us a quick tour of the studios, and on first glance, I was notably impressed. We even got to sit in the gantry of the control room and we met the producer, which was surprisingly a black woman by the name of Juliya Styles. In which her namesake is a coincidence like the American actress of similar name, but it's spelt differently.

Anyway, she was a nice person, but you could immediately see why she was the head honcho in charge.

She was making a compelling statement to all of us and showing you don't always have to lick the white man's arse to get to the top. Hashtag Black girls rock.

After the control room, we saw a bit more of the studio and then it was onto make-up and wardrobe.

Half an hour later and we were all sporting a new look for the show. I must say so for myself that we all spruced up very nicely. When we were finished, it was break time. First off, Sarah escorted us to the canteen for some much-needed refreshments and food.

STAND IN YOUR POWER

She gave us all a privilege card for the day, which entitled us to one free meal and a drink. Also, it gave us twenty-per cent off from anything in the gift shop.

When we all finished eating, we were all taken to our dressing room.

When we got in there, Sarah informed us it was one of two of the largest in the whole studio.

It had everything from Wi-Fi to Sky. A minibar, bathroom and shower. A couple of beds and a few couches and separate chairs and a table. It also housed an in-built stereo system.

I was gobsmacked and by the looks on everyone's faces. I can tell they where delighted too.

I also suspected that our opponents were getting the same treatment as us. When I asked Sarah, she concurred they were.

Forty-five minutes later, and the floor manager came into our room.

"Good evening, ladies and gentlemen, how's your experience been so far?"

"Your staff have treated us like royalty," I answered with a massive smile on my face while stuffing it with some chocolate.

"It's been nothing short of fabulous," Nina added.

"That's great to hear. So before we take you on stage and get you into your positions and mic'd up. I am going to quickly run by you the format and order of tonight's show. As I speak, the studio audience are getting into place. As you have been informed this debate is being taped and will be on TV screens four weeks from now. During taping, there will be no swearing, no conclusive racial slurs; you must be respectful to your opponents and their comments no matter how hard it will be at times, and it will be. The purpose of this debate is to find out why this

473

is a trend at the minute and both teams that have ended up in this final. You're two of the best in the country, but there can only be one winner. Whoever wins, and after the presentation, you'll be escorted by security back here. Afterwards, you'll have fifteen minutes to freshen up, and then the captain and one other representative will get ready for the media. When that's over, you'll be driven to another venue for the after-party, which you'll be mingling with some of the top television executives and industry representatives and the odd invited celebrity as well. How does that all sound?" He concluded mainly looking at me.

"That all sounds peachy sir," I answered.

"Good! Right, in fifteen minutes, Sarah will be back to escort you all to the stage and get you into positions."

"Thank you, Mr Nicholas," Kyndra added.

"Oh, there's one more thing before I forget?"

"What's that then Mr Nicholas?"

"The debate Master as some of you may already know is none other than David Almonte."

I was getting so excited at the thought of being in the same vicinity as him. He was the only celebrity I wanted to meet, and the only one I admired. The ongoing work he does in the black community is parallel to greatness. But as the debate king, he is simply the best.

"For those that don't, I suggest googling him before Sarah takes your phones away until the end of the debate. When you're up there, Mr Almonte will explain the debate do's and don'ts. Right, Team Resistance, good luck and I'll see you soon."

"See you later, Mr Nicholas and thank you," Danika concluded.

Exactly fifteen minutes later, Sarah came in to collect us. She lead the way through the corridors of the studios where we passed some celebrities. I recognised a few from the prime time show 'Cornerstones'.

As we continued through the corridors when we all reached the end, it opened out into the back of the stage.

Sarah handed us over to Mr Nicholas. He then gave us some final instructions and positioned us into our places.

Moments after, the other team were escorted out and like us; they had eleven people. Included in there were the two white women, which had my brain cells feeling confused.

But never mind that, I was here to win, and the same attitude was applied across our team.

As we were getting mic'd up, David Almonte emerged from the side of the studio. At first, he went over to the other team because they were situated nearest to the exit he came in from.

After he was finished talking and laughing with them, he came over to us. As he went up the line, he smiled and exchanged a few words with some of the others.

When he got to me, he stopped and stared at me for a few moments and then he shook my hand and asked how I was.

"How are you doing young lady? I hear you're the captain?"

"I am, and I'm a bit nervous too."

"A bit of nerves is good. Makes you human."

"For sure Mr Almonte," I said smiling.

"Please no formalities here. We are all friends at 'Let's Talk About Love."

"Okay, David, thank you."

"No worries and good luck."

As he went off, Mr Nicholas called five minutes to filming. As Resistances leader, I called everyone together for a pep talk.

"All I expect of you lot is to try your best. I know we can do this and let's bring that money back for the local youth and community centre. So repeat after me. I am beautiful. I am great. I'm not better than no one, and no one is better than me."

All together we did the chant.

"I am beautiful. I am great. I'm not better than no one, and no one is better than me."

"Come on Team Resistance."

Dominique encouraged us as we all clapped and cheered for ourselves. The opposition did some kind of intonation, but it wasn't as dramatic as ours. But they made sure we heard them. All their boasting was doing was giving me fuel and spearing me on to beat their clart.

"Sixty seconds to filming," Mr Nicholas warned.

That was my cue to take my place at the captain's podium.

When the minute had elapsed, the show began.

"Welcome ladies and gentlemen, esteemed guests, viewers at home to another edition of 'Let's Talk About Love - The Final debate. Tonight in this final we have the two teams that are competing for the £100,000 grand prize for their chosen charity or local organisation. The first team to my right is headed up by their captain. Please can you introduce yourself and your team and your chosen charity or organisation?"

"Hi David, my name is Cherelle, and my team are to my left; first off is Jemma, then Paul, Tamika, Victor, Colette, Jesse, Sandra, Frasier, Jackie and Kevin and we are Team Impact, and we are from Leicester. Our chosen charity is the 'Minority Reform Centre' based in Leicester as well."

"Thank you, Captain Cherelle, now for the benefit of our viewers at home.

STAND IN YOUR POWER

We are going to show a short clip about your team and the work you do in your local community."

After two minutes had passed, David turned his attention to me.

"Excellent stuff. So, to my left who do we have here?"

"Hey David, my name is Erykah, and my team are; first up is my beautiful best friend Nina, next to her is Dominique, then Kyndra, Quentin, My cousin Danika, Jeff and Kira, then it's Cameron, Syreena and Imani and we are Team Resistance, and we hail from London."

After the studio audience clapped, David showed our short video. Two minutes later and he was giving us all our instructions.

"Right, teams you have made it this far. First off the rules of the debate are; no swearing, no derogatory comments to be targeted at any one individual. Each team takes a turn of speaking simultaneously. If more than one person on a team buzzes to answer an opponents question, it's down to the captain who answers. Each individual has sixty seconds to answer a question, and so on. The debate will last for a total of forty-five minutes. This klaxon will sound at the end and that is the signal to stop. After the debate, the three judges will deliberate and pick a winner for the grand prize. Have you both understood the rules of engagement?"

"Yes, David," I answered. Cherelle just nodded her head and smiled.

"Teams, have you understood?"

There was a unanimous yes from all participants.

"Alright, let's get this debate on the road. Now, teams, I'm going to show you a short video on the title of tonight's debate. Black men that hate black women."

As we watched the video, everyone was transfixed. I decided to make some notes as it was the captains that were getting the debate started. After three minutes and sixteen seconds, the video was finished.

"Right Captains can you get this debate started thank you and your time starts now. And that's when the klaxon sounded. "First up is Cherelle for team impact."

"I do agree with what she is saying! You don't need to disrespect black women to date a white woman! If that's what you want to do, do it."

"Erykah."

"I'd never disrespect black men because I want to date a white man. That would be disrespecting my father, uncles, brothers and sons."

"Team impact, Paul."

"I know a lot of black women that say it doesn't bother them, have to constantly remind you that it doesn't bother them, but it does hurt them psychologically and spiritually to be rejected by their men, to be ridiculed and humiliated by the very men they fought for and have been loyal to."

"Team Resistance, Danika."

"This and I never understood white women who finds it attractive when a black man claims 'White women are more beautiful' because the kids will be black. Your mother is black. Your sister, auntie and your cousins are black."

"Team Impact, Jemma."

"Danika this doesn't need to be an argument about not all white women" we know this, but this message is for those women who feel pleasure in hearing their black men degrade their mums, their aunts, sisters and daughters name."

"Team Resistance, Dominique."

"There are many. When I'm on social media platforms, I have met them on biracial parents pages, and I had to leave because white women and even Asian women were saying crap like this. A lot of people having relations and marrying Black and they are racist. Black women wouldn't dare do this, though. You will never catch me saying Black women are undesirable. Sadly, the self-hate some Black males have. It's sad the women they date eat the mess they talk up and believe black women are less desirable and bitter."

"Team Impact, Tamika."

"Dominique I could throw out names, but I'd rather not. Surprisingly many black men use it as a pickup line. My daughter is black, how could I be with a man that belittles black women."

"Team Resistance, Jeff."

"Every race have their demonic men and woman for a reason. Truth is, those who would date outside their race are sell-outs there's plenty of good mates in your race, not teaching racial loyalty like find a reasonable person in your race is self-destruction, nature didn't make any mistakes."

"Team Impact, Victor."

"Exactly, why are you justifying yourself to someone who couldn't care less? Live your life and love the people who love you for living that life. Hope that made sense?"

"Team Impact, Frasier."

"Jeff so what you're saying we need to stick to our colours because as you claim it teaches racial loyalty? Yeah, no?"

"Team Resistance, Syreena."

"Well, I know this doesn't mean much coming from me...but I think that black women are beautiful! I never tried to be something that I wasn't, but when I was young,

I remember telling my mother that I wished I looked like Whitney Houston. She was gorgeous to me."

"Team Impact, Jesse."

"Jeff natural selection requires diversity if we were all to only date within our own "race" humanity would die off. It should also be noted that the concept of separate races is what was used to classify people, not of European descent as inferior, there is and always has been one race and that is the human race."

"Team Resistance, Jeff.

"Then tell the black women to stop disrespecting the black man?"

"Team Impact, Colette."

"Jeff You're right. 'Hey, black women, stop calling black men out on their shit then supporting and loving them!' Can we move on to the real issue now? "Hey, black men, stop being a mama's boy because she's the only one that raised you then doing an about-face and dogging all black women."

"Team Impact, Jemma."

"Jeff that is a ridiculous statement that's been said in this debate so far. You love who you love."

"Team Impact, Colette."

"There is a lot of men who have had their feelings hurt growing up. I guess you want to be cuddled and burped for the duration of your existence, huh? I don't date black men. They're broke. Always have several kids by several different women. Don't honour the sanctity of marriage by cheating and lying all the time. They're consistently breaking the law and going to jail or dying due to their ridiculous decisions. They're lazy. Dirty. Dependent. Drug abusers. Many are super sensitive and because they were raised by a single black mother and didn't know how to express their feelings in a positive manner which is why they only understand violence. You turn on the news, and they're always stealing or robbing someone. Many black men need to hush the hell up about who they choose to date and focus on bettering themselves. They probably could find a black woman who would be everything they need in a partner if they weren't so loud, violent, stubborn and trifling. See how generalised and ridiculous that sounds? Black man, are you not offended by that previous statement? All we ask is that your preference not be rooted in stereotypes and generalisations where you feel the need to bash one set of woman to date another. We hear it all the time, and it's unnecessary. You decided to date outside your race, great for you. Then why don't you get a passport and move the hell on instead of reaching back and telling us how undesirable we are."

"Team Resistance, Kira."

"A strong woman will intimidate a weak man regardless of race. Due to black men dating outside their race, incarceration rates, lack of education, lack of employment, lack of financial stability, many black women (which were named the largest group of people to graduate college with a degree) can't find suitors within our race. Instead of finding someone who is equally yoked, were told were asking for too much and to "date down". But, when we do, and the relationship goes sour, we are then ridiculed for picking a horrible mate. A never-ending circle which is why #blacklove is so essential to show that it does exist and that it is beautiful because now it's rare. I encourage all people to find who makes you happy and whole. If you're truly happy with that partner and you're internally satisfied with yourself, then there's no reason to bash anyone else. Just love and be loved."

"Team Resistance, Erykah."

"Yeah so, am I the only black woman that never bothered to care what black men or any other person for that matter thinks of me? Last I checked (1 second ago) I am great and nothing anyone can say to make me believe otherwise. Love yourself, and no one else's hang-ups will matter."

"Team Impact, Cherelle."

"I always get weirded out that some black men talking drivel about black women especially in looks, but they fail to realise that their mother is black and their daughters will be seen as black even if they're mixed."

"Team Resistance, Imani."

"And don't come secretly "sniffing" around me because you decided to marry outside your race. I don't have a problem with you marrying outside, but once you have made your decision, no need to turn back around and think you can secretly dip your hand into my chocolate cookie jar."

"Team Resistance, Quentin."

"As a black man who only dates black women, I'm gonna say this. From my experiences, I've noticed that black women act like they're unworthy of love from a black man. When we're doing the things that are expected of a 'prototypical good man', black women push us away. They say things like, 'you're too good', 'you can find someone better', 'you're boring', 'you're only treating me good because you are probably cheating on me?' It's like when black women get a good black man, they sabotage the relationship, or they run. Then they get with the 'real man dem' who are weak and ain't worth a damn, who treat them like garbage and they beg that man never to leave her side. I know you are tired of hearing that 'black women are too strong' etc. etc. etc. but on the flip side, I can honestly say that black women are afraid and can't handle a good strong black man. My woman now, she dumped me twice because she admitted that me being a good man to her scared her. Hence, she sabotaged our relationship before she finally allowed herself to accept the fact that she has a genuinely good man who loves her. We both, black men and women have been hurt by each other on societal/cultural level, and we need to allow ourselves to be loved by each other again instead of always expecting the worst from each other."

"Team Impact, Tamika."

"First, don't generalise all black women in this category of 'self-sabotage! Secondly, it sounds like you have a type; it's the women you are choosing! I can assure you that no one I know (including myself) would push a good man away because he treats you right. Hell, I'm still trying to find that guy."

"Team Resistance, Quentin."

"I've never said anything of the sort!"

"Team Impact, Jemma."

"Stop generalising us! You went on a complete rant about this. Then you come with those statements and do exactly that. Don't judge by the few you've dated. I still have a great outlook on love even though I've been broken. Every man that has left me comes back and apologises and tries to come back. Because why I'm a good woman that loved them, and they took me for granted. Stop generalising us please, thank you."

"Team Resistance, Cameron."

"Here we go! But why isn't there as much outrage when Black women date White men no one says your daddy is Black, your grandfather Black, your son Black? Always same double standard claptrap in the community.

Frankly, I don't give a damn who you love! Just Love somebody damn it."

"Team Impact, Cherelle."

"You're dating women that do not have their life together. I have never in all my existence of understanding hear a woman say to a man you're too good for me! A lot of men date women that are not on a certain level, so they can feel they did something for them, feel Superior to them, have control over them. The problem with that is. They are not on your level. They don't see you as a come up, and do better. Thus as you say sabotaging the relationship, they are not sabotaging it. They are not on your level. They are going to do what they do. Some men and women date this way. If you have a good job, got everything going for you. They don't want you. But would date someone that's not doing anything for themselves, and wonder why? Date on your level you won't have that problem. It doesn't matter if you're black, white, Chinese, Indian, etc. You are not dating on your level."

"Team Resistance, Kyndra."

"Yes, definitely not. You're seeking love from hurt women if you're constantly getting these reactions. Find a woman that's healed if she's been broken. My sisters may not agree, but it's not a man's job to heal her no more than it being a woman's job to heal him. Heal yourself. It's selfish to expect a stranger to come in and take on your burden. Anyway, avoid the types dude. Those qualities aren't the epitome of a woman. Especially good women."

"Team Impact, Tamika,"

"Stop lumping us all together. The very least we don't go around talking bad you know to other races of people. Not all black women act like that. Just the few you've come into contact with. And I can almost guarantee most of those women's problems have to do with absentee fathers, that probably look like you in the skin department."

"Team Impact, Kevin."

"That's not all black women it's women in general, and mostly one's who only know of bad experiences so when a so-called 'Good Man' comes along its so new and different they don't know how to handle the situation. If you care, help her understand and reassure her you're different than the rest of the last bad experience she had."

"Team Resistance, Erykah."

"Ever since the generation before me, a lot of black men became weak. For two generations, black women have been holding the black community together. I never understood how a black man could fix his lips to say anything negative about a black woman when they came from one. #blackgirlsrock."

"Team Impact, Paul."

"Wonderful and thorough! When you dehumanise others, you dehumanise yourself. After all, if Marcus is dating Becky, it should be because he likes her as a person, not because of her race. It's a shaky foundation for a relationship."

"Team Resistance, Danika."

"Black men and white women marriages have the highest divorce rates because many times Marcus gets with Becky not because of his desire to love and cherish a woman, but because of his hatred for black women and lust for white women, which results in divorce."

"Team Impact, Colette."

"What kind of slave mentality is that? Please provide examples of this so-called slave mentality that black women have and please don't trivialise it to having weaves or bleaching our skin. So many of us are embracing our hair and complexion because now we have makeup and hair care that's meant for us. And if you choose only to base that on what the media projects on us then you sir are portraying the slave mentality, not us."

"Team Resistance, Dominique."

"There are a lot of brothers who are not happy in the skin they're in I'll agree with that. However, we could say the same for many sisters, also. Lighter makeup, hair that isn't their natural texture, dying it blonde. We all have a role in this plight; it's just that men will voice it loudly, where a lot of times women will silence themselves on it."

"Team Impact, Tamika."

"You can't compare lighter make-up and weave to degrading your women and breeding with other women so the black can be diluted in your children."

"Team Resistance, Erykah."

"It doesn't bother me the least lil bit that they go to Becky. I mean, look at the type of black men Becky get. I don't feel bad for her because she done let the fool pump her head up about being better than us. I say, take them, please. Let Marcus ruin Becky's life and let us continue to be what we are the most educated by race and gender group in the world. They may not know who the queens are, but Becky sure does. Why do you think she makes it a point to prove how 'Black' she can be? Sisters, we are not missing anything but a consistent headache and a trip to the gynaecologist."

"Team Impact, Victor."

"Why are you dehumanising white women calling them Becky? Just making a point."

"Team Impact, Sandra,"

"Erykah, for it not to bother you, you sure have no problem degrading the black men and the white women they date! I know none of the black men I've dated has pumped my head up to make me feel like I'm better than black women, nor do I try to prove how 'black' I can be just because I'm dating a black man. Your statement discrediting black men, as if they're somehow less of a man because they happen to date white women & discrediting white women as if we're all weak little doormats, makes you no better than the men she's speaking on! Stop generalising and discrediting an entire race and/or gender-based on stereotypes! Or does that only apply when it's done to black women? Everyone's entitled to their preference. Just because yours may differ, doesn't make you any better or worse than someone else. Self-love is one thing, but to feel the need to disrespect someone else for their differences is an ugly trait no matter who it comes from."

"Team Resistance, Erykah."

"I didn't generalise black men, honey. I also never discredited anyone, but your confirmation says it all love. I also never said anything, disrespectful. What I said was the truth and just because you or another may not like it doesn't make it any less truthful. It is what it is and trust I am not bothered by it at all. I am happily engaged to a powerful, respectful, loving black man who worships the ground I walk on. So stop with the self-love speech because everything I stated says I love who I am."

"Team Resistance, Nina."

"Erykah I hear what you're saying don't listen to her, she clearly doesn't understand, or is she not reading in between the lines shall I say. I know exactly what you mean. Maybe not every interracial couple but a lot. She clearly never understood that."

"Team Impact, Sandra."

"Oh, she understood very well why do you think she felt the need to try and defend it? I ain't stun her?"

"Team Resistance, Quentin."

"The real reason Marcus is dating Becky it's because the women of his ethnicity here in the UK failed to recognise the potential this man has because he chose to speak proper English you label him as acting White because he wasn't Street enough for you, you label him as too nice, so in retrospect, you pushed him away, and then, in turn, ridicule him for a choice that you took from him by ignoring him and by rejecting him instead of recognising his potential. But hey It's all his fault."

"Team Impact, Jackie."

"Erykah honey the only thing Sandra confirmed is your hateful attitude towards anyone that likes something different! You say 'look at the type of Black men Becky get's', but yet you didn't generalise, discredit or disrespect anyone. Right, whatever. Please don't try to act like every black man that dates a white woman is nothing more than 'a consistent headache and a trip to the gynaecologist' either. I'm glad that you're happily engaged & it might be hard for you to accept the fact that a white woman can have a strong, respectful, successful, loving black man that worships the ground she walks on as well, but the reality is, it's just as possible. Now that's a fact! Not that rubbish hate you & your co-signers are spewing. And you missed my point about self-love because I said there was nothing wrong with it. You should love yourself & the skin you're in! But when you feel the need to talk down on others to prove you love yourself, it comes across as bitterness."

"Team Impact, Sandra."

"Nina I understood what she said just fine, so please don't speak for me. Now had she said 'some interracial couples', I wouldn't have said a word. But to call white women 'Becky's' and act as if we're all weak and only get the less desirable black men, please! I've only dated strong, successful men, whether they've been black, brown or white. It makes no difference. I've seen plenty of black women that date black men & they wind up cheated on, beat, etc. Point is there's strong & weak in both races. But by all means, continue to call me a cow and whatever other names you got. Classy."

"Team Resistance, Danika "

"Erm, Sandra, why are you here? I thought this was a debate for black men and black women. But I guess you were just lurking to steal pointers or something previously. Just asking since you seem like a lurker who is just making her presence known to cry because someone mentions 'Becky' and you cry, 'that's racist! Many black men date only white women that are anti-black, not all, but many of them are, and some white women will fetishise black men. And many of those men list a litany of reasons why they refuse to date black women and will then trash them to their non-black woman, who sometimes support their anti-blackness. If it doesn't apply to you, let it fly! But the way you came at Erykah makes me think otherwise. But one thing you will not do is come for a black woman on this team without being checked because someone said Becky, so you needed to defend your fetish for black porn. No one stated asking for Becky's opinion on this discussion regarding Black people and who they date."

"Team Impact, Sandra."

"Danika I'm here because I'm part of a team that's filled with black women who still wanted Jackie and me. So guess what we made it into this final. It's called diversity! You should try it sometime? But I'm sorry! I didn't see the 'Black Women Only' sign! Don't let a white woman have asked you that same question & said you were at a debate for only white women tho! Shake my head you possess such double standards? Also please show me where I cried racist, though? But I mean, if the shoe fits! Although calling white women 'Becky' is meant to be demeaning & offensive, I consider the source & could personally care less. What I did say, though, was that her statement was discrediting & generalising. I found it pretty condescending that on this particular video, talking about how black women are tired of being generalised & degraded by black men, that she chose to do the same thing to black men that date white women. I guess it's only offensive and not okay when it's done to black women though? I must've missed that part too, and I think I should just be okay with her acting as if the only black men that date white women are the ones that aren't strong or worthy enough for black women? Or the fact she acts as if they date us because we're all weak, obedient, little doormats? Disrespect is wrong no matter who it comes from and her statement made her just as bad as the men that were spoken on in the video, whether you want to co-sign for her or not! Up until she made her bitter comment, I had nothing to say, because I agreed with the video. There's no excuse for a black man, that came from a black woman, to disrespect black females just because he chooses to date outside his race. But there's also no excuse for her or anyone else to disrespect black men just because they choose not to date black women either."

"Team Resistance, Kira,"

"I love how many non-black women or whoever comes on to these debates to defend something they have no idea about or fail to understand—always concerning themselves in issues that don't necessarily concern them. Even every single time when on social media or any other platforms they're there lurking, waiting for comments, whatever you want to call it to try and defend and have an opinion on things that have no concern to them. Each to their own anyway, I guess we are all entitled to our own opinion."

"Team Impact, Jackie."

"I could honestly care less what you think of my opinion and I damn sure didn't ask for it, nor do I need your permission to give it either. If to you, my statement was me 'coming for a black woman' then you need to grow up and re-evaluate your communication skills. I didn't disrespect or attack her in any way. It's called having a debate on differences in opinions. Maybe you're not mature enough to handle that concept yet. I don't know. But based off parts of your statement, I'm gonna go with yes. Either way, find someone else to check because you failed miserably this time around. You're dismissed! Be blessed."

"Team Impact, Jesse."

"There's so many issues I have with this. I did a podcast on this very topic. Here are my grievances and feel free to push back and say I don't get it or then this video isn't for you then! One (This is a sweeping generalisation): When women are young, they say they want 'a good guy.' But at that point in life, they want excitement. So, white women classically say they want a good guy but have sex with the abusive biker. Black women say they want a strong black man but have sex with the good for nothing thug or man forever stuck on 'potential.' Then when those women grow up, they realise 'This isn't sustainable,' and go for something more stable, like the accountant. This is well and good and almost a right of passage. But when young black men make the decision to be the accountant or the history major early in life, want to date, and then are told 'You're not black enough' by their women, you ought not to expect us to stick around and wait for you to wake up. I chose to date who liked that woman and me just happened to be white. So, I did not date a black woman because of some character trait automatically I'd find positive in a white woman but negative in a black woman. I wasn't liked. So if this amounts to 'something that happened to you when you were 13,' be it. This leads me to the next point. There's a lot of projection from black women on black men who 'date out.' There is the assumption that black men can't handle a strong black woman. I've got white female friends who say that white men are just as intimidated by a successful, sassy white woman. So, it's not specific to black women in the least. That's specific to women in general. So, when a black man enters the room with any other woman other than black, there is the belief that there is some self-hate or feeling of superiority or ungratefulness for the beautiful black women who raised us. While this may be true for some, it cannot possibly be true for all. To accept one narrative for all black men who 'date out' is to accept a categorically false stereotype. There is also a lot of projection onto white women. There are historical holdovers for this one, but the assumption that white women are stealing black men from black women is a dangerous position to hold. The assumption that they are more docile and easier to handle is a reason I have been told black men date them. I assure you, my wife is a spitfire and reminds me very much of the beautiful black woman who raised me to be the man that I am. I know some black men have perpetuated this belief, so I'll give some leeway, but it couldn't be further from the truth for many of us. But, I should be able to walk into a theatre with my wife to watch '12 Years a Slave' or Nate Parker's 'Birth of a Nation' without us getting dirty stares and incredulous looks and rolling eyes and whispers and outward guffaws. Finally, the idea that black men belong with black women sounds nice on the front end, but it's reliant on racist thinking on the back end. On the front end, it shores up a beautiful culture and shouts that we deserve to exist. On the back end, when white people ask for the same thing white people with white people only then it is racist. There are dynamics of power that need to be considered there, but I'm trying to keep my point as simple as possible. Anyway, I've got a lot more to say on this topic, and I hope no one felt attacked, because I believe that black women are beautiful and worthy of love for reasons other than that they are black. I've simply chosen to love my wife, and I wish that more black women would accept her for who she is and accept our journey for what it is, rather than assuming what it must be."

"Team Resistance, Imani,"

"Sorry, I mostly skimmed your speech in my head due to its length, but I have a question: does this apply to Black men who say they won't date Black women at all? Because I believe that's the point that Danika was addressing. I think that you made some good points about interracial dating in general. Still, I don't think it addressed the specific nature of those who outright refuse to interact with black women outside of familial or sexual relations. Also, she acknowledged your fourth point by stating the issue isn't interracial dating but rather people who exclusively date one race but use 'preferences' as an excuse to hide their racial biases, ignorance, or just plain out racist agenda. I've heard this conversation before where Black women date Black men to avoid fetishism or ignorance from non-black partners. Self-preservation sounds better than saying Black men belong with Black women, and that is a legitimate concern. Still, overwhelmingly most women I know seem to assume Black men who date outside their race aren't concerned with protecting Black women. But these are just random thoughts."

Team Impact, Jesse."

"Imani, Well, if I'm attracted to brunettes, that eliminates a lot. To say 'preferences are okay' and then say 'you can't eliminate a whole race of women' is talking out of both sides of one's mouth. I could just as easily say 'I like the contrast of light skin and dark skin,' so that will necessarily eliminate certain groups, even if it is ones own. Its essentially saying, 'You may have your preferences, but you need to be willing to be surprised.' The fact is, you don't have to be willing to be surprised. You can prefer anything you want and ought not be faulted if it eliminates a group. I am not at all attracted to Asian women, and I can only couch that in negative terms if explicitly asked why. So I just say, 'I'm not attracted and give you no reason.' I could give a thousand reasons why I'm attracted to my wife, but if I took it to just the physical, I have experienced black women being distraught because they don't make the cut. But you don't have to make the cut with me. You don't even know me. A man who speaks in negative terms about black women was part of what was said here, but she also talked about hurt feelings and characteristics that are attractive in white women but not in black. I think there are characteristics in successful women that give so many weak men pause, but not just black men regarding black women. That's an insecurity I think a lot of men deal with, myself included at times. My wife and I are both successful, her a real estate agent, myself a small business owner that is growing in Leicester. I imagine if I lost my company and she was more successful, it would bring up feelings of intimidation, like I can't provide for her or that she doesn't need me in some way. I feel like I didn't adequately answer your point, though. If people are using 'preferences' to mask their racist tendencies, that's an issue. It's like white parents who have concerns when their daughter comes home with a black man. That is wrong. As for men who won't associate whatsoever or who will only have relations with black women but won't support them or stay with them, that is the mark of a child, not a man. And black women need to note the tell-tale signs early rather than hoping that somehow the man-cub will change. Women in general hope too often that they can change a man's extended adolescent attitude and outlook. Kick that man to the curb. But it ought not to ever be assumed that just because someone does have a preference, they are masking racist ideas. Get to know that man and ask honest questions first. I think a lot of people would be surprised."

"Team Resistance, Erykah,"

"Jesse, you made some good points, date who you like. But Black men need to stop talking badly about black women to justify why they are dating other women. I'm tired of the ish. I've witnessed my cousins, and other males put black women through a lot of garbage, but black women still stick by black men. It's a great insult to have black men criticise us, and not to our face but other ethnicities. I've experienced several times at work and out in public where a black male without a warrant, make negative statements about black women and how he is not attracted to black women and bash our appearance, names, and existence. At a previous job I had, a black male, who I trained and thought was nice and decent, only to discover when black people weren't around he talked badly about blacks and bragged about how he only dates foreign women. My co-workers never brought up the conversation; he just casually brought up the topic several times. Then there was this incident at a pool where I was walking past an interracial couple, and the black guy spoke negatively about black women's appearance and how he wasn't attracted to us. I guess to make the white girl fuck with him there was a group of black guys with white or Asian girls. They all were making negative comments about black women, they even went as far as to question why my boyfriend at the time was with me and not someone, i.e. (foreign, Asian, or lighter-skinned woman). I've witnessed several times black men disparage black women as if we are unworthy of dating and being loved."

"Team Impact, Jesse."

"Imani I'm sorry that is happening. I've never thought to go out of my way to talk about why I'm not attracted to someone. If someone asked me directly, I might be more inclined to say what I am and not attracted to. But I wouldn't go out of my way to denigrate black women because I'm not attracted to them (if that were the case, which it is not)."

"Team Resistance, Kira."

"This whole video and debate are about black men who constantly put down black women and feel the need to voice every second how much they hate us and that's their cause for dating outside their race. It was not for all black men who date outside their race. Like she said if you can list things that white women or whatever type of women that you like possess and that be your reasoning for dating them, then kudos to you. But to be honest, the majority of black men who date outside their race are not like that. Most of them constantly just list things they dislike about black women as a whole (as if we're all the same) and then go on to date white women just because they hate black women so much. So it's not a preference! They hate black women (or they hate themselves, so they don't want black children) so they decide to date anything except us. If they're going to do that, then the least they can do is not constantly tell us all the things they hate about us."

"Team Impact, Kevin."

"I love this. I think black women should take it a step further. How about you only worry about who's checking for you. I'm a dark-skinned black man do you think I give even two hoots about women who don't desire dark-skinned brothers? I'm also a short guy, and I have never tried to convince a woman who is into tall guys to just 'give me a try'. That's ridiculous. I focus on the women who love them some chocolate, funny, short, brothers period. I don't even romantically acknowledge women who aren't interested in me. So please, black women. Don't let these brothers with personal self-hate and insecurities make you feel bad about the skin you're in if a black man dates outside of his race that is perfectly fine. But leave black women and that negative shit out ya mouth when doing so, brother man."

"Team Impact, Jemma."

"This is why I've given up on black men. They only want black women that will struggle and stroke their ego, so that they don't have to be reminded that they're a self-hating piece of hogwash. My self-esteem isn't low enough to mess with them again."

"Team Resistance, Erykah."

"I think a lot Black men prefer the look of non-Black women, but they're not courageous enough to say that. I can't stand cowards, so I'm not interested anyway. Own your choices, and stop making it about the Black girl who told you your legs were ashy. If Black women applied the same attempt at logic, we'd be ridiculed and dismissed for 'generalising'. The pot always calls out the kettle. Who crosses off an entire race of women? Women, who are of the same race? Nobody I would want a date, and that includes White men, who don't date white women because of some behavioural stereotype. I'm an equal-opportunity rejecter of all foolishness. So we're too 'loud and masculine like' except when we're yelling at the top of our lungs, marching with signs, attempting to validate their humanity. Let brothers fend for themselves. We spend too much time worried about them anyway. Also, look at the interracial marriage stats. Go look it up. With dudes like the ones mentioned in the video! You'd think Black male and White female couplings would have much higher rates of success. If White women are so much more 'feminine and docile' why does paradise keep getting lost? Could it be that there's more to relationship success than finding someone of a different hue? Black women are finally tired of foolishness directed at us, by those who should be in our corner which doesn't mean they have to date or marry us but should mean they don't go out of their way to drive the bus we get thrown under. No loss for Black women that I can see here."

"Team Impact, Cherelle."

"If you marry the wrong person for you, then it's not going to work no matter what race either of you is. I have to say that we hear far too many black men say they don't date black women because they believe the entire race of black women fit into every known negative stereotype. But when their relationships with women of other races do not work out, they go around saying they no longer date that specific race for such generalised stupidity. And yet these idiots do not see the irony or ignorance in their actions. I read a comment once on social media from a Caucasian woman who identified herself as loud, outspoken, having a smart mouth were her exact words and brash. Because she is white, she is not denigrated for her character as black women wrongfully are. I know several black men who are in woefully unhappy relationships with white women and say horrible things about their chosen mate. Still, I never hear them generalise and say all white women are bad—more irony on men's part. Now, as for the types of men mentioned in the video. Their feelings were hurt presumably by a black girl, so now all black women are dispensable to him, but if a white girl hurt his feelings, then I guess it would mean the white girl was having a bad day and didn't mean it. His conclusion equals black women are non-essential, white girl is forgiven. I like all nationalities, but it's something about a black man that I can't leave alone. I love black men with a passion attitude and all. I'll be telling my man sometimes I don't like it when your mad and yelling at me, but at the same time it's sexy though."

"Team Resistance, Kyndra."

"In my honest opinion, Black women and black men everywhere are hurting. If Nadine did the same episode with black women talking about why they don't date black men and most of the reasons would be generalised stereotypes, most of y'all would be clapping and yaaaaaaaas'ing all over the place. Preferences are one thing, and these types of discussions are needed to find the disconnect between the Black man and the Black Woman. But if either side is not willing to take the time to have these dialogues then be quiet and move on. I think it's a mixture of pride and clutter that sits in our subconscious. We have been taught to think other races are better than our own, and it's sad. We must unlearn and relearn."

"Team Resistance, Dominique."

"From a black man; Looking back on the past, the present and towards the future, there would be no Black men without phenomenal named Black Women. Not simply the vessel or her physical gift of creating life, bringing her that much closer to the creator himself but her unbreakable soul. I must say I was fortunate enough to have a father that showed me how to treat a queen (his wife) and a mother that taught me how to find the perfect lady for me. I love women period and have felt infatuation for all different races and to shut out one race completely is to live in ignorance. But the black woman is a powerful force of nature that I fall in love with more and more every single day. It happens to be my Queens birthday today, and I want to shout her out for not only acting like royalty but also making these dreams I had on finding a black woman designed for me come true. I say, my queen, not as a possession but as a privilege to be apart of her life. Happy Birthday my lovely lady Chantel Porter you're my dream girl, and you destroy stereotypes every day simply by waking up and being you."

"Ah Dominique that is the sweetest and most romantic thing to say about Chan," I said whispering quickly in his ear.

"Thanks, Erykah, if it weren't for you I'd never would've met her."

"You're a great man, and you make my best friend a very happy woman. So you're welcome," I said back.

"Team Impact, Colette."

"They can give all the reasons they want, but we know that men are physical creatures. They are more likely to put up with negative traits from women they deem more attractive simply because of that. So Keisha has an attitude, and Tyrone doesn't like it. Becky, Maria, and Mae Ling have the same attitude, but Tyrone views it as fiery or spunk. It is simply because Keisha is ugly to Tyrone, and he despises her black skin.

STAND IN YOUR POWER

They hate black women because they are black. No other reason. It started with their mothers, and they don't want a daughter that looks like her."

"Team Resistance, Quentin."

"No, you got married because he loved you for you, when you are loud, quiet, outspoken, or introverted he will still love you. Attitude or not, he will still love you. If he as a man didn't have to change too please you then there is no need for you to change to please him. Stop policing other black women's tone and voices. You have found your voice, so why not let others find theirs and to give constructive criticism means that you are everything that you said black men hate. To criticise, you have to be outspoken, strong-willed, argumentative, and make your voice heard in a sea of comments. You were still willing to give unsolicited advice, even when your advice is the complete opposite of what everyone else is agreeing with, and you are stating without the permission or input of your husband, which takes independence. Everything you have deemed as undesirable qualities of black women are the same qualities that you possess and that you have invoked to defend yourself in this debate. You are a lot louder, stronger, and independent than you think."

Quentin's statement was the last one as the klaxon sounded out on him.

The whole debate seemed longer than forty-five minutes. The result was in the laps of the judges.

As they were deliberating, the show went to a four-minute commercial break.

During the break, we made some small talk amongst ourselves. The whole team felt we had the debate in the bag. But one thing that worried a few was what Sandra and Jackie accused me off.

It was down to three people who were going to determine whether our local Youth and Community Centre was going to get the much-needed injection of cash it solely craved.

The four minutes were up. David welcomed back our viewers. The studio audience cheered and clapped.

It was time for the result. David was handed a card. The studio lights went low. He ask Colette and me to stand either side of him.

Like in any of these kind of television programmes, waiting for that result was excruciating. The length in delivery was playing havoc with my emotions.

The palms of my hands began to sweat, and my heart was beating at a rate I've never felt before.

At that point, a spotlight shined on the three of us, and that's when Almonte delivered the result.

"And the winners of Let's Talk About Love - The final debate are." There was a long pause before he said the name.

"Team Black Resistance!" Everything went silent for a moment as time seemed to slow down, and that's when my team came hurtling towards me.

Danika got at me first, and when she grabbed me, that's when the noise came back into my ears.

"Oh my gosh cuz. We won. We won, we won, we won." She repeated over and over—while planting kisses all over my face and hugging me to death. The rest equally congratulated me, and then we all congratulated each other.

In a moment of clarity, I saw the despair on Team Impact's face. I took a moment to go over and commiserate and congratulate them.

"Thank you, Colette, you gave us a run for our money. You do have a great team tho."

"It's alright; I think your team deserved it in the end. Good luck."

"Sandra, Jackie, no hard feelings?" I said, offering an olive branch. They both decided to snub me. Oh well, I tried.

In the final moments, we were presented with the winner's trophy and a cheque for our cause for £100,000. Team Impact got runners up medals and a cheque for £25,000. On top of that, the show's sponsors gave our team £10,000 for each member. Impact's individuals got £5,000 each.

An hour later we all got showered and changed into our evening wear.

Our limousine a twelve-seater was taking us to the Spearhead Nightclub in Regent street for the after-party.

We all partied the night away into the early hours with celebrities and industry execs alike. I wasted no time in collecting autographs, and some of them even wanted my number. They said it was for future business. I was a bit sceptical but more hopeful than I've ever been.

I managed to strike up a conversation with a black guy who owned his own successful Advertising company right here in London Town.

He had a unique take on our debate and took it on another level. This is what he said; This is true, Black men do not have the power to oppress in any way. However, they do have privileges being male & often brothers deny that and either ignore their sister's oppression or sometimes help perpetuate sexist narratives that contribute to it. But in terms of actually systematically "oppressing sisters", that's not a thing. The oppressed cannot also be the oppressor. It's such a tiring negative narrative which doesn't serve any purpose. Some people always like to focus on the negative. You'll hear or see statements celebrating black women with black men co-signing and appreciating. One idiot will turn up talking crap and immediately his stupid response will be pounced on and used to generalise black men. Or you'll see or hear a negative statement and brothers calling a brother out, but that will get ignored entirely and again the focus will turn on the idiot and used to make sweeping negative generalising comments about black men. This type of behaviour is very disingenuous and highlights that 'some' just like to play the victim because it then justifies negative feelings and outbursts about some issue(s) they are dealing with which then leads to them projecting. That kind of behaviour needs to be called out. That being said as black men, we should be diligent when it comes to weeding these characters and expose anyone that disrespects black women. Black men are the most marginalised group in society and lack the necessary power to implement widespread oppression within this society. However, we should fight against any mimicking of sexism and oppression among us, which is perpetrated mass scale by whites. But at the end of the day, it doesn't serve our interest in debating 'who is most oppressed'. When it comes to black male/female relationships, we have to be diligent not to adopt the sexist mindset of Europeans. Black women are not oppressed in the technical sense by black men, but we are abused based on our gender and our demeaning behaviours, being shut out or ridiculed for certain things.

I finally got home at four am. straightaway I got undressed and placed the trophy in our cabinet.

I had the fortune of keeping it for two months out of twelve as I was the team's captain.

STAND IN YOUR POWER

As I took myself to bed, I stopped by the door and watched Donte sleeping for a few moments.

After a minute or so, I jumped into the bed with him. I then kissed my sleeping king on the forehead and cuddled up to him, and then I began to fall asleep next to a black man that was proud to be with this black woman, period.

Chapter 27 – Revaluation

I was once told to try and reach the three compositions that would yield happiness. Serenity, Tranquillity and Equilibrium. 'Erykah make them be your companions as you journey through this life'?'

Easier said than done as I pondered on those thoughts. But after winning the debate, I felt someway in achieving those feelings when Nina and I presented the £100,000 cheque at a ceremony the community centre put on.

The Owner of the building Mohammed Bekele was in attendance, and it was he and the centre manager Addisu Dibaba that made Nina and me patrons to their course.

We were delighted, and it was a well-kept surprise I had no idea about.

As far as I felt, all we were doing was lending a helping hand. Nina and I were reminded all night that we were their saviours.

But quickly as the thoughts of that evening evaded from my mind, my smile began to turn into a frown. From next week Monday it will be the day of trying to conquer one of my biggest challenges yet. Suing the assess of the Cheshire Police Force.

I did receive some good news this morning. When I was on the phone to Kyndra, she informed me that she was going on her maternity leave. So that left a gap that needed to be filled indefinitely.

She went on to say if I wanted the role full time, it was mine to pass up. I thanked her and said I'll come and see her before the court case. I needed to pick her brain on a few things. The strategies were left up to Marcus, who was due at mine in the next hour.

After I got off the phone to Kyndra, I immediately phoned Keionte, and he confirmed Kyndra's story. He said anytime in the next week during the case could I get to the station to sign a full-time contract.

I promised I would, but that meant me leaving the gym. After I spoke to Donte, he understood that I needed to follow my dreams and who was he to get in the way of that.

Besides, he kept on reminding me about what Xavi's father predicted for myself, and this felt like the start in that direction.

The irony was that little old me was trying to pursue a career in politics while I was still dealing with the establishment. Life can throw up outlandish scenarios at times. It's in those instants on how you choose to tackle what's been thrown at you, and turn it into a positive attribute.

But now I had to prepare for Marcus. I quickly kissed Donte, and he said he'll be back after Marcus had visited.

He was going out to pick up his tailor-made suit from Saville Row. Forever the show off my man is. But I do admire his style and Panache for impressing!

After we said our goodbyes and he left. I took my self into the shower. After I finished bathing, I took another fifteen minutes to get myself ready. By the time I ended getting myself ready, I had taken myself into the kitchen where I had begun to prepare lunch for Marcus and me.

I decided to make something I had for lunch once when I was dining at a Caribbean restaurant in Manchester, back in 2012. A tasty dish by the name of Rasta Pasta. I looked the recipe up online, and It's ingredients contained, Chicken, pasta, cheese, bell peppers, jerk seasoning, garlic, and green onions.

All I remember was the sumptuous taste as each piece of pasta slid down my throat. I know a man like Marcus would appreciate a home-cooked lunch, that's why I had no problem in making it.

As I gave the pasta one more stir, I lowered down the gas and went to clean myself up.

Within a few minutes, I heard the downstairs doorbell go, so I went to answer it. As I looked through the visual intercom, it was so cool to see it was Marcus.

"Come up, Marcus, the flat door is open."

Moments later, he'd reached.

"I'm in the kitchen Marcus, come on through."

"Something smells good! What is it?" He asked as he lent his briefcase against the kitchen table.

"Ah, it's nothing much."

"Doesn't smell like it."

"It's nothing! It's a little dish called Rasta Pasta."

"Rasta Pasta Hey! Sounds intriguing. But I've never heard of it."

"Oh, it's a lil' something I picked up from having lunch back home a few years ago."

"Well, I hope it tastes as good as it smells?"

"Oh, you'll be surprised."

After about another fifteen minutes, the food was ready. I served a bowl for each of us and left some for Donte for when he got home.

When we finished eating, we took ourselves into the living room. As Marcus began to empty some files from his briefcase, my phone rang.

"Hey, baby."

"Erykah, listen! Can you go into our bedroom and in my dresser can you retrieve my black notebook that's in there."

"Alright."

"Cool, I'll call you back in five minutes."

I made my way into our bedroom and did what exactly he said. I opened the drawer to his dresser and searched for the book. As I fumbled through his possessions at the back of the drawer my hand hit something hard. The outside felt soft and velvety. I took grasp of the object and pulled it out. I also found the book.

In my hands I had a purple velvet jewellery box and Donte's black book. I took myself and sat on the edge of our bed feeling curious, but I was reluctant to open of what I felt it could be. It couldn't be could it?

But as a private of a person I am about myself. I don't extend that loyalty to other peoples property.

Besides, I sensed it was for me, so I opened it and in my amazement, I gasped at the marvel and sheer size of it.

It was singly the biggest piece of bling I'd ever seen up close and personal. The rock on the ring was the size of a chicken nugget. Well, that's how it looked to my eyes.

The diamond had me gasping more, and then I screamed with joy and excitement in my voice.

That was enough to startle Marcus, because within seconds he came bursting into the bedroom, and looked almost out of breath.

"Erykah, are you alright?" He said through bated breath.

"I'm fine. But I'm in shock at the minute!"

"Oh, I thought you did yourself an injury, hence the deafening scream!"

"No, no! Just come over here quickly?"

Within a jiffy, he was sitting next to me.

"Marcus, I can't believe it, look?" I said as I shoved the box into his hands.

"What is it?"

"Just open it. You'll see!" Marcus opened the box, and the look on his face was like mine.

"Goodness gracious me. Is that what I think it is?"

"Yes, Yes, Yes! I think Donte is going to ask me to marry him."

"But hasn't he done that already?" Marcus reiterated.

"Yes, but technically no! He asked, but that was for our engagement. I didn't think he'll be proposing so soon after it."

"Well, maybe he isn't yet."

"What do you mean Marcus? Has Donte said something to you?"

"No Donte hasn't said anytime to me, hence my reaction."

"So why say that then?"

"I was answering your question with a question because you said about how you just got engaged."

"Fair enough! Well, whenever it's going to be. I hope I'm ready for it."

"You will be! But first thing first. You put that ring back and act like you don't know about it. Even if he meant for you to find it or he forget it was there when he asked you to retrieve the book."

"Either way, I now know. But I can keep it a secret."

"Good, shall we get on with the matter at hand?"

"Yes, let's go, Marcus," I said with a spring in my step and a smile that lit up my heart and soul.

Together, we both walked back into the dining area. I sat in a single chair, and Marcus sat on the three-piece settee.

He took out some files from his briefcase. As he laid them onto the table, my mind could only focus on the ring I found.

"Erykah," I heard my name being called faintly in the background. "Hello, earth to Erykah, come in." This time I heard that more clearly.

"Yes, Marcus! What is it?"

"Erykah, darling! You were daydreaming."

"Was I? Damn, I'm sorry, Marcus. Go ahead."

"Right, I'm going to outlay in full the procedures of how we are going to sue the police. Is that clear?"

"Yes, I'm hundred-per cent focused now."

"The police abuses and violations suffered by citizens that are most often litigated are known generally as police misconduct. These cases usually involve, but are not limited to, actions such as discrimination, harassment, false arrest, and excessive force."

"That's what Racist did when he spat in my drink."

"Exactly the same! But in reference to what I just said. It's more to do with how the police handled your Uncle and yourself. First, of in violation of your human rights, I will explain later on the types we will try to sue for."

"But Marcus, are we suing the police or are we including the Sandbach security as well?"

"It's my understanding your Uncle said both."

"If he says both! Then it's both."

"Right, let's carry on shall we?"

"Yes, let's do this."

"Well, to sue the police for discrimination or harassment, the victim/s, i.e. your Uncle and yourself, must show that there is a pattern of this behaviour; one incident of discriminatory or harassing conduct is not enough. So like I said back at the police station that night, I asked you if either of you was discriminated and harassed more than once between the complex and the police station inside and out for the duration of the arrest."

"Yes, we were! When the female guard called me a black bitch, the way we were unfairly treated inside the security room. During transportation, Uncle was hit upon two times after he tried to defend my honour. Then there was the mistreatment of myself and the racist remarks towards Uncle Jeb and myself again."

"That's good! So the next stage is to ascertain and prove false arrest claims. These claims usually assert that the victim's right against unreasonable seizure was violated. Which in your old case it was suggested that this is the case? So to prove such a violation, the victim or victims must show that the police did not have probable cause, or sufficient evidence to warrant an arrest. If the police had probable cause or believed that they had probable cause, then most courts will not find a violation. So we have evidence that the police had a small amount of probable cause. Still, they didn't have sufficient evidence to warrant an arrest because all they had to go on was the mere fact of the colour of your skin, which is a direct violation of their protocols! We have a case for wrongful arrest."

"That's great! So what about the way they mistreated us?"

"I got you. A claim for excessive force maintains that the police used unreasonable force under the circumstances in dealing with the victim, and typically, the victim suffers serious injury or death. So point one the guns being pulled out on you without probable cause. Point two is your claim for the alleged manhandling of your Uncle in the transportation to the station."

"Marcus, what do you mean by alleged? It happened!"

STAND IN YOUR POWER

"Erykah in a court of law it will be hard to prove unless you have sufficient evidence."

"Oh, here we go again about sufficient."

"Hang on! Maybe there is some evidence.

"How, Marcus, how?"

"We need to get hold of the CCTV cameras from the mall and when your Uncle and yourself entered the station. This will show your Uncle's injuries were sustained after the both of you left the complex and before you entered the police station."

"This is why you're the best defence lawyer in the world."

"I don't know about all that Erykah, but I'm glad you think so."

"Well, I do."

"So what I'll do is to instruct the courts today to subpoena both places to omit the evidence so they can analyse and verify it's solidity. We can use it if it becomes the most crucial piece of evidence."

"Right, also what about Racist spitting in my drink and the excessive force used in the station?"

"The spitting in your water, which we already have CCTV evidence."

"So that's three things sorted and to file for so far?"

"So far, we have discrimination from Detective McCann. We have mistreatment from McCann and manhandling from the Security guards from the complex. We are getting the evidence, and hopefully, it's there so we can file for harassment and mistreatment to you and your Uncle in the van."

"Don't forget Marcus! There's the mobile phone footage from the youth."

"Yes, I have a copy on file of when the Security guards from the complex pulled guns out on you. We did prove mistaken identity, and I'm going to use the case you won in correspondence to the gun incident."

"Wow, Marcus that's a lot of incidents we are suing them for? In all honesty! How much compensation could I get?"

"Erykah, there is no concrete definition of excessive force, so it is up to the victim to show that his or her particular situation did not call for the amount of force used by police. If you sue the police for misconduct and win, you may be awarded damages, or monetary compensation, as restitution for the violation of your civil rights and any physical or emotional injuries. The court may also require the police officers and police department involved to pay punitive damages, which is meant as punishment for the misconduct. So what I'm trying to say no one has ever been hugely successful in suing the British Police force. If, no! When we win. You're looking anywhere between £120,000 right up to £12 Million?"

When he said £12 Million, I suddenly felt light on my feet. Marcus quickly came to my aid and handed me a glass of water."

"Erykah are you alright?"

As soon as he asked that, Donte entered.

"Woah, babe, what's happened?" As he walked over and sat beside me.

"I'm okay; I've been discussing all the incidents and getting the evidence."

"So why do you seem all flustered like you gon' pass out?"

"Marcus, please? You tell him for me."

"What does he need to tell me that you can't?"

"Donte, Erykah asked me what amount of compensation she and her Uncle could receive."

"Right and what did you say?"

STAND IN YOUR POWER

"I told her no one in the U.K. has ever been hugely successful in suing the British Police force. The biggest pay-outs have been to Police officers and Police employees?"

"So what you saying Marcus! My baby can't get anything?"

"On the contrary Donte, I said if successful, they could receive any amount between £120,000 and £12 Million?"

"Oh shit, fuck, damn. You gotta be kidding me up to twelve Mill! You ain't serious right now, Marcus?"

"Ask Erykah when I'm ever wrong? I've never lost a case, and I don't intend too. Because one I love and respect every individual in the Briscoe and Gaines family and two I want justice for Erykah and her Uncle Jeboniah! Three, I need to get paid too."

"Yes Marcus, you the man! You are the man."

"According to your baby! I'm the best defence lawyer in the world."

"Yeah, I did say that."

"Cool! So Marcus, what's the next move?"

"Well, I got a couple of things to take care off for the case first. Then I got to submit some evidence. Then it's off home to my heavily pregnant wife."

"How is Nicci doing?" Donte asked.

"Nicci, bless her! She has a craving for gherkins at the moment?"

"Oh, yuck," I said in response.

"Yuck indeed. Besides her breath after eating a few. The other night she had me going out at 2 am to buy her some! So, the next day after work I went to the supermarket and bought her ten jars of the stuff."

"Do you think you purchased enough?" Donte said, laughing his head off.

"Laugh at your peril Mr Williams; your turn will come soon enough."

Immediately Donte stopped laughing, and his smile turned into a serious of expressions. He then took one look at Marcus and one more extended look at me, and then he walked off to our bedroom without saying a word.

"Oh, did I say something wrong?"

"No, you didn't! He'll be alright."

"If you're sure? Then I'll better be going. When I get home I'll be making enquires into the CCTV footage."

"I better get going too. I've got to get to Resistance to sign my contract and then I'm going out for a meal with Kyndra and Nina."

"Do you need a lift?"

"You sure it's no trouble? I can get Donte to take me."

"It's fine! If you don't mind coming to mine for half an hour. You can see who I talk too regarding the CCTV evidence! Then I'll take you after."

"Cool, let me just tell Donte."

"I'll meet you downstairs."

"In a bit."

When Marcus left, I went to tell Donte that he was going to give me a lift.

As I entered the bedroom, I heard some loud snoring. Donte was fast asleep. Poor thing. He's been so busy of late. I didn't want to wake him.

So I wrote him a note and put a couple of kisses from my lips on it, I laid it on my pillow, and then I kissed him on the forward.

I then grabbed my coat and my house keys and began to make my way to Marcus's car.

On quiet reflection, I tried to process everything Marcus had instructed today.

STAND IN YOUR POWER

I was more than ready and well equipped to take on the institution that wasn't built for us.

I wanted to make a point that some of us as a people had the balls to do what I was going to do.

My head was in awe of what could foretell if I won my case, and if I did, I'd be the first person in history to sue the British Police force successfully.

Chapter 28 - In The Presence of Evil

Never has it been in doubt from when I leave my girls side that I always come back home brimming with confidence.

Last night was the perfect antidote to my pending week of pain and hopefully, pleasure by the end of its conclusion.

Kyndra, Nina and I enjoyed a great mix of girls chat, drinks and some lip-smacking West Indian food.

But as I woke up early this morning, I knew today was the beginning of what could become one the greatest days in my life thus far, and for Marcus, if he succeeds on being triumphant, it would put him and his firm at the pinnacle of it's profession.

After Donte left for work, fifteen minutes later, Marcus texted to say he just pulled up outside my block.

Today was the preliminary hearing. There was no need for all my clan to be there. But rest assured various family and friends booked alternate days off. That guarantees someone being there to support me every day.

Of course, Danika will be there everyday as Marcus's trainee lawyer. I was so proud of her and glad she was in a place to help with my case.

On my way out, I grabbed my coat and bag. As I shut the door my phone rang. It was Kyndra, so I answered it as I made my way to Marcus's car.

"Sister Kyndra, this is a pleasant surprise. I thought you'd be taking it easy today after last nights antics."

"No can do places to be, and people too see, how you doing anyway? I wanted to catch you before you went to court."

"Well, I'm just on my way out. I got Marcus waiting downstairs in his car."

"Oh good, well I'm around the corner from your place."

"Whereabouts?"

"I'm in a little cafe on the high road."

"Okay! What are you doing up my ends?"

"I've just finished doing some shopping for the baby. Then I remembered it's your hearing today and I was wondering if you needed any support?"

"Are you sure, Kyndra? It's only the preliminary hearing the actual case if there is one, is most likely to happen in a week or two."

"Erykah, who else is going to be there to support you today?"

"Nobody."

"There you go."

"Alright, text me the address? We'll come and pick you up."

"Thanks, Erykah. See you in a bit."

After the call, I locked up the flat and made my way downstairs. When I reached, I spotted Marcus's Silver Lexus IS 250 parked adjacent to my block.

I casually walked across the road and made my way to his car. As I opened the boot to put my documents in there, Marcus hailed from the front of the vehicle.

"Morning, Erykah."

"Hey, Marcus," I said back as I shut the boot and made my way to the front of the car.

As I got in and sat down, I leaned over and gave Marcus a peak on the cheek.

"How are you doing?"

"Scared, Nervous. Did I mention scared?"

"I'm not going to lie to you. There will be times where this whole process is going to feel negative. The defendant's job is to scrutinise and object any evidence they feel is unlawful towards them."

"Before you say anymore, Marcus, Kyndra is waiting for us around the high street."

"Is she coming to the hearing?"

"Yes, too support me."

"No problem, let's go."

A few minutes later and I spotted Kyndra sitting on a bench outside.

As we parked up, she spotted us and made her way to the car.

"You can put your bags in the boot, Kyndra!" Marcus shouted out.

As she did that, Marcus looked at me and smiled. Me being my precarious self and not to appear stupid, I wondered why?

"Everything alright, Marcus?"

"Yes, I was just reflecting."

"What about?"

"The cases I've represented you in."

"And?"

"If I win this one. We, dear Erykah, will go down in the history books as the first black people to take on and sue the Police force successfully all the way to the UK Supreme Court."

"Well, I hope we can get past all the fakery this proven institutionally racist organisation has done to our people for the longest time."

"What's that I heard about fake organisations?" Kyndra asked as she got into the back of the car and settled herself onto the cream leather interior seats.

STAND IN YOUR POWER

"I was telling Erykah when we are successful and win this case."

"Hello, Marcus."

"Hey Kyndra, how are you?"

"I'm peaceful Marcus."

"That's good."

"Erykah, I have a point about what you said to Marcus. May I?"

"Go ahead."

"When you get distracted by fake people and people pretending to have your best interests at heart. Because you thought they liked you or were cool with you. If you're not focused before you know it, you're not walking your path and like myself the number of things and personal endeavours I take on outside of work; I even amaze myself. What happens is that you get swept up in an ocean of forgotten memories, and without you realising it, these little demonic cretins have turned you out, and you're looking at the world with emptiness & solitude. All this after you supposed to be this stalwart of a soldier. But instead, you're left feeling hurt and unloved. Sipping's of hatred galvanise and try to fester in your soul. But when not if, that you wake up from the monstrosity that has succumbed your core being. Two stages can happen. Point one, when you hit rock bottom and take on all the bad characteristics and ills, and when you gain a likkle strength, the only way is up. Two, this is where you galvanise and consolidate, check what tools you have at your disposal. Make a plan and stick to it. This time let nothing or no-one rid you of your purposes and your path. Moral of the story is trust, believe and love yourself first above all when others are not so welcoming."

"I can concur with all you said, Sister Kyndra. Especially the part about hitting rock bottom. Which I've been through many a time in my life."

"Ladies!" Marcus said, sounding serious as he got our attention and maintained his focus on the road.

"Yes, Marcus, what's up?" I curiously asked.

"Have any of you two heard of a guy called Gweb Lakka Miop?"

"I have?" Kyndra answered, looking very astonished like how Marcus knew of this character.

"Not me." I answered.

"Well, Erykah, you know how Nicci stay's with this kind of subject?"

"Don't I just! Your Nicci was the first pivotal person in my life. The talks we use to have while I was studying for my degree was the capitalist into why I want to get into Politics."

"Indeed, I remember. Nicci would carry on about it on the way home?"

"Sorry about that, Marcus. I know I use to keep her up late sometimes."

"Well, I'm glad it switched to the weekend in the end." He said chuckling.

"Who is Gweb Lakka Miop?" I sardonically asked.

"According to my Nicci, he is the toughest black revolutionary and master teacher of black and African culture on this planet. Who carries no fear and no let-up."

"He sounds like someone I would like to meet someday in the future."

"Erykah, I reckon he will want to meet with you. If you win this case and he gets wind of it."

"Maybe," I said with my precarious self.

"So Lakka Miop Marcus! What did Nicci say about him?" Kyndra asked.

STAND IN YOUR POWER

"Well as I was residing over parts of Erykah's case the other night. I was focusing especially on the mistreatment of her Uncle Jeb in the back of the police wagon that was transporting Erykah and her Uncle to Sandbach & Alsager station from the motorway services complex. Nicci quoted this speech word for word from her head. Amazed I was."

"Marcus, how did she lay it down?"

"She said, and I quote!" Marcus opened his phone to his notes and began reeling off Nicci's speech. "Hate can get some shit moving. We've been conditioned to suffer in peace. I love my people, but I hate my enemies. When I say, the word hate, the average negro, especially the so-called conscious ones, will immediately object and say something to the effect that hatred is an emotion. It clouds your judgement, and in the end, you won't be able to do anything? Of course, this is complete nonsense as we can historically attest to the fact that whites have hated blacks for the entirety of their knowledge of black existence. But it has not stopped them nor clouded their ability to strategise and position themselves over and above African people worldwide. It can be factually argued that it has propelled them, not impede them. So here I will state a fact that will force you to rethink what has hitherto been saying to you. Hate is not an emotion. Hatred is the principal. Now, that it's not to say that hate cannot be emotional. But what we are saying here is that it doesn't necessarily have to be. Let us consider, for example. The white scientist that is currently in a lab, as we speak, cooking up the next biological weapon, like aids, specifically intended to target black folk. Would we all agree that he the genocidal scientist hates black folk? Yes. But is he/she raging around his laboratory huffing, and puffing and convulsing in emotional fits? No! He/she is calm and calculated with his/her hatred. He/she knows what he/she must do to help his/her people continue to win and dominate this planet, and he/she is carrying out his duty mechanically, unemotionally yet still hateful. The negro has been disabled to such a degree that he/she can only understand hatred in one mode. It cannot be subtle. It cannot be calculated. It has to be worn on the sleeves of others, wildly lashing out; otherwise, he/she won't recognise it. I am honestly unsure as to why this is. I'm personally not plagued with that level of misunderstanding, so I would have to patiently meditate on it in order to come to an understanding of the cause of the issue. However, I suppose part of the reason has to do with his tendency to project his humanity onto others. Despite all of the clear evidence to the contrary, the negro continues to see the beast as merely a paler version of himself. He/she has bought into the idea that we are all the same underneath. But therefore, when whites project a smile, it interprets as a genuine cordial smile. So for him or her to recognise hate, he/she must also see a frown. In any event, what we do know is that the principles that are aside from emotional disposition. Hatred is employed by whites to help them dominate that which they see as a threat to their selfishness. Their fight for self-interest moves them to hate any challenge to their expansion, and with hatred, they can either build, and they can destroy. When nature tells them, they cannot play in the sun. That they cannot visit the stars, that they cannot biologically measure up to an African. Their hatred for such boundaries can concoct a sunscreen, create a telescope or manufacture a gun. When people tell them 'This is our land'. When nature tells them, it has a right to life. It moves them to give out smallpox blankets or to hunt in extinction. Now as a side note, at least one of you misconstrue and come at me with, would you suggest us to become like the oppressors? I'm speaking on hate as a principle. Employing hatred does make one like the oppressor anymore than killing makes someone evil. Some of us kill in order to live, while others kill for sport. The principle of killing ought not to be rejected on account of those who kill senselessly. And so the same with hatred. It's about its usage. For love can be misused/overused/underused etc. So I'll conclude by saying on principle I hate my enemies and it does not make one emotional or irrational or incapable of functionality, any more than it makes a weapons scientist incapable of carrying out the duty that he/she has set out to do."

"Wow, well after hearing that. I'm even more intrigued to cross this magic of a minds path."

"Violence is a structure European societies have always been created on. Any tribe, group, society, nation, they conquer colonise or control inevitably cascades into psychotic violence. White people created racism and sustain racism through social manipulation because as of their inherent inferiority and superiority complex," Kyndra stated.

"When one of us feels injustice. It hurts all of us," I said in response.

"Sometimes, you got to tell white people to teach their wicked people on how to treat you," Kyndra stated.

"Ain't that the truth?" Marcus said in response.

By the time we had got through all that chat, we had reached the courts with an hour to spare.

Today my preliminary hearing was being heard in an ordinary Civil court. Marcus also informed me that usually, a case like mine would take years before it even reaches the court.

The question was! How did Marcus manage not only to get my cases heard so soon but how he'd did it in such a short space of time?

His reply was simple. A judge very high up owed him a favour. He went on to say that this favour stretched back years, and although it got him the leverage to barter my case into early existence, it won't guarantee a win.

But Marcus was confident on all the evidence we had it should not only cripple Cheshire Police forces budget. It could well destroy the careers of those involved in any harassment or racist behaviour.

Fifteen minutes into my preparations with Marcus and Danika, there was a knock at the door.

"Who is it?" Marcus called out.

"It's Mr Ramsey sir. The court clerk."

"You may enter Mr Ramsey."

As Ramsey entered the room, I perked myself up in my seat.

"What can I do for you, Mr Ramsey?"

"Mr Hudson. The judge has requested your presence immediately in his chambers, sir."

"Do you know what this is about?" Marcus said, looking bemused with Ramsey's question. The judge's request miffed Danika and myself.

"The judge didn't stress why. He's requested yourself only sir?"

"I'm coming right now, Mr Ramsey."

"Mr Hudson, I'll wait outside for you."

"Thank you, Mr Ramsey."

"Marcus, what's going on?" I said seriously, feeling confused.

"Erykah don't panic cuz? Marcus?" Danika reiterated what I said in a harsher tone.

"Listen, it may be nothing. I'll be back soon enough," Marcus said, not sounding very convincing. He looked at a loss for the first time I've ever seen in him, and it wasn't breeding any confidence in me whatsoever. I was beginning to fret.

As Marcus went to leave the room, Danika caught up with him and grabbed his arm gently. Marcus turned around and looked down at her like he knew something wasn't right.

"Marcus, stop, please!" Danika demanded.

"Danika, what are you doing?"

"Marcus, can you please tell my cousin what you think is going on?"

"I'm not sure Danika what you want me to tell her?"

"I am standing right here you know," I said getting more agitated by the second.

"Marcus, please, I think you have an idea of what is going on so please can you put my cousin out of her misery before she ends up having another panic attack in front of us."

"Alright, alright in my professional opinion, it's either one or two things. It's either they have found some evidence, new evidence, that would incriminate Erykah and blow her whole case out of the water. Or two, they have decided to come to some arrangement to settle before it goes to the actual trial."

"That's better, Marcus! Now go get them."

"Yeah Marcus do your thing," I said with apprehension in my voice but there was also a fire brewing within my belly.

As Marcus went off to sort out my life in the time that he was gone Danika and I engaged in some small talk. She did her best to try and keep my spirits alive. But try as she did. I couldn't help but think the worst.

Twenty minutes later and Marcus came back with the court clerk. When they entered inside the room, the court clerk relayed some last minute instructions to Marcus and then he departed.

Marcus glided over to a chair and sat down. At first, his face betrayed his actions. He looked liked he was about to tell me my whole world was about to come crashing down on me.

But in the second phase, when he engaged my eye contact, he then opened up the biggest smile I've ever seen on him. Straight away that lifted my spirits as my mind began to anticipate on what he was about to say and although I am a cautious person by nature I couldn't help but start to feel something magical was about to be told all because of the way he was looking at me and making feel.

"Erykah, what I am about to tell you it's going to change your life forever. Now, when I tell you the first part, I don't want you to panic. Alright?"

"You're making me nervous, Marcus, but I'll try my best, to not panic." Danika took my hand in hers and gave me a look of solidarity that instantly made me feel assured.

"Good, now listen up? While I was in the judge's chambers, he also invited the Defence lawyers for the police force. The judge said that the lawyers and the police force had negotiated between themselves a lucrative deal to try and settle out of court. But for them to grant their proposal, it came with a few conditions. So, as we all sat around a table, the presiding judge said to the defence lawyers. What is your proposal? And so it went like this. 'We the Cheshire police force duly state we are first offering a formal apology to a one Miss Erykah Gaines and a Mr Jeboniah Gaines. For all the stress and harm, we have caused these two individuals. The Cheshire police force recognises that amongst their ranks, certain types do not adhere to the rules and regulations of how we operate as a constabulary within the UK. Therefore with immediate effect, those that are culpable for the crimes against your clients will be fired. We also state that if your clients agree to the terms that we are offering them. We would kindly ask your clients in the nicest possible way; please do not let this go to trial or be spreading any part of this to any media outlet or social media platform. 99.9% of the time we pride ourselves in the good work that we are doing within our community. The crimes that we solve and our general all-round fairness on how we treat the public. Therefore it is with our regret and your clients regret up until this point that we are very sorry that this happened to your client in the first place and her Uncle and that things were allowed to escalate to get to this point. We, therefore, have concluded all our internal parties involved and we can offer your client and her uncle £8 million each. We have come up with this amount as £2 Million for every individual crime committed against your clients. If your clients are happy with this amount, and they make a solemn promise to uphold their end of the bargain and sign our contract to say that they will not take us to court. Any further actions will be that the monies that will be paid into your client's accounts within one calendar month from the day they sign our contract. If your clients agree to our protocols and nothing is stated to the media within that month and if they are waiting for their money and if your clients break any of the contract conditions no monies will be paid to them. I hope this is clear to the best of yours and your client's knowledge that they understand that we didn't want to cause any malice in the first place like I said those individuals had been reprimanded and they will be duly punished before they get sacked. They will never be able to work in any law enforcement establishment in this country ever again mark our words. We will give your clients two hours from the time you leave these chambers to make a decision. The Police concluded. So if everything is alright, you can take this contract to your client, sign it and give it back to the court clerk and then we will get everything processed from there that's what the judge concluded."

"Oh my goodness Erykah," Danika said, looking as astonished as I felt.

My head began to feel numb, and I felt like I wanted to pass out. Marcus saw I was waning and quickly lifted me and escorted Danika and me outside the courts.

After around five minutes of fresh air, I managed to calm down and get my head around their proposal.

Kyndra was waiting patiently on a bench. When she spotted us, she came over.

"Hey what happened Erykah?"

"Danika, can you please tell her."

"Tell me what? Is everything alright?"

"Sister Kyndra come take a seat back where you were."

"Okay."

We all followed each other to the bench.

As we all sat down, Kyndra waited patiently for Danika to talk.

"Sister Kyndra, there isn't going to be a trial."

"What do you mean that there isn't going to be a trial. Why what happened?"

"In a nutshell, the Police decided to make a settlement without the case going to trial."

"Oh wow, that's marvellous news. Erykah you must be so pleased?"

"You haven't heard the best part yet," I stated.

STAND IN YOUR POWER

"Sister Kyndra, there are conditions that Erykah and our Uncle Jeboniah have to adhere. First off within the calendar one month from today for them to receive their compensation they are not allowed to speak to any media about the case or any social media outlet or post on any social media platform."

"I see."

"So with that being in mind? If they keep to the conditions then at the end of that month a total of £8 million each will be paid into their respective accounts that's it."

"Wow, £8 Million each. Oh my Erykah, that's sensational news."

"What did I tell you? Wait for the best part."

"You must be stoked right now?"

"Everything still feels surreal to me. I'll believe it one hundred per cent when the funds are in my account."

"Erykah if I were you. I would hire myself an accountant to help you with how your money should be sorted out. Secondly, let your bank manager know that the money is coming into your account. The last thing you need is them flagging up your account for a large transaction."

"So, Marcus, how am I going to prove it?"

"Leave it with me. I'll get the court to issue a statement for the bank and send it today."

"Marcus, why don't you leave it with me and you go get some food with the girls?"

"Danika, it's alright. I'll do it after we all have something to eat. Besides, I have to take back the contract as well. Kill two birds with one stone, so to speak."

"No problems, boss."

"Cool, let's get out here please," I said impatiently.

"Okay, let's go," Marcus reiterated.

First things first, I needed food and drink. Marcus suggested we could go over to a brassiere across the road from the courthouse. So we did.

Once Inside, I first phoned Uncle Jeb, and he was as ecstatic as I was elated. He said without hesitation; he will accept their offer. Afterwards, I called father and Bernadette. Father, bless him was thrilled with emotion and swore so many times and cried as equally too and went through all the shit I've been through in my young life and how this was retribution for a person who never should've been treated like that. He included himself in there too. I told him he was already forgiven before I came to London. He knew that, but I still had to remind him. I asked Bernie because she was the most centred person I knew to make sure father will be alright. She complied and assured me he would. Danika phone her parents and told them the good news. It was going to be a massive payday for her too. I was chuffed for her completely. But last and not least, I phone my baby. When I told him I blew his mind. I repeatedly conveyed to him through tears of jubilation that I love him so much and I also suggested we should stay at his mothers house tonight, he agreed. I also told him to gather up all his family so I could tell them my good news altogether. Plus I was going to buy their dinner for tonight.

After I finished my calls and deliberated for the last time with Marcus and Danika, I signed my contract. A courier was sending Uncle Jeb's, and he had 48 hours to sign and return his copy. I did warn him of that.

Half an hour later and Marcus came back and said that was a wrap. I was overwhelmed with emotions. I laughed, cried and sang.

After all the melee Marcus offered to take Danika home first and then myself and Kyndra.

STAND IN YOUR POWER

We couldn't help ourselves on the ride to Nik's house talking about how massive a win this was for everyone. £16 Million will become the biggest settlement ever to a civilian in the history of any of the British Police forces.

I said now my life can start and although I promised to keep my mouth shut within this calendar month. I decided once my money hit my account. I was going to tell my story to the world.

Besides, there was nothing mentioned in the contract that I couldn't.

I will no doubt become infamous from it as the woman who took on the establishment and won.

I'd imagine how many of our people my story will inspire and give some kind of hope too.

Marcus and Danika backed up my plan to pull into question the practices of this institutionally racist organisation once and for all.

Chapter 29 – Errors & Omissions

Friday the 18th December 2015 is the date that is exactly a month to the letter from when I made history and was paid out the most compensation as a civilian from the British Police force.

Inside this past month, my status as a human knowing has gone from local activist to a world-renowned celebrity.

I have gone from the girl next door to the first black woman that slated a cog in this system of oppression and domination.

From the U.K. that has interviewed me to the USA and some other places in countries within Africa, and I've been paid very handsomely for my testimonies.

In the U.K. I've appeared on shows like Breakfast with Britain and The Living Show. In the states, I've appeared on The Assessment, The Candy Collins Show and Quite Frankly, to name a few.

I've had a ghost writer tell my life story and that has become a bestseller and has made me more money than I ever thought possible I would have in my possession.

Then there is my financial advisor who told me I should invest some of my new found wealth into the forex trading market and boy did I know I would have such beginners luck. On my first ten trades I made in excess of twenty-million pounds.

That kind of business is reserved for the big boys club and now I was able to buy out some of those centres.

My family's credentials have also been brought into question. As expected, they found nothing.

It's the media's way of trying to bring down the success of black people. It just so happened to be in my family; we were scholars to professionals, and we were perfect role models for our communities. They had shit on us, period! Even father now was doing well.

What family doesn't have a few chinks in its armour so too speak?

As for Donte and myself, our lives now have been changed forever. But as much as I liked the catching's and attachments of my newly found celebrity status. I wasn't going to stray, change or forget where I came from.

Besides the Resistance Movement was now more than ever in full view of the public and political arena and I along with the rest of the movements staff. We had duties to fulfil, and nothing or no one was going to stop us from completing our mission.

So after a bumper month of going back and forth country to country, literally. Today I was giving a talk to all the students in Nina's Creative Writing classes. Then after that, Nina and I were meeting up with Kyndra before we all went our separate ways for Christmas and the New Year.

As I clutched my coat and made my way out of the mansion that we recently moved too, I got a surprise text from Donte telling me to meet him around the corner from our road.

The reason it was a surprise because I thought he was out of London today overseeing plans to build another Body Active franchise in Brentwood which is a very affluent area in the heart of Essex.

As I exited from our grounds, droplets of snowflakes began to fall lightly on me.

Instantaneously I took a scarf from my handbag and wrapped it securely over my hair. I only had it done today at Aunt Lola's salon earlier, and I was sporting a traditional relaxed shoulder-length look, which I had to change from my Mohican hairstyle now that I was moving in professional circles.

From Kensington Palace Gardens where we lived, I began to make my way to Palace Garden Mews.

As I walked past the many magnificent houses and mansions some of the other buildings in this area were embassies.

Down the road from our place, you had an area called Kensington Palace Green. To the east of my home was the memorial playground for the late Princess Diana, which is in Kensington Gardens. On the other side is Hyde Park and in-between the Gardens and my place was the Royal residence of Kensington Palace.

Kensington is the kind of area and people I'm moving around with now, and I'm living in the most expensive street in the U.K.

On my road alone you have the owner of Chelsea football club living here. Most of the residents here are the super-rich elite, also known as Global Plutocrats and they're private owners.

There are armed police officers at both ends of the street, and security huts, where Crown Estate officials control bollards that sink into the ground allowing cars to enter or leave once they have been cleared. It is hard to think of another road in London protected in this way, and that's why Uncle Sebastian is on the level he is.

Because I'm living in the most expensive street in Great Britain, the average prices for a property in this area cost around £35m to £41m. But there is this property one of the guards coming home from a meeting one evening told me about. That there was a certain Saudi Prince that owned this property which was worth in excess of £100m and was situated on 'Billionaires Row'. Now that's what you call serious wealth.

STAND IN YOUR POWER

I mean don't get me wrong you're sitting there thinking how the fuck has a girl like me end up in a street like this. The answer is simple—my connections.

Uncle Sebastian had attained the property Donte, and I are occupying by an old bachelor that was good friends with Uncle.

This old bachelor was the owner of Crown Estates who owned the road.

In the bachelor's final will, after monies and other properties were shared out between his family and friends, The Kensington Palace Gardens pad, that sat in the middle of and next too football club owners to CEOs of multinational corporations was left to Uncle's property business.

Uncle told me he has held it for three years after old bachelors death.

As soon as I came to London and rose into the position, I find myself now. It was only last week that the property we were vacating Uncle had informed us it was worth an estimated £70m and yes it was situated in 'Billionaires Row'.

Well, I nearly passed out when he told me. Equally, I asked why. His answer was a leader needed a place where she could go and find sanctuary when her world around her was continually spinning in a daze from the requests of her time and so on.

Although if ever Donte and myself were thinking to start a family and when we eventually do, this will be the best place protective wise to bring him or her up.

As I continued my walk, I bumped into the only two people so far Donte, and I have personally met and had them around for dinner last week.

"Hey guys, how are you?"

"Erykah, darling! So nice to see you. How have you been?" Kadisha asked seemingly excited.

"I'm great!"

"So where's your other half?" Ainsley asked.

"He's somewhere around the corner! He's got a surprise for me."

"Wow, ain't you the lucky one? I wished someone would do that for me now and then." Kadisha hinted while focusing her gaze on her husband.

"Oh, Kadisha! I thought I was a surprise enough every day?"

"That, my dear! Is something we need to negotiate, real quick."

"You two! What are you like?"

They were the only other Black Professional couple in the area. Mr & Mrs Ainsley and Kadisha Brathwaite. They were both older than us. Only slightly like in their mid-thirties, but it was nice to know them and handy sometimes to have them around.

Ainsley is a GP and a partner in his own practice. So as soon as I found that out. I made him my doctor.

Kadisha is a best-selling author and playwright!

Ainsley has been a great doctor too. He continues to counsel me about CBT techniques which fortuitously has helped me to manage my anxiety.

You see before Ainsley became a General Practitioner, after he left university, he landed a job at a giant Multinational Pharmaceutical Corporation in the States. It's where he met his American woman while attending one of her promotions about her first novel in a hotel function room.

But within eight months of working tirelessly, he realised he couldn't work at a place that devoured his core principles. So he left.

STAND IN YOUR POWER

Throughout his relationship with Kadisha in their first year, he did odd jobs, mostly agency based work like clerical or courier work.

It was only in their second year he was telling Donte and me at dinner last week that Kadisha and he were attending these classes that helped you to expand your mind and way of thinking.

From those classes, that's what took them both to Ghana, where Ainsley learned the techniques on how to deal with any kind of mental disorder. In the time they were out there Kadisha wrote her second novel. After four years learning about the teachings of our ancestors, Ainsley and Kadisha came to live in London. So Ainsley could study to become a doctor. After a further seven years of residency and securing his licensure, he rose the ranks over another ten years, and that's how he became a partner in his very own practice.

By then Kadisha had written her third, fourth and fifth novels that made her millions.

On the back of that, they both got married in the summer of 2010.

I got so engrossed in their story that we all ended up talking to like 2 am. Lucky it was a Saturday night. So we had the luxury to do it.

By the time I had said hello and caught up them. Donte being inpatient as he was had driven around to where Ainsley, Kadisha and myself were situated.

As he pulled up in this brand new car that I've never seen, it had a red bow tied around the white bumper bonnet.

You see, I have been taking driving lessons in secret. As I'm a pessimist at times, I didn't want to jinx anything. I finally past my tests last week and it seems my fiancé has gone over the top this time.

"Surprise!" Donte got out all excited. He was smiling like a Cheshire Cat.

"Donte, what the...?" I was flabbergasted. I didn't know what to say for once.

"Baby, don't you like it?" By my odd reaction, he asked, looking very insecure now.

"Oh gosh Donte," Ainsley said, sounding in shock too.

"He has gone all out for you," Kadisha said whispering in my ear.

"I think he's gone a little insane in the membrane," I whispered back.

"Donte, come here?" I asked politely.

"What's up, babe. Don't you like it?"

"Donte, I love it."

"So what's the problem then?"

"Don't you think it's a bit extravagant to be my first car?"

"Maybe, but you're a celebrity now, and you need a car that's befitting."

I started warming to the idea a little bit. To me, it was so flashy.

"What make and model is it?"

"If you may. Let me answer that," Ainsley requested while he interrupted us.

"Go ahead," Donte happily gave his permission for Ainsley to do so.

"Erykah darling, what you have here is one fine piece of man-made machinery. This is a 2013 Bugatti Veyron 16.4 Grand Sport Vitesse. The Vitesse (French for "speed") is a combination of the two major existing Veyron variations: the Super sport which makes 1200 horsepower from its quad-turbo 8.0-litre W-16, and the Targa-topped Grand sport. Somehow, Bugatti resisted the urge to call it the Veyron 16.4 Grand Sport Super Sport. With a starting price of £1,914,000 the Vitesse powers beyond 155 mph as vehemently as a Porsche 911 pushes above 60 mph. And the Bugatti shows no signs of strain even beyond 185 mph. You have a car here that is too fast for these ordinary streets. But with good practice, it can be mastered. But if I was a betting man, I'm going to guess that your hubby here has something else up his sleeve."

"Well, Ainsley I managed to hit a top speed of 206mph. But the car dealer said to me, and he quoted. "You might want to double-fasten your toupee's chin strap before approaching that kind of speed. At 233 mph with the top off, the Vitesse's engine power and air resistance finally fight to a draw. Affixing the top adds another 22 mph to the top speed."

"Babe, seriously I can't accept this gift," I protested in vain.

"Erykah, you won't have too. Is it an investment for our future? Hold on one sec."

As he dialled his phone, Kadisha and I looked on mystified. Ainsley just smirked.

"Yeah, you can bring it around now?"

I was still mystified.

"Donte, what's going on?"

"A few secs babe you'll see."

As soon as he said that I spotted a black car making its way slowly down the street when the vehicle reached where we stood, I spotted Donte's best friend Elijah driving it.

As he came to a halt and turned the engine off, he duly got out of the car.

"Elijah, what are you doing here?"

"Well, it's nice to see you to Erykah."

"You know I don't mean it like that?"

"I know it's cool."

"Nice car young, man," Ainsley said as he approached Elijah and extended his hand out for him to shake.

"Elijah," he answered as he shook Ainsley's hand.

"Thank you, Elijah. This is my wife, Kadisha."

"Mam."

"I'm Ainsley, Ainsley Brathwaite and we are Erykah's and Donte's neighbours."

"Nice to meet you, Mr and Mrs Brathwaite."

"Erykah, baby! This is your surprise. The Bugatti. I've only leased that for the day?"

"What did you put up as collateral?"

"One of my franchises?"

"Brave move, darling. Well, you better get it back without a scratch?" I said feeling very relieved this time around.

As he handed me the keys to my new car, I asked him what model of Mercedes it was as it's one my favourite cars. I've never seen this one before.

"What model is it?"

"It's the S650 Cabriolet."

"What was the price?"

"Almost £230,000."

"I can live with that," as I gave him a big smacker on his lips and yet again, I was embracing this wonderful man in my life.

"Right, ladies and gentlemen it's time I get going. So, Kadisha darling, mmm!" I said as I embraced her in a tight hug and gave her a peck on the check.

"Take care, Erykah! Catch up with you soon."

"Yes, we must do dinner one evening around ours."

"I'll have to check my schedule and let you know when we are available."

"You do that and get back to me."

"Will do Hun."

"Ainsley, take care," I reiterated as I gave him a quick hug too.

"See you soon, Erykah."

As they left our sides and walked in the direction of their property, I sauntered over to where Donte was who was engrossed in a chilled conversation with Elijah.

"Babe, I've got to get going otherwise I'm going to be late."

"It's cool! You go, and I'll see you tonight."

"I'll be back by 7 pm the latest."

"All good! I going attempt to cook your favourite meal."

"What did I do to deserve all this first-class treatment?"

"Nothing! Can't a man buy his future wife a gift other than the fact he's in love with her?"

All I did was smile, gave him a hug and a kiss, and I hugged Elijah too.

After saying my goodbyes, I got into my brand new whip and made myself comfortable.

As I took in the smell of the Merc's leather seats, I had a good fiddle around with all the gadgets. Once I familiarised myself with my S650. I put my car into gear and took off in the direction of South London.

When I got to the hub at the end of the street, the armed policeman as I got to know as James signalled for me to stop.

"Everything alright, Miss Gaines?" He politely asked while I electronically wounded down the window of the car.

"I'm alright, James! How's yourself?"

"Yes, Miss Gaines, everything is fine! I was just admiring your brand new set of wheels."

"Nice, aren't they?"

"Very! I've not seen this model before."

"I was told it is rare. It's a S650 Cabriolet."

"It looks costly Miss Gaines?"

"My fiancé just bought this for me."

"You're a lucky woman Miss Gaines."

"I'm feeling blessed James."

"It must've set him back a few bob?"

"£230,000 to be precise."

"Well, well! Drive safely, Miss Gaines."

"I'm always safe, James."

"Right! You take care now and have a nice day."

"You to James, see you later."

"Goodbye, Miss Gaines."

As I left James's side, I put my foot to the pedal and cruised towards Putney Bridge.

As I drove through the decadent streets of Kensington, the sweet smell of success that was ringing through my mind, bought about a massive grin to my face.

When I reached Putney Bridge, I spotted a car that nearly tried to cut across me!

As I was about to curse out the idiot driver that nearly caused me to crash, they wounded their tinted window down!

At first, all I could see was a black face grinning whiter than white teeth back at me!

"Yo, Erykah! Pullover into the first left turn after the bridge?" The voice called out after he sped ahead of me.

"Who the heck are you?" I called out angrily sneering at the face. I still couldn't see who it was from whence he passed me so quick!

Regardless, I continued over the bridge and took the first left and parked behind the car that nearly cut right across my path!

STAND IN YOUR POWER

The only reason I did was that he somehow knew my name. So I was a bit curious about who he was!

I was feeling a bit apprehensive as I waited in my car for a few minutes. But the person ahead wasn't coming out his vehicle either. Strange, I thought. Since he was the one that was so desperate for me to stop and almost killed me in the process. Eventually after a further few minutes had passed the guy got out and proceeded to walk towards my car. I still didn't recognise him.

I started to panic a little bit, and my breathing was getting a little more rapid too.

As he got nearer to my car from out of nowhere, he brandished a gun, and he was pointing it towards me.

I began to shit myself as I saw my life quickly flashed before me.

He took a few more steps closer as he cocked his gun back and began to aim at my car and me.

I only had a few seconds to open my bag and take out the pepper spray from it.

As he reached by the side of my car, he tapped the window of the driver's side and ordered me to get out.

Reluctantly I did what he wanted and proceeded to exit my vehicle.

As I stood up and shut the door behind me, he came right up in my personal space leaning in with his big ass chest over me and his gun pointing on my temple!

"Who are you and what do you want from me and how in the hell do you know my name?" Justifiably I asked with such a stinking attitude.

"Miss Gaines, you don't remember me?" He took his gun trying to lift my skirt with it.

I started to tremble and couldn't believe nobody was around. Then as I looked around, I realised it was a dead-end street. This nigger must've followed me from the Kensington high street and set me up to get me right here.

I had the spray in my coat pocket, so I waited for an opportunity to use it.

But he was too strong for me as he held my free arm with his gun hand and with the other, he started to pull my knickers down.

I tried to kick him and wriggle away, but with one of his legs, he blocked me from moving.

Now he had me pinned against my car at the end of a dead-end street and with it being dark already and minimal lighting I don't think anyone was coming to be my saviour.

"No, I don't remember you!" I said in angst.

I had to think fast about how I was going to get out of this. But I had to be smart and a little patient while using my intuition.

"You and your family were the ones that knocked me out at your cousin's engagement party."

"Oh shit! I thought you were dead?" My eyes bulged like a rabbit that got caught in headlights. By the look on my face, he knew I knew now who he was.

"I was, and now I've come back from it." He freakishly said as he began to guide his free hand into my knickers. When he found his mark, he started to stroke two fingers over my clitoris as I let out a shallow moan.

I decided my only way to get out of this was to play along and seize my opportunity when the right moment presented itself.

As he stroked on my clit a bit more, he was beginning to make me wet as he guided his two fingers into my pussy. In and out, he continued to play. Not once did I keep my eye off him.

STAND IN YOUR POWER

I moaned out a few times, and then I whispered into his ear.

"Turn me around and bend me over. I want you to fuck me so hard with your gangster dick?"

He wasted no time and did what I commanded.

He turned me and forced me a bit too hard for my liking over the bonnet.

I was now exposed over the car as I began to take off my top and bra as well!

As I stood there in all my nakedness, cold as hell, before he could come up behind me, I turned around and began to go for his trousers.

I unzipped his belt and threw it to the floor. I then undid his jeans, allowing them to fall where they eventually settled above his boots.

I guided my hand into his boxers and pulled out this niggers dick. It was already erect, and he was still brandishing the gun in his hand.

I expertly took it out and began to stroke it a few times. By the smile on his face, I could tell it wouldn't take too much to enforce my plan.

I took his penis and shoved it into my mouth as I began to suck and lick on it a few times.

When I noticed he was in ecstasy. He titled his head back and closed his eyes. I sucked and licked on it a few more times, and then I seized my opportunity.

In the next instant, I bit on his dick so hard he staggered back in pain and fell to his knees. As he whined like a baby, I got up, and full-throttled kicked him in the face. He flew backwards and onto his back, holding his groin in one hand as the gun flew further back away from his body!

Before I tried to go for the gun, I thought he still could rise and get to it before me. So I decided to get my pepper spray out. In a few seconds, I did that and ran over to him as he laid on the road still wining.

I took the spray out and aimed it first in his face as he riled in further pain. I took another swipe and sprayed on his penis as well. By now, he was in so much agony I took my opportunity to go pick up his gun.

With my top, I picked it up. As I walked passed him again, I gave him a few more kicks in his abdomen area, and then I butted the back of his head with the barrel of his gun and knocked him cleanout.

At least now, the crying stopped.

As I quickly gathered up my clothes and underwear, I got dressed, but I still was a bit shaken.

When I was dressed, I got in my car not before I hid the gun in the boot of my car.

As I drove off, I looked back in the rear-view mirror. He was still lying out cold on the floor. The rational part of me thought to go back and put him in his car in case he froze to death. The irrational part of me said he raped you and nearly forced himself inside of you.

So the irrational thought came out the winner as I sped off and left his sorry gangster ass laying where I knock him out!

As I drove on a further couple of miles, try as I might to shake the thoughts and feelings of what just happened, I couldn't hold out any longer.

I parked up at the side of a pavement and turned the car's ignition off. As I sat there, twenty questions ran through my mind.

"How did he manage to find me?' Why wasn't he taken care of back then?' Uncle Mike and his crew had some explaining to do?'

STAND IN YOUR POWER

As I sat there contemplating, my emotions took over. I suddenly burst out crying as the tears came tumbling down my face, which was ruining my make up in the process.

But right now I didn't care one iota about that. What just happened to me made me think how many more of them were out there lurking, waiting to pounce at any given moment.

After I called Donte, he immediately went crazy like a bat out of hell! After he calmed down, he ordered for me that from now on I was to have a driver slash bodyguard with me until this matter was resolved! He then said to carry on going to Nina's and that Uncle Mike and his crew would deal with the gangster.

It was evident that somehow Foster had regrouped and was probably back for revenge. Whatever was going to happen in the coming days or weeks. He just declared all-out war against the Gaines, Briscoe's and Williams families.

With that said, I carried on my journey to South London, trying my hardest to forget about my recent ordeal.

SIMON P. MICALLEF